Summer Lightning

Also by Tamara McKinley

Matilda's Last Waltz
Jacaranda Vines
Windflowers

Summer Lightning

Tamara McKinley

PIATKUS

Copyright © 2003 by Tamara McKinley

First published in Great Britain in 2003 by
Judy Piatkus (Publishers) Ltd of
5 Windmill Street, London W1T 2JA

email: info@piatkus.co.uk

The moral right of the author has been asserted

A catalogue record for this book is available from the British Library

ISBN 0 7499 0631 6 HB
ISBN 0 7499 3390 9 PB

Set in Times by Phoenix Photosetting, Chatham, Kent
Printed and bound in Great Britain by
Mackays of Chatham Ltd, Chatham, Kent

For Brandon John Morris,
the first of the next generation

Acknowledgements

Thanks to the Historical Societies in the mining towns we visited for their stoic keeping of records, and to my dearest friends, Deanna, Tony, Dianne and Alan – Christmas in Tasmania was more than special. Barry and Leeanna in Perth, you were stars – as too were Michael and Gil and darling Max – thank you for sharing so much with me.

Over eighteen thousand kilometres were travelled in the quest for this story, and my heartfelt thanks go to Ollie Cater for his love and companionship in what proved to be a traumatic journey. After all the frogs I've kissed – I've truly found a Prince!

The gentle mind by gentle deeds is known
For a man by nothing is so well betrayed

Edmund Spenser 1552–1599

Prologue 1969

Dawn was still an hour away as Miriam Strong stepped on to the verandah of Bellbird homestead. It had been a restless night filled with dreams and images from the past, evoked by the events of the previous day. Now, as she stood there and breathed in the freshness of rain-soaked grass and the sweet reminder of good red earth she felt energy and determination return. She would need them, for the battle ahead would not be pleasant.

She closed her eyes, willing the night images to fade by counting her blessings. Her life may have begun almost seventy-five years ago in the cooler green of southern Australia, but she felt she'd been born to this hot, sepia world. To the chatter of crickets, the laughter of the kookaburra, and the sigh of the warm wind in the trees. This was home and she would never leave, for it gave her strength and solace. She had ridden her first pony in home yard and had learned the vagaries of life on this outback station – the harsh lessons of the terrible beauty that surrounded her. Her life had been played out here and the echoes of its laughter and tears could almost be heard in the stillness that came just before dawn.

Bellbird Station sprawled across the isolated north-western corner of New South Wales. The homestead was a six-room Queenslander, built almost a century ago. There was the kitchen at the back, a rarely used parlour and three bedrooms. A bathroom had been added twenty years ago, and

1

the old dunny at the back of the property had rapidly yielded to the termites and the elements.

The inevitable corrugated-iron roof sloped down over the deep verandah that ran around all four sides of the homestead. Most of life was lived on this verandah, especially during the heat of summer, and Miriam had a day-bed and mosquito net set up in one corner, table and chairs in another. A collection of battered cane chairs were set haphazardly amongst the vast pots of ferns and assorted greenery that added to the cool green shade of the surrounding trees. These trees were home to galahs and budgies of every colour, and of course to the tiny bellbird whose single note was one of the purest sounds in the bush.

With a deep sigh, Miriam sat in one of the cane chairs and carefully placed the music box on the rickety table. She would think about that later. Her visitor would be arriving soon and she needed these still moments to garner strength for what was to come. How her family would react, God only knew.

Chloe, her daughter would probably tell her not to make a fuss. She didn't like trouble of any kind, preferring to hide herself away with her paintings in that great rambling house on the beach at Byron Bay. She'd always lived in a dream that girl, Miriam thought wearily. She stared out over the yard, seeing again the little girl with a halo of copper hair and green eyes that had lost none of their brilliance over the ensuing years. She supposed she was happy, but who could tell? She and Leo might be divorced, but she suspected they liked one another better now they were apart – and that had to be good. Didn't it? Miriam clicked her tongue. Too many thoughts were going round in her head, and trying to sort out her family's problems was the least of her worries.

As for her granddaughters. Miriam smiled. As different as chalk and cheese. Fiona would probably relish the adventure of the forthcoming battle, but Louise? Poor down-trodden, frustrated Louise would see it only as another problem in her life.

2

Miriam pushed all thought of her family aside as she struggled into her boots. The pain in her back helped. It was a constant reminder of her mortality. She swore under her breath as the laces took on a life of their own and refused to tie. It was absolutely bloody being old, and far from being proud of her age she cursed it. What she wouldn't do to be young and supple again. To be able to sleep through the night without bathroom visits and ride for hours across the paddocks without ending up stiff and aching for days after.

She grimaced. The alternative wasn't attractive, but she couldn't quite accept what was happening to her. She'd been a fighter all her life, she was damned if she was going to give in now. With a grunt of satisfaction she finally got the laces tied and after glancing once more at the music box, stared out over home paddock.

The sky was lighter, the first, soft pink of dawn bringing the trees into silhouette against the darker huddle of the out-buildings. The birds were stirring, the sharp sniping rasp of the cockatoos mellowed by the rolling, almost sensual croon of the magpies.

She remained there on the verandah as the day dawned, smoke drifted from the cookhouse chimney and the birds took their first flight of the day. They rose in a cloud of pink and white and grey, the tiny green parakeets and blue bud-gies darting enthusiastically amongst the galahs as they headed for the billabong. She watched them for a moment, her keen eye noting the first of the fledglings to leave their nests. A new generation was on the wing. It would soon be time to make way for them.

'But not yet,' she breathed. 'I need time to put things right first.'

She reluctantly returned her attention to the music box. The cherry wood was inlaid with mother of pearl and scarred with age. Yet, that merely added to its allure, for the scratches and gouges spoke of long journeys across the world, of time spent in some of the harshest places on earth. And as a child Miriam had tried to imagine how they'd come

3

to be there – had endeavoured to conjure up the people who'd once owned the box and kept it safe.

'Until now,' she muttered crossly as she eyed the shattered base. Yet her carelessness had set in motion a chain of events that could very easily spiral out of control if not handled properly. For breaking the music box had revealed a secret – a secret that could change the lives of her family for ever.

She ran a finger over the lid as the doubts grew. Perhaps it would have been better to lay the ghosts to rest? To accept what had been found and use it to help her family? She didn't need this – not now. And yet, how could she just ignore the find? It was the first positive proof that her suspicions had been correct. A tangible gift from the past that cried out for the truth to be told.

She fumbled with the tiny gold key and lifted the lid. The black Harlequin danced with his pale Columbine before the smoky mirrors in perfect harmony with the tinny notes of a Strauss waltz, their expressions enigmatic behind their masks.

Miriam eyed the jewel bright colours of the Harlequin's costume and the dainty frills on Colombine's dress. It was beautiful, she admitted, and probably very rare, for it was unusual to have a black Harlequin. Yet, even as a child she'd thought there was something eerie about the glazed eyes behind those masks – something prim and stilted in their emotionless embrace. She grimaced. In hindsight, perhaps they'd always known the secret they had hidden beneath them, and that was what made them appear so superior.

The music died and the dancers came to a standstill. Miriam closed the lid and tried to forget about her visitor's imminent arrival by giving herself up to the sounds and scents of a past she knew only through the stories she'd heard as a child. It was a time when she had yet to be born – but she had still been a silent, innocent witness to the drama that was about to have its final curtain call seventy-five years later.

4

Chapter One

Ireland 1893

Maureen shivered as she wrapped the thin cloak around her shoulders and waited for Henry. He'd never been this late before and she was beginning to fret. Could something have happened up at the big house? Something that meant he was unable to slip away? She gritted her teeth in an attempt to stop them chattering. The walk from the village into the woods had been long and the rain had plastered her long dark hair to her skin and the icy drips were running down her neck and into her dress. Yet it wasn't the knife of the wind that chilled her, but the thought they'd been betrayed – that he might not come at all.

Seeking shelter in the doorway of the abandoned game-keeper's hut, she leaned against the rough wood of the doorpost and smeared the rain from her face. The day suited her mood well, for the sky had remained leaden and dark-ness was fast approaching. She would have to leave soon, or she would be missed at home – and she didn't relish having to face Da, for he would demand an explanation. Yet the fear of missing Henry was even greater, for there were things that had to be discussed. Things that could not wait – not if they were to be resolved before her seventeenth birthday.

The beating of the rain on the broken thatch deadened all sound as she stood there in the fast gathering gloom, and as she peered through the deepening shadows her mind raced through the words she needed to say. They wouldn't be easy, but she had to keep faith in Henry. Surely he wouldn't desert her now?

'Maureen.'

The soft voice made her turn swiftly. He jumped from his horse, and with a sob of pleasure and relief she fell into his open arms. 'I didn't think you were coming,' she gasped.

He dropped the reins and drew her close, resting his chin on the top of her head as they sheltered beneath the tumbledown roof. 'I very nearly didn't,' he said grimly. 'My brother turned up and Father insisted we discuss the running of the estate. I'm only here because one of the mare's in foal and having trouble and I volunteered to fetch help.'

He pulled away reluctantly and smoothed the wet hair from her face before cupping her chin in his long, elegant fingers. 'I'm sorry, my darling. But I can't stay. Father's in one of his moods and I daren't be gone for too long.'

Maureen looked up into his handsome face. Henry Beecham-Fford was twenty-two, and his fair hair clung wetly against his finely sculpted head. The eyes were blue and thickly lashed, the nose long and straight above a neat moustache and sensuous mouth. She took his hand and planted a kiss in the palm. 'Can you not stay for just a moment?' she pleaded. 'I've seen so little of you in the past few days, and we never seem to have time to talk.'

He kissed her then, drawing her to him, enfolding her in his arms, the warmth of his embrace flooding through her like a furnace. She melted into him, tasting him, breathing in his scent of fine cologne and damp tweed.

'I'll meet you here, tomorrow after the hunt,' he said as he regretfully pulled away. 'We can talk then.' His blue eyes were full of humour as he looked down at her. 'Whatever it is can't be that important – we've said everything we need to right here, in this kiss.'

She stepped away from him. If he kissed her again she would be lost, and she had to keep her concentration. 'Henry,' she began.

6

He silenced her with a soft finger against her lips. 'Tomorrow,' he said firmly. 'If I stay we run the risk of getting caught, and if I'm to make any headway with Father I need to be seen to be the dutiful son.' With a hasty kiss he turned away and picked up the reins. Climbing into the saddle he reached down and stroked Maureen's wet hair. 'Go home and get dry before you catch your death, and remember that I love you,' he said. 'Have faith, my darling. We'll find a way to be together always. I promise.'

Maureen folded her arms around her waist as he turned the horse's head and galloped away. She stood there for a long while, listening to the diminishing drumbeat of hoofs and the splatter of the rain in the forest canopy. She had said nothing because it had been obvious he wouldn't have listened – he was in too much of a hurry – too afraid of their being caught. But she didn't like the thoughts that were running through her mind. Could she trust him? Or was he just using her?

Henry's family were wealthy English Protestants. They owned the land that stretched up the hill from the harbour in a spider's web of stone walls. Land that was sliced into plots hardly wider than the O'Halloran's best parlour. Land that barely produced a harvest rich enough to feed the tenants who worked it once the rent had been paid. Henry's heritage forbade their love. Would Henry have the strength to stand against his tyrannical father? Did he love her enough to risk losing everything?

She ducked her head, her arms tight about her waist as she stepped from the shelter of the hut and began to thread her way through the forest. He'd asked her to have faith in him – but could she? Did she dare to hope he would keep his promise that they would be together one day? Would he still want her once the social season began and he was occupied with hunting and shooting and dances up at the big house?

Her feet slipped on the wet leaves as she stumbled over fallen branches and around spiny bushes. She had no choice but to trust his word – not now. But God help her if she was wrong.

The wind seared as she stepped out of the shelter of the trees and on to the track that wound down the hill to the village on the shore. Her hair was whipped from her face as her skirts clung to her legs and flapped around her ankles and she leaned into the wind, chin tucked tightly into the collar of her cloak. Gulls shrieked above the harbour where the fishing boats strained at their moorings and the Atlantic waves thundered against the stone jetty, and the dim glow from the cottage windows was a welcome sight. Almost blinded by tears she struggled down the hill.

She didn't see the women until it was too late.

Henry left Dan Finnigan at the stables, and once he'd made sure his horse was dry and had plenty of feed and water, he dashed across the cobbles to the main house. The rain was heavier now, slashing the night in almost horizontal fury. He hoped Maureen had made it safely home, this wasn't a night to be abroad.

The thought of Maureen made him smile as he swiftly took the stairs two at a time and crashed into his bedroom. His love for her had come as no surprise, for he'd always adored her, even as a child. He tore off his sodden shirt and trousers and swiftly changed for dinner. Those childhood days had been the best, for although he'd been aware of the divisions in society then, there had been a greater amount of freedom – a freedom that had allowed their friendship to blossom despite their different circumstances.

He sighed as he struggled with the starched collar and gold studs. The onset of adulthood had changed that and the divisions had become even wider. What was it about Ireland that stirred people to such hatred? It was evident on both sides, in the Protestant enclaves and the Catholic slums, but surely there had to be a solution – a way of rescuing this poor, benighted country from the centuries of trouble?

He fixed his bow tie and slipped on his jacket. Eyeing his

8

reflection in the mirror he raised an eyebrow in derision. What did he know about Irish politics, let alone a solution to the eternal fighting? All he knew was that he loved Maureen and was determined to find a way they could be together. So what if she was Catholic and her father one of the trouble-makers calling vociferously for Irish Rule?

The uneasy reminder that his own father would vigor-ously object to any such liaison made him falter as he reached for the door handle. The bigotry was inbred on both sides; did he have the strength of character to defy genera-tions of Beecham-Ffords and follow his heart? Could Maureen break with the fast-held tradition of hatred for the English to run away with him?

'There's only one way to find out,' he muttered as he pulled the door open and strode along the dimly lit landing.

Beecham Hall was a square stone edifice that had been built almost a century before by a wealthy ancestor. It stood in solitary splendour amongst the hills that sheltered Lough Leigh from the westerly winds that roared across the Atlantic. The long, elegant windows looked out over mani-cured gardens and a sweeping driveway that was lined by topiary hedges. The cobbled stable-yard could be reached through an archway in a mellow stone wall that was smoth-ered in clambering roses and honeysuckle, and the kitchen garden was tucked away behind the vast laundry.

The land surrounding the house was good grazing for the cattle and horses and the woods were stocked with an abun-dance of pheasant for the shooting parties his father held every year. Fishing in the river that ran down from the Lough to the sea was plentiful, and the herd of deer in the parklands were a graceful sight in the early mornings, but a nightmare for the gamekeeper who had to fend off the poachers.

Henry had lived most of his life at the Hall, preferring the green of Ireland to the bustle and smog of London. There was room to breathe here amongst the verdant hills and on the craggy coastline. An almost mystical quality in the ruined castles and tumbledown cottages, which appealed to

9

his artistic soul. Then of course there was this house. He loved the high ceilings, the delicate plasterwork on the cornices and the cosy window seats where, as a boy, he would sit behind the heavy curtains and read. But most of all he loved the summerhouse. For this was where he could lose himself in his painting.

He stared out into the night from the half-landing, the distant sound of voices coming to him from the drawing room. The summerhouse was out there in the darkness, tucked away in a distant corner of the garden, almost forgotten since Father had had the Orangery erected at the side of the house. He fidgeted with his bow tie and wished he could forego dinner and escape to his sanctuary – to the painting that was so nearly finished. Yet duty called and, with a deep sigh, he hurried on down the last flight of stairs and crossed the hall. The grandfather clock was striking eight as he entered the drawing room.

'Where the devil have you been?' demanded Sir Oswald.

Henry eyed his father who was in his usual straddle-legged position in front of the fire. His hair glinted silver in the lamplight and the beautifully cut jacket enhanced a body kept trim by riding to hounds. 'I've been to the village to fetch Dan Finnigan,' Henry replied evenly. 'I had to change out of my wet clothes.'

'Took a long time, old chap,' drawled Thomas as his piercing eyes trawled Henry's face for any sign of duplicity. 'Sure you haven't got some tasty little colleen tucked away somewhere, what?' He snorted laughter and smoothed back his light brown hair. 'Jolly good sport, but a chap's got to be pretty desperate to be out on a night like this.'

Henry glared at his older brother, his fists tight to his sides as he tamped down on his retort. Thomas had always had a way of goading him – a way of sniffing out a weakness and trampling it in scorn.

'Ladies present,' boomed Sir Oswald. 'Hold your tongue, boy.'

Thomas' colour heightened and he turned his back on the

assembly and joined his wife. Emma was sitting on a low chaise with her needlework, eyes downcast as if afraid to be noticed.

'Come by the fire dear, and warm yourself.' Lady Miriam patted the cushions beside her on the couch. Both she and Henry knew how easily arguments broke out in this family and Henry could see how determined she was to avoid confrontation by the tilt of her chin. 'How's the mare?'

Henry didn't dare look at his father as he took a glass of sherry from the silver salver on the side-table and sat next to his mother. His brother's remark had been too close to the truth and the old bastard's mind was as keen as a rapier when it came to sniffing out trouble. 'Finnigan thinks she'll pull through,' he said evenly. 'But this will have to be her last foal. She's getting too old.'

Lady Miriam's diamonds flashed in the lamplight as she brushed her hand over her silken skirts. 'Thank you for going out on a night like this,' she murmured.

Her piercing blue eyes held him for a long moment before she looked away. But Henry had seen the questions in those eyes, the doubts, and wondered how long he could keep up this ridiculous pretence. Perhaps, after dinner, he should face up to his father – better to initiate the confrontation than to be caught red-handed and on the defensive. Yet he quailed at the thought and a trickle of cold sweat ran down his back as his father pontificated on the vagaries of having to maintain a household in southern Ireland in these times of political trouble.

Henry blocked out the sound of his voice and turned his thoughts to Maureen. He remembered how wet her hair had been. Remembered how chill the wind and how thin her cloak. It was unfair for him to be sheltered so well, to be able to sit in front of this fire warming himself while she traipsed through the rain back to the village. The ache inside him was so strong he had to stifle the groan that rose in his throat. If only they could have more time together. He hated the snatched moments, the secret meetings where every sound

11

could herald their discovery. Something would have to be done – and soon. He couldn't bear being parted from her any longer.

The dinner seemed to last for ever and the atmosphere was heavy with impending trouble. Sir Oswald ploughed his way silently through the five courses, scarcely bothering to acknowledge the presence of his family. Lady Miriam tried her best to make small talk to fill the long silences and Thomas droned on about the forthcoming election and his confidence in retaining his seat in Parliament.

Thomas' wife picked at her food, her soft brown hair dull in the gaslight, her wan little face deeply shadowed. She reminded Henry of a small grey mouse he'd once had as a pet in the nursery. But perhaps that was unkind. Poor Emma, he thought as he finally threw aside the napkin and gave up on the dinner. This last set-back was the third miscarriage in as many years – if only Thomas could restrain himself and give the poor little thing time to recover. But that was typical of his older brother. Never a thought for anyone but himself.

The servants brought brandy and cigars and Lady Miriam swept out of the room with Emma scuttling anxiously behind her. Their sense of relief was almost tangible and Henry fidgeted in his chair wishing he could leave with them. The evening had been interminable and he longed for the solitude of his bedroom, the feel of a pencil in his hand and clean, thick paper to sketch on. He wanted to capture Maureen's face – her wondrous green eyes and dark hair, the softly curved lips and rounded cheeks and the distinctly naughty dimple that appeared when she smiled. She was so perfect. How could anyone fail to love her?

His father's voice startled him from his thoughts. 'Had a letter from Brigadier Collingwood this morning,' he boomed. 'He's arranged an interview for you in London next week.' His beetling brows shadowed narrowed eyes. 'Time you did something useful instead of lounging around like some effeminate ne'er-do-well.'

Thomas' sneer wasn't lost on him, neither was his father's

12

belligerent glare. Henry took a deep breath and willed himself to remain calm. This was an old, familiar argument, but he had to remain firm. 'I have no wish to go into the army,' he said flatly. 'We've had this discussion before, and I have no intention of . . .'

'You'll damn well do as you're told, you young pup,' exploded Sir Oswald as his fist connected with the oak table and made the glassware shudder. 'I will *not* tolerate this nonsense any longer. You have a duty to the family to find a career and if you refuse to find one for yourself, then you must adhere to my wishes.'

Henry rose from the table as the colour drained from his face and the depth of his anger made him tremble. 'I have always tried to please you, Father, but it seems that is not possible. I know I have a duty towards you and Mother, but a life in the army or in the church is not for me.' He took a deep breath. 'I have a talent – a talent that I happen to think will lead to something really worthwhile if only I'm allowed to pursue it. And I can't do that if I'm in some foreign battlefield up to my neck in muck and native spears.'

'Talent!' The overhanging eyebrows lifted in astonishment then resumed their glowering presence above the smouldering eyes. 'Balderdash. You take the word of some namby-pamby, so-called artist and think you could make a decent living out of it? Tosh!' The glassware rattled again and the candles guttered as his fist hit the table. 'You're twenty-two years old. Time you grew up.'

Henry stepped away from the table, chin high, determination setting his jaw into a hard line. 'I'm adult enough to know I will never make a soldier or a cleric,' he said stiffly. 'As for the artist you so sneeringly dismiss, he's just been commissioned by Her Majesty to paint her portrait.'

He clasped his hands behind his back to stop them from trembling and stared his father down. 'Thomas made his career in politics – it was his choice. You made a career out of cotton mills and mines. I choose to go my own way. All this,' he gestured towards the panelled room, the crystal and

13

fine oak. 'All this will never be mine, and as the younger son I must be allowed to follow my own path in life. Why can't you just accept me for what I am and leave it at that? This argument is an old one and I'm rapidly tiring of it.'

'How *dare* you?' Sir Oswald's complexion was high, the grey eyes flinty with rage as he shoved back his chair. 'I've a mind to give you a damned thrashing,' he rasped.

Henry gritted his teeth, the tic in his cheek the only outer evidence of his fury as he remembered those terrible beatings his father doled out when he was younger. 'I'm not a little boy, Father,' he said coldly. 'You can't beat me into submission any more.'

'Get out of my sight,' Sir Oswald roared.

Henry had the fleeting urge to tell his father about Maureen, but Sir Oswald was itching for a fight, and there was no point in adding fuel to the fire. Without a word, Henry left the room.

'Get yer arse outta here, Paddy Dempster and don't be coming back until you're sober.'

Paddy stumbled over the doorstep of the Dublin pub as the hefty hand shoved him in the back. He could barely keep his feet and it was only the girl's arm around his waist that prevented him from falling into the gutter. This wasn't the first time he'd been thrown out of a public house, and at the age of twenty-nine, he didn't expect it to be the last. The amount of beer he'd consumed took its toll and he threw up, the vomit splashing unnoticed on his boots and the cuffs of his trousers.

'I'll take me custom elsewhere,' he yelled as he wiped his mouth on his sleeve. 'Yer stinkin' ale makes me puke anyway.'

'Ye'll be lucky any publican will serve ya, yer drunken bastard,' retorted the landlord and slammed the door in his face.

Paddy swayed as he stared stupidly at the closed door. 'I'll kill him,' he muttered, his meaty fists curling at his sides.

14

'Now, come along, Paddy. You were promising me a fine dinner, and me belly thinks me throat's been slit.' The girl nestled her head on his shoulder as she wormed her arm through his and urged him to move.

Paddy stared down at her, trying to think who the hell she was and why he'd promised her dinner. His bleary gaze softened the hard lines of her face, making the bedraggled hair and grubby neck look almost appealing. But he could smell her, even above his own stench, and the remains of the ale he'd consumed earlier roiled in his gut.

'Come on,' she persisted, her voice becoming shrill. 'Is it all night you'll be making me wait?'

'Shove off,' he muttered. 'Let a man be.' He unhooked her grasping fingers and pushed her away. He was a big man, and strong, especially with the weight of several pints inside him. The girl, caught unawares, fell against the wall of the public house and slid into the gutter.

Paddy lurched into a shambling trot. He needed to get away from her. Away from the noise of the pub and the stink of the alleyway. His guts were grumbling, the bile bitter in his mouth as her screech of venom followed him down into the darkness.

'You owe me,' she yelled as she leaped on his back. Her hands were talons reaching for his eyes, her legs wrapped around him like a vice. 'Pay up yer bastard, or I'll have the law on yer!'

He shook her off like a dog shed rain and she fell once more on to the rough cobbles. 'Give me my money,' she screamed as she rose in one swift movement and went for him again. 'Help! Police! Police! I'm being robbed,' she yelled as he pushed her away and tried to continue his unsteady progress down the lane. 'Stop thief!'

Paddy saw red – it was a cloud of scarlet that encompassed his bleary world and filled his aching head. He had to shut her up. Had to silence her before the law turned up. He turned swiftly, his large hand grabbing the scrawny neck, cutting off the stream of vitriol that was slicing through his head. Then he was squeezing, squeezing, squeezing. He needed silence, peace, time to think, to ease the terrible pain in his belly and in his head, and it wasn't until she'd stopped struggling that he realised something was wrong.

He stared in bewildered fascination as the whore's eyes bulged and her tongue protruded. He felt her go limp and released her. She fell to the ground like a rag doll. With a cautious dig of his boot he gave her a prod and when she didn't react he grunted in stupefied horror. He was for it now. The law would be here any minute and with his record his neck would surely be stretched this time.

He cast a sharp glance over his shoulder as he heard the police whistles and tramp of army boots echoing through the tenement alleyways. The effects of the beer were swept away. Nothing like the threat of the hangman's noose to sober a man, he thought sourly.

For a big man he moved swiftly through the shadows, but it was a skill honed from over twenty years of living on the outside of the law. A skill he'd had to learn very young to survive on the streets.

Paddy wove in and out of the labyrinthine jumble of rickety houses and noisy taverns until he reached the river. The Liffey was the colour of molten lead beneath the scudding clouds and sour-faced moon, and Paddy swiftly clambered over the low stone wall and hid in a narrow culvert beneath one of the bridges. He could smell the rancid waste on the riverbank and the cold green murk of the water as it slid past him in oiled silence.

He squatted in the dank and malodorous hiding place and shivered as he wrapped his arms around his waist. The jacket was worn, the shirt beneath it thin and patched. What he wouldn't do now for the mean little room in the Welsh Valleys – for the cool darkness of a coal pit that put money in his pocket and food in his belly. Why the hell had he come back to Ireland?

With a grimace he buried his grizzled chin in his collar and stared out at the reflection of the moon on the scummy water. London had proved too dangerous, and he'd escaped the law by the skin of his teeth too many times to push his luck further. Having headed for Wales he'd found work and comradeship in the tiny mountain mining village, but his sticky fingers couldn't remain idle for long and he'd almost been caught during the robbery of a nearby public house.

He scrubbed his face with his callused hands. Ireland was supposed to be a refuge – a return home to people who cared what happened to him. But Mam was dead, his brothers and sisters dispersed to all corners of the world in search of their fortune. Even the old cottage was occupied by strangers and no one knew what had happened to Da. He'd simply left home one morning and had never returned.

'I've got to get out of here,' he breathed. 'Got to find a way to make something of myself before the hangman gets me.'

Kate Kelly held the baby tightly as she stepped out of the shadows behind the curtain and watched the man run down the alley. Her heart was drumming and her mouth was parched. She'd seen his face clearly in the light from the pub, and knew she would never forget him.

A shiver ran through her as she looked back at the still figure lying in the filth of the backstreet alley. The girl looked so young, so vulnerable, with her dirty hair floating in the rain-filled gutter, her tiny hands open to the sky. Kate crossed herself and muttered a prayer as the police and army arrived. The girl was dead, for the love of God, why slap her around as if she was a piece of meat?

Kate flinched as one of the men looked up. His eyes were narrowed, searching for witnesses, and Kate melted back into the shadows. If she told them what she'd seen she would bring trouble to the family – and they didn't need that, they had troubles enough already.

The baby whimpered in its sleep and she held him close, murmuring comforting words into his downy hair. Her newest baby brother was a delight, but his arrival had exhausted Mam. Da was worse than useless when it came to helping out with the other nine children so it had fallen on Kate's narrow shoulders to keep things running smoothly until Mam was better. Not that Da was afraid of hard work to provide for his ever-growing family and would come home ashen with weariness from the tannery.

She put the baby on the mattress next to the other sleeping children and returned to the window. The body had been removed and the alley had once again returned to its raucous usual self.

'What are you looking at? I thought I heard shouting earlier.'

The soft voice made her start and she turned. 'You should be resting,' she said gently as she noticed the dark shadows around Mam's eyes and the almost alabaster sheen to her skin.

'Ach. I'll sleep long enough once I'm dead,' retorted Finola Kelly with a dismissive wave of her hand. She pulled the thin shawl around her narrow shoulders. 'So what's been happening down there? Another cat fight amongst the whores?'

Kate told her what she'd seen, making scant mention of the man she could have described so clearly. 'Let's get you back to bed,' she said, changing the subject. 'Da will be on his way and he'll be angry if he finds you up and about so soon.'

'Your Da will not have the eyes in his head to know anything. He'll be that tired, he'll fall asleep standing up.' Finola Kelly gripped her daughter's arms and looked deep into her eyes. 'Don't get caught like me, Kate,' she said urgently. 'Get out of this place before it brings you down.'

'Mam?' Kate stepped back from the ferocity of her mother's gaze. She had never heard her speak like this before. 'Is that how you see us all – a trap?'

'Ach girl, you're old enough to understand what I mean. Things are changing in the world and you're young enough to make the most of it.' The work-worn hand took a strand

18

of Kate's dark hair and smoothed it back from her face. 'You're eighteen; older than I was when I had you. Don't make the same mistake as me, thinking this is all life has to offer. You have a good head on your shoulders, Kate, don't waste it.'

'I know things are tough right now,' Kate stammered. 'But when I get back to work in the tannery the extra money will make things easier.'

'That's not what I'm saying,' snapped Finola. 'Leave Ireland. Go across the water – further if you've a mind. Don't stay here and rot like the rest of us, Kate, for this is as good as it gets for us Catholics.'

Kate felt a tingle of excitement, yet it was laced with fear. These few rooms in the back street of Dublin were all she knew. The thought of leaving her family, of travelling across the water to begin a new life amongst strangers was something she had never seriously contemplated – until now. Her imagination soared. She'd heard about the Americas and the new colonies of Australia from the families whose sons and daughters had ventured there and sent money home. She'd listened to the stories of the wide, open spaces, of the air that was supposed to be so clean and fresh it hurt the lungs, and of the opportunities to be had in these far-off places, where class and religion were no barrier to finding a fortune.

Yet common sense told her she was only dreaming. She slowly shook her head. 'I don't know . . .' she began.

Finola's hand rested on her arm. Her voice was low, with a hint of urgency about it that could not be ignored. 'Look at your future if you stay,' she hissed. 'Murder in the streets, sharing a house with three families, no money. If you stay you'll be trapped. With a baby every year and your mind turning to dust.'

She shook her head, her dark curls glinting with the first strands of grey, as she turned to look at her sleeping children. 'I want more for you than this, Kate.'

Kate eyed the other children. They lay tightly packed like

herrings on a slab, and she knew that before morning the mattress would be sodden. She took a deep breath and for the first time realised how dank and fetid the two rooms were at the top of this crowded house. In the new light of promise she suddenly became aware of the ripe and potent mixture of unwashed bodies and old cooking smells that overlaid the grime of poverty and sharp tang of urine-soaked napkins and blankets. 'But how . . .?' she began.

'I've not been laying there with me brain idle,' said Finola with a briskness that belied her obvious weariness. 'I've had a word with Father Pat, and there's a position at the presbytery in Liverpool.'

Kate eyed her mother, the hope rising above the fear of the unknown. 'Liverpool?' It wasn't the colonies, but it was further than she'd travelled before.

'Aye. They need a housekeeper.' Finola wrapped her arm around Kate's waist. 'It'll be easier work than in the tannery and three meals a day. A good start for a new life out of this place.'

Kate stared out through the window onto the rain-washed cobbles below. It was as if the girl had never existed, for there was no sign of her, no one to mourn. As for her murderer – he was long gone – an anonymous face in the darkness of lost hope that permeated these alleyways. She glanced at her mother and saw the weariness in her eyes and in the drag of lines either side of her mouth. Yes, she decided. It was time to leave if she was ever to make anything of her life.

The women were bedraggled, the hems of their homespun dresses sodden with the mud they'd been standing in as they waited for Maureen. Their expressions were grim, their mouths tight, angry lines. In silent accord they surrounded her.

Maureen did her best to hide the fear and shouted against the wind. 'What do you want?'

The screech of the seagulls and the pounding of the waves

20

against the harbour wall was the only reply as the women tightened the circle around her.

Maureen looked desperately into the faces of women she'd known all her short life. These were girls she'd played with as a child, women she'd worked with in the peat bogs and thought were friends. But there was no gleam of pity in their merciless eyes, no sign of friendship – merely a glazed, almost puritanical euphoria as they surrounded her, pressed in on her, leaving her no place to run.

'Please,' she begged. 'What is it you want?' She sought the eyes of her best friend, Regan, knowing what the answer would be – knowing the punishment they would mete out. 'Why are you doing this?' she breathed.

Regan lifted her chin, her fiery hair a demonic halo about her head, eyes bright with the light of zealous righteousness. 'As if you didn't know,' she snapped. 'We saw you with that bastard Englishman. Laying down like the whore that you are! You're not wanted here, Maureen O'Halloran.'

Her pulse was racing so fast she could barely breathe. 'Then I'll be going,' she stammered. 'Let me pass.' She took a tentative step forward.

The screams of the gulls were drowned in the banshee howl of rage as they closed in. Hands tore at her clothes, dirty nails gouged and heavy boots thudded as they stripped her naked. She could smell their sweat, their unwashed bodies and their sodden clothes as she tried to fight them off. Could feel the nails rip, the fingers pinch and poke as their hot breath steamed in the cold air. Could barely focus on the names they called her as the babel of vitriol poured down on her.

Maureen's fear gave her a strength she didn't know she had and she fought back, fist for fist, nail for nail, kick for kick. But there were too many of them, with a strength honed by hours tilling the fields and an insatiable thirst for what they saw as justice they grasped her legs and arms and turned her over until her face was pressed into the ground.

'I can't breathe,' she screamed as she tried to rid herself of the mud that oozed into her mouth and nose. She struggled to lift her head, but the air was punched from her lungs as someone jumped on her back.

Maureen kicked out, hands windmilling in an effort to rid herself of the weight and gain some air into her aching lungs. Her boot found a target and it was a minor satisfaction to hear the grunt that followed. Yet retribution was swift as the kick was returned and found her ribs.

'Keep still you bitch,' hissed Regan as she leaned forward from her perch on Maureen's back and yanked her hair. 'You can't escape, so you might as well take your punishment.'

Maureen's neck arched as the tug on her hair was increased to the point where she thought it would surely be ripped from her head. Her pleas went unheard. Her sobs and weakening struggles were ignored as the scissors were flourished and they began to hack off her hair. The blades were sharp, the aim careless and blood began to trickle warmly down her face and neck.

Maureen froze, terrified the sharp point might find her eyes, and when they were done and Regan had climbed off her back with one last, vicious jab of her knee, she collapsed in the mud.

Yet the ordeal wasn't over. Rough hands began to smear something over her head and down her body, insolent fingers relishing the anointing of punishment. It burned where they'd cut her and stung with such intensity she cried out. The fumes told her what it was and she began to whimper with fear. Tar.

'Fine feathers for a fine lady,' said one of the women with a harsh laugh as she opened the burlap sack. The chicken feathers flurried and settled. Hands pressed them down, entangling them in the tufts of remaining hair, coating her battered body until she was smothered.

'Ripe for plucking,' screeched another woman. This remark was met with screams of salacious laughter as the women stepped away, turned their backs and headed arm-in-arm down the hill towards the village.

Maureen curled her knees protectively against her chest and lay there in the mud and the rain exhausted, too sore to move, too shocked to think. She heard the voices fade as the screeching, wheeling gulls drowned them out. Felt the tar burn into her skin, its feather coating tugged by the wind. She could still feel the heat of the women's hatred and the vicious strength in their fingers. The thought of having to go back to the village was terrifying, yet she knew she couldn't stay here. Knew she must find some way of cleaning herself before the tar became impossible to remove.

She finally sat up and carefully touched her ravaged head. The scars would heal, the hair would grow back, but until it did she would be marked as surely as Cain.

Her clothes lay around her in tatters. The long hanks of black hair curled in the mud like forlorn snakes. She gathered up her cloak, which mercifully had escaped too much damage, and pulled it around her shoulders, tugging the hood over her head almost to her eyes. It was sodden with mud and rain, but it was the only protection she had against the elements.

Minutes passed before she could summon the strength to struggle to her feet. Wincing from the kick in the ribs and shivering uncontrollably from the shock of the brutality of the attack, she folded the cloak around her and stared down towards the village. She had nowhere else to go but home, but how was she to face her parents? Her father?

Michael O'Halloran was not a man to appreciate being shamed by his eldest daughter's indiscretion – especially with an Englishman – not a man who would side with his daughter once he discovered the reason behind the attack. He was fiercely Irish, with a hatred for the English landowners that coloured his view on life. Maureen knew that far from consoling her, he would take his belt to her to re-enforce the lesson that had been meted out today.

The memory of other beatings terrified her, and she wondered if she could somehow sneak into the house without him seeing. Yet she knew that would be impossible. The cottage consisted of only two rooms and she shared the alcove bed with her three younger sisters. Even if Da was away on one of his secret trips to the north there was always the chance her mother would be sitting by the fire awaiting his return.

Maureen looked over her shoulder to the woods she'd left earlier. Perhaps it would be better to try and wash away the tar and feathers in the Lough? She dismissed the idea immediately. It was a good half hour walk to Lough Leigh and it would mean crossing Sir Oswald's land and running the risk of getting caught by his gamekeeper, Fergus. She was too tired, too cold, in too much pain to even contemplate such a journey. There was nothing else for it, but to return home.

'Henry,' she whimpered as the rain washed away the last vestiges of courage. 'Where are you when I need you? Can you not hear me calling you?'

She sniffed back the tears and dismissed her words as fantasy – for how would an Englishman understand the vagaries of an Irish belief in things mystical – of course he couldn't sense her pain, her bewilderment. He was but a man – a stranger when it came to truly understanding the Irish mind. She huddled into the cloak and began the long descent towards the fishing village.

The stone cottage was one of five in a short terrace that clung to the edge of the steep hill and overlooked the harbour. The thatch needed repairing, but the windows were clean, the paint fresh on the door. The soft low of the milk cow came from the byre that was divided off from the main room and the chickens clucked their annoyance at being disturbed as she opened the back gate and stepped into the muddy yard. The light from the fire in the hearth flickered through the window and she peeked in.

Bridie O'Halloran was in her usual place beside the fire, sewing on her lap as her toe rocked the rough wooden cradle in which her three-month-old baby slept. Her eyes were deeply bruised with weariness, her thin face drooping with

24

an age beyond her thirty-three years as she sat there amongst the drying clothes.

Maureen bit her lip. There was no sign of Da. Perhaps it would be safe to confide in Mam?

Bridie looked up from her sewing as the cold wind and rain blew in to the room with her eldest daughter. 'Holy Mother of God,' she gasped. 'What on earth?' The sewing fell to the floor, the cradle and baby forgotten as she rose from the rocking chair.

Maureen closed the door and hurried to the fire. Holding out her hands to the warmth she found she couldn't stop shivering. Yet it wasn't just the cold that made her tremble – but the thought of her Da's return. 'I'm sorry, Mam,' she said stammered. 'I'm so sorry. But I didn't know where else to go.'

Bridie reached out and snatched back the hood. Her trembling fingers raced to her mouth as her eyes widened in horror. 'What have you done?' she whispered. 'Dear God in heaven what have you done?'

'It doesn't matter, Mam,' replied Maureen as she hurriedly fetched the tub from the back of the door and filled it with hot water from the kettle that always hung over the range. 'I have to get clean before Da gets home. If he sees me like this he'll . . .'

A shaft of fear shot through Bridie's eyes and a sob escaped as she made the sign of the cross. 'Quick, quick, he'll be home soon, he's only gone to Donovan's for a drink.'

Maureen's fingers were clumsy as she dropped the cloak.

Bridie's eyes narrowed and she again made the sign of the cross. 'Whose is it?' she snapped with icy contempt.

Maureen began plucking the feathers from the mess smeared on her body. Her fingers were clumsy in their haste as she glanced repeatedly towards the door. 'Henry's,' she admitted.

'Hen . . .? God love us. Does he know?' Bridie's voice was sharp, her eyes sparking with something akin to disgust.

25

'Not yet. I was going to tell him tonight.' Maureen threw the feathers into the fire and watched the flames engulf them. 'But he could only stay a minute and . . .'

The slap was as unexpected as it was sharp, burning her cheek, making her head fill with dark clouds. 'You stupid bitch,' spat Bridie. Her voice rose as she grasped Maureen's arms and shook her. 'You're no better than a whore. A stupid little tart to be used and thrown away by the likes of them. Fine words and fancy ways he might have, but he doesn't care for you – you're just an amusement to fill his time when he hasn't got anything else better to do.'

The tears came then and she turned away and folded her arms around her skinny waist. 'Your Da will kill you,' she whispered. 'Kill us both if he finds out. You've got to go. Now. Before he comes back.'

Maureen shot an anxious look to the door before she sank into the hot water and began to scrub at the mess. 'I can't go like this,' she said through gritted teeth. The combination of the tar, the cuts and bruises and the lye soap was almost unbearable – and coming so soon after the attack, her mother's reaction was devastating.

'What's happening, Mam?' The sleepy voice came from the alcove as the three little girls emerged from behind the curtain.

'Go back to bed,' ordered Bridie with a sharpness that brooked no argument. She shot anxious glances at the clock and the back door, expecting any minute to be discovered by her husband as she stuffed the remaining feathers into old newspaper and threw them on the fire. She began to mutter, the words of the rosary coming in an incomprehensible stream as she grabbed the scrubbing brush and set about cleaning Maureen's back.

'Be quiet,' she snapped in response to Maureen's cry of protest. 'You only have yourself to blame. When I think of all the times I've warned you to keep yourself pure. God only knows what Father Paul will say.'

'It's none of his damn business,' retorted Maureen as she

26

bit down on the yelp of pain as her mother scrubbed her back with a ferocity that surely wasn't needed.

Another slap, this time to the back of Maureen's tortured head. 'Mind your mouth, girl,' Bridie muttered. ''Tis bad enough you bring disgrace to this house without using such language.'

Maureen didn't bother to apologise, when Mam was in this mood it was best to keep silent.

'Who did this to you?' Bridie demanded, her voice softer now as if she'd suddenly realised how thin the walls were between the cottages.

'Every woman who could make it up the hill,' snapped Maureen as she retrieved the brush and tried to clean her arms. 'They enjoyed it too. Should have seen their faces. Even Regan Donovan was there.'

'You know what this means, don't you?' said Bridie grimly as she snatched clean clothes from the pile beside the hearth. 'We'll be shunned. Work's difficult enough to come by without this.' Her work-worn hand rested on the slender shoulder in a fleeting moment of intimacy that only two women could share.

It was a touch that told Maureen her mother did care, but she suspected Bridie didn't know how to deal with this terrible thing that had come into their lives for it was outside her understanding.

'Why, Maureen? For the love of all things holy, why did you go with him? You knew the punishment if you were caught. Look what happened to Finbar's daughter when she set up with that English soldier.'

Maureen's tears had dried, yet her resilience was at an ebb. 'I'm sorry, Mam,' she whispered. 'But I love him.' She looked up into her mother's pinched little face and tried to smile. 'And he loves me. He's promised we'll be together always.'

Bridie folded her arms around her waist and glared down at her eldest daughter. 'If you believe that then you're a bigger fool than I thought,' she snapped.

27

The thunder of the door slamming back into the wall made them jump. Bridie leaped away from the tub, her face drained of all colour. Maureen grabbed the scrap of towel and tried to cover her nakedness.

The atmosphere was electric. The silence following Michael O'Halloran's entrance laced with fear.

'Get that dirty wee whore out of my house,' yelled Michael as he filled the doorway. 'And if you so much as open your mouth, Bridie O'Halloran, I'll take me feckin' belt to the both of you.'

Maureen and Bridie were snapped from their frozen trance – each moving swiftly to allay Michael's obvious rage. Maureen grabbed the clean clothes and struggled to dress, and Bridie raced to the curtain to shield the three little girls who were watching wide-eyed through the gap.

'Get out,' Michael roared. 'Or you'll feel the leather on your backsides.'

The younger children shot out of sight and Maureen, now fully dressed, felt something akin to hatred for this bully of a father. 'It's me you want,' she said coldly. 'Leave them alone.'

He glared at her, his eyes reddened with drink and temper, his hand already unfastening his belt. 'You'll not be telling me what to do in me own feckin' house,' he shouted. His heavy boots rapped out a tattoo as he crossed the wooden floor and slowly eased the belt from around his thickened waist.

'You've shamed me, Maureen O'Halloran. I hear what my daughter's been up to from that bitch Regan Donovan. She couldn't wait to tell everyone in the pub, her Da standing there behind the bar with that self-righteous grin on his ugly face. You're going to pay for that, my girl.'

The belt buckle glinted in the firelight as it dangled from his meaty hand.

Maureen reached for the poker. And although she was trembling with fear, she knew she had to defend herself, and the baby inside her. 'Touch me and I'll hit you back,' she

28

said with a coolness that surprised her. 'I've been punished enough tonight.'

He stood there, his mouth agape. Maureen could see the confusion in his dark eyes, the shock in his face. Like all bullies, she suddenly realised, he was a coward – didn't have the guts to stand up to his own daughter.

'You can't talk to me like that,' he stammered. 'I'll, I'll . . .'

'You'll put your belt back on and sit down,' she said with an audacity that shocked her and brought a gasp from Bridie. 'And when I'm gone you're not to touch Mam or the wee ones. They had nothing to do with this – nothing at all. God help you if I find out you've hurt any of them.'

Michael walked as if in a trance to the chair and plumped down. He stared slack-mouthed at his eldest daughter as if she was a stranger – as if he couldn't believe she dared defy him.

Maureen hastily collected the rest of her clothes from the pile by the range and rolled them in a rough bundle. She glanced across at Mam who was cowering near the wall by the curtain and tried to transmit a message of courage. Then she walked across the room and out of the door, slamming it behind her in a final act of defiance.

It wasn't until she was halfway up the hill that her own courage deserted her and she sank on to a stone wall and burst into tears.

The storm of the previous night had blown itself out and the day had dawned bright and cold. The sort of day Henry relished, with the aroma of wet earth and grass tempered by the salt air coming off the sea and the warmth of horseflesh and hounds. It was good hunting weather.

He sat astride his impatient hunter and thought of his forthcoming tryst with Maureen as he waited for the whipper-in to organise the hounds. How strange she would find all this, he mused as he sipped from the stirrup cup. Yet it made a pretty picture. The old stone house was mellow in the spring sunshine, making a perfect backdrop for the excited, milling hounds, the scarlet hunting jackets and prancing horses.

His gaze trawled the assembly and came to rest on his mother. Lady Miriam was neatly perched side-saddle on her grey mare, with her long black skirt and tight jacket showing off an admirable figure for a woman in her late forties.

She caught his look and brought her mare alongside. 'I need to speak with you,' she said quietly. 'After the hunt, when your father is otherwise occupied.'

He looked across at her. Her expression was masked by the veil of her hat, but her chin was set in a determined line. 'I have things to do after the hunt,' he said firmly. 'It will have to wait.'

Her gloved hand rested on his arm. 'I have eyes in my head, son,' she said with steely warning. 'Better to speak to me about this little problem than your father, don't you think?'

Henry fingered his moustache and looked away. 'I have concerns, admittedly. But nothing for you to worry about,' he said with a calmness that belied his whirling thoughts. Had mother discovered his secret meetings with Maureen, or was this about the row he'd had with Father last night?

'There was trouble in the village yesterday,' she said grimly as she tried to still her impatient horse. 'And if my suspicions are correct, we need to do something about it. Today.'

His pulse began to race along with his imagination. 'What trouble?' His voice seemed loud amongst the stamping hoofs on the cobbles and the baying of the hounds, but the gathering was too concerned in their anticipation for the hunt to take any notice.

'Maureen O'Halloran,' replied his mother, her gaze piercing the veil.

Henry grasped her hand, the dread making it difficult to speak. 'What's happened?' he rasped.

Lady Miriam shook off his hand and stilled the mare. 'So

I was right,' she hissed. 'You fool. I warned you about getting mixed up with that dreadful family.'

'What about Maureen, mother?' His voice was edged with fear.

'What happens in the village should be of no concern to us,' she said evenly. 'As you've made that impossible, you will come to my drawing room immediately after the hunt and I will tell you what you are going to do next.'

'I'm going to find Maureen,' he snapped, pulling on the reins.

She stopped him, her grip a steel band on his arm. 'Do that and I can't help you. You know how your father will react when he hears what you've been up to.'

'I have to go, mother. I must see she's come to no harm.' He caught the expression on his mother's face and went cold. 'What is it?' he demanded. 'What's happened to her?'

She withdrew her hand and gathered up the reins. Her back was straight, her shoulders set with a long-practised determination to control any emotion she might be feeling. 'I've said all along that the Irish are barbarians, and what they did to Maureen O'Halloran merely proves my point.' She turned an imperious head towards him, her mouth set in a hard line. 'Even her family have disowned her, and I can't say I blame them.'

'Where is she?' breathed Henry.

Lady Miriam eyed him for a long moment. 'You were always my favourite,' she murmured finally as her shoulders sagged and her chin drooped. 'How could you do this to us, Henry? How could you betray my trust like this?'

'Tell me where she is,' he demanded, his impatience making him fierce.

The silence dragged and the world seemed to falter and slow as she looked back at him. 'I have no idea,' she said finally. Her hand stilled him, her gaze intensely bright with what looked suspiciously like unshed tears. 'Forget her, son. The O'Halloran girl will be dealt with, and although there will be hell to pay from your father, you must be man enough

31

to see this through.' With an infinitesimal shake of her head she seemed to gather her wits. 'I hope you learn from this, Henry, because there will be no second chances.'

Henry's impatience and fear made his hands rough as he gathered the reins. 'How did you know all this?' His curiosity would not be denied despite the urgent need to find Maureen.

'I have my spies,' she replied as she regained her composure. 'There are very few things that go on around here that escape me, Henry.'

'So you've known all along?'

She nodded curtly. 'I was hoping you'd come to your senses.' Her voice became waspish. 'Every young man must sow his wild oats. But it appears you are not in possession of your wits, or decent restraint.' She yanked on the reins and rode away.

Henry was momentarily stunned by the viciousness of his mother's retort. He'd never witnessed her wrath before, but now he could understand why she was such a perfect foil to Sir Oswald.

He backed his stamping hunter away from the gathering and watched as Lady Miriam engaged his father in conversation, neatly turning him from any sight of Henry.

'At least we have someone on our side,' he muttered. 'Though for how much longer remains to be seen.' Mother might be tough and infinitely manipulative, but she didn't hold the purse strings – didn't have the power to change generations of bigotry.

The horse was eager to be off, and fought the bit as Henry steered him away from the others and rode him through the archway to the gate that led to the fields behind the house. After a glance over his shoulder he gave the horse its head and they galloped through the cold bright morning towards the abandoned gamekeeper's hut.

Deep within the woods, the wattle and daub shelter had settled into the earth, its roof leaning precariously against a gnarled tree trunk. The stone chimney had crumbled, the window shutter drooped and the door hung on one rusting hinge. The silence surrounding this lonely little shelter was profound, and Henry could hear the rapid beat of his heart as he brought the horse to a juddering halt.

Leaping from the saddle he called her name. There was no answer and the fear was acid in his mouth as he manhandled the door to gain entry. His eyes were still full of the sunlight and the shadows were deep as he called out again.

Silence greeted him and the sense of abandonment weighed heavy.

Henry ran his fingers through his hair as he stood there in the dappled sunlight that poured through the holes in the thatch. He pushed his way back through the door and tramped around the hut looking for any sign that she might have come here earlier. There was nothing.

Grasping the reins he climbed back into the saddle and turned his horse's head towards the village. Fear overrode his better judgement. He had to find Maureen. Had to make sure she was safe. For 'trouble in the village' could mean only one thing. They had been discovered. And he knew the awful punishment Maureen must have suffered.

The village appeared freshly laundered by the recent rain, the cobbles sparkling in the early sunlight of that Sunday morning. A single, tolling bell rang out from the tiny stone church that stood overlooking the bay, and gulls hovered and swooped over a deceptively calm sea.

Henry slowed his horse to a trot as he headed down the only street towards the O'Halloran cottage. His pulse raced as men spat at his horse's feet and women hustled their children into doorways until he passed. The tension was electric. It was there in their eyes, in their stance and in the very air. Henry lifted his chin and stared ahead, determined not to show how ill at ease he felt – how vulnerable. Yet he could feel their eyes following him, boring into his back as he progressed down the seemingly interminable street to the little cottage overlooking the quayside.

A cold sweat beaded his forehead and his hands became

slippery on the leather reins as he finally drew to a halt outside the cottage and climbed down from his horse. Looking neither left nor right he strode up the narrow path and rapped on the door. He stood there, his back at almost military attention as he waited for his knock to be answered. Yet his knees were in danger of buckling and the sweat was running down his spine.

'Ye'll not be seeing that whore again,' shouted a woman from the watching crowd.

Henry turned and faced them, his fists tightly clenched at his sides. 'Where is she?' he demanded. His voice sounded sharp and youthful even to his own ears – and for once in his life he wished he had his father's bearing and command.

Regan Donovan pushed through the gathering, her red hair fiery in the sunlight, her stance insolent as she stood before him arms akimbo. 'She's gone,' she said bluntly.

'Where?' Henry's impatience was growing along with the fear.

The green eyes surveyed him, running from his shining leather boots to the windswept hair that was darkened with sweat. Regan's tongue flicked over her lips and she tossed back her hair. 'As far from you as she can,' she spat. 'Go back to your fine house, Henry. We don't want you here either.' With that she turned and with a shrill cackle of laughter linked her arms with two other girls and began to walk away.

Henry threw caution to the wind and strode after her. A murmur of unease rustled through the onlookers as he grabbed her arm and roughly pulled her round to face him. 'Where did she go?' he demanded. 'What did you bitches do to her?'

Her eyes were cold. There was no insolence in her face – just hatred. She jerked her arm from his clutches and tossed her hair from her face. 'You'll never know from me,' she snarled. Her glance flashed across the others. 'Not from anyone here,' she said triumphantly.

Henry could have slapped her insolent face. Could so

34

easily have taken her by the neck and shaken her – but despite his rage and his frustration, he knew it would do no good. Turning swiftly away he strode back to his horse and threw himself up into the saddle. 'You'll regret this day, Regan Donovan,' he shouted as he yanked the reins and made the horse prop and dance.

'Not nearly as much as you will when your Da finds out what you and Maureen have been up to,' retorted a loud voice in the crowd.

Henry was almost blind with fury as he spurred his hunter into a gallop and cut a swathe through the milling crowd. He no longer cared if he caused them injury. For the first time in his life he shared his father's hatred of the Irish.

Chapter Two

Miriam dragged herself back to the present and, after looking at her watch, realised she'd already wasted half the morning. With a cluck of impatience she returned the music box to its hiding place in the kitchen, then rammed on her bush hat and stomped down the dilapidated steps and headed for the stables.

Bellbird Station had once farmed thousands of head of cattle, now the pastures were home to some of the best bloodstock in Australia. The changes had come about gradually over the years, reaching the pinnacle of respectability when one of her stallions won the Melbourne Cup. Now they had buyers and breeders coming from all over the world and she was extremely irritated that it was unlikely she'd be around long enough to see another Cup winner.

She was out of breath and filthy half an hour later when her manager caught her mucking out the stables. 'Don't reckon you ought'a be doin' that,' he drawled.

She straightened her back and glared up at him. They were both of an age, but he had the habit of treating her as if she was positively ancient. 'Just remember who's the boss around this place, Frank, and mind your own bloody business.'

He hitched from one foot to another, his long face a picture of misery beneath the broad brim of his sweat-stained Akubra. He'd been Miriam's manager for over fifty years and should have been used to her ways by now, yet she knew he'd never quite learned to cope with one of her glares, and at the moment he reminded her of a naughty schoolboy who'd been caught smoking in the bike sheds.

'It ain't right for a lady of your age,' he said with scant regard for the consequences of such a declaration.

'Age has damn all to do with it,' she rasped as she picked up a hammer and began to repair one of the stalls. 'Isn't there something you could be doing instead of hanging around here giving me earache?'

He blushed and strolled off, his rolling gait that of a man who'd spent most of his life on the back of a horse.

Miriam's smile was wry and she watched him go. She was glad he cared enough to face up to her. Glad he'd decided to stay on Bellbird Station once he'd married and started a family. Having children around after Chloe had left for Queensland had livened the place up and she'd missed them terribly when they too had left. She'd hoped one of Frank's brood might stay on and perhaps rear another family in this good country. But it hadn't happened. The outback was too isolated – too harsh for this new generation of Australians who couldn't wait to leave for the bright lights and bustle of the cities.

The sound of an approaching vehicle snapped her from her gloomy thoughts and she turned to watch the mud-splattered utility roar over the ruts and come to a screeching halt in front of the verandah. Realising what a sight she must look and knowing there wasn't much she could do about it, she rubbed her hands down the seat of her trousers, straightened her hat and went out to meet her visitor. It was unlike Wilcox to make such an entrance – perhaps he'd got his second wind.

The utility door opened and Miriam found it rather unnerving to have to step back so she could look up into the stranger's face. He was handsome all right, but far too young to be the visitor she'd expected. 'Can I help you?' she asked.

'Jake Connor,' he drawled. 'Are you Mrs Strong?'

Miriam took off her thick working gloves and shook the proffered hand. She looked up at him again. You could tell a lot from a handshake, and his had been dry, his fingers firm but not overly forceful. 'And what can I do for you, Mr Jake Connor?'

'It's more a case of what I can do for you,' he said with a smile.

She eyed him suspiciously. He certainly didn't have the manner of Wilcox. Neither did he look like a rep or feed merchant. 'Oh, yes?'

He laughed, thoroughly at ease and not in the least put out by her brusque manner. 'You called my office. Wanted help with something?'

Miriam drew herself up to her full height – which was all of five feet and half an inch – and found that much to her annoyance she was still addressing his midriff. 'If I'd have wanted a boy to help me, I'd have asked for one,' she said stiffly. 'You've had a wasted journey, Mr Connor.'

He folded his arms and leaned against the utility with his long legs crossed at his booted ankles. He smiled down at her 'Not if you offer me a cup of tea and a piece of your famous chocolate cake.'

Miriam's eyes narrowed. How had he known about her cake? She looked him up and down admiring his nerve, and yet feeling rather peeved at how effortlessly he'd circumnavigated her brusque dismissal. His boots, she noticed were scuffed and well used, the same could also be said of his moleskins and bush hat. He might be young, and from the city, but he had the air of a man totally at ease with the dust and flies and heat of the outback. He puzzled her, and that was a fact. Cheeky with it too, she thought as she looked away.

'Pushing your luck a bit, aren't you?' she retorted.

'Not at all,' he said quietly, the amusement making his dark eyes smoulder. 'Your cake is famous in racing circles – and I ought to know, my dad's been going to the horse sales since I was an ankle biter and we always make a beeline for Bellbird's tea tent.'

She decided she rather liked this young man, and it might be pleasant to spend a little time with him before she sent him packing. For it was ridiculous to think he'd have the experience to do what she needed. 'Better come in, then,' she said grudgingly.

He opened the door of the utility and reached in for his briefcase.

Miriam's jaw dropped as she saw the other occupant. 'What on earth?'

'Meet Eric,' said Jake and grinned. 'The finest, most opinionated and stubborn cat this side of the equator. Eric,' he said to the ginger tom that was sitting imperiously on the passenger seat. 'This is Mrs Strong.'

The cat's disdainful glare studied Miriam for a moment and obviously found her beneath his contempt, for he stuck his leg in the air and bent to groom his backside.

Miriam laughed. 'Thanks,' she muttered. 'Nice to meet you too.'

'Sorry about that,' said Jake as he closed the door. 'He's always been aloof with women – nothing personal.'

Miriam watched the cat finish grooming and turn in a tight circle to go to sleep. 'I've never seen anything like it,' she said in wonder. 'Is it safe to drive with him out of a box?'

Jake nodded. 'Safer than leaving him at home. He trashes the place if I go out in the ute without him, and moves in with my neighbour until he's ready to speak to me again. My neighbour wouldn't mind, but he insists upon sleeping in the dog basket and goes on the attack if they try to move him. Her poor Alsatian's terrified of him.'

Miriam eyed the cat, which solemnly eyed her back. It was almost as if he knew they were talking about him. 'Strikes me he should see a psychiatrist,' she muttered.

Jake hitched his briefcase from hand to hand, obviously embarrassed. 'My wife tried a cat-behaviourist – it didn't work. That's why I got custody after the divorce.'

Miriam smiled as she led the way up the steps and on to the verandah. She was beginning to like this young man

39

even more. What a pity he wasn't what she needed. 'Time for tucker,' she muttered. 'Sit down and I'll brew up.'

When she returned with a laden tray he leaped to his feet and took it from her. Before she could protest, he'd poured the tea into the two thick china mugs that were chipped from age and carelessness and cut them both a healthy slab of cake.

Miriam sat in the old wicker chair and watched him. His hands might be soft, but they looked capable, the fingers long, the nails clean, unbitten and square cut. Her gaze lifted to his face and she found him watching her. 'Wilcox had no right to send someone so young,' she said baldly.

He finished the slab of cake and licked the remains of the icing from his fingers. 'I was the only one free,' he said calmly. 'Besides, I was in the neighbourhood.'

Miriam glanced at the utility. Eric was now sitting on the dashboard glaring balefully out of the window, his striped tail twitching in disgust. 'Those are Brisbane plates,' she snapped. 'Hardly local.'

'Nothing's local in Australia,' he said softly. 'We're all so spread out what's a few hundred miles between friends?' He put the mug on the table and leaned towards her. 'I might look too young, but I'm damned good at what I do and you shouldn't make judgements so quickly. Tell me what the problem is and I'll do my best to sort it out.'

Miriam raised an eyebrow. 'You seem very sure of yourself,' she snapped. 'But this is family business. I expected Wilcox – not some kid who's still wet behind the ears.'

He leaned back in his chair, apparently not at all offended by her manner. Crossing one booted foot over the other he dug his hands in his pockets and regarded her thoughtfully. 'I'm not going to win this argument, am I?' he said with a twinkle of humour in his dark eyes. 'Wilcox warned me about you. Said you were proud as well as stubborn.'

Miriam lifted her chin and tried to look stern. She was rather enjoying this sparring, but wouldn't allow him to see that. 'We're a proud family,' she said imperiously. 'We're strong because we've had to be – and if you're around long enough, you'll find the women strongest of all.'

'Too right,' he sighed. His brown eyes were bright with amusement as he looked at her across the table. 'Are you going to tell me why you need help, or are you determined to keep it secret until Geoff Wilcox is free?'

Miriam thought of Geoff Wilcox and remembered how humourless he was, how dry and uninteresting. He was excellent at his job, but lacking in personality and wit. Added to that, she thought sourly, he was certainly no oil painting.

She eyed Jake Connor and hurriedly looked away. It was difficult not to return his smile. He reminded her too much of her late husband, Edward – both men had a way with them – eyes that spoke volumes and a smile that could charm the birds out of the trees.

She pulled her thoughts together. She was prevaricating. 'How do I know you'll be up to the job?' she demanded.

His smile never faltered and there was a teasing quality to the gleam in his eyes. 'Not had a complaint yet,' he drawled.

I'll bet you haven't, she thought crossly. She eyed him for a long moment, sorely tempted to slap him for his insolence. She might be old and past it, but she knew exactly what agenda Jake Connor was working on.

Her thoughts were interrupted by the frantic yowling coming from the ute. 'Your cat's put a lie to that statement,' she said briskly.

Jake unfurled his length from the chair and ran down the steps to the utility. Eric took his time climbing down and marched, tail erect up the steps to the verandah. He surveyed the surroundings with a jaundiced eye, looked down his nose at Miriam, selected a chair with a cushion and jumped up. Fixing Miriam with his yellow eyes he began his demands.

Jake seemed flustered. 'Sorry about this. Do you think he could have a saucer of milk? I forgot to bring any.'

Miriam was trying hard not to laugh as she poured the

milk and pushed the saucer towards the cat. Sitting up at the table, Eric put his front paws neatly on either side of the saucer and began to lap. 'Does he always eat at the table?' she asked with barely disguised sarcasm.

'Usually,' said a red-faced Jake. 'It's beneath his dignity to eat from the floor – just as it is to chase birds.'

'Good,' retorted Miriam. 'The fledglings are only just beginning to leave the nests and I don't relish wholesale slaughter in my front yard.' She eyed him for a long moment, the silence broken only by the lap, lap, lap of the cat's tongue.

'I found something yesterday,' she began hesitantly. 'Something which could change things in this family – not necessarily for the good.'

He sat up, his interest obvious, and she was once again forcibly reminded of her long-dead husband. For Edward had also loved mysteries. 'What was it?' he asked, his gaze steady, his expression serious.

She looked away and chewed her lip. If she told him then the secret would be out and she would have to run with it. Yet how could she remain silent? It had been too many years since the truth had been told – it was time to finish this once and for all.

She fixed him with a glare. 'I'll show you, but you must promise to keep this to yourself until I'm absolutely sure I want to take things further.'

Jake nodded and Eric sat on his cushion watching her, the milk still studding his whiskers.

Miriam struggled out of her chair and shook off Jake's offer of help. 'I might be crook, but I'm not yet helpless,' she snapped with such an appalling lack of grace she immediately apologised. 'It's just bloody being old, you'll have to excuse my manners,' she said gruffly.

He smiled at her and returned to his chair as Miriam hobbled indoors to fetch the music box. She'd done too much this morning and her knee joints were throbbing in time with the dragon of pain that was unfurling in her back. She

42

shuffled into the kitchen and swiftly took a couple of the pills her doctor had prescribed for moments such as this.

When she returned to the verandah, Jake was leaning against the railings, one slim hip pushed out, his neat rear end jutting as he watched the activity in the yard. From where she was standing, Jake's rear was a very pleasant sight, and Miriam had to tear her gaze away so she could concentrate on the matters in hand. There might be snow on the roof, she thought with surprise, but by jingo there was still fire in the hearth.

'There,' she said as she placed the music box on the table between them. 'My proof that I've been cheated out of my rightful inheritance.'

She watched him turn the key and open the lid. Saw how his eyes followed the dancing figures and how his brow wrinkled in puzzlement.

When the music stopped and the dancers became still, Miriam carefully pulled out the secret drawer that had remained hidden all these years and was now badly broken. 'I dropped it,' she explained. 'Otherwise, I would never have known it was here.'

Jake's eyes widened as he saw what had been hidden, and he looked up at her for permission before he reached out and put it in his hand. 'My God,' he breathed. His dark eyes found her again. 'Do you have any idea what this is? Of what it's worth?'

Miriam was a little put out that one so young should fully understand what he was looking at. 'Oh, yes,' she said quietly. 'I know exactly what it is.'

His face was still alight with amazement. 'But where did it come from?' he asked in an awed voice. 'And why was it kept hidden?'

'That's a very long story,' she said as shadows of the past eclipsed the warmth of the sun. 'I hope, that by the time I've finished telling it, we'll both have a clearer idea of how we can solve my predicament.'

*

Fiona Wolff took off the crash helmet and leather jacket and stored them away in the Kawasaki's panniers. She ran her fingers through her hair in an effort to comb out the tangles and hurriedly applied lipstick and eyeliner. Snatching a glance into the handlebar mirror she decided that would have to do, she was late already and her father, Leo, would be going ballistic.

The exhibition of Leo's sculptures was being held in Brisbane's premier gallery, and as Fiona ran up the steps and showed her invitation to the doorman she wondered if perhaps she should have taken more care with her clothes. The gathering was obviously high-powered, the dress code far from casual, and she felt a little out of place in mini skirt, long white boots and a sleeveless skinny rib sweater.

She shrugged off the doubt. She was comfortable and cool which was more than could be said about the silly women who were draped in furs and diamonds despite the temperature having soared into the high nineties.

Fiona took a glass of champagne from the waiter and looked around the room. Leo's sculptures were magnificent against the black marble floor, the lighting enhancing the sensuous curves and delicate features of what the family called his harem. For Leo only sculpted women. They were his passion and his downfall. The reason he and Mum had divorced.

She meandered happily through the mêlée, content to remain unnoticed for a while as she reacquainted herself with his women. Here was the cool alabaster elegance of Charlotte, the black hauteur of Naomi, the elfin sexuality of Sara. There was voluptuous Roseanne and motherly Kim, and over in the corner by the fountain was Beth. Beautiful, tragic Beth, who'd never conquered her fear of reality and had lost the battle against her addictions despite Leo's nurturing.

Fiona sighed. Leo's hand had never been surer than when he'd sculpted Beth, for he'd caught her frailty, and the darkness of the demons in her eyes as she bent to look in the pool. How right he'd been to have her searching endlessly in the glassy water for something that was merely a reflection of her lost hope. Yet this parade of women was a testament to his unfaithfulness – a history of a wanton lifestyle that had ultimately destroyed his marriage and Fiona had found it hard in those early days to forgive him.

She took a sip of the chilled champagne and grimaced. It was too sour for her liking and was, as usual, giving her the hiccups. She put the glass down on a windowsill and remained hidden by the surrounding foliage that had been brought in by the exhibition people especially for the occasion. Her father was close by and as it had been six months since she'd seen him, she wanted to observe him for a little while.

Leo, resplendent in a red velvet smoking jacket, was talking to a statuesque blonde who looked as if she'd been transported here from ancient Rome. The long white dress was draped from one elegant, bronzed shoulder, the folds moulded to her exquisite figure by the rope of gold at her waist. The golden theme was duplicated in the band on her upper arm and the chain around her neck.

Fiona smiled as she leaned against the wall and watched. Leo was positively drooling, but doing his best to hide it. What was the bet he'd found his next model, and his next mistress? Yet, why not? He was a handsome man, her father. With a leonine head of silver hair, eyes that were startlingly blue and a figure not yet wracked by too much booze and a poor diet, he could still cut a swathe.

'What are you up to, hiding yourself away?'

Fiona turned at the sound of the voice and grinned. 'Hello, Mum. Didn't know you'd be here. Are you exhibiting as well?'

Chloe shook back the cloud of auburn hair, her bracelets jangling on her slender wrists. Her green eyes drifted over Fiona and came to rest on Leo. 'My paintings are being exhibited next month. I'm only here because someone's

45

got to watch out for the silly old bugger,' she murmured. 'Given half the chance he'll step on the wrong person's toes.'

'You mean the blonde?'

Chloe nodded. 'Married of course – to Brendt.'

Fiona understood immediately. Brendt came from a rich and influential family with fingers in the political pie as well as on the pulse of the stock markets. On his grandfather's death, Brendt had diversified the family wealth into shipping and real estate as well as the media and mining and was said to be as ruthlessly ambitious as the old man. Rumour had it he was the steel hand in the velvet glove that steered Australia's Chancellor of the Exchequer.

'Better rescue him then, before he has her stripped and washed and sent to his room.'

Chloe's laugh was soft, her eyes dreamy as she put an arm around Fiona's shoulders. 'It's lovely to see you. I didn't think you'd be back in time for Mim's birthday, let alone for this.'

Fiona smiled at the family name for her grandmother. Miriam herself had begun it when she was tiny and couldn't get her tongue around her name, and it had just caught on and carried through into the following generations. 'Wouldn't have missed either,' she said firmly. 'My Bellbird summers are still very special. Besides, I'd finished the photo shoot in Brazil, and I needed to come home to get the films developed properly.'

Chloe's gaze drifted away and trawled the room. 'I hope National Geographic pay you enough,' she murmured. 'I hardly ever get to see you any more.'

Fiona saw her toes peeking from beneath the emerald caftan, and realised her mother had forgotten to put any shoes on again, but as she was used to her dreamy attitude to everything, she ignored the omission. As an artist Chloe could get away with being eccentric – in fact it almost enhanced her reputation. 'Better rescue Dad,' she reminded her.

'Darlings,' he boomed as he opened his arms to greet them. 'Come and kiss me before I fade away.'

Fiona giggled as she kissed his cheek and was clasped to his chest in a bear hug. She was used to his theatrics – probably something to do with his Bohemian ancestors. 'Hello, Dad.'

'Leo, darling,' he breathed in her ear. 'Dad sounds so old. Can't let the side down by letting all these people know how decrepit I really am.' His smile belied the admonishment and his kissed her forehead. 'You smell wonderful,' he murmured. 'What's that in your hair?'

'Brazilian shampoo,' she replied with a giggle. His remark was typical, and it was why she and Mum could ultimately forgive him anything. For although her sister Louise regarded him as a dirty old man, they realised he genuinely loved women. He adored watching them, adored shopping for them, adored listening to their gossip. But most of all he loved their scent, their softness, even their ability to unsheath their claws when on the attack. It was because of his innate understanding of the female in all its forms that he was such a great artist.

Fiona stood back as Chloe was embraced and kissed. They made a handsome couple with Chloe's drift of hair so bright against his silver, her sinuous curves fitting so well against him.

'Where's your sister and that dreadful husband of hers?' Leo cast his gaze around the room.

'In the bar, I think,' replied Chloe absently as she picked up a glass of champagne and surveyed the room. 'Ralph's bumped into a banking colleague.'

She pronounced it phonetically as they all did behind his back. Rafe was far too precocious for such a prat.

'Talking business, no doubt,' grumbled Leo. 'Has the man no soul? I sweat blood getting this damn exhibition together and he prefers to discuss banking.' He snorted and slammed his glass down on a nearby table. 'I'm going to haul him out of there.'

Fiona stilled him by putting a hand on his arm. Leo was not the most tactful of men when it came to his son-in-law. 'I'll get them,' she said firmly. 'You need to stay here and charm your public.' She leaned towards him, her voice low. 'Just leave the blonde alone – she's married to Shamrock Holdings.'

He smoothed back his hair and grimaced. 'Enough said,' he replied. 'Go and get your sister and we'll crack open another bottle of champagne. Gallery's paying.'

Fiona watched Chloe thread her arm through his as he led her through the chattering crowd. There was no point in wishing things would change between her parents, for they seemed happier, closer, much more content with each other. Divorce had not been cruel, but had brought friendship and a deeper understanding of the other's needs. In fact, she thought as she left the room and crossed the atrium, they probably saw more of one another now than they ever did before.

The bar was all steel and glass, bright from the sun that poured in through the roof. Richly coloured paintings hung on the wall and soft leather couches and chairs had been set around low tables for those who needed a drink after seeing the price of Leo's work.

Fiona saw her sister immediately and was shocked at how pale and thin she looked. That black dress is doing her no favours, she thought as she crossed the room. And as for the boyish haircut – it only emphasised the sharp cheekbones and deep shadows around her eyes.

Plastering a smile on her face, Fiona approached the table. Ralph was in full flow, bending the ear of a florid man in a garish waistcoat and expensively cut suit. 'Here you are,' she said brightly. 'Leo's asking for you.'

Louise began to rise from her chair, shot a glance at Ralph and sat down again. 'Can't you see Rafe's busy, Fiona. Leo will have to wait,' she hissed.

Fiona frowned. She'd seen that anxious glance, the hesitant, almost hunted look in her sister's eyes. 'That's not

48

going to stop you, though, is it?' she persisted. 'Come on, Louise. Dad's going to open another bottle of champagne.'

Louise looked nervously at Ralph who ignored her as he stood up and shook hands with his colleague. Once the man was out of earshot he turned venomous eyes on Fiona. 'I'll thank you not to interrupt an important meeting,' he snapped. 'And I'd rather you didn't encourage Louise to drink – she's on a diet.'

Fiona looked down at her sister. 'Diet? What diet?' she asked baldly. 'You were thin enough already.'

'She's lost two stone,' Ralph interjected. 'Down at least two dress sizes. I think she looks wonderful.' His frosty gaze travelled over Fiona's figure and his sneer was a clear indication of his thoughts.

Fiona had never had problems with her weight – she didn't mind being a few pounds heavier than she should – and had realised long ago she would never be a stick insect and philosophically accepted the fact. She looked at Louise and realised there was no point in telling both of them what she thought – that Louise looked half-dead. 'And how do you feel about losing so much weight?' she asked gently.

'Great.' Louise smiled over-brightly as she stood up and attempted to smooth the creases of her short black dress. 'You should give it a go. It's basically vegan, with no fat, no wheat and no dairy products. Of course tea and coffee and booze have to go as well, but the weight just drops off.'

Fiona looked at her aghast. Of course the weight dropped off if you starved yourself, she thought crossly. 'I like my meat almost raw, my beer cold and lashings of cream on my strawberries – life's hard enough without becoming a martyr to these 60s food fads.' She pulled out a pack of cigarettes and lit one just to show Ralph he couldn't bully her like he could her sister.

He glared at the cigarette and waved his hand to disperse the smoke before turning his attention to Louise. 'I said that would crease,' he muttered. 'Should have worn the Mary Quant I had sent from London.'

Louise plucked at her dress again. 'They'll drop out once I'm on the move,' she said with a nervous breathiness. 'Besides, the dress you bought was too tight. It wouldn't have been appropriate.'

'I think I know what is and is not appropriate,' he murmured as he took her arm. 'And if you hadn't gorged yourself on all that chocolate it wouldn't have been too tight.'

'It was only two little chocolates, Rafe,' she protested softly. 'I thought I deserved a treat after being so good.'

'No pain, no gain,' he declared loftily and steered her out of the bar. 'You wanted to lose weight, and I'm trying to help you – but if you persist in breaking the diet then you only have yourself to blame if your clothes don't fit.'

Fiona realised her mouth was open and hastily clamped it shut. Ralph had always been full of himself, but now he was becoming a bully.

Poor Louise, she thought as she finished her cigarette and stabbed it out in an ashtray. Why the hell doesn't she leave him? They've got no kids and that ridiculously flash house on the river would fetch a bomb – certainly enough to buy Louise something more suitable to live in. As for the diet. She blew a silent raspberry. It was bad enough when Louise went veggie, but this was downright ridiculous. Doesn't she realise how ghastly she looks – or how much damage she was doing to herself?

'Osteoporosis here she comes,' muttered Fiona as she followed them out of the room. 'Liver damage, vitamin deficiency, and a skin like paper that's going to crease far more easily than that damned dress. I'm going to have a very long talk with Louise.'

But she soon found that getting Louise alone was not an option. Ralph kept her firmly by his side, working the room, networking for future business with his merchant bank, barely giving Louise's family any attention at all. They left an hour later with a promise to meet at Bellbird Station at the end of the week.

Leo watched them leave. 'What's that dreadful man done to my beautiful little girl,' he wailed. 'I tried talking to her, but she doesn't see what he is – can't understand why I'm concerned for her.'

'Mim will sort him out,' said Chloe as she pulled the long purple velvet cloak over her emerald silk caftan. 'She's a firm believer in three meals a day and no nonsense. Ralph will have his work cut out if he tries to interfere.'

She turned to Fiona and wrapped her in an embrace that was clouded with Chanel No 5 and a faint hint of turpentine. 'See you at Bellbird, darling. And take care on that bike.'

'Your mother is the most beautiful woman in the world,' sighed Leo as they stood together on the steps and watched her float down to her car before roaring off in a cloud of exhaust fumes and screeching tyres. 'But I do wish she wouldn't drive – has the attention span of a gnat and absolutely no sense of direction.'

Miriam finished speaking and the echoes of the past filled the ensuing silence.

Jake looked across the table at the redoubtable woman opposite him. Miriam Strong was aptly named, despite her bird-like appearance. For beneath that frail exterior lay the core of steel and determination which had won her respect throughout the racing world. Yet there was something in her eyes that told him all was not well, and he wondered if the discovery of the contents of the secret compartment was only a part of what ailed her.

Jake stared off into the distance, the bustle in the yard merely a background noise to his thoughts as he dug his hands in his pockets and leaned back in the chair. He had no idea where this story was heading, but was intrigued by her tale, remembering how his own grandmother would have him and his sisters spellbound as she recounted her life as a pioneer.

With a glance at his watch he realised the day was disappearing and he had yet to find accommodation for the night.

'Are you in a hurry to get somewhere?' Miriam's voice broke into his thoughts.

Jake smiled. Nothing much missed the old girl, that was for sure. 'I was just wondering where the nearest roadhouse was,' he said.

She waved a dismissive hand. 'You can stay here. Got a spare room until the end of the week.' She eyed him beadily. 'Family's coming up for my birthday. Lot of nonsense if you ask me. Complete waste of petrol.'

Despite her words, Jake could see she was looking forward to seeing them, the brusqueness merely a defensive ruse to hide her true feelings. 'If you're sure?' he murmured.

'Wouldn't offer otherwise,' she retorted.

Jake grinned and leaned forward, his arms resting along his thighs. 'I don't need to be back in the office for a while, so thanks. It'll be a nice change to get out of the city.'

'If you're so clever, how come you can just leave the office when the mood takes you?' Miriam's gaze was piercing.

'I'm a partner, and due some holiday. That's why I volunteered to come up here.'

She put her head to one side as she regarded him, and Jake was once again reminded of how bird-like she was. 'Come from the country, do you?' she asked.

He nodded. 'Dad's got a property out near Ballarat. My older sister still lives there with her husband.'

'Why did you leave?'

He shrugged. 'I found living in the outback too stifling. But that doesn't stop me from going home as often as I can.' He decided to change the subject. 'You realise that what you're planning could be financial suicide, don't you?' He kept his tone soft, to take the sting out of his words.

'I was afraid you'd say that,' she replied. Her gaze drifted to the music box. The lid was down, the dancers still, the music silent. 'But I thought that if I told you the story it might shed light on things that so far have not been explained.'

52

She leaned forward, her gnarled hands clasped on the table. 'Hindsight can be a wonderful thing, Mr Connor. When the passion goes out of a situation we are able to see things far more clearly.' She smiled at his confusion. 'I'm hoping it will all make sense eventually,' she murmured.

He had no idea what she was talking about, but decided it wouldn't hurt to let her go on with her story. 'So, did Henry ever find Maureen?'

Miriam's eyes were misty with memory, and Jake wondered whose voice she heard. For it was as if she was listening to the story being re-told – as if a much-loved person had come to sit beside her and was leading her back to the past.

Chapter Three

Miriam could hear his voice so clearly, could feel his presence. It was as if the finding of the secret cache had released his spirit and she took strength from it – for this was her father's part of the story – his legacy.

'Henry knew Maureen couldn't have gone far, even if she'd travelled through the night.' Miriam sighed. 'He sat astride his horse at the crossroads, his frustration and shame still with him after the confrontation with Regan. He didn't know what to do. To all intents and purposes, Maureen had disappeared. She hadn't gone to their meeting place, and had left no message in the rotten tree stump.'

Miriam looked into the past and heard his voice, so clear even after all this time. 'He wondered then if she had ever truly loved him. Wondered if he loved her enough to track her down. For if he did, then there would be no turning back. His choice would be made and there would be little redemption.'

Maureen had sought shelter in the abandoned hut and was in a restless sleep when her mother came looking for her. 'Wake up,' she ordered. 'You can't stay here.'

'I'm waiting for Henry,' Maureen replied.

'He won't be coming,' Bridie snapped. 'Get up and follow me. And hurry. I don't have long.'

'He will,' she persisted. 'He promised.'

'Will you listen to yourself?' Bridie's hands were on her hips, her face a mask of contempt. 'The man won't want you now – neither will his family. Best to leave before there's even more trouble for us all.'

Maureen felt the chill of acceptance despite her deep hope that Bridie would be proved wrong. 'I must see him,' she said urgently. 'I must hear it from his own mouth before I leave.'

Bridie gathered up the bundle of clothes and thrust it at her daughter. 'Ye'll hear nothing you want to hear,' she said darkly. 'Let me know what is best, for once.'

Maureen hesitated and was roughly nudged in the back. 'I've not all night to be wasting. Yer Da will wake up soon and I have to get back. Move, girl.'

Maureen reluctantly followed Bridie into the cold, still night. A full moon lit their way as they traipsed through the woods and emerged on the far side of the hill, well away from the village. 'How did you find me?' she asked tentatively as she hurried to keep pace with her mother.

'I know more than you think,' she muttered.

'Where are we going?' Maureen clambered over a fallen tree and snagged her skirt. She was clumsy with weariness, and still reeling from the earlier attack.

'A place I know that no one will think of looking for you,' Bridie replied with a coldness that brooked any argument, and a determined pace that was hard to match.

Maureen's thoughts were in turmoil. If she left without speaking to Henry she would never know if he had betrayed her. Yet, if she defied her mother there was no telling the humiliation she might have to bear. They walked in silence for almost an hour until they came to a small stone dwelling that was almost hidden amongst the rocks that clustered down the steep hill.

'What is this place?'

'Shepherd's bothy,' replied Bridie. 'You'll stay here until I get back.' Bridie pushed Maureen through the door and handed her a packet of bread and cheese.

Maureen looked at her mother, trying to read her mind, to understand what she meant by all this subterfuge. 'Where are you going?' she asked. 'Why are you doing this?'

Bridie's expression softened for the first time that night. 'You're my girl,' she said simply. 'Despite the disgrace you've brought on all our heads, I cannot just abandon you.' She squeezed Maureen's arm and turned away. 'Stay here. I'll be back soon.'

Maureen watched her climb back down the rocky hill and disappear out of sight. She slumped down on the dirt floor and leaned against the weathered stone wall. Weariness, fear and heartache closed in with the silence and before she'd taken more than a couple of bites of the food she fell asleep.

The sun was high in the sky when Bridie returned. She eyed Maureen and brushed a hand gently against her daughter's bruised cheek. 'It's time to leave,' she said softly. 'Here. Take this. You can buy a seat on the stage and passage over the water, and this is the address of the convent who will take you in when it's time.'

Maureen looked at the small leather purse Bridie placed in her hand. She felt the weight of it, heard it jingle and knew what it was. The tears, held back for so long, coursed down her cheeks.

'Hush, my *acushla*, my *mavourneen*,' crooned Bridie as she put her arms around Maureen. 'He's not worth the tears.'

The two women stood there in the mean little stone shelter and acknowledged and strengthened their ties of kinship and heritage as the sun crossed the sky and the clouds began to darken the day. Then they parted. Bridie tramped back to the tiny fishing village, to a life ruled by bigotry and a violent husband. Maureen traipsed further and further from all she'd ever known towards an uncertain and terrifying future.

There were only two roads out of the village. One to the next hamlet along the coast, and one east, to Dublin. His love for Maureen was too strong to just let her disappear from his life. He had to find her. Had to know if she returned his love.

The decision made, Henry gathered up the reins and kicked his horse into a gallop.

Several hours later he realised he was on a fool's errand. The hunter was blowing, its vast lungs wheezing like an old organ as they came to a halt on the brow of a hill. Standing in the stirrups, Henry surveyed his surroundings. Hills and valleys of verdant green rolled before him beneath a sky of scudding clouds. There was no trail of dust heralding the passage of a wagon, no lonely figure traipsing the dirt road. The only sound was the wind in the grass and the snort of the hunter. With a heavy heart he turned and headed back to Beecham Hall.

'So, you've decided to return home.' Sir Oswald's voice was dangerously calm as Henry entered the morning room. 'I know all about the O'Halloran girl, so spare me your lies.'

Henry felt a stab of elation that was mixed with fear. 'Have you seen her? Where is she?'

'I've dealt with it,' retorted Sir Oswald. 'It need not concern you any more.'

'She does concern me, Father,' he blurted. 'I love her.'

'Don't be ridiculous,' Sir Oswald boomed. 'She's a bog Irish slut who thinks she can trap you by getting in the family way.'

Henry blanched. 'Family way?' He licked his lips, his pulse racing as he stood before the awesome presence of his father. The shock of this pronouncement sent his thoughts into a maelstrom. Why hadn't Maureen told him? How could she have kept such a secret from him?

Sir Oswald poured himself a large whiskey and eyed his youngest son over the rim of the glass. 'Had her whining mother here earlier, sporting a black eye as usual and begging me to help get her daughter out of the mess you've both caused.'

'How long ago was this?' Henry's elation made him careless of his father's reaction.

Sir Oswald slammed the glass on a small side table and clasped his hands behind his back. 'About ten minutes after

57

you went sneaking off,' he roared. 'Blasted woman inter-rupted the hunt and I had to come back here and sort out your mess.'

'You don't need to sort out anything,' snapped Henry. 'If Maureen is carrying my child, then we'll be married at once.'

'Over my dead body,' roared Sir Oswald. 'She'll be packed off to England and the brat adopted.'

The gasp that greeted this statement made them all turn. Emma rose from her chair, her pallor heightened by angry spots of colour on her cheeks. 'How can you be so wicked?' she hissed. 'This is Henry's child. Your grandchild. You can't just give it away.'

'Sit down woman,' Sir Oswald roared. 'This is none of your damn business.'

To everyone's amazement, Emma disobeyed him. 'Yes it is,' she retorted. 'You wanted an heir, and so does Thomas, but it's becoming obvious that I'm incapable of providing one. This baby is the solution,' she ploughed on. 'It will have Beecham-Fford blood and Thomas and I could easily arrange a discreet adoption.'

'Thomas,' roared Sir Oswald. 'Deal with your wife. And if she can't keep her mouth shut – get her out of here.'

The courage seemed to drain from Emma as she sank back down on the chair and hung her head. But her outburst had strengthened Henry's resolve and although he had yet to find Maureen, he was damned if he was going to let his father ride rough-shod over him – especially now his child was part of the equation.

'The child is mine, and not for adoption,' he announced coldly. 'And I intend to marry Maureen. There is nothing any of you can say that will change my mind.'

'Money talks, boy,' snarled his father. 'Wouldn't mind betting she's halfway to England by now with my gold in her pocket, and not a thought for you.'

Henry glared at his father. He'd never loathed anyone quite so much in his short life, and hoped he never would again. 'I intend to find her – she's going nowhere unless it's with me.'

'Henry,' interjected Lady Miriam with a tone that brooked no interruption. 'I admire your obvious devotion to this girl, and your honourable intention to stand by her. But you must not allow her attractions to blind you to your duty to this family.'

Henry opened his mouth to reply and was silenced by her withering glare.

'Do you realise what a scandal like this would mean to Thomas' political career – to your father's standing in the world of commerce?' She stood, her long riding habit swishing around her ankles as she walked slowly towards him.

'Do you wish to see our good name trampled – our reputation the brunt of snide gossip – our social standing mocked?' She answered her own questions with a shake of her head. 'With wealth there comes duty and service to those less fortunate. This girl is not only Catholic, but working class. Unlike you, she has a full understanding of her place and will accept her lot.'

Her hand was gentle on his arm as she looked up into his face. 'I beg you to reconsider, Henry. We must all make sacrifices at some time or another, and I have no doubt this girl will marry soon enough and have plenty of other babies to keep her occupied. You know what these Catholics are like.'

Henry shook off her arm, appalled at her lack of feeling. 'There does not have to be a scandal,' he said hoarsely. 'Maureen and I will be married, and once the fuss dies down we can return home.'

'Naïve young fool,' blustered Sir Oswald. 'Wise up, boy. If you leave now, you can forget any help from me – or anyone else in this family.' His glare encompassed everyone in the room. 'The very idea of bringing that Irish whore into my house – let alone her brat,' he snorted. 'Probably isn't even yours.'

The silence was thick with emotion as Henry stood before his father. 'Naïve, I might be. But my conscience and my heart will not let me abandon her and our child,' he said with a firmness that belied his racing pulse and dry mouth. 'If it is your wish to turn your back on me, then so be it.'

Sir Oswald's colour was high, his eyes sparking with distaste as he regarded his youngest son. Then he turned away and headed for the door. 'You are no longer welcome in this house,' he said coldly as he turned in the doorway.

Henry took a step towards him. The disbelief was sour in his mouth. He'd never in his darkest moments dreamed his father would actually go through with his threat. 'Father,' he pleaded. 'Don't . . .'

'Only a son may address me so,' Sir Oswald interrupted. 'You no longer have that privilege.'

Henry watched him close the door and listened to the ring of his departing footsteps. The tears were blurring his vision and there was a lump in his throat that threatened to choke him as he turned to look at the others.

Thomas' hand was at Emma's elbow as he helped her from the chair and, grim-faced, steered her out of the room. The look of helpless sympathy she shot at him as they passed almost tore Henry apart.

Lady Miriam stood there for a long moment, the differing emotions clear in her eyes. 'Oh, Henry,' she finally breathed. 'What have you done?'

His pain was overwhelming. 'Will he ever forgive me?'

She shook her head and dabbed her eyes with a scrap of lace. 'I hope she's worth it, my boy.' Her kiss was warm against his cheek and he could smell her favourite rose perfume as she embraced him.

Henry was determined not to let his mother see the agony he was going through, and when she placed something in his hand he could barely make out what it was through his unshed tears.

'It's not much, but it'll give you a fresh start, should you find her,' she murmured with a sigh. 'Perhaps, if you go far enough away your father will mellow – but don't expect too much of him. He's cast from a mould that is set fast and unlikely to bend. He will never accept a catholic in the family.'

She kissed him again and Henry clung to her, knowing this would probably be the last time he would ever see her.

When she finally drew away from him her composure was at breaking point. 'Goodbye, son,' she said through her tears. 'God speed.'

Maureen had said goodbye to her mother several hours before, now the night was closing in as she tramped over the hills towards the staging post where she could buy a seat for the long journey to Dublin.

Every part of her ached, but it was nothing compared to the pain in her heart. She was leaving home and everything that was familiar, her reputation in tatters, the Judas coins of Beecham-Fford jingling in her pocket. She'd been a fool to believe Henry loved her. A fool to believe he would stand by her in the face of trouble.

She crested the brow of the hill and paused for a moment to catch her breath. Looking around her she realised she could no longer see the village, or the trees that shielded Beecham Hall. The silence closed in and she became aware of how small and insignificant she was against the vast green backdrop of the empty countryside. With a deep sigh she once more picked up her bundle, and lifting her skirts from the dewy grass, began the descent towards the distant lights of the staging inn.

Her thoughts were in turmoil as she tried to come to terms with her situation. The child in her belly had quickened in the past few hours – had become more real, and therefore, more precious. Her feet tramped across the tough, lush grass of the Kerry land that had been stolen from her forefathers and she made a vow. The English might steal everything else belonging to the Irish, but they would not be having her baby.

She heard the sound of galloping hoofs and the rattle of wheels and wearily stepped from the track into the grassy ditch to let them pass. Her mind was sluggish, her eyelids heavy for the want of sleep as she pulled the hood of her cloak over her face and turned from the dust that billowed from beneath the wheels and stamping hoofs.

'Maureen? Maureen!'

Startled, she looked up. Disbelief numbed her as Henry climbed from the phaeton and gathered her into his arms.

'Thank God I found you and you're safe,' he breathed. 'Why did you run away? Why didn't you tell me about the child?'

She stood immobile in his embrace before pulling away, her composure an icy shield between them. 'What are you doing here?'

He frowned, the confusion clear in his eyes and in the hesitant way he tried to gather her back into his arms. 'I've been trying to find you all day,' he stammered. 'I've been half out of my mind with worry. I thought I'd never find you in time.'

Maureen regarded him, her love for this man willing her to forgive him. Yet she knew she had to remain strong. For, after all, did she not have his blood money in her pocket? 'And why would you be trying to find me? Our business is done.' She took the purse and shook it in his face.

'Maureen,' he began, and was halted by the sharpness in her voice.

'Is this what I'm worth, Henry? A handful of silver?' She could see his confusion, the shame reddening his face, and was tempted to throw the coins at his feet. But, as much as she hated to keep this money, she had no other means of survival and it would be an empty gesture.

He licked his lips. 'You're more precious to me than all the silver in the world,' he stammered. He cleared his throat. 'What's happened to you, Maureen? Why are you this way with me after all we've been to one another? The money was nothing to do with me. My father . . .'

Maureen grasped the hood of her cloak and swept it away. 'This was the price I paid for loving you,' she said flatly. 'What now, Henry?'

62

She saw the horror in his eyes as he took in the tortured scalp and tufts of hair, the bruises and scratches on her neck and face. Her determination faltered as she saw his unshed tears, but she knew that one moment of weakness would be her undoing. 'And what of our child? Is that to be sold for a handful of silver as well?'

Henry knelt at her feet, mindless of the restless horses, the rolling phaeton wheels and the dust staining his trousers. 'You are both beyond price,' he cried with earnest intensity. 'More precious than any jewel. I would rather die than lose you.'

Maureen began to tremble, whether it was from emotion or the cold, she had no way of knowing. Yet her chin remained determined despite the yearning to take him in her arms. 'Fine words, Henry. So you will come with me over the water? Leave your family, your money, everything behind?'

Henry wrapped his arms around her hips, his cheek resting on the small mound of her belly. When he spoke, his words were soft, tinged with love and pain.

' "Come live with me and be my love, and we will all the pleasures prove, that hills and valleys, dales and fields, woods or sleepy mountain yields." ' He raised his fair head and looked up into her eyes as he finished the quotation. ' "There I will make thee beds of roses and a thousand fragrant posies, a cap of flowers and a kirtle embroider'd all with leaves of myrtle." '

Maureen's tears were warm on her face as she slowly sank to her knees within his embrace. 'That's beautiful,' she whispered. 'I wish I knew how to put words together like that.'

He kissed away her tears, wary of the bruises, mindful of the deep scratches. 'The words are not mine – I wish they were. But the sentiment is perfect for this special moment.' He cupped her face, lifting her chin so she drowned in his eyes. 'The poem's called "The Passionate Shepherd to his Love", by Marlowe. I wish I knew all of it,' he said with a soft laugh. 'But I promise to read it to you one day.'

63

Maureen clung to him then, lost in his embrace, garnering strength and courage from the warmth of his love. Yet, as they finally pulled apart and he helped her climb into the phaeton, she caught sight of something that sent a deep chill to her very core.

A large black crow was watching them from its perch in a nearby tree, and the yellow eyes were cold and knowing. Maureen's Celtic instincts warned her that this was a harbinger of a darkness that would follow them wherever they chose to run. A prophet of doom who would see them pay for their sinful union.

Miriam emerged from those dark days and blinked in the sunshine. 'They caught the packet steamer to England,' she said quietly. 'They thought it would be the start of a brave new life, but neither of them were prepared for what actually came about.'

Intrigued though he was, Jake could see the bruise of weariness beneath her eyes. 'You're tired,' he murmured. 'Perhaps we should leave the rest of the story for another time?'

She eyed him thoughtfully and shook her head. 'Time is the one luxury I don't have,' she replied. 'I'm an old woman, Mr Connor, and my father's story has remained untold for too long. If I'm to have any chance of proving how he was cheated – and no doubt murdered for that thing in the music box – then there's no more time for rest.'

'Murdered?' Jake's eyes were wide with amazement. 'You never mentioned murder.'

'I know,' she said bitterly. 'I don't want to believe he was – but the more I think about it, the more certain I am that Kate was right.'

'Kate?' He looked confused again. 'You mean Kate Kelly?' He straightened up in the chair and blew out his cheeks. 'What on earth has she to do with all this?'

Miriam looked out to the yard. Frank was organising the evening ride-out and the horses were milling, their coats

glossy in the afternoon sunlight, the heads proud and beautiful. A stab of pride made her smile and an immediate sense of
well-being flooded through her. 'You'll see,' she murmured.

Jake brought his overnight bag from the ute and dumped it in
one of the spare rooms. It was a nice room, with the late
afternoon sun streaming in at the windows that overlooked
the home paddocks, the polished floor gleaming. There were
still reminders here of Miriam's daughter and he took a
moment to acquaint himself with her.

A line of dolls stared down at him from a shelf, their bale-
ful glass eyes making him feel a little intrusive. The pictures
on the walls were replicas of some of the world's greatest
paintings and he recognised Monet's *Water Lilies*, Van
Gogh's *Sunflowers* and Degas' *Dancing Class*. The books
also followed the same theme – works on the great artists,
biographies and one large tome on the history of art through
the Middle Ages.

He looked around in surprise. For the daughter of a well-
known and respected horse breeder, he would have expected
gymkhana ribbons, riding trophies and pictures of her
favourite ponies, but there was nothing equine in the room at
all. The omission spoke volumes. Miriam's daughter did not
share her passion.

His smile was wry as he pulled out a fresh shirt from his
bag. He thought he might have something in common with
Chloe, for he too had been a child of the outback who had
not shared his parent's passion for battling the elements.

Life on an isolated station had to be the toughest way to
earn a living, and although he missed the clean air, the wide
open spaces and the majesty of the Never Never, he knew
how stifling it could be. With the same faces, the same gossip, the endless round of country dances and picnic races
where the sons and daughters of the pastoralists found their
future partners so they could begin the cycle all over again.
He sensed Chloe had felt the same, and had escaped. It
would be interesting to meet her.

65

Miriam was in the kitchen carving thick slices off a mutton joint and slapping them on to a plate. Eric had taken over the empty wood basket and was watching every move she made, a line of drool pendulous from his chin.

'Can I help?' Jake asked tentatively as he opened a tin of cat food he'd retrieved from his bag. He'd never been much use in the kitchen and his ex-wife had banned him from theirs. Now he lived mostly on take-outs and supermarket meals for one that would cook in ten minutes in the microwave.

'Not much to do,' Miriam replied. 'Cold mutton, mash potato and pickled beetroot doesn't take a lot of thinking about.' She wiped her hands down her trousers and eyed the cat. 'I think he's expecting more than just tinned food,' she said with a hint of asperity. 'You spoil that animal, you know. Wouldn't last five minutes out here with the feral moggies we've got on the place.'

Eric sniffed the cat food and stuck his nose in the air. He sat neatly at Miriam's feet, his tail curled around his paws, eyes fixing her with yellow determination.

Jake shuffled from one foot to another as Miriam gave in and added a few scraps of mutton to the saucer. 'He's good company,' he muttered. 'Something warm and living to come home to at the end of the day.'

Miriam eyed him sharply. 'How long have you been divorced?' she said gruffly.

'Five years,' he replied as they sat down at the scrubbed table and helped himself to the mashed potato.

'Time you found someone else,' Miriam muttered. 'It's not good to be on your own for too long. Get set in your ways – become selfish.' She looked across at him. 'I know what I'm talking about. Been on my own for most of my life.'

Jake nodded. 'It's probably too late already,' he mumbled through mash and mutton. 'What woman in her right mind would put up with Eric?'

Miriam eyed the cat. He was now sitting up at the table

with a voracious eye on their food. 'If you taught him some manners and reminded him he was a cat and not a human, you might find some woman who would take you both on.' Her smile was warm as she returned his grin. 'Just how old are you?' she asked.

Jake was getting used to her way of asking impertinent questions and decided he'd play along. 'Thirty-two,' he replied. 'How old are you?'

'Old enough to know better than tell you,' she retorted.

They got on with their supper almost in silence, and after the plates had been pushed away, Miriam put her head to one side and studied him keenly. 'D'you like horses?'

Jake was a little disconcerted. He liked them well enough and often hired a hack at the weekends. But he could take or leave them. 'I like looking at them,' he replied. 'And I enjoy going to the races with Dad when time allows.'

'Come on then. I'll show you around.'

They left the table, pulled on boots and headed across home yard. The horses were back from their evening ride and the men were busy rubbing them down and settling them in for the night. Miriam took him through the vast stable-yard pointing out brood mares that had dropped winning foals, and giving him a history of every horse in the place.

Jake was impressed. The yard was spotless, the tack shining, the straw clean. And as for the horses – even he could see how magnificent they were. How his dad would have loved to be here, he thought ruefully. He could have bent Miriam's ear for hours gossiping about training and races and jockeys – for he'd followed form all his life and probably knew as much about Miriam's business as she did.

Miriam had reached the end of the line of boxes and was leaning over the half-door. 'This is Pagan,' she said proudly. 'We can trace his bloodline right back to Archer.'

She must have seen this meant nothing to him and went on to explain. 'Archer was the first horse to win the Melbourne Cup,' she said. 'That was back in 1861. His owner walked him five hundred miles from Nowra, here in New South

Wales all the way down to Melbourne in Victoria, and he still won the race.'

She stroked the long chestnut nose. 'This old devil never won the Cup, but he's been a champion in his time and has sired some good racers.'

Jake noticed the Shetland pony standing in the lee of the stallion's bulk. 'What's the pony doing there?'

'Keeps the old boy company. They go everywhere together, and if Snapper is taken away from him, he plays up so badly none of us can get near him.'

'Snapper?' Jake eyed the fat little pony and smiled. It was pure Thelwell, with its long pale mane and tail and shaggy brown coat.

'Put your hand anywhere near him and you'll find out. They might look sweet, but they're crook little buggers if they're feeling mean.' She shut the top half of the door and switched off the light. 'Had me a couple of times,' she muttered. 'And if it wasn't for Pagan needing his company, I'd sell him off.'

They returned to the homestead after Miriam had introduced him to Frank and some of the stable-lads. She made tea and they settled back at the kitchen table. Eric was draped across the log basket again and Miriam bent to stroke him.

'I wouldn't,' warned Jake sharply. 'He bites.'

Miriam nodded and sat down. 'Another Snapper,' she said and smiled. 'Seems we have the same taste in animals, Mr Connor.'

'Please, call me Jake.'

She eyed him for a long moment. 'My family call me Mim,' she said eventually. 'I suppose it doesn't matter if you do the same seeing as how you're about to become privy to my secrets.'

She leaned forward, her eyes very green in the kerosene lamplight. 'What I'm about to tell you over the next couple of days is between us. Understand? I will let my family in on it when I'm good and ready – and not before. Do I have your word?'

Jake nodded in agreement, but at the same time wondered how long Mim could carry this off. For a high-profile battle such as this one promised to be could never be kept secret, and her family would need to be prepared for the furore that was inevitable.

She seemed satisfied and nodded. Then after a moment of silence she began retelling the story. 'Henry and Maureen married and settled in London. They rented a couple of rooms above a shop in Fulham and Henry set about trying to find work. It was Maureen who found employment first, and she kept the roof over their heads by working in a laundry.'

Miriam sighed. 'My poor father was at his wits' end. He didn't stand a chance you see. His accent and rather obvious background made people wary of employing him. His so-called friends from university shunned him once they met his new wife, and his bastard of a father had put the boot in by blackening his name amongst those likely to offer him employment in their factories. All of this affected his paint-ing, of course. He'd taken most of them from the house in Ireland, but couldn't find anyone to buy them, and now, humiliated by his young, pregnant wife having to earn their keep, his spirits were very low.'

'What about the money his mother gave him?' asked Jake quietly. 'Surely that would have been enough to set them up?'

Miriam nodded. 'It was over four hundred pounds – a for-tune in those days. But he knew they couldn't afford to fritter it away. In the end it provided their only means of escape.'

Jake frowned. 'Escape? But they'd already left Ireland. Surely they could have bought a business with the money – a house – they would have been set up nicely?'

Miriam shook her head. 'It didn't work like that, Jake,' she said sadly. 'In those days a man of Henry's background was hampered at every turn if he tried to straddle the oppres-sive class system. High society shunned him, the genteel middle class were disapproving and the working people scorned and distrusted him. It's not like today when anything

69

goes and the worth of a man is seen in what he can achieve, not in the class he was born into.'

'So what did they do?'

Miriam leaned back in her chair and folded her arms. 'Henry became a remittance man,' she said sadly. 'He used the money his mother had given him to book passage to Australia.' She looked down at the table. 'Unfortunately he and Maureen were not the only people on that ship who were seeking to make a new life.'

The dockside was bustling with noise and movement. Wagons carrying top-heavy loads were pulled over the cobbles by heavy-footed drays, and the stench of manure and unwashed bodies was overlaid by the pungent tang of salt water and the spices being unloaded from a nearby ship.

Gulls swooped and screeched overhead and porters sweated as they manhandled the first-class passengers' heavy suitcases and trunks up the gangplanks. Pickpockets and whores weaved through the mayhem, sharp-eyed for opportunity as carriages trundled into the dock and disgorged their passengers. The shouts of the hawkers and the sailors mingled with the stamp of horses and the low hum of excited passengers as they waited to board the SS *Swallow*.

She towered over the docks, swaying with the rhythm of the tide, her three masts and two funnels reaching for the sky. Her steel hull rasped against the rope fenders on the dockside as she tugged against the restraining hawsers and the rigging snapped with the wind against the wooden masts as smoke drifted from the funnels. The *Swallow* had been built ten years before in Glasgow and weighed over eight thousand tons, was propelled by a single screw and could do about nineteen knots. With four decks she could carry almost fifteen hundred passengers.

Henry put his arm around Maureen's thickening waist and drew her close as they eyed the great ship and the bustling crowd that eddied around them. He wished she could feel the same excitement for the adventure ahead, but knew that beneath her composed exterior there lay a deep sickness for home and Ireland. There had been no reply to her scrawled letter he'd helped her write, no sign they had been forgiven by either family for the shame they'd brought them.

''Tis awful big,' she breathed. 'Are you sure it's safe?'

Henry smiled at her naïvety. 'She's made the trip several times with no mishap. All these people wouldn't be getting aboard if they didn't think she was safe.'

Maureen didn't look convinced as she watched the crates and trunks being stored in the hold, and the parade of finely dressed first-class passengers making their way up the gangplank. She seemed to shrink beside him as the cut-glass accents sailed down from the upper decks. 'We'll not be up there, will we?'

He shook his head, remembering the cruise he'd taken only a year earlier with his parents. 'We're travelling third class,' he muttered regretfully. 'The money won't stretch, and we'll need as much as possible once we land in Australia.'

Maureen tugged at the ribbons of her new bonnet and pulled up the fur collar of the coat Henry had surprised her with this morning. Her hair was still very short and although it was growing into a delightful cap of ebony curls, Henry knew she still felt vulnerable in public.

He regarded her as she watched the ebb and flow of people around her and saw her brighten when she recognised the lilt of southern Ireland. 'Perhaps it won't be so bad,' she said with studied cheerfulness. 'At least I'll have me own kind to chat to.'

Henry eyed the rabble of excited Irishmen and their women who were tramping up the third-class gangway loaded down with children and bags. He would find things very different on this voyage, he realised. For he was no longer one of the élite, but a part of the mass. Yet he had known that marrying Maureen would change everything, and he did not regret his decision. Life was about to become far more interesting. He could forget the horrors of London and in the six months it would take to reach Australia, he could plan for their future.

'Let's get on board,' he said as the excitement fluttered inside him. 'It's getting cold down here.'

Neither of them noticed the still figure that leaned against a stack of wool bales. But if they had, they would have perhaps wondered at the strange intensity of the watcher's eyes, and felt the chill of foreboding.

Kate tugged at the tight-fitting jacket and straightened her bonnet. The new skirt and blouse had been bought with the last of her wages, and her boots were shining with polish. She grasped the bag that held her worldly possessions and tried to remain calm. Yet it was difficult. The sounds and the sights of this London dock merely enhanced the feeling that this was the beginning of a new life in a new world, and she could barely keep still.

'Are you sure this is what you're wanting, Kate?'

She looked up into the kindly face and nodded. 'It is, Father,' she breathed.

'We'll all miss you,' he said dolefully. 'It's a fine little worker that you are, and no mistake.'

Kate thought of the hours of scrubbing floors in that draughty, chill presbytery, of preparing dinners for the six priests and the unwelcome attention she'd received from one of them. She shivered as she remembered how frightened she'd been when he'd suddenly appeared at her bedside. How horrified when he'd attempted to climb in with her – to touch her in places no priest should touch.

She'd managed to kick him, hard – just where it would hurt the most, and after that had barricaded her room at night. But he'd made a habit of following her during the days. Of appearing unexpectedly when she'd thought she was alone.

Knowing she wouldn't be believed, she'd said nothing and began to plot her escape. It was when Father Pat had told her he was travelling south on his way to a conference in Rome, that she realised this was her best opportunity.

On the long journey south she'd confided to him her dreams of distant shores and the chance to really make something of herself, and he had surprised her with his enthusiasm and the swift results of his search for her new employment. Her fare had been paid by Mr Reed, a widower returning to Australia, who had engaged her to help him with his two small children. Now, here she was waiting to board the SS *Swallow*.

'Thank you for getting me the post, Father,' she said with a smile. 'I don't know how I'll ever repay you.'

His expression was solemn. 'I'm thinking you've earned the right to a fresh start, Kate,' he said quietly. 'These last two months could not have been easy for you.'

Her eyes widened as the full impact of his words sank in. 'If you knew, then why didn't . . .?'

'There are rules and regulations we must be seen to be following, Kate. But rest assured, the church will put things to rights.' He straightened his shoulders and smiled. 'I'll make sure your letters reach your family priest so he can read them out, and once you have settled in your new home I hope you will carry on with your learning. You've a bright head on your shoulders, and I'm thinking that one day you will make all of us very proud indeed.'

Kate blushed and bent her head. Her reading and writing skills had come on rapidly during the short time Father Pat had taught her, and there didn't seem to be the words to thank him for all he'd helped her achieve. 'It was good of you to spare so much time,' she murmured.

'It was a pleasure, Kate.' He glanced over her head and waved. 'Seems this is goodbye,' he said cheerfully. 'I see Mr Reed waiting for you by the gangway.'

Kate bobbed a curtsy. The mixture of fear and excitement was potent, and after he'd given her his blessing, she weaved her way through the crowd and headed towards the first-class gangway.

The knowledge that she was leaving behind all she knew was tainted with sadness, for she would probably never see her family again. And yet the horizons that were opening up to her could not be ignored, and there was a spring in her step as she approached the tall, sun-browned man who was her new employer.

Patrick Dempster had managed to elude the police and after returning to London had scraped together enough money to book steerage on the SS *Swallow*. Now, as he stood on the quayside and breathed in the intoxicating aromas and listened to the sounds around him he was impatient to begin his new life. For he knew this was his last chance and he was eager to see what it was like on the other side of the world.

He'd heard about the gold and precious gems that were there for the taking if only a man had the guts to search for it. Had heard of land that stretched far beyond any man's sight that could be had for a few pence an acre. This brave new world was a gift for men like him. Men who had no ties and were used to hardship. Men who lived on their wits and were not afraid to stand up to a challenge.

The excitement fluttered in his belly as he looked above the milling, shifting crowd to the towering masts and funnels of the great steamship. It would soon be time to board her, but he wanted to hold on to this thrill of expectancy for as long as possible. Needed to feel the excitement build until he could barely stand to resist it. For experience had taught him it would be all the sweeter if he waited until the last minute to taste the full flavour of this adventure.

He found some wool bales that had been unloaded and stacked in preparation for collection and leaned against them. His curious gaze drifted over the crowd that milled around him and settled on a young couple. They meant nothing to him, but his innate ability for scenting something askew piqued his interest.

Patrick spat out the straw he'd been chewing and watched them from beneath the brim of his hat. The woman seemed ill at ease, constantly fiddling with her bonnet, nervously clinging to the man's arm. He, on the other hand seemed calm enough and it was obvious he was trying his best to put her at ease. Yet there was something wrong about what he was seeing, and Patrick frowned as he tried to figure out what it was.

He regarded them thoughtfully, his eyes narrowed in the bright spring sunlight that bounced off the warehouse windows. There was little doubt the man was a gent. It was in the set of his shoulders and the arrogance of his chin and, as they walked past him, he caught the rounded vowels of an expensive English education and the glint of a gold watch chain. But it was the woman that intrigued him the most, for despite her fashionable clothing, her accent was pure Kerry.

Patrick picked up his bag and followed them. What was a girl from Kerry doing with a man like that? She was no servant, that was obvious by the way she clung to him. Perhaps a mistress then and this was their last farewell before he sailed away?

Patrick grimaced and shook his head. What the hell did it matter? The man would be travelling first class and he would never see him again, and the girl would go back to whatever slum he'd found her in.

He hitched his bag over his shoulder and put all thoughts of the oddly matched pair aside as he began to whistle. It was a fine day and he was determined to enjoy the feel of cobbles beneath his feet, for it would be six months before he stepped on land again.

He suddenly caught a glimpse of rapid movement within the crowd, and his senses, honed from years on the streets, picked up trouble. Before he'd taken a further step, two youths emerged from the jostling crowd and Patrick recognised the practised moves immediately.

The first youth ran full tilt into the man Patrick had been watching, and with profuse apologies and a sleight of hand worthy of a magician relieved him of his gold watch and chain. This was rapidly passed to the second youth who melted back into the crowd.

Patrick's sharp eye for the main chance had not deserted him, and he eased the bag from his back and followed. The return of such a watch would surely mean a generous reward – and it might do him some good to have a wealthy patron on board.

There were no cries of alarm from the quayside as Patrick weaved his way through the mêlée and kept the dirty green cap in sight. No doubt the mark hadn't even noticed his watch was missing.

He saw the boy dodge behind a horse and cart and make his way into the shadows of what looked like an abandoned warehouse. Patrick hid his bag behind a stack of chicken baskets and eased into the darkness – he'd need both hands free if it came to a fight. He followed the sound of the boy's breathing and the scrape of his boots on the crumbling stone floor.

The youth yelped in fear and pain as Patrick's grip on his neck pinned him against the wall. 'Hand it over,' he growled.

'Don't know what yer on about,' the boy rasped as he kicked and squirmed.

'The watch and chain.' Patrick was sweating. Time and his patience were running out and the kid's sidekick could show up any minute. 'Where is it?' He squeezed a little harder.

'In me pocket,' the boy squawked.

Patrick held him pinned to the wall as he searched the greasy trouser pockets. The boys had been busy today, he realised with a grim smile. He pulled out several wallets, a bracelet and a fob, some fine lawn handkerchiefs and the watch. He lessened his grip, but kept a hand on the boy's chest as he inspected the cache.

'You can keep this lot,' he muttered. 'I'll take the watch and the money.'

'You can't . . .'

'Oh, yes I can,' snarled Patrick as he gave the boy a shove. 'Now clear off and find some other place for your tricks.'

He watched the boy scamper through the gloom towards

the back of the abandoned building, and heard him clamber up some steps and run away. He was reminded of his youth, of the times he'd pulled the same stunt and had his booty stolen from him by the bigger, stronger boys until he was able to fight back.

Patrick pocketed the money and with the watch in his hand, he retrieved his bag and headed back to the ship.

The couple had drawn to a halt beside the gangway and were looking up at the ship. Patrick realised they were not yet aware of the theft, and for a moment he was tempted to say nothing. Then he thought of the reward he would doubtless get and he stepped forward.

'Begging yer pardon, sir. I believe this belongs to you.' His tone was as obsequious as he could get it. 'Caught a young pickpocket making off with it and gave chase.'

The man's hand flew to his waistcoat pocket and the colour drained from his face. 'Good God,' he breathed. 'And I never felt a thing.'

Patrick glanced at the woman who was eyeing him with suspicion and he quickly looked away and handed over the watch. 'Quick as the little people, they are, to be sure. Have to have the eyes in the back of the head to catch 'em.'

'Thank you, mister . . .?

'Patrick Dempster, sir. At your service.' He tried not to show the disdain for his own grovelling but if it meant some money for his trouble he could put up with that.

'Henry Beecham, and this is my wife, Maureen.' He hesitated, his fingers dipping fruitlessly into the shallow pockets of his waistcoat. 'I'm embarrassed at my lack of change at the moment,' he declared red faced. 'But please believe me when I say how grateful I am to you – and how much I admire your honesty.'

Patrick eyed him, the thoughts spinning around as he digested this new information. The tight-fisted bastard wasn't going to pay him a penny. How he wished he'd kept the damned watch. Could have got a good price for it.

Then his bitterness cooled and he looked from the girl to

77

the man and realised what it was he'd sensed earlier and not been able to pinpoint. This was a remittance man. Banished by his family because of the Irish girl by his side. He relaxed. He'd play this one carefully. For despite the fact the man had no coinage on him, the wealthy always gave their wayward sons enough money to keep them comfortable. 'Will you be sailing today, sir, or are you here to see someone off?' he asked.

Henry patted his wife's hand and smiled down at her. 'Yes, we're sailing today, Mr Dempster.' He looked back at Patrick. 'Are you?'

Patrick nodded. 'But I don't expect we'll see one another again, as I'll be travelling steerage.' He tipped his hat and again glanced at Henry's wife. She was still watching him, the mistrust clear in her eyes – and he knew his charade hadn't fooled her at all.

'I wish you and your wife well,' he added as he prepared to turn away.

Henry's voice stilled him. 'My wife and I would be pleased if you would join us for dinner, Mr Dempster.' He looked defiantly into Patrick's face. 'It seems we are to share similar travelling arrangements.'

Patrick saw the look of horror on the woman's face and kept his gaze downcast as he accepted the offer and the two men shook hands. He didn't want either of them to see the glint of hope he knew must be in his eyes.

He again shot a wary glance at Beecham's wife as he bent to pick up his bag. He'd have to play this very close if he was to win her over. The girl was obviously sharp and he suspected that if he didn't get her on his side his enterprising, half-formed plan would fail.

But what a plan, he thought as he followed them up the third-class gangway. For Beecham was already in his debt, and the idea he'd had earlier was taking shape. He had six months to hone that idea to perfection and then he would take it to Beecham, who would have no choice but to agree. He'd make sure of that.

Chapter Four

Fiona climbed from the pool and wrapped the towel around her waist. The sun was dipping fast and after the heat of the day the night promised a welcome coolness. She towelled her hair as she closed the safety gate and padded barefoot back to her ground-floor unit. There was still some paperwork to catch up with after her long absence, and she wanted to check the folio of pictures again before she delivered them to the magazine editor.

The two-storey apartment block was perched on a hill that overlooked the river and the city of Brisbane. There was the communal pool and a gym as well as a couple of spas and a children's crèche, and Fiona was constantly reminded of how lucky she was to have had the chance to buy the unit before the prices shot through the roof. For the exclusive block was far enough away from the busy freeway not to hear the endless traffic that began before sunrise and went on until long after dark. Yet it was close enough to the river to be able to get into the city on one of the water taxis and was much sought after by business people.

She padded into the lounge and closed the door. It was good to be home again, to have her own space and familiar things around her after camping out in the humid rainforests of Brazil. A relief to know she could please herself and not have to run around after a man.

She smiled fondly as she thought of Barney. He'd been a

good bloke, funny, easy to talk to – but a disaster at relationships. They had both understood that his job as a reporter meant he'd be away for a lot of the time, and that hers was just as time consuming – but Barney never thought to tell her before he left for an assignment, and she'd lost count of the times she'd expected him home, only to get a phone call two days later from outer Mongolia or somewhere equally as remote. Over the two years his apologies wore thin and so did her patience, and when he didn't turn up for a special weekend they'd planned, she packed his bags and had taken them to the newspaper office and dumped them on his desk.

Fiona pushed all thought of Barney to the back of her mind and surveyed her home. The white tiles were cool beneath her feet, the lounge large and square with a tiny kitchen at one end. She'd deliberately chosen white for the leather suite and the walls, and had jazzed it up with bright rugs and cushions. She would have liked plants, but they would only die during her long absences, so there was no point.

Not one for ornaments and frills there were only a few family snapshots arranged on the two low coffee tables, and her books were lined neatly on shelves. Some of her own work was displayed on the walls alongside the framed award she'd won last year for a series of photos she'd taken of Aboriginal children in the outback.

Her bedroom looked over a small patio, which in turn looked over the pool area. The floor-to-ceiling windows took up most of one wall and delicate muslin curtains kept out the sun. The bathroom was en-suite, but there was a second bedroom and bathroom down the hall.

She stripped off the wet bikini, plumped down on the double bed and finished drying her hair. If she could get her work done tonight, then she could set out for Bellbird first thing in the morning and have Mim to herself for a while. It had been ages since they'd had a good gossip, and she'd been looking forward to what she called her Bellbird

Summer – the two weeks when the family got together again at the outback homestead.

Fiona grimaced as she realised her hair had taken on a life of its own. What she wouldn't do to have smooth, shining hair that didn't corkscrew into a tangle every time it got wet. It wasn't even Mum's glorious copper either – just a rather murky brown. She threw the brush aside and glared at her reflection. The Brazilian sun had brought the freckles out again, and although her tan made the blue of her eyes quite startling, she wished she hadn't inherited Leo's rather patrician nose.

She turned away and pulled on jeans and a T-shirt and went to rummage in the fridge for something to eat. With a pasta salad and a glass of chilled wine at her elbow, she picked up the phone and tried again to ring her sister. But her efforts were thwarted by the answering service, and she gave up.

Louise waited for Rafe to unlock the door and did her best to appear relaxed. Rafe had been distant all evening, and they'd driven home in silence. Not a good sign. When Rafe was in this mood it could be days before he spoke to her, and, as usual, she had no idea what she'd done wrong.

Her thoughts were in turmoil as she walked across the marble floor and headed for the kitchen. Had she said or done something to displease him? Perhaps he hadn't liked her talking to that theatre director for so long – but Ed had been so interesting, she'd forgotten the time – and it was Rafe's suggestion she keep the financial director amused while he went off to talk to someone from another firm.

She fumbled with the kettle and almost dropped it as she filled it with water. These protracted silences made her nervous, and the longer they went on, the more jumpy she got. 'Coffee?' she asked as she heard his footsteps approach.

He grabbed a carton of orange juice, slammed the fridge door, and eyeing her coldly left the room.

Louise leaned against the cold white counter and gripped

the edge. 'Don't do that, Rafe,' she said into the silence. 'At least tell me what it is I'm supposed to have done.'

There was no reply, merely the heavy tread of his feet on the blond pine stairs.

Louise turned and stared at the window. The light made it impossible to see the garden, or the sky, and she was faced with her own reflection. The reflection of a stranger. A thin, pale stranger who gripped the sink as if her life depended upon it.

'I hate this,' she murmured. 'I'm not putting up with it any more.' With those brave words still ringing in her head she left the kitchen and made her way up the stairs.

The house was enormous. Set on ten acres of prime riverside real estate, it had five bedrooms and bathrooms, three reception rooms and a games room, all kept neat by two maids who came in twice a week. The garden had a pool and spa and that too was cared for by outside help. In moments such as these, Louise despised it and often felt she was marooned in a luxury hotel – for this had never felt like a home – more like a show house. Perhaps, if they'd had children it would have been different, but Rafe had explained how inconvenient that would be with their lifestyle and Louise had reluctantly come to accept he was probably right.

She made her way along the landing and hesitated momentarily before she opened the door to their bedroom. There was no sign of Rafe, but she could hear the shower going in the bathroom. Undressing quickly, she slipped on her nightdress and wrapped herself in a towelling robe. She was sitting at her dressing table when Rafe entered the room.

'I do wish you'd talk to me,' she said with deliberate lightness as she creamed off her make-up. 'If you don't tell me what's wrong, how can I possibly put it right?' Her pulse was racing and her mouth was dry, but she determinedly sat where she was and went through the nightly ritual.

She watched Rafe in the mirror as he gathered his clothes

for the morning. His face was set, his mouth a thin line of disapproval. She turned on the stool and gripped her hands tightly together on her lap as he faced her.

'I know what you're up to, Louise,' he said coldly.

'I'm not up to anything,' she retorted. Yet the colour rose in her face and her hands twisted and worried the towelling belt around her waist as his penetrating glare never faltered. Why does he always make me feel so guilty when there's nothing to feel guilty about? She made a determined effort to appear calm and composed.

'Your face gives you away,' he snapped. 'I'm not stupid, Louise. I know you've been having an affair with that man you were talking to tonight.'

Her eyes widened and her face drained of all colour. 'Don't be ridiculous.' The words tumbled out before she could think and she bit her lip. 'I've never met him before tonight,' she muttered.

'Ridiculous?' he said icily. 'Me? Ridiculous? I think you should examine your own behaviour before you start accusing me of that, Louise. Do you know how embarrassing it is to have your wife flirting with every Tom, Dick and Harry she meets? How sickening it is to see a middle-aged woman making a fool of herself with men half her age?'

'I wasn't,' she gasped. Yet a tinge of guilt made her wonder if perhaps she had been flirting with Ed and not realised it. He was handsome and very pleasant to talk to and he'd made her laugh, which felt good.

Rafe opened the bedroom door. 'We won't be going to Mim's by the way. I've got a business meeting.' He shut the door firmly as if to emphasise his wish for the conversation to be over.

Louise sat on the stool and stared at the door. She was almost frozen with shock, and yet her mind was whirling with the things she would have liked to say to him. Yet she knew they would never be voiced, for, if she thought about it, perhaps her behaviour tonight had been a little flirtatious. She'd spent a long time chatting with Ed, and Rafe had always been jealous. She should have known what his reaction would be.

'Stupid, stupid, stupid,' she muttered as she dropped the dressing-gown on the stool and climbed into bed. The sheets were freshly ironed and smoothly cold against her skin as she settled into the pillows and let her mind wander over the distressing little scene that had just been played out.

Rafe was a good husband and she didn't know how she'd survive without him. He'd taught her how to dress and how to comport herself in high society. He'd schooled her in polite conversation and the politics of banking, and provided her with a home and a lifestyle that other women would give their eye teeth for. He was generous with his money, never questioning her when she asked to buy something, and so supportive over her diet he was constantly telling her how wonderful she looked. How many times had he told her his jealousy was only his way of showing her how much he loved her? She'd behaved like a fool.

Yet it was cruel of him to cancel the annual trip to Bellbird when he'd known how much she'd been looking forward to it. She turned her face into the pillow as the first hot tear rolled down her cheek. Perhaps, if she tried harder to please him he would change his mind and forgive her. For she didn't want to lose him, she loved him too much.

Miriam said goodnight to Jake and closed her bedroom door. The dragon of pain was unfurling again and she would be glad to sink into bed and let the tablets do their work. Her discarded work clothes were flung over the back of a chair and she decided they would do for another day, she didn't have the energy to get the copper boiler going.

She placed the music box on the dressing table and turned the key. The lilting waltz echoed around the room as she pulled on her long cotton nightgown and climbed into bed.

It had been a strange sort of day she mused as she watched the tiny, dancing figures and waited for the pills to get into her system. But it was pleasant to have Jake's company, even if she didn't approve of Eric sleeping on his bed. Damn cat, she thought with a smile. Certainly knows what it wants.

She nestled into the pillows and let her mind be soothed by the music, and as the medicine began to ease the pain she found she could concentrate on the next part of the story. For she would need to get everything right if Jake was to understand how much this meant to her.

Closing her eyes she drifted towards sleep, lulled by the rhythm of a ghostly ship ploughing across the ocean.

Maureen gripped the railings and turned her face into the wind. It was good to be on deck after the stifling and rather fetid atmosphere of their quarters below decks. Perhaps the cold, salty blast would take the edge off the sickness which had been with her for so long, and had not been improved by the pitch and roll of the ship.

She couldn't understand why she felt so ill, for she'd accompanied her uncle on his fishing boat many a time, and had positively revelled in the dip and toss of the enormous Atlantic waves. Her fingers rested protectively over the burgeoning swell of her belly and she smiled. She'd never been pregnant before. Perhaps that was the answer?

She took a deep breath and tried to ignore the niggling doubt as she stared out over the vast grey ocean. All women had morning sickness, she told herself. Hers was just a little more severe because of the voyage. The pain she was experiencing was probably a legacy from the kicking she'd received back in Ireland, and although it made it difficult to sleep sometimes, she thought perhaps it was a little better today. The baby seemed active enough inside her, kicking and squirming. No doubt the discomfort would disappear soon, just as the bruising had done, and she was just needlessly fretting.

Maureen glanced over her shoulder at Henry. His fair hair was glinting in the weak sunlight, feathered by the wind as he sat in the canvas chair and concentrated on the sketch he was doing of one of the passengers. It was good he'd found

85

something to occupy him, she thought. Even better that he was being handsomely paid. Word had soon gone around and there was a long list of people wanting their portraits done to mark this momentous voyage.

She watched his hand, so sure with the pencil against the creamy paper, his head bent to his work, his eyes bright with concentration. He was so talented, so desperate to make his name and prove his father wrong. If only things had been different. If only they could have stayed in London and found a sponsor.

As she turned back to stare out over the railings she felt a sharp stab of pain. The gasp was involuntary and she tried to smother it by biting hard on her lip. Determined not to let Henry see her discomfort, she wrapped her arms around her waist and waited for it to ease. Her fingers gently explored the slope of her ribs, knowing this was the source of the pain – remembering the heavy kick of the boot that had put it there. At least they hadn't killed her baby, she thought as she closed her eyes and swallowed the moan that threatened to escape.

'Are you all right?' Henry's voice startled her.

She leaned against him as he stood behind her on the tilting deck, and gave him a swift smile of reassurance. 'Just a little sick to the stomach,' she said lightly. 'I'm thinking I'll lie down for a wee while.'

'Do you want me to come with you? I'm almost finished here.' His blue eyes were concerned as he looked down at her.

She shook her head. 'No, no,' she said swiftly. 'I'm better on me own, and will probably be asleep before you know it.' She kissed his cheek, tasting the salt from the spindrift, feeling the chill of the wind and knowing she was not being honest with him. Yet she consoled herself with the thought that she'd managed to hide her discomfort for almost five months now, and there was no point in worrying him when there was nothing he could do.

Maureen held fast to the wooden railing as she made her

way down the narrow stairs to the third-class sleeping quarters. She could hear a baby crying and the strains of a fiddle weaving its way through a babble of chatter. There was no doubt about it, she thought as she made her way slowly towards her curtained-off compartment, the Irish knew how to make the best of things.

The tiers of bunks offered little privacy but for the heavy curtains they could pull across at night. Maureen and Henry were in the section for married couples, and further towards the bow were the women's bunks. The men and youths were quartered at the stern, and it was from here that most of the noise emanated. Meals were taken at long trestle tables and benches, which were set up between the two sections. This area had become the hub for gathering to gossip and exchange homespun philosophy as they played their fiddles and drums and sang the old songs of Ireland.

She ducked her head to avoid the overhead bunk and sank on to the lumpy mattress. The pain was easing a little, but it had left her light-headed and queasy. Tugging the rough blanket over her shoulders she lay down and curled her knees to her chest. If she could only sleep, then perhaps she'd begin to feel better. She was so tired – so very tired that everything had become an effort.

Kate hurried down the steps, her face flushed from the pace she'd set to get from the first-class cabins down to the third. Her hair had been whipped by the wind and her cheeks tingled as she jumped the last two steps and headed for Maureen's compartment. She had only an hour before the children would need her again, and she wanted to see if her friend was feeling any better.

'Hey, Kate. Come give us a dance, girl.'

She smiled at the familiar voice, and shouted back. 'I've better things to be doin' than dancing with you, Seamus Dooley.'

'Oh, darlin',' he called back from the depths of the rear quarters with mournful pathos. ''Tis breakin' me heart, y'are.' This declaration was met with cat-calls and jeers from his cronies.

Kate grinned and carried on walking at a fast pace. Seamus Dooley had a nerve, that was for sure, but despite his dark good looks and his glib tongue, she had no intentions of getting herself mixed up with him. He had a roving eye, and a way with the women that would surely get him into trouble one day, and she wanted no part of it. For what was the point of making this journey to the other side of the world if she settled for the first handsome man she came across?

It was quieter in the married quarters, for most of the passengers had realised it was more pleasant on deck during the day. Kate slowed down, her footsteps barely making a sound as she approached Maureen's curtain and peeked around it.

Maureen's eyelids fluttered and she smiled. 'What are you doing here, Kate?' she murmured. 'Thought you were supposed to be watching the wee ones.'

'It's lunch time,' she said as she perched on the edge of the mattress. She was rather pleased she'd remembered not to call it dinner, for the toffs had dinner at night. 'Mr Reed likes to have the girls with him in the dining room.'

Maureen winced as she rose to lean on her elbow. She tried to mask it by yawning. 'I must have fallen asleep,' she murmured.

Kate wasn't fooled. She noted how pale Maureen was, how the shadows still lay around her eyes despite the morning sleep. 'Is the pain very bad?' she asked softly.

'Ach, it's nothing,' Maureen said with a dismissive shrug. 'I'll just be glad to get me feet back on something that doesn't toss me here and there.'

'Don't you think Henry ought to be told?' persisted Kate.

'No.' The retort was sharp. 'He's enough to worry about. Leave it, Kate.'

Kate eyed her friend and wished there was something she could say that would convince her to see a doctor. For this constant sickness wasn't right, neither were the sharp pains in her side. Yet she could not betray Maureen's trust and tell Henry.

'I'm sorry, Kate,' murmured Maureen. 'I didn't mean to be so sharp.' She gave a wan smile. 'You're a good friend to both of us and I don't think you realise just how much I appreciate that.'

Kate patted her hand and smiled. 'There's no need to be apologising,' she said lightly. 'You just concentrate on getting your energy back.'

Maureen lay back down and closed her eyes and Kate sat holding her hand until she was sure she'd fallen back to sleep.

They'd met shortly after the *Swallow* had left London. Kate had been rushing down to the third-class quarters with her bag after helping Mr Reed settle the children for the night, and had bumped into Henry and Kate as the ship pitched sharply in the swelling sea. Kate had seen the helpless way Henry was trying to deal with Maureen's sickness and had taken over. It was the start of a blossoming friendship and Kate became confidante to both of them.

Maureen had told her about their flight from Ireland, and their reason for coming on this voyage. Henry had confided his hopes and dreams of becoming a well-known artist despite his father. Kate admired their courage, and hoped that one day she would find just such a man as Henry, who would love her and protect her and do anything to keep her.

She rose from her perch on the horsehair mattress and tucked Maureen's hand beneath the covers before pulling the curtain. She'd spent longer down here than she'd meant, and she would have to run like the devil if she was to get back to the top deck before she was missed.

Kate raced down the narrow corridor. As she gathered up her skirts and tore up the steps she didn't see the figure looming ahead of her. She ran straight into him, bouncing off his broad chest like a child's ball.

She gasped as she teetered on the top step, arms windmilling to keep her balance. Strong hands gripped her around the waist and she was hauled to safety. They both sank in a heap on the deck.

'Thank you,' she gasped as she straightened her skirts and pulled the hair from her eyes.

''Tis a pleasure,' came the reply as his hand grasped her wrist and he pulled her to her feet.

Kate looked up and froze. It was a face she had seen before. A face she could never have forgotten. 'I, I . . .' she began.

'Not to be worrying yourself,' he said brightly. 'The name's Patrick Dempster, but me mates call me Paddy.' He held out his hand. 'Pleased to make your acquaintance.'

Strength came from the knowledge he'd never seen her before and didn't know what she'd witnessed – yet the shock of seeing him again, and of realising they would be travelling together for at least another two months almost made her speechless. 'Kate,' she mumbled. 'I have to go. I'm late already.'

She picked up the hem of her skirt and began to run. She needed to put distance between them. Needed to get the feel of his hands washed from her in the clean, cutting salt air.

But escape was illusory, for she could hear him calling after her.

'See you again, Kate.'

Chapter Five

Fiona hadn't slept well and she'd put it down to jet lag. But as she packed the motorbike panniers for the coming journey, she realised that her worry over Louise was probably a part of it. She'd tried ringing earlier, and had still got the damn answering service.

Chewing her lip, she eyed her watch. There wasn't much time, the trip to Bellbird would take at least a day and a half, but if she got a move on, she could beat the city rush-hour traffic and be at Louise's in about half an hour. The decision made, she locked the unit, donned the crash helmet and steered the motorbike out through the security gates. Within minutes she was roaring down the freeway and heading for Story Bridge.

The sun was barely over the horizon when she pulled up at the imposing gates and let the bike engine idle as she kept her finger pressed on the intercom button.

'Who is it?' the muffled voice answered impatiently.

'It's me, Fiona. Let me in, Louise.'

There was a long moment of silence, and then the security buzzer went and the gates began to slowly draw back. Fiona eased the bike through them and roared up the gravel driveway.

The house was imposing, and pretentious with white stucco and graceful balconies that positively reeked of money. The lawn was as smooth as a billiard table, the trees and shrubs clipped into order and the white sail that was suspended over the pool at the side of the house was almost glaring in the rising sunlight.

Fiona switched off the bike and kicked out the footrest. She swung her leg over the seat and removed her crash helmet. Shaking out her hair, she strode up the white marble steps to the colonnaded portico.

'What the hell do you mean by coming so early? What's the matter?' Louise was in her dressing-gown.

Fiona pushed past her and entered the cavernous hall, her boots ringing on the marble. 'Where's Ralph?' she asked shortly.

Louise looked momentarily confused. 'He's already gone into the city. Did you want him for something?'

'No.' Fiona walked into the kitchen and sat down at the counter. She helped herself to coffee from the percolator and spooned in sugar and cream. 'It's you I came to see,' she said eventually. 'I just didn't want Ralph sticking his nose in.'

Louise folded her arms around her waist, her face set and angry. 'You've got some nerve,' she said sharply. 'You come barging in here at some unearthly hour of the morning and the first thing you do is insult Rafe.' She stood on the other side of the counter and glared. 'This better be good, Fiona.'

Fiona realised she'd handled things all wrong as usual. She'd forgotten how prickly her sister was in the mornings, and had run off at the mouth without taking this into consideration. 'I left several messages on your answering service. If you didn't want to see me, then you should have rung back.'

'We didn't get home from the cocktail party until after midnight. I was going to phone you later this morning.' Louise looked defensive, the long, thin fingers plucking at her dressing-gown sleeve.

Fiona eyed her for a long moment. She knew Louise too well, and she'd bet a dollar to a cent she'd been crying. Her determination to discuss the ridiculous diet faltered. If Louise was already upset, it would merely cause a row. But it was the reason she'd come, and her conscience wouldn't allow her to back down. Row or not, Louise had to see what a dangerous thing she was doing.

'Why don't we have some breakfast,' she offered. 'We could go to that little place down by the river. Remember the bacon sandwiches they do? And the hot chocolate with the marshmallow floater? You used to love it.'

Louise shook her head vehemently. 'You know I'm on a diet,' she said crossly. 'Surely you didn't come all this way to discuss breakfast?'

'I did, actually,' replied Fiona as she set her coffee cup down on the counter. 'I'm worried you're not taking care of yourself,' she said quietly.

'You're just jealous I've lost a lot of weight,' retorted Louise.

Fiona ignored her. 'Don't you think it's gone far enough?' she said mildly. 'Lose much more and you'll fade away.'

'I don't have to listen to this,' snapped Louise. 'You're the last person I'd come to for advice on diet and nutrition. If you've nothing else to say, you can leave.'

Fiona climbed off the stool, grabbed her startled sister by the arm and hauled her into the downstairs cloakroom. 'Take it off,' she snapped, tugging at the dressing-gown.

Louise struggled to get away from her, but Fiona was too quick. She ripped the gown away and had to stifle the gasp of horror at what she saw. Louise's ribs stood out like the carcass of an old warship, the hip bones jutted beneath the tiny band of her lacy panties and her breasts were non-existent.

'What are you doing to yourself?' she breathed. 'Louise,' she rasped as she forced her sister to face the mirror. 'Look at yourself, dammit!'

Louise glared at her reflection and pulled the dressing-gown back over her bony shoulders. She tied the belt forcefully and pushed back her short hair. 'If you weren't my sister, I'd have you up for assault,' she said icily. 'Why can't you mind your own damn business?'

'But you can't want this,' gasped Fiona. 'You're literally starving yourself to death.' She saw the flinch in her sister's eyes and knew she was finally getting through. 'What is it, love?' she murmured as she took her in her arms. 'Why are you doing this?'

Louise froze in the embrace, her arms at her sides, her chin lifted in defiance. 'It's my hormones,' she said stiffly. 'I eat when I want, but I just can't seem to put on weight.'

Fiona pulled away, stung by the obvious lie. 'It's because you're unhappy,' she said firmly. 'You've lost control of everything else, but what you put in your mouth.' She gave a grunt of disgust. 'Wise up, Louise. This is a dangerous game you're playing.'

'Have you quite finished?' Louise's eyes were arctic with fury.

'No,' retorted Fiona. 'I'm going to keep on until you see sense. Perhaps once Mim's seen what you're doing to yourself, you'll realise the truth of it.'

Louise pushed past her and stepped into the hall. 'We can't make Mim's birthday,' she said defiantly. 'Rafe's got an important conference which will take all weekend.'

Fiona wasn't going to let her get away with it. 'That doesn't stop you coming,' she said shortly. 'You could ride with me.'

'Not bloody likely,' retorted Louise with a grimace. 'You're deadly on that bike. Besides,' she added, determination bright in her eyes, 'Rafe needs me here to help entertain. I don't have time to visit Mim.'

'Bullshit!' Fiona was past caring and gave her temper free rein. 'That bloody husband of yours is a bastard. Can't you see he's deliberately organised this meeting so you can't visit Mim? Haven't you realised he's cowered and manipulated you to such a point you don't know which end is up?'

Louise pressed against the wall as Fiona took a step towards her and barked in her face. 'Wake up, Louise. He's set you up here in this marble mausoleum and effectively isolated you from the world. The first thing he did was pour scorn on your acting, so you gave it up. Then he took a dislike to all your friends and banned them from the house. Now it's your family.' She was out of breath and panting. 'Who's next, Louise? Is there anyone left?'

Louise's face was waxen. 'How dare you?' she hissed. 'What the hell do you know about anything? You've never been married. Never managed to keep a man for more than five bloody minutes. You swan all over the flaming world without a care in your head for anyone else – least of all for the family. What right have you got to come round here and throw your rather obvious weight about? Eh?'

Fiona itched to slap her silly face, but she held back. 'You've never been a bitch, so don't start now,' she warned. 'This isn't about me and you, or even you and the family. This is about respecting yourself. About feeling worthy enough to stand up to that bastard and walk away.'

Her voice was soft as she headed for the door. 'You don't have to live in his shadow, Louise. You're bright and lovely and perfectly capable of living without him.'

'Why should I? We aren't all like you, living like a gypsy, swapping men when the fancy takes you. At least I'm not a tart.'

Fiona dropped her chin and stared hard at the marble floor. She would need all her willpower to resist the urge to take the silly cow by the neck and give her a shake. 'The family are expecting you at Bellbird,' she said stiffly. 'If you don't come, then I will make sure they know why.'

She looked across at her sister who was standing trembling against the wall. 'I don't fancy Ralph's chances once Leo gets hold of him, so I'd sort it out, and quick.'

'Get out!' shouted Louise, her voice rising to a high-pitched scream. 'Get out, get out, get out!'

Fiona slammed the door behind her just as a crystal vase sailed close to her head and crashed to the floor of the portico. She ran down the steps, slammed on the helmet and kicked the motorbike into a roar. With a spume of gravel

95

flying from beneath the wheels she tore down the driveway and out into the street.

Come hell or high water, she vowed, she'd make Louise see sense. And if that meant dealing with Ralph herself, then she would find a way.

Jake's dream was confused. He was on a sailing ship bound for Australia, but he thought he could hear the insistent ring of a telephone. It didn't make sense. He forced his way up through the layers of darkness into the daylight and found himself staring straight into Eric's yellow eyes.

The cat was perched on his shoulder, the deep rhythmic purr vibrating right through the blanket as the claws paddled the wool and the penetrating gaze never faltered.

'Get off,' Jake muttered as he wrestled with the cat and the blankets and clambered out of bed. Padding out of the room he entered the kitchen. There was no sign of Mim and the telephone was still ringing.

'Hello,' he said tentatively.

'Who's that?' demanded the female voice at the other end.

'Jake Connor,' he said with a yawn as he scratched his chest. 'Who are you?'

'Where's Mim?'

Jake frowned and bent to peer through the window. He could see only part of the yard and a corner of the fenced-in paddock. 'Not in sight,' he muttered. 'Probably in the stables.'

'Damn.' There was an exasperated sigh followed by a long silence.

Jake stood there, his bare feet cold against the stone floor, his pyjama trousers at half-mast. He hitched them up. 'Can I give her a message?' he asked when the silence had become uncomfortable.

'Who the hell are you? What are you doing in Mim's kitchen?'

Jake had had enough. 'I'm visiting,' he said tersely. 'More's to the point, it's cold in here and I'm not dressed yet. Who are you and what do you want?'

96

There was a soft giggle at the other end of the line. 'Sorry,' she muttered. 'You must think I'm very rude. I'm Fiona – mean anything to you?'

Jake realised she was testing him to see just how familiar he was with the family. He rubbed his chest absent-mindedly and grinned. 'You're Mim's youngest grandchild. Chloe's daughter.'

'Fair enough. Are you any good at remembering messages?'

He raised an eyebrow. Who did Fiona think she was dealing with – a half-wit, or school kid? 'On a good day I can remember most things,' he said in mock seriousness. 'But when it's a full moon I get a little hazy.'

There was the giggle again and Jake decided that although she had to be the most annoying person he'd talked to this morning, he did like the sound of her laugh. It was deep and sexy, with a touch of devilment that piqued his interest.

'Will you tell Mim that Louise and Ralph may not be coming to her birthday party after all?' She paused. 'I think that should be enough to get her on the phone and haul his arse over there,' she added with asperity.

Jake hitched up his pyjama trousers again. 'I suppose you're not going to tell me what all this is about?'

'You're right. I'm not,' she replied. There was a pause. 'Tell Mim I'm on my way and should be at Bellbird sometime tomorrow – probably early evening.'

Now that was a piece of news to brighten his day. It would be interesting to meet this rather fiery, suspicious woman. 'Right oh,' he said cheerfully. 'Catch you later, then.'

'How long are you staying, exactly?' Her tone was guarded.

'As long as it takes,' he said, knowing he was being irritating, but wanting to get his own back.

'What's that supposed to mean?' she snapped. 'Just who the hell are you, and why are you staying with Mim? What's going on over there?'

'I'm not going to tell you,' he said blithely, the laughter bubbling up in his chest.

The line was abruptly cut with the slam of the receiver at the other end and Jake was left standing there half-naked and grinning.

Miriam had done almost two hours in the stables, now she was tired. She left the yard and tramped slowly through the long grass to her favourite tree and sat down on the wooden bench Edward had built in their first year of marriage. It was scarred by the elements and the paint was gone, but it offered shade and tranquility and she needed time to recoup her strength and think.

Her night had been restless, with the images of the past coming to her so strongly she could still feel their presence now she was awake. She smiled, despite her weariness. The spirit of those who peopled her dreams and her memories still lived on and she could almost picture Kate's bustling, joyous energy and her father's gentle but firm determination to do what was right. The sun seemed to lose its warmth as she remembered Patrick's dark presence and she shivered.

'Are you all right, Mim?' came the soft voice.

She looked up. She hadn't been startled by his approach even though she hadn't heard it, just rather grateful to him for coming at such an opportune moment.

'Ghosts,' she said wearily. 'They never really leave us, do they?'

Jake didn't answer, merely joined her on the bench and stretched his long legs before him. He tilted his hat over his eyes and dug his hands in the pockets of the moleskins as they shared this companionable moment in the sibilant heat.

Miriam felt her strength return in the presence of this quiet man. He might be young, she thought, but there's a stillness about him that brings contentment. She would have liked to ask him about his wife, about the divorce, but knew it would be intrusive. Yet she wondered why such a man had had a troubled marriage – perhaps these particular still waters ran very deep – perhaps she'd seen only one side of Jake Connor.

She sat next to him in the shade of the pepper tree and listened to the hum of bees. The sounds of the stable-yard drifted on the breeze and the occasional caw of a crow filtered through the squabble of the parakeets. As far as she was concerned, Bellbird Station was the nearest she'd ever get to Heaven, and she hoped that when she did finally solve the mystery of life after death, it would be in a place like this.

Jake cleared his throat and, sitting up, straightened his hat. 'There was a call for you earlier,' he said quietly. 'From Fiona.'

She felt a pang of something akin to panic. 'Don't tell me she's had to go away again,' she said sharply. 'She promised she would visit.'

Jake shook his head. 'It's Louise and Ralph who won't be coming.' He must have thought he'd seen disappointment in her face. 'Sorry, but that's all Fiona said.'

Miriam stood up and rammed her hat back on. 'No need for you to apologise,' she said shortly. She eyed him sharply. 'What's his excuse this time?'

Jake shrugged. 'Fiona didn't say.'

He towered over her as they walked back to the homestead. She glanced up at him. 'What's so funny?' she snapped when she saw the smile playing at the corners of his mouth.

'Fiona said you'd be crook about it,' he drawled.

'She's right,' retorted Miriam as she stomped up the steps and crashed through the screen door. 'Make yourself useful while I sort this out. The kettle's over there.'

Miriam dialled Ralph's office, spoke to his secretary and waited. 'Ralph,' she said before he could get past his initial greeting. 'I hope you and Louise are coming to Bellbird as planned.'

'I'm tied up here, unfortunately,' he replied, not sounding in the least regretful. 'Can't make the journey after all.'

'That's a pity,' said Miriam with the same lack of regret. 'I

99

was hoping for some advice on a rather nice little windfall I've come into. But no matter, I'll ring Baxter instead.'

She waited. William Baxter was the chief executive of Ralph's closest competitor and the two men loathed one another.

'I may be able to reschedule,' he said with studied non-chalance. 'But it could take some time.' There was a pause and the riffling of paper. 'Can't you discuss this windfall with me over the telephone?'

'Not really,' she said evenly. 'I was hoping to keep this in the family, but if you can't . . .' She left the rest of the sentence hanging, knowing he wouldn't be able to resist.

'I'll see what I can do,' he said briskly. 'But I am a busy man, and I can't promise anything until I've spoken to my people.'

Miriam replaced the receiver. 'Pompous prat,' she spat as she took the mug of tea from Jake and plonked down in the kitchen chair.

'No luck then?' Jake was leaning against the cupboard, the mug of tea steaming in his hand.

Miriam laughed, the dimple appearing in her cheek. 'Want to bet on it?' She ran her fingers through her thick, greying hair. 'He'll come all right. Nothing like the hint of money coming his way to get Ralph's dander up.'

Jake shifted his lean hip to a more comfortable position against the battered kitchen cupboard. 'Fiona said she'd be here sometime tomorrow. Probably late afternoon,' he said almost as an afterthought. 'I'd better move out and leave you to your family celebrations.'

She masked her pleasure at hearing of Fiona's imminent arrival with her usual brusqueness. 'You'll do no such thing,' she ordered. 'I haven't finished telling you about my parents. And you'll need to know it all if we've any chance of making sense of things.'

'It might not necessarily be that easy,' replied Jake as he set his mug down. 'Memories can play tricks, and we can be totally convinced of something and still be proved wrong.'

His expression was serious as he looked down at her. 'I wouldn't pin your hopes on it too much, Mim. We could be heading for a fall.'

She eyed him sternly, determined not to let him see how affected she was by his pessimistic outlook. 'So you don't think I stand a chance?'

'Not really,' he confessed. 'Not from what you've told me so far.'

'Then it's time I told you the next part of the story, and we'll see how you feel about things then.'

She pulled herself out of her chair and took the bottle of tablets from the shelf beside the range. Swallowing two with a gulp of water, she wiped her mouth on the back of her hand. She saw him watching and grimaced. 'Got a bit of a headache, but I'll be right.'

He followed her into the hall and through the door into the parlour. It was a pleasant room, one in which time had stood still. Running the full depth of the house it had windows overlooking both the front yard and the back paddock. The chairs were deep and covered in chintz, the curtains made in the same faded material. A thick carpet covered most of the wooden floor, and the jumble of old-fashioned, heavy furniture shone with loving attention. The focal point of the room was the stone chimneybreast and the painting which hung above the hearth.

Miriam stood back and watched as Jake crossed the room and stopped before the painting. It was always interesting to see what people thought of it.

'Did your father paint this?' he asked as he tried to decipher the almost illegible signature.

'Yes, it was his last.'

'I'm no expert,' he murmured. 'But the quality of the work is amazing. The capturing of the light, the pathos of the figures – it's wonderful.' He turned to face her. 'This sort of painting is really fashionable. If it was cleaned, you could get a fortune for it. I hope it's insured?'

'It's not for sale,' she said abruptly as she sank into one of

101

the armchairs. 'But it is insured.' She gave a sigh. 'Though if it was ever lost or stolen, or even damaged – no amount of money could ever replace it. It's about the last thing I have to remember him by.'

Jake leaned against the mantelpiece and folded his arms. 'What about his other paintings? Surely he must have had quite a collection by the time he died?'

Miriam stared at the painting, the memories sharpened by the all too familiar scene. 'They had to be sold,' she said abruptly.

'Why?' he prompted.

'All in good time,' she said with profound sadness. 'But to understand why that particular painting means so much to me, you will need to know the story behind it – and the price paid to keep it.'

For the first time in his life Paddy Dempster experienced a sense of belonging, and hadn't felt the need to thieve or cheat his fellow travellers. His friendship with Henry Beecham had flourished over the past four months, and much to his surprise, he found he actually liked the man despite his heritage. Maureen of course was another matter. She was too sharp, too knowing, and although he'd done his best to make her like him, he'd had to be content with her cold politeness. It was Henry who mattered. Henry who would ultimately fall in with his scheme and help him to make a fortune.

Paddy enjoyed the close quarters of the steerage accommodation and the camaraderie that had sprung up between the unmarried men. There were women too – young, single and with an eye to snaring a man before they reached the Australian shores. Yet Paddy had eyes only for Kate.

He was sitting at his usual place on deck, smoking a pipe and watching Henry sketch when he spotted Kate coming towards him. Henry must have seen the alertness in him, the all too casual neatening of his collar, for he paused in his work and watched Kate's progress along the deck. 'I see our

Kate has cast her spell on you, Paddy,' he said with a chuckle. 'I'd be careful though, she's quite a handful for any man, and I don't fancy your chances.'

Paddy carefully knocked the dottle from his pipe and threw it overboard. 'She's quite a prize,' he murmured as he admired the way her skirts swayed from the hip. 'A man would be a fool not to try.'

'I'll put in a word for you,' muttered Henry as he winked. 'But I wouldn't hold out much hope of that one succumbing to your charms. Far too level headed.'

Kate flushed as she caught Paddy's eye and swiftly turned her attention to Henry. 'I've a few minutes to meself,' she said. 'I was hoping to talk with Maureen, but I can't find her.'

'She can't be very far away,' Henry replied, his glance sweeping over the crowded deck and animal pens where the cows and goats and chickens were housed. 'Why don't you sit awhile and chat with Paddy? Maureen's bound to come along soon, and it's time you and Paddy got to know one another better.'

Paddy saw the hesitation and the uneasy glance Kate shot at him and felt a twinge of doubt. It was as if she was afraid of him. Yet he'd done nothing to frighten her, had kept a discreet distance when they found themselves alone and had always been polite. He shifted along the narrow bench. 'Come Kate,' he said softly. 'I'll not bite.'

Kate smoothed her skirts and sat on the very edge of the wooden bench. 'I can't stay for too long, the children will be waking from their afternoon nap.'

Paddy noticed the tension in her, the way she perched at the furthest point away from him and wondered why this was. He'd been delighted to find she was so friendly with Henry and had hoped this would be to his advantage. Yet despite Henry's jovial attempts to bring them together over the past few months, Kate seemed determined to remain aloof.

After an exchange of a few stilted words, they sat in

103

uneasy silence as Henry returned to the portrait he was doing of a rather stern dowager. Paddy breathed in the scent of Kate as he admired the way her skin had darkened in the hot sun and her breasts thrust against the thin cotton bodice. He licked his lips as he watched a single tear of sweat trickle down her neck and disappear into the cleft just visible beneath that tight bodice.

She was ripe and ready and he felt a stirring deep within him as his gaze trawled from the slender neck to the sensuous mouth and dark eyes. Kate Kelly might appear to be the picture of disdain, the proper lady, but in his imagination he could see her lying beneath him, hair wild, legs wrapped around his hips, her mouth open in pleasure as he took her.

She turned her head and stared at him. It was as if she could read his mind. 'I'll be going,' she said as she stood. 'Tell Maureen I'll catch up with her tonight.'

Paddy watched the way her hips moved beneath the thin cotton and knew he could wait no longer. Kate Kelly had to be tamed – and he was just the man to do it.

Supper was over, and Maureen waited until Paddy left the table and joined the other men in their raucous game of cards. She reached across and took Henry's hand. 'I wish you wouldn't encourage him,' she said.

Henry's blue eyes widened. 'He's a good chap,' he replied. 'Taught me a thing or two. We wouldn't be half so comfortable if Paddy hadn't got us those extra blankets and the milk and vegetables.'

Maureen shivered and pulled the shawl more firmly around her shoulders. The nights were bitter despite the awful heat of the days, but Paddy's constant presence made her uneasy. 'I don't trust him,' she declared. 'And neither does Kate.'

Henry patted her hand. 'Silly girl,' he murmured. 'Paddy might be a bit brash and rough around the edges, but he's a good heart. He means no harm and I find his company amusing.'

104

Maureen knew the time had come to voice her concerns. 'I've seen men like that before,' she said with an urgency that made her shrill. She made a concerted effort to lower her voice, but her tone lost none of its edge. 'He's not a true friend, Henry. He stays with us because he thinks he can profit from you.'

Henry's blue eyes were puzzled as they regarded her. 'I have nothing Paddy would want,' he said evenly. 'There's little enough money and we carry no valuables. I think your imagination is running away with you.' He smiled then and grasped her hand again. 'I'm a big boy, now, my darling. I am quite capable of looking after us, so don't you be worrying your pretty head about Paddy.'

Maureen could have slapped him. She snatched her hand away and pushed from the table. 'Don't patronise me, Henry,' she hissed. 'I might not have had your education, or your experience, but in some things you are a fool. At least give me the credit to recognise when one of me own is up to no good.'

'I'll have no more of this, Maureen,' he said stiffly. 'Paddy could easily have pocketed my watch back on the docks, and not once has he suggested a reward or hinted that he wants more from me than friendship. The subject is closed.'

Maureen strode away from the table, the rage building inside her, the furious tears blinding her as she headed for their compartment. She loved Henry with a passion, but dear god he was a fool. Why couldn't he see what she did? The return of the watch had been a clever ploy – his constant presence, his helpful advice and the extra allocation of milk and blankets were all a part of his plan. Though what that plan was, Maureen had to admit ignorance. She just knew there was something decidedly untrustworthy about Paddy Dempster, and the sooner the ship docked and they could be on their separate ways, the better.

Kate closed the door on the sleeping children and turned to find Peter Reed watching her. 'I'll be going now, sir,' she said as she bobbed a curtsy. Father Pat would have been proud. She'd come a long way since those awkward first days in the presbytery.

He smiled and the cobweb of lines creased at the corners of his eyes. 'Always rushing to be somewhere,' he drawled. 'Are you never still, Kate?'

'It's very late, sir, and I promised to see my friend tonight.'

'Ah.' He lifted a brown eyebrow. 'So there's a man, is there? Might have guessed.'

Kate grinned. 'No sir,' she said. 'Maureen's expecting her first, and I've promised to keep her company tonight.'

Peter Reed lifted his glass. 'Stay and have a drink with me, Kate,' he offered. 'You're much better company than those other stuffed shirts. Should have known better than to travel first class.'

'It wouldn't be right, sir.' Yet she lingered. Peter Reed was a handsome man, and she had seen the simpering glances thrown at him by the rich young women travelling on this upper deck. 'I'm sure there are lots of young ladies in the first-class drawing room who would be much better company,' she said.

'They don't have your energy, your curiosity and lust for life.' He poured himself another drink and eyed her thoughtfully. 'You will do well in Australia,' he said finally. 'You have the right qualities.' He must have seen his compliments were making her uneasy, for he put down the glass and opened the door for her. 'Go on, Kate,' he said softly. 'And enjoy your evening.'

Kate left the stateroom and hurried down the thickly carpeted hall to the stairs that would take her down to the decks below. She had come to like Peter Reed. He was a kind and courteous employer, interested in her dreams and aspirations but never overstepping the mark. His voice was deep, the drawl edged with a strange twang that was neither Irish nor cockney, but brought with it a hint of the harsh lands of Australia which he had made his own.

Stopping to catch her breath, she leaned against the railings and stared out at the water. The moon was high in a cloudless sky that was liberally sprinkled with bright stars. A glow shimmered in the rolling waves giving the night a touch of magic as the great ship ploughed towards an endless horizon.

'The sailors call it phosphorescence,' said the voice behind her.

Kate turned. 'What are you doing up here?' Her voice was sharp and he was much too close for comfort.

Paddy scratched his chin. 'I often come up here at night,' he said. 'It's quieter, and there's more space to walk and to think.'

Kate moved away from the railings, but Paddy's bulk was barring her escape. 'I promised Maureen I'd visit,' she said as calmly as she could. 'I'll be missed if I'm late.'

Paddy sketched a mocking bow and offered his arm. 'Then let me escort you, Kate.'

She glanced swiftly around. They were quite alone.

Paddy took her hand, tucked it into the crook of his arm and smiled down at her. 'There, that's better,' he murmured.

Kate reluctantly kept pace with him. To run would seem foolish, and if she was sharp with him it could cause all kinds of trouble. He was big and strong, and although she was tough, she knew she was no match for him should he guess at her abhorrence. She would have to play along and just hope the opportunity for escape would present itself quickly. All it would take would be a passing sailor, or a strolling couple and she could leave his side with no fear of giving him offence.

They walked in silence along the weathered deck, their footsteps muffled by the deep and ever-present rumble of the great steam engines. The ship ploughed on, dipping and rising with the waves, the stars looking down with cold disinterest.

Kate could feel the heat of his arm beneath the shirtsleeve. Could feel the tension in him as they approached the flight of steps that would take them down to steerage. It matched her own. For she could hear his shallow, rapid breathing and was all too aware of the deep shadows cast by the crates lashed to the decks and shrouded in tarpaulin.

His arm tightened on her hand. His grip on her shoulder swung her deep into those shadows and, before she could cry out, he'd thrust her hard against the wooden crate and his mouth was smothering her.

Kate fought back, pummelling him with her fists, kicking out with her boots, desperately trying to avoid that all-encompassing mouth and sour tongue that forced its way between her lips.

Paddy pressed against her, his arousal digging into her belly as he lifted her skirts and grasped her thigh. His hands cupped her bottom and lifted her from the deck, ramming her once again against the crate and pinning her there while he fumbled with his trousers.

Kate's scream was lost in her throat as the endless, smothering kiss engulfed her and his fingers delved inside her. She wriggled and squirmed and kicked out to no avail. He meant to have her and there seemed no way to stop him.

Her arms flailed, weaker now. He was forcing her legs apart, thrusting himself forward, seeking out the thing he wanted. Her desperate fingers touched something cold and smooth. She grasped it. Lashed out blindly with a strength honed by terror – and found her mark.

Paddy's mouth opened as the iron bar hit his head. He froze, his eyes puzzled. Then his hands slipped from her and he fell heavily to the deck.

Kate couldn't move. It was as if she had lost the use of her legs as well as her senses. She watched him fall. Saw his already damaged head hit the deck with a sickening thud before he lay sprawled at her feet. There was blood. She could see the dark trickle of it stain the bleached wood.

Paddy groaned and his hands began to claw at the deck.

Kate was galvanished into action. She dropped the

108

crowbar, leaped over his inert form and raced for the stairs, pounding down them as if her life depended upon it. Tearing past the animal pens she raced for the lower stairs to the sleeping quarters. Ignoring the ribald laughter from the others who were enjoying their last few moments before turning in, she hurried from the communal area and headed towards the darkness and comfort of her bed.

She pulled the curtain and sank into the mattress, curling up into a ball, her face buried in her pillow. After the tears came a calm decision. She would say nothing to Maureen, she had troubles enough, but she would find the opportunity to speak to Henry in the morning. There had to be some way he could protect her from Paddy.

She was snatched from her troubled dreams by the rough hand that was suddenly clamped over her mouth. His weight dipped the mattress and she could see the glint of his eyes and smell his sweat as he leaned over her.

'You'll keep quiet about what happened tonight,' Paddy whispered. 'Or I'll have you locked up in the brig for trying to kill me.' He nuzzled her face with his chin. 'It can be our little secret,' he whispered.

There was no escape from the hand that so effectively pinned her to the pillow. Her eyes were wide with the fear of him.

'Dare to speak of this and I'll let it be known you're free for the asking. That you were more than willing and things just got out of hand.' He nuzzled her again, his stubbled chin rasping against her cheek. 'No respectable man will employ you again to look after his brats, so I'd be very careful, Kate. There's only one other profession a girl like you can go into when she has no references, no sponsors – and I wouldn't like to see that happen – not to someone who will one day be my wife.'

Kate stared at him in horror as he grinned down at her. She flinched as he plucked at the sheet and pulled it down. A moan of despair filled her throat as his fingers traced a trail over the thin nightgown, scorching a path over her belly and the mounds of her breasts.

'I will have you, Kate,' he murmured. 'You can be certain of that.'

The *Swallow* steamed towards Port Philip on 15 April 1894. Eight babies had been born during the six months at sea – four people had died and a sailor was lost overboard during a squall off Cape Horn. There had been three weddings and countless engagements on board, but only time would tell if these matches would survive the gruelling battle ahead.

The blast from the *Swallow*'s funnels merely added to the excitement as Maureen and Henry joined the other migrants and clung to the railings.

'Our new homeland,' Henry shouted above the noise. 'Look, Maureen. Look how beautiful it is.'

Maureen stood within the circle of his arms and gazed out over the water. 'It's as blue as Our Lady's robes,' she breathed in wonderment. 'Sure, and I've never seen anything so glorious.'

'Look at the way the sunlight sparkles on it like stars,' he said pointing excitedly. 'It's so bright it almost hurts the eyes.'

Maureen shielded her eyes with her hand and looked towards the shore. The *Swallow* was steaming through the heart of a horseshoe of land, and on this side the giant red cliffs soared above pale yellow sand that was fringed with lacy waves. Beyond lay a land as green as Ireland. Her heartache for home was a pain deep within, and it hurt far more than any other she'd experienced on this endless voyage.

'We're home, darling,' Henry said softly into her hair. 'Let's promise each other we'll make the most of every opportunity this wonderful country offers us.'

Maureen was almost blinded by tears as she turned in his arms and held him tightly. 'We have each other,' she said softly. 'It's enough.'

Henry lifted his face to the sun and took a deep breath. 'Our children will flourish here,' he said. 'We must see to it they never have to experience what we've been through.'

Maureen nodded, her heart too full to put her feelings into words, the nagging pain in her back making it difficult to concentrate.

'You'll never guess,' said a breathless voice. Kate shoved her way through the tightly packed crowd at the railings. 'Mr Reed's asked me to marry him!'

'Congratulations.' It was good to see Kate again, she always brought such life and exuberance with her, and the past few weeks had been dull without her.

Kate shook her head, her black hair as always slipping from its pins and tumbling over her shoulders and down her back. 'I turned him down,' she retorted.

Maureen looked at her friend in puzzlement. 'Why? I thought you liked him – and he's rich as well as handsome.'

Kate laughed. 'I like him well enough to be sure, but not enough to marry him.' She shrugged nonchalantly. 'Besides, he really only wants a mother for his little ones, and I'm not ready to settle down yet.'

Maureen put her arm around Kate's shoulders. It had been an age since they'd had a chance to gossip, for Kate had suddenly packed her bags and with no real explanation had moved up to the top deck. 'We've missed you these past few weeks. But I suppose Mr Reed needed you close with the children going down with fever?'

Kate shrugged again, her eyes not quite meeting Maureen's. 'It was just more convenient to be on hand,' she said lightly. 'Seemed silly running back and forth all the time.'

Maureen watched her friend. There was something different about Kate – something secretive, and she had a suspicion Paddy was behind it. For Kate changed the subject when questioned too closely, and Paddy had become sullen when he learned of Kate's defection to the first-class stateroom. He'd tried to hide it, but Maureen wasn't fooled, and as his friendship with Henry grew ever stronger, she became more uneasy.

Kate wriggled into the gap beside Maureen and clung to the rail. 'Will you look at all that space?' she breathed. 'And the size of the sky. Did you ever see anything quite so . . . so . . .' She seemed to finally run out of breath.

'Big?' prompted Henry and laughed. 'Oh, Kate,' he said fondly. 'I'm glad we met. The trip wouldn't have been half so much fun without you.'

Kate's expression changed and there was a hint of tears in her eyes. 'I'm going to miss you two,' she sniffed. 'But me spelling's much better now, and I promise to write every month once we're all settled.'

Maureen took her in her arms and the two girls clung to one another. It was like leaving home all over again and the heartache was almost too much to bear. For, like Mr Reed and his children, she and Henry would be getting off the *Swallow* here in Port Philip. Kate would remain on board for the final leg to Sydney where she'd been promised a job as a housekeeper.

They drew apart and Maureen was about to turn back to the railings when she noticed Paddy standing apart from the others, his gaze dark and intense as it rested on Kate.

She was about to say something when the gnawing pain in her back gripped like a vice. With a sharp intake of breath, her hands flew to her swollen belly. The vice clenched ever harder. Gathering strength it filled her being until everything else was eclipsed.

'Maureen! What is it?' Henry's voice was filled with anguish, but she could only just hear him through the roaring in her head.

'Quick, help me get her below,' ordered Kate. 'The baby's on its way.'

Maureen panted. 'It can't be. It's not due for another two weeks.'

She'd barely finished speaking when she felt something warm and sticky on her thighs. Looking down she saw the drops of bright red blood on the bleached decking. She'd seen enough births to know her baby was not going to wait. Without protest she let Henry carry her back down to their berth and gratefully sank on to the hard mattress.

'Get the doctor,' ordered Kate as several other women milled round, filling the restricted space. 'She's before her time and I've never done this sort of thing alone before.'

Henry sped off up the stairs and Maureen took a firm grip of Kate's hand as the pain began again and grew steadily to an agonising crescendo. 'Help me, Kate,' she gasped. 'I'm frightened.'

Kate shooed away the others and held on. She tried to soothe her with gentle words of encouragement, but Maureen could hear only a muffled, disjointed voice coming through the black waves of pain. 'It's coming,' she cried. 'Oh, my god it's coming. Do something, Kate. Help me.'

'Bring your knees up and push,' ordered Kate. 'Here,' she said as she thrust the handle of one of Henry's paintbrushes between her teeth. 'Bite on this and push like buggery!'

Maureen bit down. She had the hysterical urge to giggle through her tears, but the pain was coming again and the need to push this baby out had become the most important thing in the world. She gripped her knees until they were either side of her belly. Gathered all her strength, bent forward and pushed as hard as she could.

'Good girl,' encouraged Kate who was now at the other end of the bunk. 'I can see its head. 'Tis a proper Irishman, with black curls. Now give me another push.'

Maureen was sweating and breathless, her senses spinning. The pain seemed to have encompassed her entire body, rekindling the fire in her ribs, soaring through her lungs, thudding in her head. Almost bankrupt of energy she garnered the last of her strength and pushed.

As the baby slid from her, the knife of pain stabbed her side, drawing up into her lungs with such intensity the air was punched from her chest. She fell back on the pillows and

113

clawed at her throat. Her heart was pounding, her lungs empty. She couldn't cry out, couldn't breath.

'What's the matter?' Kate's fearful voice came to her from so far away she could barely make out the words.

Maureen's fingers ripped at her collar as she drummed her heels against the mattress. She had to find some way of getting air – of ridding herself of whatever was squeezing the life out of her. The terror increased as the drumbeat of her heart filled her head, slowed to a heavy thud and muffled all sound. It blacked out the meagre daylight and she turned her head towards Kate – towards the distant sound of her infant's cry.

Henry stumbled down the stairs after the medic, the tense, nervous excitement tinged sharply with fear. The baby was coming too soon, and Maureen had not been well for most of the journey. He'd hoped that a few weeks on land would help her regain strength for this moment – but things had spun out of his control. He'd never felt so helpless.

As they walked down the narrow companionway they heard Kate's frantic calls and Henry was in a lather of frustration. The bulky figure in front of him was moving too slowly and there was no room to pass him. 'Hurry, hurry,' he urged. 'Something's wrong.'

'Women get overexcited at moments like this,' the doctor replied as he maintained his steady plod. 'I'm sure there's no need to worry.'

Kate came flying towards them and threw herself at the doctor. 'You've got to help her,' she screamed as she dragged on his arm. 'She's not breathing.'

Henry pushed them both aside and raced to the compartment. He skidded to a halt and fell to his knees beside the bunk. Maureen lay on the mattress, her mouth open in a silent scream. Her skin was like marble, tinged with blue around the mouth, the deep gouge of her nails clear on her neck.

'Let me pass.' A firm hand hauled him out of the way as

114

the doctor dropped his bag on the floor and quickly examined her.

Henry was only partially aware of Kate standing beside him. Only distantly able to recognise the thin wail of a newly born baby. All his concentration was fixed on Maureen. She was so still, so pale – so remote and unlike the girl he loved. He silently willed the doctor to wake her up – to find out what had gone wrong and make it better. For life without her was unthinkable.

The doctor finished his examination and stood up. His face was solemn, his eyes not quite reaching Henry's as he spoke. 'Your wife is dead,' he said mournfully. 'I see she has recently suffered a broken rib, and that could have been the cause.' He put his pudgy hand on Henry's shoulder. 'If so, she was on borrowed time. I'm sorry.'

Henry wondered if he'd heard him correctly. 'No,' he muttered. 'She can't be dead. We were talking only minutes earlier.' He wet his lips and looked from Kate to the man before him as the silence stretched and his tortured thoughts whirled.

'What broken rib?' he asked, the confusion numbing his senses. 'She never said anything.'

The doctor packed his medical bag and adjusted his pince-nez. 'The broken rib is a fairly recent injury which, with lack of treatment, had not knitted well. She must have been in some pain, but no doubt she didn't wish to worry you,' he said flatly. 'The exertion during labour was the defining factor in this most tragic affair. Nothing any of us could have done.' He looked over his pince-nez, his eyes doleful. 'The stoicism of some women never ceases to amaze me,' he said.

Henry stared at him, numb with shock, incapable of speech.

'I'll make the arrangements to have your wife prepared before she's taken ashore, Mr Beecham. And don't worry about my account – there was nothing medical I could do.'

Henry stood there and heard the man's footfalls fade into the distance. Then the sheer horror of the last few moments washed over him and the bleak reality of Maureen's death hit him. He fell to his knees and took her hand. It was already cool to the touch, lifeless. He stroked her face, needing only to touch her. She'd left him. Broken her promise and left him bereft on the very shores of what should have been their new home, their new life together.

The first tears streamed down his face and he pulled her into his arms and held her. The remorse over not realising just how ill she must have been, was unbearable.

'I'm sorry,' he wept. 'So sorry. Please forgive me for not seeing you were in so much pain. For not realising how ill you really were.'

He had no idea of how long he'd knelt there with his dead Maureen in his arms, and when the light touch on his shoulder drew him momentarily from the darkness of his pain he shrugged it off.

'Henry,' said Kate softly. 'Henry you have to let her go. The men are here to prepare her for shore.'

He rocked Maureen in his arms and kissed her face for the last time before he reluctantly laid her back on the mattress. 'Goodbye my darling, my *mavourneen*,' he whispered into her dark curls. 'I love you. Will always love you.'

Kate took him by the arm and he let her lead him away, down the corridor and into the deserted dining hall. He slumped down on a bench and with his arms on the table he bent his head and wept.

'I'll sit with him,' said the gruff voice.

Kate looked up into Paddy Dempster's face and felt a chill of foreboding run down her spine. 'You're not wanted here,' she said with a sharpness that made Henry look up.

'Paddy?' he said through his tears. 'Paddy, she's gone. My Maureen's gone.'

Kate watched as, after shooting a glance of triumph in her direction, Paddy sat down next to Henry and put his arm around his shoulders. Kate felt isolated and alone, and although she didn't like to leave Henry, she had things that needed doing. She looked down at the tiny baby in her arms and back at the man so deep in mourning he was lost to her. Bundling the baby in a blanket she'd plucked from another bunk, she hurried up the steps to the deck. She had to find Peter Reed before they docked. He would know what to do, where to go, how to handle things like funerals and accommodation.

Peter Reed proved to be a tower of strength. He quietly and efficiently organised for Maureen's body to be taken from the ship and transported by carriage to a local funeral director. He arranged for Kate and Henry to be put up in a cheap, but clean hotel on the waterfront, and paid for fresh milk to be delivered each day for the baby.

'I don't know how I'll ever repay you,' said Kate as she stood on the step outside the hotel. It was two days later and Maureen had been laid to rest in the tiny cemetery earlier that morning. There was, thankfully, no sign of Paddy.

His slow smile creased the corners of his grey eyes and drew lines on either side of his mouth. Peter Reed tipped the wide brim of his hat. 'You could reconsider my offer of marriage,' he drawled.

Kate shook her head. 'It wouldn't be right,' she said softly. 'We both know why you asked me, and it wouldn't work – not without love.'

He dug his hands into the pockets of his riding breeches and shrugged. 'Can't blame a bloke for trying,' he said in his slow, easy drawl. 'You'll be quite a catch for some man, Kate, that's for sure.'

Kate watched as he climbed on to the back of his horse. He was a good man. Wealthy and handsome, with a warmth and generosity she couldn't fault; she suspected she was letting a golden opportunity slip through her fingers. Yet she would be cheating both of them if she changed her mind.

He tipped his hat again and rode away, the red dust lifting from beneath the horse's hoofs, veiling him from sight.

Kate returned to the suite of rooms they had rented at the

top of the hotel. There were two bedrooms and a sitting room, each jammed with cheap furniture that filled every available space. Fly screens covered the windows and homespun rugs covered the uneven floor. A glass door led out to the verandah that ran the length of the upper floor, but despite the comfortable cane chairs that had been set out there, the flies made it impossible to stay long.

The heat was almost unbearable and Kate's cotton dress clung damply to her skin. She opened a window and quickly closed it again. The hot wind was swirling the dust up from the street, smothering everything in a fine red powder.

Kate gave a deep sigh and turned away from the window. She felt marooned and afraid for the future after the shock of Maureen's death. She'd seen nothing of this new country and her plans had been wrecked. Peter Reed had gone to his property, which by all accounts was in the middle of nowhere, and Henry had barely spoken to her since they'd landed. Yet Kate knew the time was fast approaching when she would have to make Henry take stock of their predicament. The money would soon run out, and decisions had to be made as to what they would do next.

Her gloomy thoughts were banished by the sound of the baby's whimper and she crossed to the basket she'd placed on a chair. The baby was snuffling in her sleep, her tiny thumb hooked between her lips. Kate smiled as she gently took her out of the basket, and with the warmth of the child close to her breast, went in search of Henry.

She found him sprawled across his bed, his face puffed from weariness and sorrow. He hadn't shaved since they'd left the ship, and his hair was unkempt. He opened his bleary eyes. 'Leave me,' he ordered. 'Can't you see I'm in mourning?'

Kate looked from the man to the baby in her arms. 'I thought you might find some comfort in your daughter,' she said quietly.

'I don't want to see it,' he said as he turned his shoulder and buried his face in the pillow.

118

Kate bit down on the angry retort. 'She's your daughter,' she persisted. 'A part of you and Maureen.'

Henry sat bolt-upright on the bed, his hair wild, his eyes fierce. 'Take it away,' he shouted. 'If it hadn't been for that,' he jabbed a finger at the sleeping baby, 'Maureen would still be here.'

Kate stood in the doorway as Henry turned his back on them and the baby began to cry. This was not the Henry she knew. Not the man who'd been so loving to his wife, so excited about their coming child. The sympathy she had felt for him was swept away in a flush of fury.

'That's not true,' she snapped. 'This wee scrap had nothing to do with the kicking that broke Maureen's rib. You can't blame her for what happened.'

'I can, and I do,' he said bitterly from the depths of the pillows. 'I want nothing to do with her.'

Chapter Six

Miriam sat back and looked at the man opposite her. 'So, you see,' she murmured. 'My father didn't want me.' With a long sigh, she looked down at her hands. They were an old woman's hands, she realised with a jolt. Thin and heavily veined, the knuckles broadened by toil in the stables, they were stark evidence of the span of years since her unfortunate birth.

Jake's voice interrupted her ruminations. 'Reckon he was feeling guilty,' he replied. 'He hadn't taken any notice of Maureen's obvious discomfort. No wonder the bloke went into decline.'

She looked at the young man opposite her, saw the understanding in his eyes and realised she was dealing with someone who, perhaps, had some experience of real pain. No matter he was younger than she'd expected. No matter he flirted outrageously with her and didn't give an inch in their sparring. He was a man she felt she could trust implicitly, and with that knowledge came peace.

'You're right, of course,' she said finally. 'He couldn't bear the thought he'd somehow been responsible for her death. I was just a terrible reminder of his loss – the cause of all his troubles.'

Jake didn't insult her by making any comment on her statement. He just nodded. 'None of this could have been easy for poor Kate, either,' he murmured. 'Landed with a grieving man and an unwanted baby in a strange new country, she must have wondered what she'd let herself in for.'

'Kate was resourceful,' replied Mim with a fond smile. 'Not one to sit on her heels and wait for help to materialise, she found work in the hotel. It paid enough for their board and lodgings and gave her a chance to settle into the ways of things out here.'

'Good on her,' said Jake. 'Sounds a tough little sheila.'

Miriam nodded. 'Tougher than she looked, and mature beyond her years,' she agreed. 'But there were certain situations she couldn't control, and it was to be my father's downfall eventually.'

The sounds from the stable-yard faded as Kate's voice drifted to her, and Miriam was once again transported back to a time beyond her memory.

Kate had finished clearing up after dinner and was helping Cook prepare the vegetables for the following day. The hotel was full as usual, the passengers from the big ships choosing to stay awhile before they began their long treks into what the people here called the Outback. Cook, a fat woman of indeterminate age from the East End of London seemed unperturbed by the heat and chattered on about her plans to travel to the gold fields to catch up with her errant husband.

Kate only lent half an ear to the cook's prattle. Despite being winter, it was like a furnace in the tiny kitchen, the range belting out the heat, driving the barometer way past the nineties. The sweat made Kate's hair cling to her neck and her thin cotton dress was damp and limp. She was thankful that stays and petticoats were deemed unnecessary in this new country, for she wouldn't have lasted five minutes in this heat otherwise.

Yet her real concern was the reappearance of Paddy Dempster. He'd arrived two days ago, and he and Henry had been closeted upstairs for hours each day, and in the bar at night. Kate had managed to avoid him, locking herself in her room at night, making sure she was always surrounded by other people. She had no proof, but was certain Paddy was scheming – and that what he planned would involve Henry's last few pounds.

She muttered a reply at the necessary points of Cook's long diatribe against her feckless husband as they peeled endless potatoes and dropped them in the pot of salted water. Her hands were swift and capable, but Kate's thoughts veered from one problem to another.

It was almost three months since Maureen's death and still the child had not been named – had not been embraced or acknowledged by her father – and Kate was at her wits' end. How to make Henry see the damage he was doing, not only to himself, but to his child, with his drinking, his late nights and dubious relationship with Paddy – the days spent lying in bed feeling sorry for himself?

Kate's patience was wearing thin, her need to escape the drudgery of this hotel kitchen had become a burning desire that must soon be satisfied. For she could feel the pull of the great empty land beyond the confines of the city. Could almost hear the call of the wild, untamed miles she had yet to explore.

The potatoes were finally finished and Kate dried her hands on a scrap of towel and went to fetch the baby. The basket had been covered with a length of netting to protect her from mosquitoes and flies, and was set on a chair on the back porch in the hope of catching any breeze that came off the water.

'She looks healthy enough,' muttered Cook as she waddled out of the kitchen to get a breath of air. 'But she ain't yours.' Her bright sparrow eyes regarded Kate sternly. 'Don't wanna get too fond of 'er,' she said sagely. 'Her dad will probably send 'er back to England now the mother's gorn.'

The fear of just such an event had kept Kate awake at night, and she'd been comforted only by the thought that Henry's family would no more take in Maureen's child than an orphaned mongrel. In fact, she'd realised bitterly, the

122

mongrel had more of a chance. Poor, wee scrap – it seemed no one loved her. Kate shook her head. 'Not likely,' she said flatly. 'He's stuck with her, like it or not.'

'Hoping to nab 'im fer yourself, then are ya?' Cook laughed, making her chins wobble and her rolls of fat quiver.

Kate reddened. Were her feelings for Henry that obvious? She picked up the baby who was crying and in need of changing. 'You've a suspicious mind to you, Bella,' she retorted above the baby's squalls. 'This poor wain's mother is barely cold in her grave and here y'are matchmaking.'

Bella wiped the sweat from her face. 'I got eyes in me 'ead, love. I seen the way you moon around after 'im.' She shook her many chins. 'You're wasting yourself on that one. 'E ain't got a thought in his 'ead for either of you – not now he's got the fever.'

Kate chewed her lip. The talk of gold and precious gems was all she heard in the bar and dining room and the fever that Bella mentioned was rife amongst the new arrivals pouring off the migrant ships in search of riches beyond their dreams. She'd assumed Paddy had joined the rush, and had been surprised when he'd turned up again. Surely Henry had not become sufficiently aware of anything around him to be caught up in this madness? She stilled, the cold thrill of dread running across her shoulders. Unless this was the reason Paddy had returned?

She became aware of Bella watching her and shook back her hair. 'He has not the eyes in his head to be listening to such things,' she retorted on the defensive. 'He's still grieving.'

Bella's eyebrows shot up. 'If you believe that, dearie, you'll believe anything.' She folded her arms beneath her pendulous bosom and eyed Kate fondly. 'I seen 'im, love,' she said softly. 'Him and that Paddy, talking half the night away in the bar. Wouldn't mind betting they're plannin' something.' She grimaced. 'Him and 'is lordship is thick, I know that much.'

Kate eyed her sharply. So Bella had also noticed Paddy,

and his influence over Henry – it wasn't just her imagination. 'I've got to be going,' she said as she hastily grabbed the basket. 'See you in the morning.'

Bella's meaty hand stayed her departure. 'You'll 'ave to work fast if you don't wanna be left 'olding the baby,' she said grimly. 'Once a man gets the fever, he's lost all sense.' She nodded sagely. 'Take it from me, dearie. I know what I'm talking about.'

Bella's words rang in her head, the note of truth all too clear as she turned away and hurried up the dark stairs to the top floor. Henry knew nothing of prospecting. Paddy was as smart and cunning as a snake. The combination could be deadly to all of them – especially to this little nameless baby. It was time to confront Henry with his responsibilities. Time to stop this madness before it went too far.

Paddy had just left and Henry was staring out of the window, his thoughts drifting and inconsequential. The street below was bustling beneath the flickering street lamps. High-stepping horses pulled elegant carriages, bullocks hauled heavy loads to the crack of the whip and pedestrians took their lives in their hands as they attempted to avoid the traffic.

He watched a particularly well-dressed woman lift her skirts as she negotiated the piles of dung that littered the street and tried to ignore the raucous shout of a bullocky. He saw her become flustered and noticed how her bodice clung to her in the heat. She should have followed Kate's example and rid herself of stays and undergarments, he thought. It might not be seemly back home, but here it was downright commonsense.

His thoughts briefly turned to Kate and he smiled. He couldn't have coped without her tough, uncompromising loyalty, and he was glad to call her friend – but sooner or later he would have to put some order in his life and plan his next move.

Henry's gaze fell on the pile of papers and maps on the table. Paddy's enthusiasm had been beguiling, and as he

124

stood there at the window he felt the first tug of something other than grief. It was an opportunity, he admitted silently. Yet he had no real enthusiasm for mining, even if the prospect could bring him a fortune. The need to paint had returned. The burning desire to capture this strange, lawless place on canvas was drawing him out of his misery, making him restless.

With a sigh he turned from the window and dug his hands in his pockets. He didn't really know what to do, and that was a fact. Paddy was persuasive, his scheme intriguing – but could he really trust him? Both Maureen and Kate had expressed their doubts, and he was wise enough to realise that a woman's intuition was a powerful thing.

His thoughts churned as he thought over his predicament and Paddy's offer. He needed money to survive in this strange, new land, yet to be a painter was all he'd ever wanted. Without Maureen there was no purpose in his life – no real reason to remain here. For each day brought back a memory of her – a fading image of her standing on the deck, her warmth in his arms, her dark head resting against his shoulder.

Hot tears threatened and he blinked rapidly. No one could replace her in his heart. No one could understand the heaviness of his guilt at having ignored her obvious discomfort during the voyage. Yet how to explain to his family? How to keep his pride and return home after all that had happened? And what of the child? He was trapped.

He sat down at the table and pulled out a fresh sheet of paper from his writing case. Mama would know what to do for the best.

Sitting there deep in thought he was startled by Kate's unannounced entrance. 'I wish you'd knock,' he said gruffly. 'It isn't seemly to barge into a gentleman's room without warning.'

Kate wore a determined expression and Henry's spirits plummeted further. He knew that look and it always brought trouble.

'It's time we discussed the future, Henry,' she said firmly. 'I need to know what your plans are for this wee one.'

Henry eyed the child in her arms and looked away. 'You seem quite capable of looking after it,' he said gruffly. 'I don't see why you shouldn't carry on doing so.'

Kate hitched the child in her arms as she approached him. 'I have other plans,' she said firmly. 'She's your child. You look after her.'

He looked at her aghast as the child was dumped in his lap. He automatically grabbed her before she fell from his knee and was surprised at the solidity of one so small. 'Kate, take it away,' he ordered as she began to wail. 'I don't know what to do with it.'

'You'll learn,' she said, her voice, strangely muffled. 'And while you're at it, think about a name for her. She can't go through life being called *it*.'

With that Kate slammed out of the room and he heard her footsteps thud down the stairs and the crash of the back door.

Henry eyed the squalling, red-faced infant and in desperation experimentally bobbed her on his knee. 'Hush,' he said firmly. 'Stop that.'

To his amazement the child obeyed almost instantly, and he found himself being regarded solemnly by two very green eyes. Henry felt awkward holding her as they stared at each other for a long silent moment. Then the child smiled.

Henry felt a surge of something so powerful he had no word for it. The emotion tore through him, warming his heart, bringing life to a soul he'd thought had died along with his wife. For the baby had Maureen's dimple in her plump little cheek.

He carefully shifted her into the crook of his arm and examined this tiny stranger. How had he never noticed the likeness to Maureen, he wondered? For her hair was the same ebony, her eyes the same emerald, even her brows arched in the same winged crescent. Icy fingers ran down his

126

back as he remembered how he'd refused to even look at her before now. How he'd handed her over to Kate and ignored her.

Blinded by tears of remorse, he felt the tiny hand grasp his finger and the dam of anguish and love was breached. For this was his child. Maureen had sacrificed her life to give him the most precious of gifts and he had almost lost her. 'Never again will I deny you,' he whispered into the damp curls. 'Never again will I leave you.'

The baby gurgled, her fist tightly wrapped around his finger, the dimple playing in her cheek. It was as if she knew and understood what he was saying and was welcoming the attention she had so long been denied.

He breathed in the warm, freshly bathed smell of his daughter's skin, revelling in the miracle of her life, wanting to make up for the lost months when the future had seemed so pointless. The green eyes looked up at him and he felt a love so deep and overwhelming there was no way to express it but in a kiss.

His lips softly touched the downy head and he closed his eyes. 'I'll call you Miriam,' he breathed. 'For in this new world you will have to be strong – just like your grandmother.'

'Kate hadn't gone very far, merely down the street to the corner and back again,' said Mim. 'She wasn't at all sure she'd done the right thing, but had guessed rightly that only shock tactics would work on my father.'

She smiled at Jake. 'Kate crept back up the steps and peeked through the keyhole. What she saw gladdened her heart, but also brought sorrow. For now my father and I had become acquainted – bonded is the modern phrase for it I believe – she was free to leave.'

'Why should that make her sad?' Jake ran his fingers through his thick, black hair. 'Surely the reason she made Henry take notice of you was because she wanted to make a proper life for herself?'

'You men are all the same,' Mim retorted. 'Wouldn't see what was in front of you if it wasn't painted in neon.'

She looked at his face, saw the lack of understanding and sighed. 'Kate was in love with Henry,' she said in exasperation. 'Yet she knew it wasn't the time to declare her feelings. Knew Henry didn't see her as anything more than a friend. But she also knew that no matter how long it took, she would find him again and tell him of her feelings. For this was the man she was meant to be with – the man of her heart.'

'Oh.' Jake leaned over the back of his chair, chin on his folded arms. 'So what did she do?'

'She packed her bag, said goodbye, and left.'

Miriam fell silent as she remembered Kate telling her how hard it was to leave Henry that morning, for their parting had been frosty.

'It's none of your damned business,' Henry snapped. 'Leave it, Kate, before we both say something we regret.'

'I'll regret it more if I say nothing,' she retorted, hands on hips, her face hot with the effort of keeping her temper under control and her voice down so as not to waken Miriam.

'Paddy will cheat you,' she said evenly. 'He's using you to back him in this hare-brained scheme because he thinks you've got money to burn. If you're stupid enough to give him any you can kiss it goodbye, 'cos he'll never pay it back.'

'Who made you the expert on Paddy?' he barked. 'What the hell is it to do with you how I invest my money?'

She stared at him in horror. 'You haven't given him any, have you?'

Henry lifted his chin and stroked his moustache. 'I've invested in a claim,' he said stiffly. 'Paddy and I have gone into partnership. Not that it's any business of yours.'

'Jesus, Mary and Joseph,' she breathed. 'Me mother said a fool and his money were soon parted, and you've got to be the biggest fool there is.' She saw how the colour drained from his face. Saw his eyes harden as he looked

128

down at her. But she wouldn't be cowed. 'How much?' she demanded.

He looked away, his fingers straying once again to his moustache. 'Seeing as how you've been well paid for looking after Miriam these past few months, that's none of your business,' he said firmly.

She eyed him for a long moment. Any money she'd been given had been spent on Miriam. It was unfair of Henry to make barbs like that when he knew full well she'd never taken a penny for herself. Her temper rose, and in one long burst of energy she told him exactly what she knew of Patrick Dempster.

'He's not to be trusted,' she finished. 'Tell him you've changed your mind and want the money back. There are other things you could do with it than throw it away on one of Paddy's get-rich-quick schemes.'

He cleared his throat and turned back to her. His face had lost all colour and his eyes were bleak. 'I'm sorry, Kate. I had no idea.' He looked away, his shoulders slumped. 'But it's too late to change things,' he said flatly. 'Paddy left last night for New South Wales to stake our claim. Miriam and I are to follow in a few days once I've sorted out the rest of the supplies.'

'Oh, Henry,' she said with a sob. 'What have you done?'

He winced at her words, perhaps hearing the echo of his mother's. Then he raised his chin and squared his shoulders. 'I've secured a stake in the future of this rich country for Miriam,' he said stiffly. 'Paddy knows about mining having worked in the pits in Wales, and is willing to teach me. I have the money to back the enterprise and so we agreed to a partnership.'

He went to the small table and picked up a sheaf of documents. 'Here are the deeds to the claim, as well as the prospector's licenses. I've had a solicitor draw up a partnership agreement, so it's all legal and above board.'

Kate was about to pour scorn on his bits of paper. She'd been here long enough to realise this was a rough and ready country, where legal documents meant very little in the heat of a gold rush. Then she looked up into his handsome face and was unable to voice her concern. There was hope in his eyes for the first time since they'd landed. A brightness in his face and a strength of purpose in his stance she didn't have the heart to destroy.

'I wish you luck,' she murmured. 'You're going to need it.'

Miriam was weary, the pain gnawing at her, making it difficult to concentrate. Yet she knew she must, for the family would be arriving soon and she needed to finish the story. She eyed the man sitting opposite her. His long legs were stretched either side of the delicate chair, his elbows leaning on the carved back. The doubts were legion, for she had no real concept of what she was getting involved in. No real understanding of the consequences of trusting this stranger with her most precious memories.

'I'm beginning to understand the reasoning behind your story, Mim,' he said thoughtfully. 'But don't you think you should rest for a while? You look tired and it's late.'

It was as if he could read her mind, and once again she was thankful for his presence. Wilcox wouldn't have understood at all, and would probably have run out of patience with her by now. 'I am tired,' she admitted. 'But it's best we finish this tonight.'

He looked doubtful, then, when he realised she would not be put off, insisted on pouring them both a brandy. 'For purely medicinal purposes,' he said with a soft smile as he handed her the crystal balloon glass.

Miriam closed her eyes as the alcohol warmed her throat and slowly spread through her. 'Thanks for not questioning my need to tell you everything before the others get here,' she said as she put the glass on a nearby table. 'I have my reasons, as you will shortly realise.'

They sat in silence, each with their own thoughts.

The sky was darkening. It would soon be night, and

Miriam could hear the squawking of the galahs and parakeets as they executed their final flight of the day and settled in the trees. It was a sound she had lived with all her life, and the knowledge that one day she would no longer be here to listen to it frightened her. She picked up the glass and took a deep swallow to steady her nerves. It was as if she could hear the clock ticking her life away.

'Mim? Are you okay, Mim?'

Jake's concerned voice seem to be coming from a great distance and Miriam had to force herself to appear calm and coherent. She finished the brandy. 'It's those ghosts again,' she said with a shaky laugh.

'I really think we should call it a day,' said Jake as he stood up. 'You're obviously worn out, and none of this could be doing you any good.'

'It is,' she said with determination. 'I can't rest until I've finished.' She smiled to soften her words. 'I've a need to do this, Jake. I would be failing myself if I simply gave up because I was tired.'

Jake eyed her for a long moment, but remained silent.

Miriam watched the different emotions flit into his expressive eyes, saw the doubts, the arguments against what she was doing and knew there could be no turning back. He had to know it all if he was to help her.

'My father, Paddy and I travelled many dusty miles after we left Port Philip,' she said into the silence. 'We traipsed from one mining camp to another in search of gold and precious gems, our belongings stacked in the wagon, our horses growing older and more weary as the years passed.'

She fell silent as she remembered how the dust would rise in a halo above them as they plodded through the bush – how the jolt and tilt of the wagon had become her lullaby – and how her father used every spare moment to capture the extraordinary light of the outback in his paintings.

'I was a child of the diggings,' she murmured. 'It was a solitary life, for most of the miners had left their families

131

back in the cities, but I had nothing to compare it with, so accepted the way things were.'

'How did your father cope with a small baby if he was down a mine all day?'

Miriam shrugged. 'He told me he paid the wife of a hardware merchant to look after me when I was tiny, and when we moved on to the next digging he found a miner's wife who was willing to care for me during the day when he was at work.'

She smiled at Jake. 'As I grew older I became more independent, and earned my keep by sifting through the mullock heaps for anything the miners might have missed. So my playground was the mullocky, my toys the discarded rubbish that littered the diggings, my friends the grizzled, suspicious men who worked the diggings. But I was content.' She sighed. 'Thankfully I was a good child and didn't give anyone a hard time – perhaps I'm making up for it now?'

'It could explain your stubbornness,' he said with a straight face.

She nodded, the smile making the dimple play in her cheek. 'Maybe,' she murmured. 'But I prefer to call it tenacity.'

They grinned at one another and Mim took strength from him. 'It was 1905 when things came to a head,' she began. 'None of us could have foreseen what her arrival at the diggings would mean. None of us could have possibly guessed at the tragedy that was to follow.'

Kate drove her mules and wagon into the mining settlement of Wallangulla. With her hands lightly guiding the reins, she sat on the buckboard and looked around her as the mules plodded past the mullock heaps and deep, square shafts that plunged vertically into the red earth. She was aware of the curious stares, aware she was considered an oddity in this tough man's world. Yet she'd become inured to those stares, inured to the suspicion that greeted her arrival, for she'd been travelling to camps just like this for the past five years, and they held few surprises.

Wallangulla was an untidy collection of bark huts, wattle humpies and canvas shelters that sprawled across the ironstone ridges that rose out of the black soil plains of northern New South Wales. Mules and horses slumbered beneath the sparse timber that gave poor shelter in the overwhelming heat, and a group of ragged women and children were sifting through the mullock heaps that littered the ground at every turn.

Yet, contrary to its appearance, Kate knew this place was regarded as sacred by the local tribe of Aborigines, for Wallangulla, translated from the local dialect, meant hidden firestick – a reference to the fierce storms that were frequent on these ridges, and could kill a man, his dog and his mob of sheep with one blow.

Kate ignored the insolent stares of the men and the speculative glances of the women as she steered the mule through the ramshackle settlement. She knew from past experience that once she'd announced her reason for being here, they would accept her gladly.

The site she finally chose was set on a flat mesa beneath a scattering of box and eucalyptus trees. The view was spectacular, stretching out to a horizon that was hazed with heat beneath a bleached sky. Scrub and trees were dwarfed by distance, and a lone crow circled above her, its mournful cry echoing in the silence. With only a winding dirt track linking it to the main camp, her choice of site offered privacy and discretion – two of the most important attributes for her business.

The sun glared down as Kate eventually stood outside her tent and surveyed her work. The wagon had been unloaded, the mules hobbled and cropping at the sparse groundcover of tough grass. Her supplies were neatly stacked inside the vast canvas shelter and there was now a smouldering campfire over which a billy was beginning to boil. Her board had been nailed to a tree at the end of the

133

dirt track, now all she had to do was tidy herself and wait for her first customer.

With a smile of satisfaction she dabbed the perspiration from her face and stepped inside the tent. The canvas soared to almost six feet at the centre, stretching across the dirt floor into a broad living area, which had been divided by screens into three compartments. One for storage. One for sleeping – and one for business.

Kate glanced around the main compartment as she tucked the rifle out of sight and checked the bullets in the tiny pistol she always kept in her pocket. Furnished like a parlour, it held two comfortable chairs, a table draped in a favourite shawl and a phonograph. At night, this area would be lit by the oil lamp she'd placed in the centre of the table.

She took off her sweat-stained hat and fanned her face. The heat was almost unbearable despite having erected the tent beneath the cover of trees, and she longed for the luxury of a cool bath. Stepping into her sleeping quarters she gave a sigh. Not much chance of that out here, for the only water on the ridge was in the sulphur pools, and that was hot and fit only for bathing, or watering the animals. Drinking water had to be bought and transported almost seventy miles from the nearest sheep station's tank.

Using some of the water she'd collected earlier from a nearby pool, she stripped and washed. Within minutes of drying herself she was sweating again, and she wistfully remembered how different it was in Sydney, where a cool breeze came off the sea, and shelter could be found beneath shady verandahs and in green parks. Despite her years of travelling, she'd never become used to the stifling atmosphere of these distant mining camps, and philosophically accepted she probably never would.

As she tucked the cotton blouse into the long, cambric skirt and buckled the belt around her waist, she wondered how much business there was here at Wallangulla. Her ultimate destination was much further north, but she'd heard the rumours about this place and had taken the detour from

White Cliffs out of curiosity. From what she'd seen so far, the rumours had to be false, for why had the miners stayed if there was nothing of worth in the ground?

Kate pocketed the tiny pistol and began to pin up her hair. It was long and as unruly as ever and she'd been tempted to cut it many times, yet Isaac's quiet advice had stopped her. She smiled as she fixed the last pin. Dear Isaac, how wise he was to understand she needed to keep her femininity despite the months spent on dirty, dusty tracks – of living like a gypsy and being surrounded by rough and suspicious characters.

She turned from the ewer to her bed – the one luxury she took everywhere. Made of wrought iron, it could be taken apart easily and stacked in the wagon. The springs squeaked beneath the feather mattress as she sat down, and the brass knobs on the bed-head glimmered in the pale light seeping through the canvas.

Her fingers stroked the deep red velvet pile of the bedspread as she regarded her few belongings. Hairbrushes and powder boxes lay on the small dressing table, and the hazy light winked in the golden threads of an Indian shawl she'd draped over a stack of boxes. The shawl was of the finest silk, bought from a Chinese miner down on his luck.

Kate reached for the music box that sat on a low chair by the bed. It had been a gift from Isaac, brought across the frozen boundaries of Russia as he'd fled yet another pogrom – his only link to a tragic past – his gift to Kate in the knowledge she would treasure it always.

She turned the key and opened the lid. The black Harlequin and his Colombine danced sedately to the haunting music, their masks hiding their thoughts as they twirled before the tiny mirrors in mechanical perfection.

A tear trembled on Kate's eyelashes as she watched them. If only she could have returned Isaac's love – made him happy. She closed the lid as the music faded. Poor Isaac, she thought. You were so generous with your time and your

135

knowledge – but you deserve much more than I was able to give – I hope you find the right woman one day.

Her thoughts were interrupted by a call and she hastily put the music box away and checked her fob watch. It was unusual for her customers to call before sunset. She patted her pocket, felt the hard reassurance of the pistol and stepped from behind the screen.

The man was tall, shaggy haired and bearded and looked like the thousands of other men who lived in the mining settlements. Yet she would have recognised him anywhere.

Paddy swallowed. His mouth was suddenly dry, but his heart was hammering against his ribs and all the old yearnings rose up to torment him. Kate had matured into a beautiful woman, and his passion for her had not faded over the ensuing years. 'So I wasn't mistaken,' he said finally.

'Unless it's business you're wanting with me, then you can leave,' she said coldly.

'Ach, Kate,' he said softly. 'You are a sight for sore old eyes and no mistake.' He took a step forward and breathed in the familiar scent of her. 'Have you not a kiss for me after all this time?'

'I have nothing for you, Paddy,' she said with a flatness that matched her eyes. 'Go back to your wife and daughter. Leave now, and that will be an end to it.'

He was disconcerted to realise she knew of Teresa, but he still took another step forward, the heat in him overcoming all reasoning. Grasping her waist he pulled her to him. 'We've unfinished business, Kate,' he murmured as he bent to capture her mouth. 'And this time I mean to have my way.'

The hard jab of something solid dug into the flesh beneath his ribs.

'Get out.' The words were softly spoken but there was an edge of cold determination in them.

Paddy stilled, well aware of what she held to his midriff. 'You wouldn't dare,' he hissed.

Her dark eyes were steady, her face set. 'Are you willing to bet on that?' The small pistol dug deeper and her finger twitched on the trigger. 'This is a lawless place, Paddy. I'm a woman alone – I have to defend myself. I'll take me chances.'

He released her and stepped back. She was magnificent in her stance and defiance, with flashing eyes and a heightened colour to her cheeks. If only she knew how much he wanted her, how much he loved her. 'Bet you wouldn't dismiss Henry so swiftly,' he snarled.

Her chin rose and her shoulders went back. 'Henry is a gentleman,' she retorted. 'He would never take such liberties.'

So that was the way of it. Jealousy tore through him and he had to clench his teeth and his fists to stop him from reaching for her again. 'Henry's a fool,' he snarled.

'Fool or not, I prefer to do any business with him in future. Don't come here again, Paddy.'

He stood before her, unsure of what to do next. He'd lost face – lost all chance of having this woman – and now he had to bear the thought of Henry having her. 'You'll be sorry for this, Kate Kelly,' he growled. 'No one does this to Patrick Dempster.'

Henry couldn't understand the foul mood Paddy was in. Then he heard of Kate's arrival at the camp and knew that once again Paddy had been thwarted. He hurried to the tent on the edge of the diggings and called her name.

Kate emerged between the canvas flaps and Henry's mouth went dry, the words dying as they stood there in the dwindling light, their eyes devouring one another in the ensuing silence.

She's beautiful, he thought as he absorbed the slender figure, the olive skin and dark eyes. He looked in awe at the sleek, shining hair that had been tamed into lustrous black coils at her nape. Kate had become an assured woman in the intervening years.

137

But what must she think of me? His rough hands twisted his disreputable hat as he realised how far down the road he'd travelled since their last meeting. He knew only too well that his clothes were filthy and ragged, his hands made ugly with the engrained dirt from his work down the mine. He fingered the straggling beard and ran a nervous hand over his collar-length hair. He could smell his own sweat – a pungent reminder of how far he'd let his standards drop since leaving Port Philip.

'Henry?' Kate took a hesitant step towards him. 'Henry, is that really you under all that hair?'

He tried to make light of it by grinning, but he could feel the shame heat his face and it was impossible to meet her eyes. 'At your service, Kate,' he said with a stiff bow. 'My apologies for my appearance.'

'Ach, I've seen worse,' she said with a dismissive shrug. She threw her arms around him in an energetic hug that almost knocked him off his feet. 'It's so good to see you again,' she laughed.

They stepped from the embrace, each of them suddenly shy. 'I've a billy on the boil,' said Kate brightly. 'Sit yourself down and tell me all your news over a cuppa. How's Miriam? Do you find time to paint? Have you found your pot of gold yet?'

Henry stroked his beard to hide the smile. Kate hadn't changed despite the sophisticated hair and the fine quality clothing – she was still full of energy, still beguiling with her almost childlike curiosity and enthusiasm for life. He watched the expert way she hooked the billy from the fire and noticed the absence of a wedding ring. A quick calculation confirmed she had to be twenty-nine or thirty now – so why had she chosen this way of life and never married?

Their eyes met over the smoky vapour that rose from their tea. 'I can see the questions in your eyes, Henry Beecham, but I'll tell you nothing until you answer me. How is Miriam?'

Henry smiled. 'Why don't you ask her yourself?' he said quietly. 'She's over there making a fuss of your mules.'

Miriam drank the last of her second brandy and settled back into the cushions. 'I can still remember that day,' she said. 'It was the eve of my twelfth birthday.'

She fell silent as she recollected the rust-coloured earth and the sepia canvas shelters beneath dust-laden trees that dropped with the heat. Sulphur tainted the air from the mysterious green pools of water to be found in the niches and hollows of the black and red ridges, and the whine of winches hauling up the buckets came back to her, along with the steady plod of horses and mules and the rattle of wagons against the scree.

She remembered how she'd been in awe of the vista from the top of the ridge. It had seemed endless, stretching in a great sweep to every horizon, dotted with scrub and bush that harboured snakes and kangaroos and a myriad of colourful birds. And above it all was an enormous sky. Bleached from the heat of the sun during the day, it would become a curtain of black velvet after sundown, strung with stars so numerous she couldn't count them.

She realised Jake was waiting for her to speak, and she smiled back at him. 'Short-term memory loss in the aged can be a nuisance,' she said briskly. 'But the real curse is being able to remember the past so clearly. Makes one too aware of the passing years.'

Gathering her thoughts she began again. 'My father had told me about Kate and the way she'd cared for me as a small baby, but I had no recollection of her before that day of course, yet I liked her instantly. She had the sort of face that invited friendship – a warmth I was immediately drawn to.'

Miriam softly laughed at the memory. 'She didn't grab me and kiss me like some of the women did in the camps, but softly took my hand and led me to a chair and handed me a mug of tea.'

'You must have had a lot of questions,' said Jake.

She eyed Jake and shook her head. 'Children were taught in those days to be rarely seen and definitely not heard. I was content just to sit there and listen to my father and Kate talking.' She smiled as she paused. 'I've always found you can learn far more by being silent and watchful, than by rushing in with questions.'

Jake raised a dark eyebrow, but had the sense to make no comment.

Miriam returned to her narrative. 'Kate was fascinating to listen to. She'd travelled to so many places – seen so much more than me and Dad. She was also fascinating to watch as she used her hands to illustrate something, her eyes to portray fear and horror as well as laughter – she was a great storyteller.'

'I bet she was careful when it came to telling you what her profession was,' said Jake with the suspicion of a smile in his eyes. 'Not a really suitable topic for young ears.'

She looked at him, puzzled by what he could mean. Then it dawned on her and she laughed so hard she got a stitch in her side. Once she'd regained her composure and wiped her eyes she put him straight. 'Kate wasn't whoring,' she spluttered. 'She travelled the diggings for quite another reason.'

'Go on then, surprise me.' Jake folded his arms, the challenge in his eyes. 'I suppose you're going to tell me she was a lady miner?'

Miriam shook her head and stifled the giggle. 'Close, but not close enough.' She cleared her throat and made the mental effort to pull herself together.

'After Kate left Port Philip, she booked passage on a ship to Sydney. She quickly found work as a housekeeper for a wealthy Jew who lived in the city. Isaac Levinsky was a dealer in fine gems, a man who'd escaped the Russian pogroms and lost all his family in the process. He'd come to Australia on one of the migrant ships from Germany and like so many of his kind, made his fortune here.'

Miriam switched on the lamp at her elbow and watched the light reflections dance in the crystal brandy balloon.

140

'Isaac was a lonely man. Deeply religious, he spent the sabbath, as well as most evenings at the synagogue, or studying the *Talmud*, he was a respected scholar. When Kate first went to work for him she had to learn the customs of a Jewish home. They were numerous, ranging from separating meat from fish and dairy products, to using special knives and not serving certain dishes.'

'It's a minefield,' muttered Jake. 'My father-in-law ran his home on the same lines, and I was forever getting into trouble for doing the wrong thing.'

Miriam looked across at him and wondered if that had been a part of the reason for his marriage failure. She would ask him later.

'Isaac realised fairly quickly that Kate was bright, much too bright to be wasting her talents keeping house. He began to teach her about the precious stones he kept in his safe. Taught her how to value them, to see the flaws and how they should be cut and polished.'

Miriam paused. 'But he also taught her how to dress – how to deal with buyers and sellers – how to talk knowledgeably about the latest play at the theatre, the latest popular reading.' Miriam smiled. 'He wanted her to feel at ease in polite society, for he knew that one day Kate would be a wealthy woman.'

'How could he know that?' Jake's expression was puzzled.

'He saw her potential,' she explained. 'Kate was with him for almost seven years, and by the time she was competent enough to take to the tracks, she was impeccably groomed for her future.'

'Isaac was in love with her, wasn't he?'

Miriam nodded. 'Oh, yes, there was no doubt about that. He even asked her to marry him – which was a huge risk. For by marrying a *goyim*, he would be shunned at *schul* and at the synagogue.'

Miriam looked back down at her hands. 'But that wasn't the reason she turned him down – not really – you see she

141

still loved my father and had this indelible faith that they would meet again. She loved Isaac as a friend, a mentor – perhaps even a surrogate father – but she couldn't love him as a husband.'

'So she set off for the diggings?'

Miriam smiled. 'She built up quite a reputation as a buyer. Travelling from camp to camp, she bought straight from the miners. This was unusual in those days, for the miners often walked hundreds of miles with their parcels of gems so they could sell them in the cities. What Isaac and Kate realised was, that this took time and energy for very little profit – kept the miners away too long from their diggings – so why not take the business to the camps?'

'Sounds a risky enterprise,' muttered Jake. 'It was all a bit lawless back then.'

'That's why she always carried a pistol and a loaded rifle. Sometimes she also hired a man to accompany her, especially if she'd had a very successful trip.' Miriam paused. 'Things haven't changed that much,' she said finally. 'The suspicion, the greed and the jealousy is still rife in those outback mining communities – I know of at least three buyers who carry loaded guns, even these days.'

Jake nodded and shifted in the chair. They had been talking for over an hour and were both tired.

Eric pushed his way through the door, tail erect, legs stiff with importance. He jumped on to the arm of Miriam's chair, eyed her speculatively and then made himself comfortable on her lap.

'Strewth,' hissed Jake. 'He's never done that before. Must like you.'

Miriam stroked the soft fur and felt the answering rumble of Eric's purr. 'I can't say I like cats much,' she said with a laugh. 'Perhaps that's why he chose me to sit on.'

Jake raised his eyes to the ceiling and sighed. 'Probably,' he muttered. His gaze drifted from the slumbering cat to the painting above the fireplace. 'You were going to tell me why that was so important to you,' he reminded her.

Miriam looked at the sepia tones and the extraordinary light her father had captured in oils. 'It was his last gift to Kate,' she said softly. 'He gave it to her the morning he disappeared.'

Chapter Seven

Louise sat beside Rafe as the taxi took them through the late evening traffic towards Fortitude Valley and the city airport. She didn't want to question the reason behind his sudden change of heart, for he'd been so loving and kind over the past twelve hours it would seem churlish to complain. Yet she couldn't quite dismiss the thought that something must have happened for such a change in him.

Brisbane looked magnificent, the glass towers glistening blue and green beneath a starry sky, their mirrored facades reflecting the ferries on the river and the necklace of car headlights that were strung through and around the core of the city. She gave a deep sigh of satisfaction as she leaned back into the soft leather. Rafe made the ordinary, everyday hassle of travelling so easy. This car to get them to the airport, a private plane to fly them to Bourke, and a hired four-by-four to get them out to Bellbird Station. So why did her sister's accusations ring so clearly in her head?

'Have you spoken to Mim, lately?' Ralph fastened the locks on his briefcase and put it on the seat between them.

'Not for a few weeks,' she admitted. 'I've kept meaning to, but we've just been so busy.' It was a poor excuse and she knew it. She glanced at her husband and was immediately wary. His scrutiny was intense, watchful and overtly suspicious. She ran her tongue over her dry lips. 'Why?' she asked, her tone wary.

He turned away, his profile one of studied nonchalance. 'Nothing. I just wondered.'

There was a long silence and Louise, thinking the exchange was over, the subject closed, began to relax. Rafe's voice put her back on guard.

'You would tell me if Mim had confided in you, wouldn't you, Louise?' His voice was dangerously soft, the usual precursor of trouble.

Her gaze met his and she steeled herself for whatever was coming next. 'Of course,' she replied. 'But Mim doesn't confide in me, never has,' she said with a firmness that belied the thud of her pulse. 'It's Fiona who's Mim's favourite.'

'So you know nothing of this windfall?' His scrutiny held her.

Louise frowned and shook her head. 'News to me,' she said.

He seemed to accept her lack of knowledge and stared out of the window. 'No doubt we'll learn more when we get to Bellbird,' he said softly.

Louise tucked the information away to examine later and fretted over how to appease him and bring him back to his good mood. 'Thanks for changing your mind about going,' she said into the ensuing silence. 'I wouldn't have wanted to miss her birthday party.'

He turned to her, his smile reproachful. 'Since when have I denied you anything, Louise? No matter how inconvenient it might be.'

'Inconvenient?' It was almost a whisper and she hated herself for being such a wimp. Yet it had become so familiar she found she couldn't stop herself.

'I'm in the middle of some very delicate negotiations,' he told her. 'Shamrock Holdings have approached my bank and I can't really afford to be away from the office.'

Louise looked at him in horror. 'Shamrock? But isn't that part of Brendt's company?'

'What of it? Brendt has turned that corporation into one of the wealthiest in the world. I'm not going to turn his business down because it might upset your grandmother's sensibilities.'

Louise remained silent. Mim's lifelong hatred of Brendt's family had been made clear to all of them from a very early age. In fact they'd heard so much about it that none of them really took it seriously any more. Yet she was concerned that Rafe was thinking of doing business with them.

'Why has he come to your bank?' she asked hesitantly.

'Because we are in a position to offer the most favourable terms,' he replied. He patted her hand and clasped it on his lap. 'Don't go worrying yourself over business,' he said with an indulgent smile. 'I know what I'm doing.'

Louise sat and looked out of the window. She had been a company wife for almost twelve years, and in that time had learned a great deal about the business being done and the gossip that followed the movers and shakers in the banking world. Even if she hadn't known about Brendt and his family through Mim, she'd heard enough about them to realise they were not to be trusted. If Rafe was determined to have dealings with that particular clan, then he had to be very careful indeed. For like his forebears, Brendt was about as straight as a coiled snake.

Miriam's thoughts were a jumble of scents and sounds from another age, intermingled with a parade of faces she knew and loved, most of whom were long gone. She moved restlessly in the chair and wished she had a blanket to pull over her shoulders. The dragon of pain was sleeping, but it was a cold night and she could feel the same chill she'd experienced all those years ago. The chill of winter – of mystery – and inexplicable loss.

'It was what the Aborigines called a three dog night in that isolated mining camp and, despite the animals curling at my back and feet, I was still cold. I lay there staring into the darkness, my father's snores coming from the depths of his blankets, our breath forming an icy layer on the makeshift canvas shelter.'

Miriam paused as she once again felt the chill of that night. 'I snuggled against the brindle bitch that yapped and twitched in its sleep, my thoughts wandering as I waited for the first sight of dawn when I would have to leave the tenuous comfort and face the outback winter morning. Despite my childish pleasure at having reached the great age of twelve only a few weeks before, I was old enough to accept the lack of presents or special treats.'

Miriam smiled, the memories so sharp and clear it was as if the present was no longer real. 'Money was tight as usual, for despite Dad and Paddy's long hours underground they had not found anything significant. Now we were down to our last sack of flour and screw of tea.'

'It must have been tough on you,' murmured Jake. 'An experience any modern child would find it hard to imagine.'

Miriam laughed. 'No doubt the social workers would have been brought in if it had happened nowadays. We've all grown too soft, too dependent on hand-outs and the prop of a nanny state.' She shrugged. 'I accepted my life and the hardships with a nonchalance honed by experience and the lack of knowledge of anything different. Dad would find his fortune. It would just take a bit of luck. I never allowed the thought that luck seemed to have passed us by and tried to imagine how it must feel to sleep in a feather bed, like Kate.'

She clasped her hands on her lap. 'How I envied Kate that brass bed and the velvet cover. I thought she must be very rich indeed to own such grand possessions.'

'She probably was rich,' said Jake. 'The buyers are usually the only ones to make any money out of the miners.'

'I was a kid, what did I know?' Miriam retorted. 'I was far more concerned with my feelings for Kate, and the obvious affection she shared with Dad. Since Kate's arrival, I'd noticed how Dad had begun to take more care of himself. He'd trimmed his beard and hair, washed more frequently, and had made a point of keeping at least one shirt clean for when we visited Kate's tent.'

Miriam smiled. 'Dad didn't always take me on his visits.

147

Thought I had no idea of the long evening hours he spent with Kate when he expected me to be asleep. But there was little privacy in the camp, and I would have to be deaf, dumb and blind not to see how things were going between them.'

She chewed her lip as she remembered wondering how it would be to have Kate as a mother – for she'd soon realised it was a possibility – and had come to the conclusion it might be fun to travel through the outback with an assured welcome at all the camps. Fun to see a city as bustling and glamorous as Kate had described Sydney. For she'd never seen a city, much less an ocean, and she was curious.

Lost in her memories she relived those precious few hours when innocence and youth had still been with her. And yet they had not been enough to shield her from what was to come.

Dawn had finally filtered through the patched canvas, bathing their cramped, makeshift home in a golden glow which made the icy remnants of their breath melt tearfully down the lumpen seams. It was time to get up, to rekindle the fire and put the billy to boil. Yet she was reluctant to leave the warmth of the dogs and her blanket, for thoughts of her father marrying again had brought her long dead mother to mind.

Dad still felt her loss, she was certain, for she'd caught him looking at the miniature he'd painted before they'd left England, and had noticed the unusual brightness in his eyes. Miriam had only the miniature and Dad's loving stories as keepsakes for a mother who'd died giving her life, and she treasured them. Would it be a betrayal of her memory if they loved someone else?

Miriam became impatient with her thoughts. She pushed the dog aside, eased out of the blanket and crawled through the flap in the tent. There was work to be done before Dad woke, and the day was already begun. With her mother's ragged shawl wrapped tightly around her shoulders she breathed in the air that was tainted by the warm sulphur

148

pools which steamed on the edges of the settlement. It felt good after a night in the cramped tent, and although this was an isolated, rough place, she had inherited enough of her father's artistic soul to appreciate its beauty.

Frost sparkled on the ridges and wisps of cloud were impaled on the highest branches of the few trees that had survived the latest drought. Tendrils of smoke rose from cooled campfires, dogs scavenged the rubbish and the patient mules stood drowsily in slivers of sunlight cast between the tumbledown dwellings. All was silent in the sleeping settlement but for the doleful caw of a circling crow.

Despite having slept in all her clothes, Miriam was shivering as she cracked the ice on the bucket of water and began to wash. Her teeth were still chattering as she dried off with a scrap of towel and rolled down her sleeves. The shawl was threadbare, the hem of her dress too short to cover her ankles and naked feet and the bodice was tighter than ever. Yet none of this bothered her, for the dress would do a while longer, and her feet, like all the other children's were hardened to the rough ground.

She raked the almost toothless comb through her curly black hair and winced as it caught in the tangles. How she wished hers was as straight and easy to manage as Bridie Dempster's. With a sigh, Miriam looked over at the low canvas shelter Bridie shared with her parents. They were a boisterous lot, but for once it was quiet.

Paddy had been a part of her life ever since she could remember, and although she learned very quickly to keep out of his way when he'd been drinking, she enjoyed the stories he told her when he was sober. Much to her father's consternation, he'd shown her tricks he'd learned as a boy on the Dublin streets. He had a twinkle in his eye and a soft brogue in his voice she found fascinating, and when he swung her in the air and danced the jig she would scream with delight and beg for more.

Paddy had married Teresa fairly soon after they all left

149

Port Philip. Bridie was their first born, and the only survivor from a brood of four. She was two years younger than Miriam, and they had formed a close friendship in the adult world of the mining camps. Bridie had long red hair and hazel eyes that shone with flecks of gold in the sunlight, and Miriam thought she was beautiful. Yet Bridie had a way of getting them both into mischief, and they'd felt the back of Teresa's hand on more than one occasion.

As for Teresa, she often sported a black eyes after one of Paddy's drunken bouts, but the whole camp had witnessed her legendary temper and knew Paddy didn't always get his own way. It was said Teresa once laid him out with an iron cooking pot, knocking him cold for several hours. A much chastened Paddy shrugged this off as nothing, but it was noted he didn't go on a drunk for a long while after.

Miriam had collected wood for the fire and was in the process of making damper from the last of the flour when her father stepped through the canvas flap and squatted beside her.

His rough hand ran over her hair before cupping her chin. 'Good morning, my little angel. And how are you this fine day?'

Miriam looked into his blue eyes and was warmed by his love. 'Itchy,' she retorted with a laugh. 'The dogs have got fleas.'

He laughed with her, his gaze flitting to the dirt track that ultimately led to Kate's tent. 'I was wondering if you'd mind . . .' He hesitated, saw the amusement in her eyes and nervously licked his lips before he carried on. 'I have a gift for Kate,' he said quietly. 'It's the painting I finished the other day.'

Miriam eyed him for a long, silent moment. 'I thought someone else was interested in buying it?' She put a hand on his arm in an attempt to take the sting out of her words. 'We need the money, Dad. This is the last of the stores.'

He looked down at his hands. The long, artistic fingers were hardened by toil, the nails ingrained with dirt from the

150

mine, and yet Miriam knew he had lost none of his touch when it came to his paintings. They were selling for just enough to keep them from starvation.

'I know, but I can paint another,' he muttered. Then he lifted his chin and looked into her face. 'I want to give Kate something special. You know I care for her, don't you?'

Miriam handed him the tin mug and he held it gingerly as he blew the steam. 'Of course, Dad,' she replied. 'I like her, so why shouldn't you?'

He was silent for a long moment and Miriam could tell he was deep in thought. 'She would make a good mother,' she encouraged softly.

Henry's eyes lit up and his smile made him appear care-free and young. 'So you have no objections if I ask her?' he said breathlessly.

Miriam shook her head, dipping her chin so he couldn't see her laughter. 'Eat the damper and finish the tea first. Then you can give Kate the painting before you go to work. Paddy isn't up yet, so there's plenty of time.'

Miriam came back to the present, her eyes filled with tears. 'He did as he was told, but I could see the impatience in his hands, in the restless shifting of his feet in the dirt as he ate his breakfast. He was eager to be with Kate.'

She wiped her eyes and blew her nose. Her voice was muffled with emotion as she spoke again. 'I kissed him goodbye and watched him walk away, the painting under his arm, a spring in his step. It was the last time I ever saw him.'

The mansion was perched on a hill overlooking Sunrise Beach on the Sunshine Coast of Queensland. The lights from the expanding and fashionable resort of Noosa could just be discerned through the trees, but they were no match for the blaze of light pouring from every window of the white stucco building. As the chauffeurs waited by sleek limousines and the guard in the gatehouse watched the security monitor, the family inside were entertaining.

151

The dining hall was starkly white, lit by a blaze of crystal chandeliers, warmed only by the priceless Persian carpet that covered most of the marble floor and the valuable paintings on the walls.

Brendt sat at the head of the long oak table and eyed his guests. A glow of well-being flooded through him as he lifted the crystal glass to his lips and sipped the champagne. Grandfather would have been proud, he thought. For his guests numbered several statesmen as well as a smattering of some of the world's greatest financial wizards. Their women had obviously raided the beauty parlours as well as their jewellery safes, and it was gratifying to know how important his dinner parties were in the social calendar.

He watched his wife as she chatted to their guests, and once again congratulated himself on taking his mother's advice. Arabella was the daughter of an English earl. Educated at Roedean, she'd spent a year in Switzerland at a finishing school and had been working in an exclusive art gallery in London when he met her. She had all the qualities he needed for a wife – but held no illusions about her – for she was as ambitious and ruthless as he, and if by some freak of chance he should lose everything, she would walk away and not look back. It made for an exciting marriage, for they were both turned on by power and money, and their sex life was dynamite.

He looked away from her and regarded his mother who was deep in conversation with a government minister. At seventy-three, she was the consummate hostess, with the hauteur and exquisite manners of a grand matriarch. Her lustrous hair had faded somewhat over the years, but she had never resorted to dying it, saying she intended to age gracefully. Now it was cut short and brushed from her face, highlighting the sharp cheekbones and hazel eyes. Emeralds glittered in her ears and at her throat, the pale cream of her silk dress enhancing a flawless skin and a figure that was envied by women ten years younger. No one would ever have guessed at the hardships she'd endured as a child.

152

Brendt caught her eye and smiled as he raised his glass to her. She was her father's daughter, her ruthless ambition masked by velvet determination and a tenacity that never ceased to amaze. Her judgement was flawless, for she never permitted emotion to cloud her decisions. Even before the old man had died, she had become Brendt's mentor, his guide; the rock upon which their dynasty was founded. She had seen in him, her eldest son, what had been lacking in her other children – her own will to win – her own voracious grasp for the chance to beat off the competitors.

Brendt sipped the champagne as he watched her. Mother had married young. Father was a wealthy land developer with fingers in many pies when he'd died of a heart attack at thirty-two. His mother had never remarried, but Brendt suspected she still occasionally took a lover. She had emerged from mourning to take over Father's empire with a deft hand and had made it even more prosperous. A wealthy woman in her own right, she could easily have retired years ago. Yet she still enjoyed the cut and thrust of the business world and Brendt realised it was this that kept her young.

He thought of the secret files they had on their business associates, and as he sipped the champagne, his gaze drifted over his guests as he brought up a mental list of their misdemeanours. There were two alcoholics – reformed, but terrified of being discovered. A drug addict – freshly out of rehab but still hooked, and two bankers with expensive lifestyles even their income wouldn't cover. Two high-flying entrepreneurs with more than a passing acquaintance with the Russian mafia, and a former prostitute with a new name and fictitious history who'd managed to snare herself a millionaire banker. Last, but not least, the top lawyer who preferred the company of small children to that of his model wife.

He blinked as a shudder of distaste ran over him. He could understand corruption in most forms and positively encouraged it if it was going to profit his enterprises – but paedophiles really were filth. Brendt thought of his own two little girls asleep upstairs. If he had his way, he thought coldly, the bastard would be castrated without anaesthetic.

Brendt wiped his lips on the linen napkin, as if by doing so he could rid himself of the sour taste in his mouth. The lawyer was useful to him – for the moment – but when he'd outlived his usefulness, Brendt would see to it that he didn't live long enough to molest a kid again.

His thoughts were interrupted by the butler. 'What is it, Morris?'

'Mr Black has just delivered his report. Nothing out of the ordinary, but I've been asked to point out the last two paragraphs for your immediate attention.'

Ignoring his guests, Brendt took the neatly typed pages and read through the main report swiftly. Black was a good man to have on his payroll. Quick and efficient, with scant disregard for how he got the information, the former policeman and army captain could submit a detailed character reference within hours of the request.

He'd certainly done his homework on Ralph, he thought with a glimmer of cold satisfaction, but unfortunately it didn't tell him much more than he already knew. There had to be something dirtier about the man. Black would have to dig deeper.

His hands began to tremble and his mouth went suddenly dry as he scanned the final two paragraphs. He read the closely typed words again and when they had finally sunk in he crushed the report in his fist.

Miriam Strong was the one person he couldn't cower – the one person he and his family feared most of all. Now she was poised to destroy them – poised to open the closet and expose the secrets they'd kept hidden for so many years. She had to be stopped.

154

Chapter Eight

Jake turned restlessly in the bed and tried to will himself to sleep. But the images refused to disappear, and he was left with stark reminders of his own childhood – and his failed and ultimately tragic marriage and subsequent loneliness. It seemed as if he was destined to live his life on the outer edges, to be the observer, never the participant – except when it came to his work. He threw off the blanket and ran his fingers through his hair. Thinking like this would get him nowhere.

He stood at the window for a long while, looking out at the darkness, his thoughts meandering, but always returning to the same crucial moments of his life when fate determined change. Those moments would be with him always, but after hearing Mim's story, they seemed more haunting than ever.

Giving up on sleep, Jake pulled on his clothes. Eric was slumbering deeply and merely twitched his whiskers as Jake removed his thick jacket from the bedpost. He carried his boots as he crept into the hall and winced at the shriek of the rusting hinges on the screen door. He stood on the verandah for a moment, listening for signs of having disturbed Mim. But was greeted only by silence.

Poor old duck, he thought as he sat on the top step and pulled on his boots. She's far too frail to be dredging up old enmities. Certainly past the age when she should be up until after midnight, recounting her life in the hopes it will shed light on a long-dead mystery.

Jake stood and rubbed his hands down his worn jeans. He admired her for her courage and her tenacity, but was that enough in the light of what she was asking him to do?

Stepping down into the yard he headed for the paddocks that were bathed in moonlight. He had to be careful not to get emotional – not to be swayed by anything other than cold, hard fact. For if he did, he would only give her false hope – and that would be too cruel after all she'd been through. Yet he knew that if they could come up with something more tangible, this could turn out to be the biggest career move in his life.

He set a brisk pace as he strode through the long grass. The night was cool, but not uncomfortably so, the moon bright enough to show him the way. He looked up at the stars and remembered how, as a boy, he'd been in awe of such a display. That awe hadn't diminished, he realised, as he came to a standstill and surveyed the mighty heavens that encompassed this vast outback land. He could see the majestic sweep of the milky way, the five points of the Southern Cross and the legendary figure of Orion with his hunting dogs. They were clear and bright, some of the stars winking blue, others red or white – a majestic sight that made him feel insignificant in the scheme of things.

Jake dug his hands in his pockets and resumed his walk. Because of Mim, his head was full of memories, of people and places he'd known during his life – of things he'd done and not done – that had changed his life's pattern and set him on this lonely course.

He was seven when his mother died, and although his memory of her was hazy, he could still retain certain images of her. Of her standing by the range, her fair hair in damp tendrils on her neck, her hands white with flour. Of her riding with the stockmen, helping with the shearing and swearing as she attempted to get the old ute started after the wet. Of her dancing with Dad after the picnic races. She'd always seemed so energetic, so vital, how could she have been taken so suddenly?

Jake stared out to the horizon, the tears threatening even after all these years. Her death had left a void he'd been trying to fill ever since – and now he knew he never could. A mother's love could not be replaced once you'd basked in it – a mother's arms were like no other, her understanding and devotion unquestionable and never subjective.

He climbed to the top of a low hill and looked out at the moonlit vista that spread to every horizon. The homestead had seemed empty without her, the sheep station a harbour of sad memories. His grandmother had taken him and the other kids over until Dad won the battle against depression and the bottle, but as soon as he was able, he'd left home. Despite his Dad's disappointment that he wouldn't be staying to carry on the family business, it hadn't been difficult to persuade him that he needed to go to a proper school if he was to become anything but a homesteader and sheep farmer. The school of the air had given him a good grounding in the basics, but as he matured he'd realised he needed more stimulus, and like thousands of others before him had escaped the isolation of an outback station and headed for the city.

Jake tramped down the hill and set off at a cracking pace for the meandering creek in the distance. It glimmered coldly beneath the moon, the guardian trees stark silhouettes against the night sky. It had been on a night just like this when he'd met Rachel, and they'd danced until dawn, leaving the party only when they realised they were the only guests still there.

Beautiful Rachel with her black hair and eyes and her olive skin. She had a way of making him laugh, a way of making him feel the richest, most privileged man in the world. Until he broke her heart.

Out of breath, he came to a halt beneath a tree. The ancient limbs dipped towards the slow-running creek, the roots gnarled and twisted in the earth giving home to countless

157

numbers of insects. He chose the sawn stump of another tree and sat down, pulling his collar up against the sharp breeze, digging his hands in his pockets as memories of their wedding day flooded back.

Rachel and her mother had accepted his refusal to convert to Judaism, but her father had not. Denied the privilege of being married in synagogue, they had the ceremony performed in the less illustrious surroundings of a Sydney court-house. Neither of her parents had attended, but as the years went by, Rachel's mother had eventually persuaded her father to accept the inevitable. The birth of their first child was to be the healing of the breach – and it was – for a time.

Jake dipped his chin and stared down at his feet. Her name was Esther, but they called her Sunny, for that was her disposition, and the colour of the joy she brought. She was eighteen months old when she developed a high fever that no amount of care seemed to diminish. The rash came shortly afterwards and she'd lain limply in his arms as they were driven at high speed to the hospital. Sunny died of meningitis a few hours later.

With a deep, trembling sigh, Jake remembered how Rachel had clung to him, had begged him for comfort as their baby lay waxen in death on the hospital bed. But he'd been too shocked, too deeply into his own mourning to have the will to tend her needs.

After the traumatic funeral where he'd carried the tiny white coffin and lowered it into its final resting place, he'd shut himself off from Rachel. Buried himself in his work, coming home late, leaving early before Rachel woke, they lived separate lives. For he couldn't face the empty nursery, couldn't face the dark shadows of longing in Rachel's eyes – couldn't accept that yet again fate had stolen someone he loved. He was deaf to the pleas, blind to what damage he was doing to his marriage – dumb in his ability to express his pain.

Rachel left him a year later.

Jake scrubbed his face with his hands and stood up. The links between him and the hapless Henry were all too clear. In hindsight it was easy to see the mistakes he'd made – easy to understand why she'd left him. Yet at the time he'd regarded her leaving as a further betrayal – a further sign that he was destined to go through life on a solitary path. For he had lost everyone he'd ever loved – how could he trust love again?

Miriam had heard him leave, and watched as he strode away from the homestead and headed for the pastures. It was clear he was unsettled, but it was no business of hers – she just hoped he wouldn't fail her.

She pulled on trousers and a sweater, dug her feet in her old slippers and, after picking up the music box, headed for the kitchen. Despite her weariness, she knew she wouldn't sleep any more tonight. Her mind was too full of memories to give her peace – the thoughts of what she was trying to achieve giving her an adrenalin buzz.

Having made a mug of tea she sat down at the battered old table and looked around her kitchen. It had been very different the first time she'd seen it – but that had come later – much later.

Miriam and Bridie were sifting through the mullock heaps, looking for anything that had somehow escaped their fathers' notice. 'I'm sick of this,' grumbled Bridie as she pushed back her sweaty hair and sat in the dirt. 'Why don't we go and see what we can pinch from the store?'

Miriam shook her head. 'We nearly got caught last time,' she muttered. 'And your Dad would beat you half to death if he knew what you were up to.'

Bridie laughed as she got to her feet and ran her hands down her filthy trousers. 'He wouldn't, and that's a fact,' she said in her lilting Irish voice. 'Me Da told me he thought old Wiseman was a crook, makin' a profit out of us poor diggers.' She grabbed Miriam's arm. 'Come on, Mim. I need you to stand guard.'

159

Mim pulled away from her and sat down, her arms folded across her skinny chest. 'No,' she said firmly. 'It's wrong. He has to make a living like we all do.'

Bridie flicked back her hair and eyed Mim speculatively. 'You can have a share of anything I get,' she wheedled.

Miriam shook her head and looked away. She'd been tricked into going with Bridie last time and had been horrified when her friend showed her the things she'd stolen while Mim was innocently talking to the storekeeper. She didn't like being used, and certainly didn't want to repeat the agonies of what to do with the stolen booty Bridie had forced upon her. Bridie would be furious if she knew Mim had returned everything when Wiseman's back was turned. 'I'm not going,' she said flatly.

'Scare baby,' taunted Bridie. 'Just like your Da. You won't achieve nothing by being so goody-goody – I don't want to be your friend any more.' She turned away, her red hair flaming in the dying sunlight, her bare feet skipping over the sharp scree and withered grass.

Miriam felt the heat of shame in her face and fought to keep the tears at bay. Bridie's words had stung, but she knew they weren't as painful as the conscience she would have if she allowed her to have her way. Yet Bridie was her only friend. They had been playmates since she was two – and she couldn't imagine not being with her.

She got to her feet and tramped slowly out to the rabbit traps they had set the day before. Dad would be back soon, and if the traps were empty she had no idea what she'd do for supper. Perhaps she should have followed Bridie's example and taken the risk?

She dismissed the idea as she threaded her way through the trees. Dad would want an explanation, and she knew she wouldn't be able to lie to him.

There was a rabbit and a goanna in the traps, and Miriam reset the wires and carried the bounty back to camp. They would eat well tonight. Perhaps it paid to be honest after all – perhaps this was a lesson learned for the future? She skinned the rabbit and prepared a thin stew, then salted down the goanna and hung it in the meat safe for tomorrow. Having tidied what she could and washed away the dirt of the day, she sat by the camp-fire and waited for her father to come back from the diggings.

'Is yer Da not back yet?' asked Paddy as he sauntered into camp an hour later.

Miriam looked up at him and shook her head. 'Isn't he with you?'

Paddy ran his filthy hands over his beard, his gaze meandering over the camp. 'Yor man left about three hours ago.' He finally looked down at her, his eyes bright with an intensity she couldn't understand. 'He's probably courtin',' he said with a rumbling laugh. 'I'm thinking young Kate is far more attractive than digging in a black hole all day.'

Miriam watched him take the sack off his shoulder and drop his spade before he pushed through the flaps of his tent. Perhaps he was right, she thought. But it was unlike Dad not to tell her he would be late. She eyed the pot of stew and took it from the fire. It would remain hot long enough for them to eat when they got back from Kate's.

Kate emerged from her tent, her face lit by a smile. 'Well, hello,' she said cheerfully. 'And to what do I owe this pleasure?'

'I've come to tell Dad his supper's ready,' replied Miriam. 'Is he inside?'

Kate frowned. 'What makes you think he's here, my darlin' girl? I've not seen him since this morning.'

Miriam didn't know what to say. If he wasn't with Paddy, and he wasn't with Kate, then where on earth could he be? The onset of fear was paralysing.

Kate put an arm around her shoulders. Her voice was light, but Miriam could hear the edge of concern that sharpened it. 'Is he not down the shaft, Mim? Have you asked Paddy?'

Miriam nodded, the tears threatening. 'He says he left the

shaft about three hours ago. But he didn't come back to the tent, Kate. I don't know where he's gone.'

'Hush now. Don't fret, darlin'. We'll find him, don't you worry.'

Miriam let her take her hand and together they went in search of Henry.

Jake was surprised to see Mim in the kitchen when he returned from his walk, but understood why she too had found it difficult to sleep. The old ghosts had a habit of keeping a person awake once they'd been invoked.

'I'm cooking breakfast,' he said brightly. 'It's a beautiful day, and I haven't been this hungry since I was a kid.'

'Been out vanquishing ghosts, have you?' she asked with a smile.

He returned her smile. 'Vanquishing – what a good word. Makes me feel I should be wearing shining armour and be astride a white charger.' He found a frying pan and with a little butter, began to fry bacon. As the delicious smell wafted through the kitchen he sliced bread and tomatoes and onions. 'Have you vanquished your ghosts?' he asked quietly.

'Not yet,' she said with a firmness that belied the dark shadows beneath her eyes. 'But now I've got my own private Sir Lancelot, I'm hoping to eventually.'

Jake turned the bacon. 'Don't expect too much of me, Mim,' he said carefully. 'I can only do so much – it's all up to you really.'

She gave a great sigh and poured another cup of tea from the pot. 'I know. But I've been thinking about things, and I've got a growing suspicion I know how we're going to achieve our goal.'

He turned from the range and eyed her curiously. 'How?'

'The bacon's burning,' she said. 'And if you put the eggs in like that they'll burst and spit everywhere.' She hauled herself out of the chair and pushed him aside. 'I can see why your wife banned you from the kitchen,' she teased as she forked the bacon expertly from the fat and replaced it with bread.

Jake watched as she put the eggs in another pan and covered them with a lid. 'You were saying you had an idea,' he prompted.

'All in good time,' she said with infuriating disregard for his curiosity. 'Let's eat, and then I'll finish telling you about that last day in the diggings.'

Miriam watched Jake mop up the remains of his breakfast with the last slice of fried bread. It was good to see a man eat at her table again – good to watch a healthy appetite at work. It was as if Edward had returned.

'Strewth,' said Jake as he put his hand on his belly. 'Reckon I'm fit to bust.'

The illusion was swept away by the broad Australian accent. For her beloved Edward had been an American, with the twang of Texas in his voice. 'In that case it's time I got on with the story. Fiona will be arriving today.'

They cleared the dishes and tidied up, then went into the parlour.

'I feel happier telling you my secrets in this room,' she muttered as she pulled back the curtains and looked out of the window. 'It's probably because of my father's painting.' She turned to gaze at it for a moment. 'His spirit's there, you see. In the brushwork, the colours, the light and texture of the subject.'

'Have you never wanted to paint?' Jake rested his hip on a windowsill, hands deep in the pockets of his jeans.

Miriam shook her head. 'A special talent isn't necessarily handed down to every generation,' she said with a smile. 'My daughter's the artist, and her daughter, Fiona is a very talented photographer.' She chewed her lip. 'Louise also has a talent, but it's not for art. She could be a fine actress if only she'd cut loose from that mongrel Ralph.'

She saw the gleam of curiosity light his dark eyes and again shook her head. 'I'm waffling,' she said firmly. 'You'll meet them all soon enough, and can make your own judgement. For now, I need to finish the most important part of the story.'

She made herself comfortable in an easy chair. Bolstered by cushions and two of her tablets she took him back to the past.

Kate looked down at Miriam. She was only twelve, and yet her world was falling apart. They had searched throughout the rest of the day with no sign of Henry, and Kate was beginning to fret. Something terrible must have happened to him – yet she knew she must not transmit this awful thought to the child at her side.

'We have to start a search,' she shouted over the rumble of voices. She stood on a box and tried to make the gathering listen. 'Henry must have fallen down one of the shafts. I want you all to check your own and then we'll begin on the others.'

'There's a hundred and one bloody abandoned shafts around here, lady,' shouted one of the miners, his be-whiskered face shadowed in the light from the dancing flames of the torches they carried. 'We could search all bloody week and not find him.'

Kate looked down at Miriam, who had never left her side throughout. The child was white faced, as still as a statue, her narrow shoulders set in determination. 'You've got to give it a go,' she shouted back. 'There's enough of us.'

'It's bloody madness to go poking about in the dark,' grumbled another miner. 'A man could break his flaming neck.'

Kate gripped Miriam's hand. 'Yer a bunch of cowards,' she yelled. 'Give me a torch. I'll do it meself.' She dropped from the box and snatched a flaming torch from the nearest hand. 'Come, Miriam, stick close to me. We'll find him, don't worry.'

'I'll be coming with you,' shouted a voice. Another joined in and was followed by a chorus. The miners circled Kate and Miriam, their torches dancing in the chill breeze that had sprung up since sunset. 'Where do you want us to be starting?'

Kate breathed a deep sigh of relief. She hadn't really wanted to go down into the tunnels, but she would have done so if necessary. 'We have to do this properly. Divide up into groups of four or five and each group take a section of the diggings. Search every shaft – the used, the abandoned, even the ones that have had cave-ins. He must be down one of them.'

She watched them leave, the torches flaring and eventually dimming as the miners fanned out over the diggings. Her mind was working fast, and yet she couldn't show Miriam her dread, her dark suspicion that Henry would not be found. The miner had been right – there were too many shafts – too many hiding places where a man's body would never be discovered if it was hidden well enough.

'I'm going to take you back to my tent, darlin',' she said softly. 'You can sleep on my bed if you like.'

'I want my daddy,' sobbed Miriam. She lifted a tear-stained face. Her twelve years meant nothing – she was just a child again. 'Where's my daddy, Kate?'

'I don't know, *acushla*,' she murmured. 'Come now. Let's get you something to eat, and when you've had a little sleep we'll maybe find out something.' Her mind was racing over the possibilities as they headed back to her tent. The dread was growing as time passed, but she must not let the child see it – neither must she give her false hope.

Kate put a sleeping powder in the warm soup and soon she had Miriam tucked beneath the red velvet cover on the feather mattress. She looked down at her for a moment, remembering the times when she'd watched her sleeping as a baby. The years and the poverty had not yet taken the childish roundness from her little face, or sharpened the features, and the baby could still be seen in the curled and dimpled fist that held so tightly to the velvet cover.

With a deep sigh, Kate turned from the bed and lowered

the wick on the lamp before leaving the tent. There were things she had to do. Things that couldn't wait until morning.

Henry's tent was in darkness, and Kate took a dry tree branch and lit it from the embers of a nearby campfire. She pushed through the flap and was totally unprepared for the sight that greeted her.

Henry's possessions had been thoroughly ransacked. His painting materials were scattered across the dirt floor, the pillows and mattresses ripped, the clothes dumped in a corner. An unfinished painting had been slashed, the easel snapped into pieces. The empty kerosene cans, that had been scoured and used as drawers, were upended, their contents strewn to all four corners of the tent. His saddle bags had been emptied and the last of his stores had disappeared along with his pick and shovel.

She looked down at her feet and picked up the shattered miniature he'd painted of Maureen so many years before. It had been trampled, ground into the dirt by a heavy boot and was almost unrecognisable. She put it in her pocket as the rage began to build. Honesty in the diggings was rare – but this? This was savage. Why steal the food? Why wilfully destroy everything Miriam held dear – especially on such a terrible day? How could anyone do that?

She turned slowly, taking in the carnage. If the main purpose for coming in here was to steal, then why rip up the mattresses? The miniature was worth money, so why leave it behind and trample it? Her thoughts whirled, then steadied, and her rage chilled to an icy fear. Was the theft merely a ruse to hide a more sinister intention?

Kate faced the open flap in the canvas and eyed Paddy's tent. She could see his dark shadow flickering against the sheeting in the lantern light as he sat with his wife and daughter. He seemed unconcerned by Henry's disappearance. Why wasn't he out searching with the others? The two men were partners, after all.

As she stood there amongst the chaotic mess she

remembered her last conversation with Henry this morning and the chill deepened. Henry would not be coming back – and there was only one man who stood to gain from his disappearance. Only one man who was capable of such violence. But how to prove it?

She took a hesitant step towards Paddy's tent, then stopped. She had witnessed his violence before and even with the pistol in her pocket, she knew she would never get the truth from him. To question him now would put him on his guard and Miriam in danger. Miriam had to be protected – it was what Henry would have wanted.

Kate quickly gathered up the few items of clothing and personal belongings that were still in one piece and stuffed them into the saddlebags. She put the art materials back in their roll of canvas and added it to the rest. With a quick glance around the poor dwelling she hurried out to the horse. Slinging the saddlebags over its bony back, she unhobbled it and quickly led it to her tent.

With a sigh of relief she saw the child was still sleeping, warm and safe where she'd left her. Kate found she was trembling so much she had to sit down. Her hands shook as she checked the pistol and the rifle and set them on the table by the bed. She eyed the music box. Isaac would know what to do, she thought as she poured a stiff brandy and swallowed it in one gulp. But he was too far away. The burden was hers, and she would have to decide what to do next if Henry wasn't found tonight.

After a long interval of deep silence, Kate began to pack. She moved quietly around the tent so as not to disturb the sleeping Miriam and one by one her stores and belongings were loaded in the wagon. As dawn threw a thin line across the horizon she tethered Henry's horse to the back of the wagon and harnessed her own mules between the traces.

'Is Daddy back yet?' came the sleepy voice from the bed.

Kate gathered her into her arms and gave her a hug. 'Not yet, *acushla*. Come. Let's have some breakfast.'

They sat either side of the campfire, neither of them

167

hungry and making only a token attempt at eating the eggs and bacon. They both stilled as one by one the miner's groups returned from their night's search. They had found no trace of Henry. It seemed he'd simply vanished.

The men and women drifted back to their canvas dwellings, their shoulders drooping from weariness and the deep sadness that comes with losing one of their own. It might have been a common occurrence, out here in the Never Never, but it never failed to remind them what a tenuous life they were leading.

'He'll come back,' Miriam insisted. 'We can't leave.'

'We must,' said Kate as she stood and smoothed back her hair. 'It's not safe here for you any more.'

Miriam looked puzzled. 'Why? If we leave then Daddy won't be able to find us.' The tears rolled down her face and she sniffed. 'I'm not afraid, Kate. Not if you stay with me.'

Kate felt an ache for the child as she took her in her arms. How to tell her she feared Paddy? How to explain to a twelve-year-old that he was quite capable of murder, and that her father would never come back?

Her thoughts were interrupted by the sight of Paddy striding towards them. 'Go in the tent, darlin', and stay there,' she murmured.

Miriam stood in the shadows of the big tent, stiff with fear as Paddy loomed over Kate. Their voices were raised and the whole camp had come to a standstill.

'Where is it, you bitch?' he yelled. 'I know you and him were thick as thieves. He must have given it to you.'

'The only thief around here is you, Patrick Dempster,' Kate yelled into his face. 'And it's over my dead body before you lay one finger on those deeds. That's if I had them. Which I do not.'

'You're lying,' he shouted, making a grab for her.

Kate's hand moved like a striking snake, the pistol glinting in the morning sunshine as she drew it from her pocket. 'Touch me and I'll shoot,' she said coldly. 'I have plenty of witnesses to say you were molesting me.'

168

'They won't open their gobs for you, you whore. Give me the deeds, or I'll have the law on you.'

Kate was white faced, but her hand was steady, the pistol aimed for Patrick's heart. 'I don't have them,' she said icily. 'As for the law – look around you. There's no law here. Not a trooper for hundreds of miles. We make our own justice in the diggings, Patrick – you know that – and so do I.'

Patrick must have noticed the belligerent glares, and the air of menace that emanated from the watching miners. 'Don't think you can escape me by running away, you bitch,' he snarled. 'I'll find you one day – you and that snivelling brat – and I'll take what's mine. You can bet on it.'

Miriam closed her eyes and tried to blot out the sound of his voice, the sight of his angry face, the heat of his rage. 'Kate and I left the diggings soon after that. We headed for Sydney and Isaac.'

Jake remained silent, his gaze fixed to the painting, his expression thoughtful.

'I don't know how long it took to get there, but it seemed forever. I spent most of the time either asleep or crying. The nightmares were the worst, though. I kept imagining him down in the dark, surrounded by snakes and creepy-crawlies, hurt and unable to call out for help.'

Miriam opened her eyes and because her memories of that time had been so dark, she was startled by the bright sunlight that poured in at the windows. 'We arrived in Sydney to find that Isaac had been taken into hospital with pneumonia, and his house was locked up and deserted.'

She blew her nose and dabbed her eyes. 'I never saw him. Kate refused to take me on the hospital visits, but he was a good man, and loyal too.' She smiled through her tears. 'He died shortly after we arrived in Syndney, but he'd left a will in which Kate inherited everything. The house, the business, the stock of gold and gems he had in his safe. His prediction had been correct – although for all the wrong reasons. Kate was suddenly a very rich woman.'

Fiona eased the motorbike around the long, undulating bends of the country road. The deep shadows of the overhanging trees were momentarily slashed by glares of sunlight, which made it difficult to judge distances. It was beautiful country out here, she acknowledged as she finally opened the throttle and tore down the straight. Miles of green pasture stretched towards every horizon, with hills and valleys dotted with sheep and cattle and horses. It was good grazing country, with plenty of water, the perfect setting for Mim's stud.

She finally saw the first of Mim's paddocks, and after fifteen minutes she came to the wrought-iron gates. The wire fencing was replaced by a fancy brick wall on either side of the entrance, with the legend BELLBIRD STATION inscribed in stone plaques. Jacaranda trees guarded the entrance and followed the wide meandering track north, their purple blossom bright in the sunlight.

Fiona got off the bike and opened one of the gates. She couldn't help thinking, as she always did on her frequent visits, that it was all a bit different from when she was a child. She still remembered the narrow dirt track that once could barely be seen beneath the tangle of scrub and bottle brush, and the five-bar gate that seemed to be permanently hanging off one hinge.

Knowing that anticipation was an important part of coming back here, she slowed the bike and enjoyed her surroundings. The widened track wound its way towards the homestead she still couldn't see. The avenue of jacaranda dappled the glare of the sun, and the surrounding hills were low and softly rounded, almost voluptuous in their thick coat of strong green grass – the horses grazing this bounty, sleek and graceful.

Bellbird homestead finally came into view as she reached the top of a low hill, and she took a moment to reacquaint herself with it. The homestead sat squarely to one side of the yard, its white paint and red corrugated-iron roof bright splashes against the pale green pepper trees and eucalypt. The corrals and stables had taken on the ochre of their surroundings, alleviated only by the spreading branches and red foliage of the poinciana trees that sheltered the outbuildings and Frank's cottage.

Her anticipation turned to impatience and she turned up the throttle and roared down the hill. She brought the bike to a standstill beside the dusty utility and after a glance at the Brisbane plates, realised Mim's visitor was still here.

She took off her helmet and shook out her hair as she climbed from the bike. It might be interesting to put a face to the voice over the phone, she thought as she reached for the screen door, for her imagination had taken flight during their conversation.

Her hand stilled as she heard the murmur of voices coming from the parlour, and she listened for a moment, puzzled by the conversation. It was unusual for Mim to use that particular room unless she had important visitors – but the topic she was overhearing was an odd one to have with a stranger.

Deciding she could no longer eavesdrop – for they must have heard the motorbike – she slammed through the screen door and announced her presence. 'Hello,' she called. 'Anyone at home?'

'In the parlour, Fiona,' came the reply.

Fiona pushed open the door and did her best to mask the shock as Mim stood to greet her. Mim had always been small, but now she looked shrunken and suddenly very much older. Fiona was unable to ignore the painful slenderness of the arms that enfolded her and the delicate, brittle feel of her body as they embraced. 'Are you okay?' she asked fearfully.

Mim drew back and smiled. 'As right as I'll ever be now I've seen you,' she said firmly. 'By the way, dear, this is Jake Connor.'

Fiona turned and found she had to look up to see his face

171

as they shook hands. 'We've spoken on the phone,' she finally managed.

He's very handsome, she acknowledged as she withdrew her hand and stuffed it in the pocket of her jeans. Tall, well built, sexy. There had to be something wrong with him. No man was that perfect. She brought her wandering thoughts into line. 'You never did explain why you're here,' she said, her tone rather more blunt than she would have preferred.

'All in good time, dear,' said Miriam briskly as she turned to plump the cushions on the couch.

But Fiona had caught the look flashed between Jake and Mim and recognised it as a shared secret – a conspiracy. Her curiosity was piqued even further. 'What are you up to, Mim?' she asked.

'Why should I be up to anything?' the elderly woman retorted. 'Sit down, Fiona and keep Jake company while I make a fresh pot of tea.'

Fiona stood her ground. 'I don't want tea,' she said flatly. 'I want to know what's going on.'

Mim sighed. 'Oh, dear,' she murmured. 'I might have known you'd cause trouble.'

Fiona opened her mouth to defend herself and was swiftly silenced by Mim's glare.

'Jake is from Brisbane,' said the old woman. 'He's here to help me with something. It will all become perfectly clear soon enough, but you'll just have to be patient, and wait until the others get here.' She walked out of the room and closed the door with a sharp click as if to put an end to the conversation.

Fiona looked at Jake. 'I suppose you're not going to tell me what this is all about, either?'

He shook his head, his dark eyes filled with laughter. 'I wouldn't dare,' he drawled. 'Mim might be small, but that glare's enough to stop a stampeding bull in its tracks.'

Fiona's brittle mood disappeared and she giggled as she plumped down on the couch. 'Too right,' she agreed. 'It's only Frank who seems oblivious to it.'

172

She looked out of the window and saw the manager crossing the yard. Perhaps Frank had an inkling to what all this was about, she thought. I'll grab him later and get him to spill the beans. When she looked back, it was to find Jake watching her with a curious, penetrating gleam in his eyes.

'How much did you hear before you came in?' he asked quietly.

Fiona felt herself redden, but she returned his gaze defiantly. 'I don't listen at doors,' she said defensively.

'Really?' he said solemnly. 'The screen door must have been jammed quite tightly for you to have taken so long to get through it.'

He smiled and she noticed the way his eyes crinkled at the edges. He really was sex on legs and at any other time she might have made a play for him, but at the moment he was pissing her off. 'Were you watching me?' she demanded.

Jake leaned against the mantelpiece, his arms folded, the smile still playing around his mouth. 'Not intentionally, but I couldn't miss the noise of that bike, and there's a clear view of the steps from here.'

Damn, she thought furiously. The bloody man had an answer to everything.

Chapter Nine

Frank's cottage was set on the far side of home yard and overlooked the gentle slope that ran down to the billabong. Shaded by trees, the verandah was a pleasant place to sit of an evening, and Frank was happily watching the ducks and the parakeets fly down for their last drink of the day. His pipe smoke drifted with the breeze that wafted down from the surrounding hills – it was a good way of keeping the mosquitoes at bay.

'G'day, Frank. How ya going?' Fiona settled into a cane chair beside him.

'Good,' he mumbled around his pipe. 'Got a new man working for me, so I gotta bit of peace for a change.'

'About time you shifted some of the workload, Frank.'

Frank, a man of few words, nodded and carried on smoking his pipe.

Fiona eyed the long, weatherbeaten face beneath the battered bush hat and wondered just how old Frank was. She remembered him as a child, and he'd seemed ancient then – yet he didn't really look any different now despite the passing years. 'Mim doesn't look well,' she began. 'I was shocked to see how frail she is.'

Frank nodded again and after a long silence, drew the pipe from his mouth. 'She'll be right,' he drawled. 'Just getting old like the rest of us.'

Fiona bit her lip. She didn't like to acknowledge the truth

that her grandmother was mortal. 'Seventy-five isn't that old,' she protested.

His hazel eyes were direct as he regarded her. 'It is when you've spent those seventy-five years out here in the Never Never,' he said gruffly. 'Mim ain't one to slow down, neither. Caught her mucking out the other day.' He grinned, making the corners of his eyes crinkle into a web of lines. 'Got me ear chewed off, but I'm used to it.'

Fiona rested her elbows on her knees and stared out over the darkening landscape as the cicadas began their pulsing rasp. The billabong glimmered silver as the birds settled for the night, and the last of the galahs were black silhouettes against the rising moon. She should have brought her camera, but it was back at the homestead.

'Do you know anything about this Jake Connor?' she asked eventually. It didn't do to barrage Frank with too many questions at a time.

'Good bloke,' muttered Frank around the stem of his pipe. 'Met him once or twice in the stables. Reckon he don't let Mim get away with nothing, quite livened the old girl up.' This was a long sentence for Frank and he fell silent.

Fiona struggled to keep her patience. Good bloke, or not, she wanted to know why he was here. 'Did Mim tell you anything about him?' she ventured. 'They seem on the best of terms. He's already calling her Mim, as if he was one of the family.'

Frank shook his head. 'Don't tell me nothing,' he mumbled. He leaned back in his chair and propped his booted feet on the verandah railings. 'Reckon it might have something to do with that music box, though,' he drawled.

'What music box?' Fiona was instantly alert.

Frank shrugged. 'Dunno,' he muttered. 'But she fair made a mess of it when she broke it.'

Fiona felt like shaking him – but Frank would eventually tell her all he knew – just in his own time, and at his own pace. She kept her voice even, her impatience under control.

'Why would Mim bring someone all the way from Brisbane to look at a broken music box?'

'Dunno.'

Fiona felt she was pulling hen's teeth, and wished his wife was still alive. At least you could have gleaned some sense from Gladys. 'Unless it's an antique?' It was a prompt which garnered no response. 'But you've seen it, haven't you?'

Frank stretched and tapped the dottle from his pipe. 'Ripper bit of workmanship, with the figures and all,' he mused. 'But not worth much after she broke it, I reckon.'

Fiona realised he was keeping something from her. It was in the shifty way he refused to make eye contact. 'How did she break it, Frank?'

He scraped the toe of his boot on the verandah floor. 'Fell off the bloody ladder,' he muttered. He rubbed his bristled chin and hurried on through Fiona's gasp of horror. 'She didn't tell me she was gunna get up in the rafters. I heard the crash and found her in the hall.'

'Bloody hell, Frank,' snapped Fiona. 'You should have called me. Was she hurt?'

He shook his head, his expression doleful. 'Nah. Only her pride and a bruised backside. Fair tore into me for trying to help, but I made sure she was right before I left her.'

Fiona lit a cigarette and smoked it in silence. The music box had to be worth something for Mim to go to all that trouble, she thought. Especially if it was the reason behind Jake's appearance at Bellbird. Yet it couldn't explain the frailty, the sudden ageing of her beloved Mim. 'Has the doctor been?' she asked.

'Coupl'a times over the past few months,' he replied warily. 'But she told me it was only for a check-up.' His heavy lidded eyes regarded her with solemnity. 'She wouldn't let me call him after the fall, but I've been keeping watch, and she's seems fair dinkum.'

Fiona put her hand on Frank's arm. 'Thanks,' she said quietly.

He looked down at her, the slow smile illuminating his

face. 'Reckon Mim wouldn't like you asking me all these questions, Fiona. Very private lady.'

'I know,' said Fiona with a sigh. 'And it's damn frustrating.'

Miriam drew the curtains and smiled. Poor Frank, she thought. When Fiona gets her teeth into something she worries it like a dog with a rat – she might have known she'd try and pump Frank for information. 'Never mind,' she murmured as she brushed her hair and prepared for bed. 'She'll know everything soon enough if I decide to go ahead with this.'

Turning back the sheet, Miriam climbed into bed. The pain was with her constantly now despite the pills, and she breathed a sigh of relief as she sank into the pillows. The days had been too long, the nights restless. The sooner she resolved the puzzle of the music box, the better, for time was growing ever shorter.

Miriam closed her eyes. She didn't know how long she could keep up the pretence, and although she hated having to lie to everyone, there were more important things to think about. 'Mortality is a state of mind,' she whispered. 'Hold on, Mim. Just hold on.'

She let her thoughts wander back to the years in Sydney, and as sleep finally claimed her she returned to her youth. To the time when her path was to collide again with that of Bridie Dempster's.

The years in Sydney had dulled the pain, and Miriam had finally come to accept her father would never return. Yet she hadn't forgotten him, and often, in the still moments of the night she would play the music box, and as she watched the dancing figures she would remember the time they had had together. Those moments brought him close and kept his memory alive – the music bringing solace.

Kate had taken on the role of guardian and they had settled in Isaac's house. It was quite old by Australian

177

standards. Built in the early 1800s, it was one of the first brick houses in Sydney and looked over the water. Miriam loved to wander through the rooms and look at the antiques and the precious books. Loved to sit at the window and watch the boats on the river as they steamed into the harbour. Life was so very different in this beautiful city, and she often wished her father could have shared the experience.

Kate no longer travelled, preferring to run her business from Isaac's headquarters. She had seen to it that Miriam studied the books and improved her handwriting and reading. She had also taught her how to conduct herself in society – for as a respected and wealthy woman, Kate was often invited to prestigious gatherings and Miriam was getting to the age when she too would begin the social whirl.

When Miriam turned fifteen in 1909, Kate enrolled her into a school for young ladies. This institution was run by two elderly sisters who'd come out from England to find husbands. When they failed to do so, they had turned their hand to educating the daughters of the wealthy colonists in the ways of etiquette, refinement and deportment. It was no easy task, and they often despaired at the hoyden ways of these spirited girls who seemed more at home on a sheep station than in a drawing room.

Miriam hated every minute of her enforced education. She had found to her disgust and chagrin, that she had no talent for the piano, was worse than useless at watercolour painting and seemed possessed of two left feet when it came to the dance classes. The strictures of what she saw as an outdated discipline frustrated her. After years of doing as she pleased in the mining camps, this was more like a prison, and she longed for the year to end.

Miriam climbed down from the carriage and gathered her books. She was hot and uncomfortable in the restricting jacket and pencil-slim skirt that made her walk like a hobbled horse. The broad-brimmed Panama hat was just a plain nuisance. It sat on her thick, unruly hair like a pea on a drum, stuck in place with hatpins that scratched her scalp. She ran a finger beneath the collar of the high-necked blouse and wished the ruche of lace wasn't quite so determined to tickle her chin.

Her hand stilled as she caught sight of Bridie Dempster being handed down by a footman from a carriage. The man wore the same green and gold livery as the coachman, and the shining, expensive-looking carriage was obviously private.

Miriam bit her lip, uncertain of what she should do. They had not seen one another for four years, yet she could still remember the last time she'd faced Paddy's wrath – could still feel the hurt that Bridie hadn't bothered to visit after the tragic disappearance.

As Miriam dithered, Bridie made the decision for her. With one swift glance of recognition, Bridie's chin went up, and with her gaze averted, swept past in a rustle of silk.

Miriam's relief was tinged with sadness. They had once been close – now they were to remain strangers. She noted the richly embroidered jacket and the matching skirt. Bridie's hat was one Miriam had seen in a little millinery shop in the city and she knew it cost a small fortune – yet, unlike her own, it sat perfectly on the shining coils of auburn hair. Paddy must have found his pot of gold, for how else could this show of wealth be explained?

Miriam followed her into the reception hall and watched as Miss Prudence welcomed her. This was obviously her first morning – and yet Miriam couldn't understand why Bridie was here. She was only thirteen, and yet she already had a sophistication Miriam could only dream about – an aura of self-assurance that made her the focal point on entering a room.

'Young Ladies,' called Miss Prudence as she clapped her hands for silence. 'I wish to introduce Miss Bridget Dempster. Miss Dempster will be with us for the rest of this term and I am sure you would like to join me in thanking her for the splendid Orangery her father has provided for the school.'

179

Miriam joined in the polite applause and noticed the gleam in the hazel eyes as they surveyed the room and finally settled on her face. She felt a chill of foreboding as the message was silently relayed. The challenge had been set. Bridie would not tolerate gossip about her lowly beginnings – and would fight tooth and nail to keep them secret.

Miriam turned away and headed for her first class. She would say nothing of Bridie's past and tell Kate nothing of her arrival – or of Paddy's donation to the school – for it would only cause trouble. The Dempsters had become a topic of great anger to Kate over recent years, and although Miriam didn't understand why, she realised it would serve no purpose to add fuel to the fire. There were only a few weeks left until the end of term. What harm was there in keeping Bridie's presence secret?

It was three days later when Miriam discovered just how dangerous Bridie could be.

Miss Prudence and Miss Faith stood on the narrow dais having summoned the girls from their afternoon classes. Their faces were austere, their black clothes merely enhancing the pallor of their skin. 'It is my sad duty to report a theft,' said Miss Prudence, the spokesman of the pair.

A soft gasp was followed by a rustle of whispers amongst the thirty girls. Miriam turned her head to speak to her friend Amy when she was stilled by the intensity of Bridie's scrutiny. The hazel eyes were cold, the mouth set, and yet there was an air of triumph in the tilt of her chin.

'A diamond brooch has disappeared.' Miss Prudence talked over the whispers until there was silence. 'You will remain in the hall until a thorough search has been done.'

'That must be Bridget's brooch,' whispered Amy. 'I saw her with it earlier.' She wrinkled her nose. 'Stupid to bring such a valuable thing to school. Any of the servants could have taken it. I don't see why we have to stand here half the afternoon when a quick search of the kitchens will probably unearth the thing.'

Miriam had a sick feeling in the pit of her stomach as she

180

turned once again to find Bridie watching her. 'What time of day was it?' she murmured to Amy.

Amy patted her fair curls and eyed her reflection in a small hand mirror. 'Just after luncheon,' she replied, careful not to shorten the word. 'We were changing into our dancing shoes.' Her blue eyes were wide as she regarded Miriam. 'Why?'

Miriam shook her head. 'I was just curious,' she muttered.

It was over half an hour later when the elderly spinsters returned to the reception hall. Most of the girls had settled on the window seats to read, whilst others stood in corners and gossiped. 'As you are no doubt wanting to prepare for the Governor's Ball tonight, you may leave early,' said Miss Prudence. 'The brooch has been found.'

With a sigh of relief, Miriam marked the passage and closed the book. Amy was already heading for the door – in a hurry to get home as usual. Miriam had never known anyone take so long to get ready for anything.

She smiled as she gathered the rest of her things. The ball would be her first formal outing, and promised to be fun, for Kate was going to finally introduce her to George Armitage who would be escorting them. George, a widower with seventy five thousand acres of land in northern New South Wales, had squired Kate to many functions over the past few months, and Miriam had noticed the sparkle return to Kate's eyes.

'Miss Beecham. Would you come with me please?'

Miriam felt the colour drain from her face as she turned to look into sour eyes. 'Of course,' she stammered. 'What's happened? It's not Kate, is it?'

Miss Prudence ignored her and led the way, Miss Faith following behind Miriam. They entered the study and the door was closed. 'What explanation do you have for this?' asked Miss Prudence as she placed the brooch on the desk.

'None,' said Miriam truthfully. 'I've never seen it before.'

'Come now, Miss Beecham.' There were high spots of colour on the gaunt cheeks, but the eyes remained cold. 'It

181

was found amongst your sheet music.' She sat upright in the leather chair, her fingers interlocked before her.

The colour rose with the heat of indignation. 'Well I didn't put it there,' retorted Miriam.

'You will be expelled,' said Miss Prudence. 'Your ... guardian is on her way to collect you.'

'I didn't steal the damn thing,' shouted Miriam. The years of coaching, of elocution and polite social graces went out of the window as she fought to clear her name. 'Amy saw Bridie with it before the dance class, and I wasn't even near the music room today.'

'You will be silent.' The grey eyes bored down, the steel trap of her mouth drawing a thin line above the pointed chin. 'Miss Dempster was distraught when she found the brooch was missing at luncheon. She came to me, begging me not to make the name of the perpetrator public. She knew what a scandal it would cause – how badly it would affect the reputation of the school. You have her to thank for me not calling the police.'

'The p . . .?' Miriam sat down with a thud on the nearest chair. 'I can't believe you think I'm a thief,' she gasped. 'What would I want with a brooch when Kate has a whole safe full of diamonds and precious gems?'

'What indeed?' interjected the angry voice in the door- way. 'Miriam, pull yourself together.' Kate stormed into the room, dragging a tearful Amy by the arm. She picked up the brooch, turned it to the light and inspected it closely. 'Just as I thought,' she snapped. 'It's no more diamond than that win- dow. Glass imitation – a good one, but not good enough to fool me.'

The spinster sisters sat rigidly in their chairs, their faces ashen, mouths agape as Kate took off her gloves and settled herself on a chair.

'You should be watching what you're saying when you accuse my Miriam of stealing,' she said with menacing soft- ness. 'She'd no more steal than you – especially from the likes of a Dempster.' She fairly spat the word as she glared at

182

the two elderly women. Without turning her head she snapped. 'Amy, tell them what you saw. And tell it all, mind, or I'll be having words with your father, so I will.'

Amy blushed to the roots of her blond curls. With her eyes downcast she told them how she'd seen Bridget sneak into the music room. She'd followed her, curious as to why she should be acting so furtively, and had seen her fiddling with a music case which clearly wasn't her own – for Bridget's was of white kid and very unusual. She'd assumed she was playing one of her tricks on someone and had thought no more about it until this afternoon.

'Why didn't you say something earlier?' asked Miriam. 'You could have saved me a lot of trouble.'

'I know, and I'm sorry, Mim, truly sorry. It wasn't until I came back to fetch a book I'd forgotten that I saw Kate, and she told me what you'd been accused of. I realised then what Bridget had been up to in the music room.' The long-lashed blue eyes were swimming in tears. 'Forgive me?' she whispered.

Miriam took her hand. 'Of course,' she replied.

'Well now,' said Kate as she gathered her gloves and stood up. 'Seeing as how we've sorted things out we'll be getting on with the rest of the day. Miriam will not be returning to your establishment, ladies. I have no wish for her to be socialising with the likes of Bridie Dempster.'

She leaned over the desk until she was on a level with their eyes. 'If one word of this gets out – from you or that little harpy Bridie – you'll find yourself in court, the pair of you. And I'm warning you – being accused of slander is far more expensive than some damn Orangery. I suggest Miss Dempster is persuaded to take her nefarious habits back to the slums she came from.'

'Come girls.' Kate swept out of the room like a schooner before the wind, the two young girls bobbing behind her like a flotilla of sailboats.

Jake was sitting on the verandah, deep in thought. Mim had left him in a quandary. There was nothing tangible for him to work on – no real proof to guide him. Hearsay, rumours, family enmities were powerful outside the context he would be working on, but too easily dismissed as frivolous. And yet he could understand why it was so important to Mim to go further. For once out in the open, the press would have a field-day and the mud would stick. He wanted to help Mim, for he admired her – but how to figure out a way of doing so was the rub.

He yawned and stretched and vaguely wondered where Eric was. It wasn't unusual for him to go walkabout, but the bush was rather more dangerous than the streets of Brisbane, and Jake hoped Eric hadn't picked a fight with a snake.

'Mind if I join you?' Fiona pushed through the screen door.

Jake smiled and hitched along the bench to make room. 'Not at all.' He noticed how the soft light from the hall made a halo of her hair and quickly looked away. Fiona was having a strange effect on him, and as she sat down he caught the scent of perfume and was reminded of Rachel. And yet the two women were worlds apart in looks and mannerisms, for Rachel had been sleek and sophisticated, and Fiona was more of a tomboy.

'You look like a man with the weight of the world on his shoulders,' she said after a long, awkward silence.

'I'm a man on edge,' he said gruffly. 'If you're here to pump me with questions, I'll say goodnight.'

'Touchy.' She lit a cigarette and blew smoke. 'I happen to care about Mim, that's all. You can't blame me for wanting to know what's going on.'

He rested his arms on his knees and turned his head to look at her. She was very beautiful, even in her suppressed anger. 'Mim has sworn me to secrecy until tomorrow,' he said quietly. 'I am not about to break my promise – so you'll just have to be patient.'

'Fair go, Jake,' she said through another stream of smoke. 'I come back to Bellbird for my annual summer visit to find a strange man in league with my grandmother and you

184

expect me not to be curious? And what's all this about Mim's fall, and some damn music box?'

Jake stood up and rammed his hands in his pockets as he leaned against the railings. Staring out over the dark pastures, he tried to keep the laughter out of his voice. 'There you go again. I think I'd better leave.'

Her hand rested lightly on his arm as she came to stand beside him. 'No. Don't,' she said softly. 'I'm sorry. I shouldn't try and make you break your promise, but it's so frustrating not to know what's going on.'

They were silent for a moment and Jake was very aware of how close she stood, of how her perfume mingled with the night scents and made his pulse race. 'I'm sorry, too,' he said finally. 'It must be very unnerving for you. But I promise Mim isn't being conned or manipulated. This is just something she needs resolved, and I happen to be the one who might be able to help her.'

Their conversation was interrupted by the most terrible screeching and yowling. It came from the shadows at the side of the house, and as they both looked over the railings, Jake realised what it was.

'Looks like Eric's bitten off more than he can chew this time,' he muttered as the dust flurried around the furiously fighting cats.

'Who the hell is Eric?' Fiona peered into the darkness.

'My cat,' said Jake grimly. He hovered close to the railings, unsure of what to do for the best. Then he became aware of Fiona's stare of astonishment and felt the embarrassing blush flood his face. 'Eric's top cat in our neighbourhood back home, but I think he's picked the wrong fight this time.'

'Bloody hell,' gasped Fiona. 'You brought your cat out here? You must be insane.'

Jake looked away, acknowledging she was probably right – but then she didn't know Eric, and leaving him behind had not been an option.

Eric appeared at the foot of the steps, head erect, ears

bloodied, his legs stiff with self-importance. As he marched
up the steps and eyed his audience it was as if to say, that's
sorted them out, now what about a bit of applause?

Fiona giggled and bent to stroke him.

Jake was about to warn her not to take the risk but was
silenced by Eric's complete acceptance of her attentions.
The cat began to purr as he wound himself around Fiona's
legs and all Jake could do was stand there in amazement.

Fiona bent to pick him up.

'I'd be careful,' Jake said sharply. 'Eric allows only a certain amount of liberty taking, then he bites.'

'You wouldn't bite me, boy, would you?' crooned Fiona
as she nuzzled his fur with her nose.

Eric's yellow eyes regarded Jake with an insolent glare
before they closed in ecstasy and he dribbled down Fiona's
shirt collar.

Jake watched Fiona and saw how the moon was reflected
in her eyes and how the shadows enhanced the creaminess of
her skin. Life was complicated enough, but he had a feeling
that if he stayed on Bellbird Station for too long, it would
become more so.

Chapter Ten

Miriam had risen early and after confirming with the station cook that the men would have their special meal tonight, prepared lunch with Fiona's help. With the spare beds freshened with newly laundered linen, Fiona remade the bed on the verandah while Jake transferred the cat and his belongings to the empty drover's cottage. It had seen better days, and although it had been abandoned when the new bunkhouse was built ten years before, it was dry and the bed not too uncomfortable.

The homestead was filled with the scent of the fresh flowers that had been flown in earlier with the mail and the rest of the supplies. They had dusted and swept until the battered wooden furniture and the scratched floors gleamed – and had even persuaded Jake to climb on chairs to remove the spider webs that hung like cargo nets from the beams.

After they had finished cleaning, Fiona insisted upon taking her photograph, and although she was reluctant, Miriam had dressed carefully in a sprigged cotton dress and had brushed her hair into sweeping waves which framed her face. Now she sat on the verandah with the insolent yellow of the golden wattle as a backdrop and attempted to keep still. There were so many things to remember, so much to do – this really was a waste of time, and she'd always hated having her photograph taken. Yet she couldn't disappoint Fiona, and after all, she mused, what harm was there in taking a few minutes out to please her granddaughter?

She stared into the camera lens and fiddled with her rings. The diamond was loose on her finger, as was her wedding band, but this was a special occasion and by wearing it she felt closer to Edward. Allowing her mind to wander as the shutter clicked and the camera whirred and Fiona told her to look this way and that, she thought of how the pictures might turn out. They would show a stranger of course – a woman aged before her time as all women were who spent their lives out here in this harsh country – not the girl she knew was still hidden deep inside.

She sighed. Where had all the years disappeared? And how would they remember her when she was gone? She hoped she would stay in their minds as a loving thought, just as her father remained with her. Her ruminations were broken by Fiona's voice.

'Okay, Mim. That's it.' Fiona was winding the film on, releasing it from the back of the camera and stowing it away in a pouch. 'Should be able to get these developed tonight,' she said with a smile. 'I've brought my equipment.'

Miriam looked at her in surprise. 'So quickly? Don't you need to send them away?'

Fiona shook her head, her cloud of hair dancing in the breeze. 'Not any more,' she said with a laugh. 'In my job it would be a disaster.'

Miriam left her chatting with Jake. Fiona was always animated when she talked about her travels, her career and her ambitions and Miriam smiled as she made them all a pot of tea to wash away the dust. Fiona looked very pretty in that dress, even if it was too short. It was a pity she didn't get out of those damn jeans more often.

As they sat on the verandah and waited for the others to arrive, Miriam settled into the cushions and regarded her isolated kingdom. It was pleasant here in the shade, she thought as she stared out over home yard. The reflected heat was swimming on the tops of the iron roofs, leaving puddle

188

mirages on the dark red earth and dappling the shadows beneath the trees. But here, in the cool green of the sheltering trees the heat was bearable, the breeze a relief after their frantic house cleaning.

She thought about her family and the coming party as she watched the lazy flight of a hawk as it drifted against the blue. Her expectations were mixed. It would be lovely to see them all again – to sit around the table like in the old days and chat about inconsequential things – but how would they react to her revelations? She twisted the rings on her wedding finger and pleaded silently with Edward to help her get through what could prove an exhausting and traumatic day.

'I feel in the way,' said Jake as he finished the cup of tea. 'Why don't I leave you to your family and come back in a couple of days? My family property is only a few hours away, and I promised them a visit.'

'Are you running out on me, Jake Connor?' Mim fixed him with a glare that didn't quite hide the amusement twitching at her dimple.

'Yes,' he admitted with an answering grin. 'I've told you my opinion about what we'd discussed, but as you seem determined to ignore my advice, there's no point in me staying. I think it's best to leave before the proverbial hits the fan.'

'You'll bloody stay here and help me out,' she snapped. 'You don't know how awkward my family can be.' She ignored Fiona's gasp of contradiction and tilted her head to one side and eyed him with sparrow bright intensity. 'I thought you were my Sir Lancelot?' she teased. 'Armour gone rusty has it?'

Jake stood and stared out into the yard, obviously ill at ease. 'That's not fair,' he muttered. 'I can't be expected to rescue you if you refuse my help.'

Miriam silently acknowledged that he was right as she looked past him to the holding yard. Her attention was caught by the corralled horses. Something had stirred them up. Running back and forth, bucking and swishing their tails

189

they seemed intent upon doing themselves damage and Frank was swearing loud and long as he tried calming them. She quickly realised it was nothing to worry about. They were just full of oats and would quit once they'd been out for a run on the gallops. But they did look magnificent, and she felt a glow of pride.

Jake turned and looked from Mim to Fiona. 'Can't you persuade her to change her mind?' he asked.

Fiona looked up and shrugged. 'Fair go, Jake. I haven't been let into this little secret. I'm the last person to ask.' She grinned at his obvious frustration. 'Besides,' she added. 'You know Mim. Once her mind's made up, nothing will change it. Reckon you backed the wrong horse, Jake.'

'This isn't about backing a damn horse,' he muttered as he ran his fingers distractedly through his hair. 'This is about . . .'

'Jake.'

Miriam's sharp interjection stilled him and he sighed. 'All right, all right,' he conceded. 'But don't blame me if it all goes crook. I tried to warn her, but will she listen?' He let his breath out in a long, exasperated sigh.

Miriam did her best not to laugh, for Jake reminded her so much of Edward. It was there in the set of his shoulders, in the passion and the sheer frustration of having to lose an argument. She had enjoyed the sparring then, and was enjoying it now. Strange how things didn't change all that much in the world, she thought as she turned towards the sound of an approaching vehicle.

'Here they come,' she said brightly. 'Take that scowl off your face, Jake – it spoils your good looks.'

Leo had insisted upon driving Chloe, for although this was home, she'd been known to lose her way. Chloe drove with scant attention to what road she was on, preferring to listen to the radio and letting her mind drift. On one memorable occasion she'd taken the wrong highway and had ended up in the middle of Adelaide.

Miriam embraced her daughter and was swamped in a

190

cloud of Chanel No 5 and scarlet chiffon. Clinging to her, Mim relished the contact after such a long absence – for they lived so far away from one another that visits were necessarily rare. Chloe was a little more rounded, but it suited her, and anyway, she thought, Chloe was still her little girl, her darling, even though she was past fifty.

Leo dumped the luggage and cases of champagne on the verandah and opened his arms to enfold Mim in his embrace. 'How's my favourite girl?' he whispered in her ear. 'I hear you're twenty-one again today. Happy birthday.'

Miriam giggled and slapped him playfully on the arm before disentangling herself from his enthusiastic embrace. She'd always liked her daughter's husband, and she realised in that moment that Jake was very like him. They were men who genuinely liked women, and she felt at ease with both of them. Having introduced them to each other she left them happily discussing the new British Mini that was set to revolutionise motoring as she opened the first of her presents.

It was an exquisite silk shawl, hand painted by Chloe. She kissed her warmly and admired the delicate butterflies and tiny peach blossom that drifted across the pale green silk and disappeared into the feathery fringe. 'This must have taken a long time, Chloe,' she said as she draped the gossamer silk over her shoulders. 'It's wonderful, darling, and just right for today.'

Fiona then presented her with a tooled leather photograph album, and as Miriam turned the pages she felt the tears threaten. For Fiona had obviously taken a great deal of trouble to find the right pictures. Here was her father, stiff and awkward in sepia as he posed beside the mining office in White Cliffs. Kate sat in uncharacteristic primness beside George for their wedding picture, and Edward grinned as he nonchalantly leaned against a fence post and rolled a cigarette. Chloe smiled out from beneath a summer straw hat as she sat on her first pony. Then came Louise and Fiona, little girls laughing together as they posed in their knitted swimsuits by the billabong.

191

Miriam kissed Fiona and held her for a long moment. 'Thank you,' she breathed. 'I will treasure it.'

Jake stepped forward and handed her a small package tied with gold ribbon. 'Willcox warned me,' he whispered. 'I hope you like it, because I had fun choosing it. Happy birthday, Mim.'

She pulled the ribbon and opened the paper to reveal a book of poetry. It was Byron, her favourite. 'I see you understand my tastes,' she said, and smiled her thanks.

Louise and Ralph appeared moments later and once Jake had again been introduced as a passing visitor, and Miriam had unwrapped the expensive handbag and gloves she would never use, they sat down for lunch.

The table had been set up beneath the trees behind the house. The silver and crystal winked against the startling white of the linen cloth, and the basket of flowers in the centre made a colourful splash. The old cane chairs had been given a new lease of life by the addition of new cushions, and the china was Kate's precious Crown Derby dinner service that had been unearthed from a cupboard and carefully washed.

The talk was lively, the laughter easy as lunch progressed. Miriam sipped her wine and nibbled at her food as she watched the others plough through the smoked salmon and prawn entrée and then help themselves to the delicious roast beef. Dessert was fresh fruit salad with lashings of cream. It had taken a great deal of organisation to get the fresh fruit and fish here in time, and she had Frank to thank for that. Dear Frank. She'd be lost without him and his contacts at the flying mail service depot.

She sipped from her glass of champagne as plates were finally pushed to one side and cigarette and pipe smoke drifted in the still air. Talk was desultory in the sibilant heat of the afternoon, the laughter soft and almost sleepy. Her family made a pleasant picture on this beautiful day and she committed the scene to memory before it could be destroyed by what would come later.

Chloe's broad-brimmed straw hat was weighted down with a profusion of roses that matched the scarlet of her dress. For someone with hair that colour, red should have been avoided, but Miriam thought she looked stunning. No wonder Leo adored her.

Her gaze roamed to Fiona who was in animated conversation with Jake. She watched them for a moment, noting how engrossed they were in each other, and wondered if this blossoming attraction would continue once she'd told them the real reason he was here.

Louise was chatting to Frank, who had plastered down his hair and put on a clean shirt for the occasion, but was obviously feeling a little lost. Gladys had been dead just less than a year, and had been the conversationalist of the pair. Miriam felt the absence keenly, for she and Gladys had been through some hard times together, and their friendship had been a strong one.

Her gaze moved on round the table. Leo's hat brim had been firmly pulled down over his brows and he leaned back in his chair puffing on a cigar, eyes closed in a blatant attempt to ignore Ralph. Ralph was fidgeting with his glass, ill at ease in his city suit and patently wishing to be elsewhere. He'd tried to corner Miriam earlier about the imaginary windfall, and she'd fobbed him off with a vague promise to reveal all later, but he was clearly impatient for the party to end so he could get down to business.

Miriam rather enjoyed the feeling of keeping Ralph stewing for a while, and smiled at Leo as he opened another bottle of champagne. She was already a little tipsy – but that was probably more to do with the two pills she'd taken rather than the amount she'd drunk. At least the combination kept the pain at bay, and she had two more pills tucked away in case she needed them.

'I propose a toast,' called Leo. He looked down at her from the other end of the table. 'The French have a more fitting name for their mother-in-law, and it suits Mim perfectly. To Mim. *La belle-mère*. We salute you on your seventy-fifth.'

193

The glasses were raised to a shout of agreement before they demanded she speak.

Miriam pushed back her chair and stood. 'To my family,' she said simply. 'May they continue to love me.'

Silence greeted her, and the bewildered faces turned towards her, the eyes full of questions as she sat back down. 'Of course we will,' spluttered Louise. 'What a strange thing to say.'

Miriam looked into the face of each of them. Jake refused to meet her gaze, Fiona looked suspicious and the others just plain puzzled. 'Drink the champagne,' she ordered. 'You're going to need fortifying.'

A mutter of concern went around the table as they dutifully sipped. The relaxed mood of the afternoon had changed, now there was tension in the air.

'Sounds ominous,' rumbled Leo. 'You're not about to confess you've committed some heinous sin, are you?' He tried to make light of the solemn atmosphere by chuckling. 'You don't have a hidden past as a call girl – or a toy boy tucked away that we should know about?'

Miriam smiled at his teasing and was about to reply when Fiona interrupted. 'Come on, Mim. Don't keep us in suspense.'

Miriam hitched the shawl over her shoulder. Why did the young have to be so impatient? 'I have two things to tell you,' she began. 'Both of them will come as a shock, and I'm sorry to spoil my lovely party. But it's rare for us all to be together, and this is my only chance.'

She saw Frank push away from the table. 'Don't go, Frank,' she said swiftly. 'You're as much a part of this family as anyone, and what I have to say will affect you too.'

'If this is family business, perhaps your visitor should leave,' declared Ralph in his pompous manner.

'Jake stays,' she retorted as she shot the younger man a look of apology and ignored his silent plea to say nothing. 'You'll understand why soon enough.'

Miriam gathered her thoughts as her fingers stroked the

194

silken fringe on the shawl. Which piece of news should she reveal first? Neither of them would be welcome, but the time had come and she had to make a decision.

She took a deep breath. 'I have inoperable cancer,' she said baldly.

Gasps of horror were followed swiftly by raised voices and the onset of tears.

Miriam held up her hand for silence as the questions flowed. 'It's in my back and spreading. I've accepted the diagnosis, and have no wish to lose my dignity and my quality of life by being radiated and stuck in a damn hospital. So please don't argue with me, and don't try emotional blackmail either. Neither will change my mind.'

She looked at her daughter and granddaughters, noted the bewilderment, the anguish and the tears. 'I'm sorry for telling you like this, my darlings, but I thought it best to be blunt. Cancer is just a word, and we all have to die sometime. I've had a good life, a very ordinary life really, in which I've been privileged to know love in all its forms. Don't cry for me – I'm not afraid.'

She gathered their hands as they came to kneel beside her chair. 'I have pills to deal with the pain, and as you can see, I'm content,' she consoled. 'This is my home and I wish to remain here, amongst the people I love. And when I'm gone, I'd like to be buried next to Edward.'

This declaration brought another storm of tears – of pleas to get a second opinion – of suggestions for radical treatment in the best hospital Australia could offer.

'No,' she said firmly. She pulled from the clutching hands and picked up her glass. Having taken a sip, she put it back on the table. 'Please sit down,' she said quietly. 'There is another matter I wish to discuss.'

Miriam waited until they were once more settled at the table. The beloved faces were ashen, the frivolous mood dashed by her revelation. Her heart went out to them, for she knew what a shock it must have been, knew the next few minutes would be a further trial. She found she was clenching the table napkin in her lap and smoothed it out. Her pulse was racing, the heartache for what she was about to do almost silencing her. And yet this was something she couldn't leave undone. She had come too far for that.

She saw Fiona and Louise cling together as they struggled to maintain their composure. Noticed how Chloe automatically turned to Leo in her moment of distress, her tear-stained face buried in his jacket. Caught the gleam of speculation in Ralph's eyes as he watched her over the rim of his champagne glass. Frank's hat brim was pulled low, but she could see the tension in him by the way his hands were tightly clenched on the table, the knuckles showing white beneath the weather-beaten flesh.

Jake's gaze was bleak, his face drained of colour as he sat there, isolated from the family, and she thought she finally understood what it was that haunted him.

When she felt they were in good enough shape to listen, Mim cleared her throat and began to speak. 'You have all asked about Jake,' she said. 'And although I haven't been totally honest with you, he has fast become a friend.'

She smiled across at him. 'A good friend who has given me honest advice. I'm just sorry I can't take it, Jake. But I was never very good at that sort of thing, and I'm too old to learn new tricks.'

She looked around the table. 'Jake is a lawyer. He's here because I've decided to sue Brendt Dempster and Shamrock Holdings.'

The announcement was greeted with a stunned silence.

'Mum, you can't,' pleaded Chloe finally. 'You're ill, and in no fit state to dredge up old family feuds. Let it rest.'

'Not much of a lawyer if he's persuaded you to take on that crowd,' snapped Louise giving Jake a glare of disdain. 'Don't listen to him, Mim.'

Miriam held up her hand for silence. 'Jake advised me not to take things further, but I don't agree. The Dempsters stole my inheritance – your inheritance – and I need to make sure they don't get away with it any longer.'

'Don't be ridiculous,' barked Ralph above the ensuing babble.

Miriam turned to him. 'Why is it ridiculous?' she demanded.

'Because you won't win,' he snapped.

Miriam cocked her head and eyed him thoughtfully. 'And why is that?'

'They have money, position and influence. You wouldn't stand a chance.'

'All the more reason to sue them,' she snapped. 'It's time the Dempsters got a taste of their own medicine.'

'You stupid woman,' he growled as he flung his napkin across the table and stood up. 'Why risk everything for some ancient feud that should have been buried years ago along with your father? Don't you realise this court case could not only ruin you, but me as well?'

Miriam felt the loathing rise in her throat – it had a bitter taste. 'At least I'll get my day in court,' she said with dangerous calm. 'Win or lose, Dempster will have to face the truth and be exposed as a liar.'

She took a pause. 'But I'm interested in why my suing the Dempsters should affect you.' She eyed him with a coldness that stilled him. 'Unless you're in league with them?'

The silence was profound as all eyes turned to Ralph.

'Are you?' Miriam demanded.

He ran a finger around his collar and needlessly straightened his tie. 'I'm brokering a business arrangement with Shamrock Holdings,' he said gruffly. 'It's in the very delicate early stages at the moment, and something like this will cause untold trouble to me and to the bank. We're investing a great deal of money, and it's high risk enough without your troublemaking.'

He ran a finger around his collar again as Miriam glared at him. She noticed the beads of perspiration on his forehead and the defiance in his eyes. 'Lie with dogs and you'll get fleas,' she said coldly.

'You must have very firm proof,' said Fiona, who had

197

remained silent throughout. 'What made you decide to do this after all these years? And why now? When you're so ill.'

Every face was turned towards Miriam in the ensuing silence. She swallowed hard. 'That's the other thing I need to discuss,' she said as she firmly avoided their eyes. 'I might not have as much evidence as I should, but . . .'

'For heaven's sake,' stormed Ralph. 'Are you telling us you're taking Dempster to court with no bloody proof? You're insane, woman, bordering on the dangerous. Should be locked up.'

'Don't talk to my grandmother like that,' snapped Louise. 'Sit down and be quiet Rafe. This isn't helping at all.'

Miriam saw the naked terror that shot into Louise's eyes after delivering this little speech, and the way Ralph went almost white with fury as glared down at her. The shock of realisation made her feel sick and she wondered if he ever got violent – had ever hit her – or worse. Louise had to be protected, but how? Ralph manipulated her like a puppet – she was no more capable of leaving him than of committing armed robbery.

Miriam took a sip of water. Her nerves were in shreds. It had been hard enough to face them all without the added worry over Louise. She looked at Fiona and tried to smile, but the muscles in her face were stiff with anguish. 'I was hoping for support,' she said quietly. 'But it seems I must do this alone.'

Fiona reached over the table and clasped her hand. 'Without proof you don't have a case,' she said gently. 'Jake's right, Mim. You can't do this.'

Miriam looked at the faces surrounding her. She patted Fiona's hand and resumed her straight-backed posture. 'I have some proof,' she announced. 'But I know I will need more if I'm to succeed in bringing the Dempsters down.'

She waited for the protests to die, noting they were not quite as vociferous as before. Curiosity had obviously got the better of them. 'We need to find the deeds,' she said into the silence. 'Once we have those the case is won.'

'Deeds? What deeds?' Ralph had lost all colour and his eyes were steely.

'The deeds to the mine. They will prove beyond doubt that my father and Patrick were partners, and that Patrick cheated this family of their rightful claim.'

Fiona clapped her hands. 'A quest,' she laughed. 'How exciting. When do we start?'

'Wait on, Fiona.' Chloe took off her hat and shook out her hair. 'Mum's dying. This is no time to go looking for something that was probably lost or destroyed years ago. She should be taking it easy, resting, making the most of the time we've got left with her.'

'Fair go, Mum. This is just the sort of thing to keep Mim going. And if we do find them, think about how great she'll feel getting her own back at last.'

'I think you're all on a fool's errand,' muttered Ralph. 'Chloe's right. The deeds probably don't exist any more and the whole thing will just be a waste of time.' He turned to Miriam. 'If you want my opinion . . .' he began.

'That's the last thing we need,' Fiona snapped. 'Go back to your bank, Ralph. We can manage without you.'

Ralph stood, his back stiff, a nerve jumping in his throat. 'Louise, say your goodbyes. I'll wait for you in the car.'

'I'm not going,' Louise said quietly. She looked for support from the others and Chloe leaned forward to rest her hand on her shoulder. 'I want to stay here with Mim.' She cast her eyes to her hands that were twisting in her lap.

'Too right,' said Miriam quickly before Ralph could open his mouth. 'I'll need Louise here to help me in the search, so you run along, Ralph.'

He stood there, his hat in his hand, the fury clear in his eyes. 'You'll regret today, Miriam,' he warned softly.

Chapter Eleven

The family sat beneath the trees in silence. They heard the roar of the car engine and the screech of the power steering as Ralph turned the rented four-by-four and sped away. Chloe kept a tight grasp on Louise's hand, murmuring encouragement and attempting to allay her terror of what Ralph might do. Leo returned from the homestead with a bottle of brandy and each of them welcomed the fire it brought as they tried to digest the events of the last hour.

Frank was, surprisingly, first to break the silence. 'Reckon you're one stubborn old sheila, Mim. But if it means that much to you, I'm willing to help.'

Miriam smiled at him. 'Thank you,' she said. 'I knew I could count on you, my old friend.'

'You can count on me and Leo, as well,' said Chloe. 'There's no rush to get back to Brisbane, and I can always cancel the exhibition. But I don't want all this fuss to wear you out, Mum. You should be resting, not taking people to court.' She leaned across the table and took Mim's hands. 'Please reconsider,' she begged. 'The feud between grandfather and Paddy is long over – let sleeping dogs lie.'

'I can't do that,' she replied. 'Having discovered the first piece of evidence I would be failing my father if I didn't pursue this to the end. He deserved justice, and I'm damned if I'm going to let him down.'

'What is this evidence?' Louise was sitting white-faced

between her parents, her thin features sharpened by a slash of sunlight coming through the trees. 'Must be pretty conclusive for you to go this far.'

'On its own, it's merely circumstantial,' she admitted thoughtfully. 'But tied in with the deeds it would be dynamite. That's why it's so important to find them.'

'And what if they no longer exist?' Louise was persistent.

'Then I'll use what I have,' Mim said firmly.

'It isn't enough,' muttered Jake. 'A court would throw the case out before it began.'

Fiona turned to Jake and eyed him thoughtfully. 'You seem to know more about this than any of us,' she said. 'What exactly is this evidence?'

'None of your business,' snapped Mim who was sick and tired of the whole thing. The lovely day had been ruined, and although she was the cause of all the trouble she was aware of the pain returning and the need to rest. 'And don't try pumping Jake, he's given me his solemn promise not to say anything.'

'But why?' Fiona's frustration was clear in her voice.

Miriam hesitated. She really wasn't sure of the answer herself, but instinct and experience warned her not to trust any of them with her secret. Not that they were dishonest – just likely to talk – and one never knew who might be listening. Ralph had already shown his true colours and Louise was cowed enough to tell him everything she knew. This meant she could tell no one, for it wouldn't be fair to leave Louise out of the secret. And if Dempster got to hear of her find, there was no telling what would happen.

She looked around the table. 'Find the deeds and I'll tell you,' she said finally. 'There's a lot of boxes and cases in the attic. I have no idea what's in them, but suggest you try there first. Most of it belonged to Kate.'

Kate married George Armitage on a summer afternoon in 1909. She wore a white skirt and blouse made of the finest lawn and carried a posy of Cooktown orchids. The delicate pink blossoms had also been threaded through her dark hair. Miriam had no doubts this was a love match and attended her wearing a pale lemon dress. A corsage of hibiscus was pinned at the waist and another in her hair. The groom, handsome in a new suit, his moustache and hair gleaming with pomade looked clearly nervous.

George was a man of few words, with an endearing shyness so endemic amongst the outlanders who lived on their isolated properties. Tall and lean, with brown eyes and a drooping moustache, he was toughened by the elements, and tanned from the hours he spent in the saddle attending his cattle. His slow, Queensland drawl disguised a quick mind, and he had pursued Kate with a strength of purpose that surprised them both.

As they left the church and climbed into the buggy, he confided his astonishment to Miriam. For he'd never thought someone as beautiful and lively as Kate would ever accept his proposal. Miriam had liked him from the start. In a way he reminded her of her father, for both men shared the same stillness, the same quiet contemplative manner and stubborn determination.

Content to be leaving the city, Miriam and Kate thankfully shed the restrictive finery and donned clothes more suitable for the outback. It would take several weeks of travelling before they caught their first glimpse of George's property.

The buggy stopped as they crested the final hill and George tipped back his hat. 'Welcome to Bellbird,' he drawled. 'It ain't much compared with that fancy house in Sydney, but it's home.'

Kate tucked her hand in his and kissed his cheek. 'Home is where the heart is,' she murmured. 'And it's here, with you and Mim.'

Miriam was embarrassed by Kate's rather clichéd romanticism, but understood the emotion behind it. For Kate had finally found love – had finally put the past behind her and was beginning a new life.

Miriam sat on the seat beside them, awed by the beauty

before her. It was late afternoon and the sky was streaked with vermilion, the dying sun casting an ethereal glow over the valley below. Bellbird homestead nestled beneath sheltering trees, the weather-beaten timber walls softened by the translucence. Outbuildings sprawled around the flattened earth of home yard and a wisp of smoke feathered from a chimney. Cattle grazed on the slopes of the surrounding pastures, hock deep in the long, green grass. A stillness pervaded the scene, a sense that nothing had changed since the first settler arrived in this isolated corner of New South Wales, and at long last Miriam felt she was coming home.

George slapped the reins and the horse began the gentle descent into the valley. On closer inspection the homestead was tumbling down and the roof wasn't the only thing that needed repairing. As he handed Kate down and led her up the termite-chewed steps, Miriam could see she was already planning how to put things in order.

The kitchen, which had seen no woman's hand since the death of his wife ten years before, was a shambles. The cooking range was filthy and smoke had blackened the wall behind it as well as the beam above. Chairs and tables were covered in farming manuals, old boots and horse blankets and the stone sink hadn't been scrubbed for a decade.

George shooed out a couple of chooks that had laid their eggs in the wood box and knelt to stroke his ancient dog which was slumbering in front of the range. 'Sorry about the mess,' he said shyly as he caressed the silken head of the Queensland Blue. 'I asked one of the lubras to tidy up, but she obviously didn't bother.'

Kate took the pins out of her hat and rolled up her sleeves. 'I'll not be cooking in this until it's clean,' she said firmly. 'Get me water, a scrubbing brush and a bucket,' she ordered.

'Don't you want to see the rest of the house?' George looked chastened, and a little afraid. When Kate was in this mood anything could happen.

'One shock is enough,' she muttered. 'I've no doubt the whole place needs fumigating.' She turned to Miriam.

'Don't unpack a thing,' she ordered. 'We'll be sleeping in the tent for now.'

It took weeks to turn the shambolic house into a home. Kate and Miriam scrubbed and brushed until the cobwebs were banished, the floors gleamed with polish and the range sparkled in a new coat of blacking. George, with the help of a couple of native jackaroos, fixed the roof and the verandah railings and repaired the steps and the screens. New curtains were put up at the windows, pictures hung on walls and Kate's fine rugs lay on the floor.

The carter's arrival some months later was greeted with shrieks of joy. For now Kate could display her fine china in the glass cabinet and dress the parlour with comfortable chairs and the long velvet drapes she'd brought from Sydney. Her crystal was placed carefully on the dresser and the few ornaments she'd kept after selling the Sydney house were displayed on little tables. The grand piano was given pride of place beneath the window and Kate's Indian silk shawl was draped over it.

The final touch was hanging Henry's painting above the new stone fireplace and toasting their achievements with champagne. Now she and Miriam could call it home.

Miriam watched as the others began their search of the attic. Leo was directing operations and holding the ladder whilst Fiona and Louise rummaged about with a torch and handed down boxes and cases. Jake had taken himself off somewhere, and Chloe was drifting about in the kitchen attempting to do the washing up. Her family were working together, just as they always had, she thought. Their strength in one another would carry them through what was to come.

Miriam was exhausted, the core of pain growing ever more demanding as she left them to it and went to her bedroom. After taking another two pills, she stripped off her clothes and sank into bed. It had been a long day – and a traumatic one – yet it had been right for her to tell them about the cancer, right to warn them of the coming trial. For they were the people she loved most – and secrets had a way of hurting far more than any truth.

She pulled the sheet over her shoulders and lay there in the gathering gloom. Night fell swiftly out here, and behind the shuttered windows she could hear the jingle of harness and the soft clip-clop of the horses' hoofs as they crossed home yard. A man's voice drifted with the breeze and the sound echoed a reminder of another time – and brought a resonance and colour to her memories of the early days, and of a man called Edward.

Miriam celebrated her sixteenth birthday at Bellbird Station in 1910. She could now ride as well as any man on the property, and had earned a reputation for being a tomboy. Yet she was aware of the changes within herself, aware of the side-long glances of the drovers and the young men she danced with at the country gatherings. Yet, despite devouring every romantic novel she could lay her hands on, she had yet to feel the rush of emotion and longing portrayed in these heated tales, and wondered if she ever would.

Edward Strong was twenty-two when he arrived at Bellbird Station. Miriam stood in the doorway of the barn and watched the stranger ride into homestead yard. He had an easy way with him as he swung from the saddle and led his horse to the water-trough, and she noticed how his brown hair glinted amber fire in the sun as he took off his strange looking hat and wiped the sweat from his face.

She leaned against the doorpost and studied him. He wasn't a tall man, she realised as George emerged from the tool shed and greeted him, but he was well proportioned and looked good in the travel-stained trousers and checked shirt. He walked with the slow, easy gait of a man who'd spent most of his life on a horse, his boot heels lifting the dust, the silver spurs and the buckle on his belt glinting in the sun.

She stood there in the shadows as the two men discussed the work ahead, and was intrigued, not only by the stranger's clothing, but by his accent. For although she'd never met one, she was certain he was American.

George led him across the yard to the bunkhouse where he introduced him to the drovers and ringers. Miriam returned to oiling the saddles and preparing the tack for the following day. She would meet him soon enough, but for now there was work to be done.

The drought had lasted two years and had finally broken a month ago. The brittle grass had returned to its lush green, the puddle in the billabong had swollen to lap the steep banks on either side and the stone-bedded creeks were gurgling with clear, swiftly flowing water. Miriam knew it would be difficult to find the wild horses this year, for there was no end of places they could water now the rains had come.

'Who's that?' Kate emerged from the stables and shielded her eyes from the sun as she watched George and the stranger stroll over to the cookhouse.

'Horse-breaker, I reckon,' she replied. 'George said he was coming this week.'

'I hope George lets me ride with them this year,' said Kate as she swept back the strands of hair that had strayed from the neat coil at her nape. 'I'm getting quite good on horseback, and housekeeping is awful tiresome.'

It was a hope Miriam shared, but kept to herself. It was unlikely George would let Kate run with the brumbies – his late wife had been killed when she fell from her mount during a cattle stampede – and even though Kate thought him over protective, they both understood why he was so.

Miriam glanced across the yard. The horse-breaker had emerged from the cookhouse and was rolling a smoke, his broad shoulder and narrow hip propped nonchalantly against the doorpost as he yarned with a couple of the other men. He seemed perfectly at ease despite having only just arrived, and at first sight he was no different to any of the other young men who came to Bellbird looking for work. Yet there was something about him that fascinated her and as the day wore on and she completed her chores she found herself watching for him.

'George won't let you ride out on the round-up if you keep making sheep's eyes at the breaker,' said Kate as she passed by with the feed for the chooks.

Miriam climbed over the fence and dropped down into the yard. 'I don't know what you're talking about,' she retorted, the colour rising furiously in her face. 'Shouldn't you be getting the tea? It's late, and George will be hungry.'

Kate shot her a knowing look. 'He's very handsome, so he is, but he's from Texas,' she said as if that should explain everything. 'I've heard tell that Edward Strong has a gypsy soul – he'll not stay long, Mim, so don't be breaking your heart over him.'

Miriam busied herself with gathering the twine that had bound the hay. Edward Strong, she repeated silently. The name suited him.

'Mim,' said Kate sharply. Her hand plucked at Miriam's shirtsleeve. 'Don't be wasting your time, darlin'. He's a rover – a passing fancy that any young girl would tilt her bonnet at. Don't be fooled because he's different. He's still a man, and they're all the same under the skin.'

Miriam put her hands on her hips and turned to face her. 'Fair go, Kate,' she blustered. 'Give me some credit for having a brain.'

Kate's mouth twitched. 'It's not your brain I'll be worrying about,' she said softly as she picked up her skirts and turned away.

Miriam frowned. She had no idea what Kate was talking about, but she dismissed the problem by plotting a way to approach George and gain his permission to join the round-up.

She waited until tea was over and Kate was occupied with doing the dishes. George was sitting on the verandah, enjoying his evening pipe. This would be the only chance she had to talk with him in private. 'I'd like to run with the brumbies this year,' she began. She was not one to beat about the bush and knew George appreciated her getting to the point.

'Too flamin' dangerous,' he grumbled around the pipe stem. 'Brumby run's no place for a woman. Kicking and biting and leading you a dance all over the flamin' country. They're a mean lot, especially the stallions.'

Miriam sat in the chair beside him. She'd expected this reaction and had come prepared. 'I've been riding ever since I came here,' she said firmly. 'I help with the cattle muster, the dipping and in the corrals. You know very well women are as tough as men out here. We have to be.'

He eyed her for a long moment, the smoke rising from his pipe as his moustache drooped to his stubbled chin. His face was as brown and creased as an autumn leaf, his arms as knotted as rope, but his eyes were bright with humour.

'Kate warned you'd give me an argument,' he muttered. He took a long while to relight his pipe. 'Reckon you'll be right,' he drawled finally. 'But I don't want no whinging, and if you get in the breaker's way you'll never do it again. I pay him more than any man on the place and can't afford to waste his time looking out for you.'

The excitement for what lay ahead coursed through her and she flung her arms around his neck and kissed his cheek. 'Thanks, George. I won't let you down.'

'Better not,' he grumbled, trying to look stern, but perhaps remembering the time when he'd first joined the annual muster. 'Not a word to Kate,' he warned. 'She'd have me guts for garters for letting you go and not her.'

'Then let her come with us,' she begged.

George shook his head. 'Neither of us are coming this year, Mim,' he drawled. 'I'm getting too long in the tooth and Kate ain't skilled enough despite what she thinks.' He eyed her from beneath his brows. 'I don't wanna risk losing her, not after it's taken such a long time to find her.'

Miriam was still awake long after Kate and George had gone to sleep and the house had fallen silent. Yet she was up before dawn, her swag packed and ready for her adventure. Kate shot her an enquiring look as she hastily finished breakfast, but if she knew about George's decision she said nothing.

Edward emerged from the barn armed with saddle blanket and tack. 'I guess you must be Miriam,' he said in a deep drawl. 'Glad to have you along, ma'am.'

Miriam's hand was swamped as his fingers curled around it, and she looked up into darkly lashed eyes that were the colour of wild violets. On closer inspection he was even more handsome than she'd thought. His nose was long and straight, the brows dark, the chin cleft beneath the morning stubble. 'G'day,' she managed.

He waited for her to collect her own saddle and then walked with her to the horse corral. Tongue-tied and awkward, Miriam realised it was the breadth of those shoulders and the way he held his head made him appear so tall, for in reality he could only have been about five foot ten. Desperate to appear nonchalant and adult, she searched for something intelligent to say.

'That's a strange kind of hat,' she finally managed as they reached the fence.

He grinned as he tugged the broad brim further on his brow. 'It's called a Stetson, ma'am,' he drawled. 'No self-respecting Texan would leave home without one.'

Miriam was furious with herself for blushing and hastily looked away. He was having a strange effect on her, and his proximity merely enhanced it, for she could smell the fresh, laundered scent of his shirt and the warmth of his skin. Yet it was his smile that sent shock waves down to her very toes, and his deep drawl that was enticing, and she finally understood the breathless prose of all those penny paperbacks she'd devoured.

With the horses cut from the paddock, the shoeing over and swags packed, the mustering group mounted up. Two packhorses carried axes, shovels, crowbars, fencing wire and yards of calico. There was no cook, each rider had to fend for themselves. It would take them about three days to get to Twelve Mile Creek.

Miriam was used to spending long hours in the saddle and had always enjoyed the company and rough humour of the men who worked on Bellbird. Yet this trip held a kind of magic, for as they rode deep into the vast plains of the outback she felt more and more drawn to the man with the laughing blue eyes and the deep Texan drawl.

Edward Strong rode long in the stirrup like the drovers, but there the similarity ended. His boots were ornately tooled, with a low heel, unlike the Australian ones, which were flat and plain. Instead of moleskins, he wore leather chaps and denim trousers, held at the waist by an ornate leather belt that had a buckle of silver with a lump of turquoise at the centre. His hat brim was wider than the standard bush hat the others wore, and the crown was higher, circled by a band of snakeskin and decorated with an eagle feather.

Over the next three days Miriam watched him as he rode the big gelding, his gloved hand easy on the reins. It was as if man and horse were from the same mould, she realised as they made camp on the third day. Each had strength in their lithe frames. Each had a noble carriage of their heads. Each blended in with the rusty brown landscape of this outback land. Miriam realised she was falling in love – and despite all of Kate's warnings, she couldn't resist.

Twelve Mile Creek was a low channel of clear water that twisted and turned like a King Brown over a sandy bed that gradually tapered off and disappeared into the bush. Even to the inexperienced eye the horse tracks were obvious amongst those of emus, kangaroos and goannas.

Edward Strong's quiet drawl stilled all conversation. 'I guess they won't come here for much longer. See those marks? That's where the mustangs have pawed holes in the sand to suck up the receding water.'

He tipped back the brim of his Stetson and eyed the leaden sky. There had been no rain for the past three days. 'They'll

210

move on to where there's plenty of water. This creek ain't gonna last much longer despite the recent rain.'

'How many do you reckon come here?' breathed Miriam. His heavy lidded blue eyes regarded her for a moment. 'About fifty to a hundred, I guess. Hard to tell with the ground all churned up.' Then his smile lit up his face, making him appear almost boyish. 'Better get some sleep, it's an early start in the morning, ma'am.'

Miriam could feel the blush spreading over her face and she looked away. It was as if Edward Strong was fully aware of the effect he was having on her – it was there in the twinkle of his eyes and in the smile tugging the corners of his mouth. She didn't sleep well that night, and it had nothing to do with the hard ground beneath her blanket.

Breakfast was damper and tea swallowed hot and fast before sunrise. Saddling up, the group left camp and explored the other waterholes. They had made their way carefully through the bush and were edging ever closer to the furthest waterhole from the property when Edward signalled for them to stop.

'Look,' murmured Edward as he reined in his horse next to her. 'Over there.'

Miriam followed his pointing finger and stifled a gasp of delight. Fifteen or twenty young horses milled around the sandy riverbed, pawing at the ground, dipping their noses in the water. Their coats were dusty, but their muscular physiques were magnificent.

'Are we going to take them now?' she whispered.

Edward was leaning towards her, his saddle creaking as he moved. He shook his head, the blue eyes mesmerising. 'No point. We haven't got a corral fixed up and we'd never catch the bastards.' He tipped his hat and reddened. 'Apologies for the language, ma'am.'

Miriam, who'd long forgotten the lessons learned at the Academy for Young Ladies, didn't know how to respond, so she turned her attention back to the wild horses.

The lead stallion lifted his head from the water and sniffed the air. He was a magnificent palomino with a coat of caramel and a mane and tail of platinum. His nostrils flared and his ears went back. With a shrill whinny he warned the others and after rearing up he turned with the grace of a dancer and herded his harem together before chasing them away. Strong muscles gleamed in the early sunlight, the mane and tail flowing like liquid silver as the mares and colts thundered before him. Dust rose in a great cloud that drifted like a curtain between the watchers and their prey.

'How are we ever going to catch them?' Miriam was enraptured by the almost sensual fluidity of that stallion, yet the thought of such a magnificent animal being trapped and tamed didn't sit well with her.

Edward adjusted his hat, his eyes intense with the light of some unspoken humour. 'Ain't gonna be easy,' he drawled. 'Mustangs don't reckon much on getting caught. That stallion's probably taken them miles away by now.' He took off his sweat-stained Stetson and rubbed his sleeve over his forehead. 'Horses gotta drink. I guess they'll be back soon enough, ma'am.'

His smile made her pulse race and she looked away. She would have to be careful with this man. He was far too handsome – far too aware of the chaos he wrought within her – and she knew that her inexperience could get her into deep trouble.

It took all the next day to build the yard just below a ridge. The nearest water was only five miles away, and the open plains country was firm and good for galloping across, with enough sparse timber to give cover. When it was finished they had a large, three-sided corral with slip-rails that could be quickly shoved into place. The yards of calico were run in strips out from the wings of this edifice and nailed to fence posts that had been planted earlier.

The following morning was frosty, the sun still two hours below the horizon as they broke camp. Miriam was as tense as an overwound clock as she saddled her best horse and rode with the others to the main billabong.

212

Edward Strong had coached them carefully and now, as the sky lightened, they were spread out over several hundred yards, crossways to the light breeze. Under cover of the sparse stand of timber they waited, tension growing – their breath wraiths in the cold air as a couple of yearlings, a foal and two mares emerged from the shadows.

'Why can't we take them now?' Miriam whispered.

Edward put a finger to his lips. He was lying along his horse's neck, camouflaged as they all were amongst the dancing shadows of the trees. 'Wait,' he mouthed.

Duly chastened, Miriam lay along her pony's neck and did as she was told. Her pulse raced and her hands felt slick inside her riding gloves, as she studiously ignored the man beside her and watched the horses.

They came one behind the other in an orderly queue like housewives going to church. There were several good-looking colts, a few mares with foals at foot and the palomino stallion. A family group, for the stallion would have run off the younger colts unless they were his own. They drank deeply as several more groups joined them. Splashing and pawing they drank until their stomachs were distended. Satisfied, they stood nonchalantly cropping at the vegetation unaware of their audience.

Edward's stock-whip cracked. 'Yeehah!' he bellowed.

The startled brumbies thundered off, the stallion biting the mares' rumps to urge them on to greater speed.

Edward's shouts were echoed by the others as they cracked whips and joined in the race. The stallion galloped away from the direction the men had wanted. The stockman on that side urged his horse into a lathering gallop to head him off and get in the lead. They all knew that if he didn't make it they would lose the herd. For if the stallion broke through, the others would swiftly follow.

Much to Miriam's disgust she was regarded as a green-horn and, surrounded by dust and the thunder of many hoofs, was relegated to gallop full tilt behind the herd to help keep up the stragglers. Her hat blew off, and her hair escaped

213

from the pins and streamed behind her as the excitement took hold and she became as one with the wind and the thundering herd.

She was aware of the wingman going alongside the stallion and of the other stockmen forcing the animal to turn the herd in the right direction. They were fast approaching the ridge and with shouts and whip cracks the brumbies were made to keep up the pace. Ears flat, nostrils distended the wild-eyed, magnificent animals flew across the open ground, hoofs and manes flashing in the early sunlight.

Miriam joined in with the men to make as much noise as possible as they came into sight of the calico wings. Edward had explained it was important to frighten the hell out of the brumbies so they remained grouped and on one path – straight between the wings of calico and into the yard.

Edward dropped back from the lead as the front-runners raced between the calico, and he joined Miriam and the others at the tail to urge the rest of the mob on. Miriam was riding faster than she'd ever done before as she and her mount caught the excitement of the chase, and the thrill of running in harmony with the wild horses.

The yard was only feet away when the brumbies suddenly realised they were trapped. Skidding and propping, they tried to break out of the pack and turn. Eyes wild, manes flying they baulked and jostled, screaming their fear and defiance.

But there were too many horses jammed between the calico wings – too many men making too much noise – they had nowhere else to run.

Miriam yelled and cracked her short stock-whip as they herded the brumbies towards the open end of the corral. The sheer weight of numbers forced the reluctant beasts on and, one after another, they entered the corral.

The stock boys were ready. They rammed in the slip-rails and quickly secured them with green-hide halter shanks.

Miriam was breathless, sweating and elated. She had

214

completed her first run and would never forget it. She looked at Edward, hoping for approval and the chance to share the thrill of it all. But he was fully occupied.

'Get around the outside of the yard and try to keep 'em off the rails,' he yelled above the drumbeat of hoofs and the shrill whinnies. 'They could easily smash 'em down and get away.'

With the enemy of man on all sides the brumbies eventually began to calm down and Miriam slid wearily from her saddle.

Edward rode up and as his horse pawed the dust, he yelled down to her. 'No time to rest. You wanted to work, so work. Get back on your horse until the mustangs have gotten used to you. Talk to them, or give them a song, but make sure they see you. It's important they get used to horsemen before we have to muster them back to the ranch.'

Miriam blushed, her angry retort dying as he wheeled his horse away. She clambered back into the saddle, her temper tightly checked. For despite his rudeness, she could understand the logic. But it was to take over another hour of circling the yard to calm the brumbies and by that time she was too exhausted to care.

The muster lasted three days. Days in which Miriam clung to the saddle, determined to see it through. She had little strength left for flirting or day-dreaming and fell asleep the moment she climbed beneath her blanket.

The stallions were cut from the herd to stop them fighting, and apart from one or two, they were set free. Miriam and the men rolled up their swags and tuckerbags and prepared for the long journey back to Bellbird Station. The horses had quietened considerably after their enforced stay in the corral, and once the stock horses had been infiltrated into the mob as coachers, the brumbies seemed reasonably content to be herded south.

Miriam and the others arrived at Bellbird station two days later, almost falling from their saddles in weariness. None of them had slept during the journey home, for it had been

215

impossible to make camp with no corrals and over two hundred brumbies in tow.

Miriam filled the tin bath and soaked the dust and sweat away as she chattered endlessly to Kate about the thrill of the chase and the way Edward had so cleverly caught the brumbies between the calico.

Yet the adventure wasn't yet over, for although Edward was the best-paid man on the Station, he would remain on Bellbird for five or six weeks. He would be paid the usual stockman's wage of three pounds, plus twenty-five shillings a head for each horse broken. Because of this generous wage, George limited the breaker to four a week, reckoning that any more than that would be a rush job.

Miriam was kept busy with her usual chores, for George and Kate had flatly refused to let her help as off-sider to the young American. Yet Miriam could always find some time in the day to watch Edward at work.

The pound yard was round and built with a series of gates that lead off to other yards where the unbroken horses were kept. Twenty or so would be drafted off at a time and led into the pound yard where the young Texan would swiftly check them over. A few were sick or lame, some too young and undeveloped. They wouldn't be broken this year.

Some of the brumbies were already carry the BB brand of the station, having been handled as foals and left to run with the others until they were old enough to break. These colts were nervous, their memories of the searing branding iron obviously still sharp as they fought against the heavy snaffle bits in their mouths. Others had the white hairs on their withers that were the clear sign they'd once been saddled and ridden. These were drafted first and swiftly dealt with so Edward could get on with the real business of breaking.

Miriam had finished her chores for the day and was perched on the top rail of the pound yard watching Edward deal with the second of the two stallions they'd brought back. It was the flashy looking palomino.

The horse went berserk and tore around the yard as the

216

off-sider kept his horse alongside, weaving back and forth as the stallion tried to break away from the fence. Finally cornered, the palomino stood trembling with legs splayed and ears flat as Edward approached.

Miriam held her breath as the off-sider closed his horse in, pressing the stallion against the railings so Edward could swiftly ease on the bridle.

The palomino reared, eyes wild as Edward hung on to the reins, heels digging into the earth. 'Whoa, boy. There, there,' he murmured. 'I ain't gonna hurt you,' he crooned.

The stallion was having none of it. He fought the bridle, twisting and turning, shaking his head, pulling back and trying to rear up.

Edward hung on, the reins biting into his leather gloves as the stallion yanked and propped and shook his head. 'That's a good fella,' he called softly. 'So full of yourself, aren't you, boy?'

The stallion was straddle legged, head down, breathing hard as the lightweight droving saddle was carefully eased on to his back. His eyes rolled and showed white, the ears flat to his head, nostrils flaring as Edward tightened the girth.

Miriam was transfixed. The enmity from the brumby was tangible. It froze like a coiled spring. She could see the dark patches of sweat on Edward's shirt as he grasped the pommel and flung his leg over the quivering back.

The palomino shot into the air like a rocket. Bucking and kicking he landed with a thud, then dipped his head and corkscrewed in a tight, vicious circle. Edward's hat flew off and the off-sider swiftly got out of the way of the deadly hoofs.

'Open the outside gate,' yelled Edward as he somehow maintained purchase and eased his pull on the reins.

The stallion saw his chance and in one gigantic surge raced for the open gate and freedom.

Miriam's pulse drummed as the other men rode out after him. They would try to turn the stallion by shouldering him away from his headlong path, the swift change of direction

217

making him slow down. But the stallion was obviously vicious and she prayed Edward was strong enough and experienced enough to survive that hectic race across the plains.

She stood on the top bar of the pound yard and tried to see what was happening, but was frustrated by the cloud of dust that rose from beneath the pounding hoofs. Her heart was banging against her ribs, and her mouth was dry as she waited for the outcome of this enthralling battle. How she wished she'd saddled her own horse and could join in the fun – but it was far too late for that.

As she waited fretfully, one hand shielding her eyes from the glare, she prayed he'd return unscathed. Then, as another dust cloud rose into the molten sky, a wave of thankfulness shot through her. There, on the horizon, was the unmistakable silhouette of Edward and the stallion.

The palomino might have been exhausted, but his will to be free obviously still overrode everything. He propped and danced and lashed out with his back hoofs every time he sensed the man on his back might be weakening. They rode back in this fashion, each as wilful as the other.

Miriam forgot she was supposed to be helping Kate with tea, and watched, entranced, as finally man and stallion grew weary of the game. The palomino's head drooped as he plodded around the paddock and Edward almost fell from the saddle and led the horse into the holding yard. The stallion bent his neck and drank deeply from the trough, seemingly unconcerned as Edward undid the girths, eased off the saddle and rubbed him down.

Miriam came to stand on the other side of the railings as Edward dumped the saddle and climbed over. 'Good on you,' she said quietly. 'Thought you were a gonner there.'

Edward pushed back his hat to wipe away the dust and sweat. The blue eyes still sparkled with humour despite the tough day. 'That's one fine mustang, ma'am,' he said as he glanced back at the stallion. Then his gaze fell on Miriam and his voice softened and grew more intimate. 'But I guess we shouldn't be too hard on him. Don't want to kill his spirit completely,' he murmured.

Their eyes met and in that moment of silence something magical happened. For like the palomino, Miriam had come under the breaker's spell.

Chapter Twelve

Fiona lay beside her sister and stared up at the ceiling of their old bedroom. It was strange to share a bed with her after so many years, but with Ralph leaving she had no need to sleep on the verandah. 'I can't believe Mim's dying,' she murmured. 'Nothing will ever be the same once she's gone.'

'I know,' replied Louise. 'This place has always been a second home, but . . .' She fell silent.

Fiona knew what she meant. Bellbird was Mim, and she couldn't imagine the place without her. Couldn't possibly imagine this could be the last of their Bellbird summers.

'Mim's artful, I'll give her that,' she said eventually. 'The announcement she made about the court case certainly gave us something else to think about.' She shifted restlessly on the pillow. It was a warm night and Louise had always generated heat. 'Do you think we'll find the deeds?'

'Who knows,' murmured Louise. 'Mim's always had a thing about the Dempsters, and I can see her point. But we don't know how much of it was true. She was a kid when it happened, and all she really has to go on is the stories Kate told her.'

She fell silent for a moment. 'But I like to think there are some deeds somewhere – it would make Mim so happy to be vindicated.'

'Mmmm. But there's a lot of stuff to get through, and with Mim so ill, we could run out of time.' Fiona changed tack, not wanting to think about her grandmother's imminent death. 'That was pretty brave of you today,' she said. 'Ralph was furious.'

Louise shifted her head on the pillow and ran a hand over her cropped hair. 'I just wanted to stay here,' she murmured. 'Nothing brave in that.'

Fiona turned her head and eyed her sister. The pale moonlight fell on Louise's face and made it waxen. 'I saw the way you looked when you realised what you'd said,' she retorted. 'Why are you so frightened of him?' A terrible thought made her rise on one elbow. 'He doesn't bash you, does he?'

'No. He's never lifted a finger to me.' She took a short, trembling breath. 'He doesn't need to,' she whispered.

Fiona saw the single tear squeeze through the long lashes and meander down her sister's cheek. 'Oh, Louise,' she murmured. 'What has he done to you?'

The slender fingers found the tear and brushed it away. 'Nothing,' she said firmly. 'Ralph is a good husband. I don't know why you all think he's such an ogre.'

Fiona rolled on to her back with an exasperated sigh. For a minute there she'd thought she was finally getting through to Louise. 'We've had this conversation before,' she said softly.

'Don't be like that, Fee,' pleaded Louise as she touched her arm. 'I'm sorry I was such a bitch the other day, but you caught me on the hop and I was just being defensive.'

'Why? There's no reason for you to defend yourself, or Ralph to me. I'm your sister – my love for you is unquestionable.' She turned on her side until they were face to face. 'Can't you see it's because we care that Mum and Dad and I have to give you a hard time? I don't like to see you so thin and obviously unhappy. Why do you stay with him, Louise?'

Louise buried her face in the pillow, the tears trickling into the cotton. 'He's given me so much. Made me what I am, taught me so many things. I'm scared to leave him, Fee. Not because of what he might do, but because I'd be lost without him.'

Fiona didn't reply. Her thoughts were in turmoil. Louise knew she was in a fix, but until she was made to realise her own worth she wouldn't have the courage to leave this abusive marriage. Ralph might not have hit her or physically harmed her in any way, but the drip, drip, drip of fault-finding, of making her depend on him for everything, had done a powerful job of work on Louise.

'I know you don't understand,' said Louise softly. 'But I love him. He's my rock – the one person I trust implicitly not to let me down.' She shifted in the bed and lay with her hands beneath her head. 'He told me once that if I ever cheated on him he would kill me – and then kill himself. That's real love, Fiona. And I'll never have the chance of it again.'

Fiona kept her opinions to herself. Ralph certainly knew which buttons to press, but she doubted very much his threat would come to anything. Clever and manipulative he might be, but a candidate for murder and suicide was out of the question. Ralph was basically a coward – all bullies were. 'Just promise me something, Louise,' she began.

'What?' Her tone was wary.

'Promise me you'll think about what I've said while you're here on Bellbird. This is a chance to take stock, Louise. A chance to live beyond his shadow. I think you'll find that life isn't so terribly complicated without him – not with the family behind you.'

Louise sniffed and rolled over. 'Goodnight,' she muttered.

Fiona lay there in the moonlight, wide-awake and restless. She would have to be satisfied for now, but perhaps the coming days would show Louise the strength in the real, undemanding love of her family, and make her question her motives for staying in a marriage that was slowly making her invisible.

Bellbird Station was wreathed in early morning mist as Jake stepped out of the wooden shack and watched Eric stalk through the long grass. He stretched and breathed in the

222

crisp, clean air before hitching up his pyjama trousers. It was time to leave. The search for the deeds could take some time and if they were found – which he doubted – then he had no qualms about putting the case forward. Yet Miriam had made it plain, that either way, she expected him to prepare the papers and lodge them with the courts, and he could only do that in Brisbane.

He ran his hand over his chin and grimaced. He needed a shave and a shower, and this might go part of the way to banish the cobwebs of a restless night. He grabbed his towel and wash kit and headed for the men's bathroom block at the back of the cookhouse. Standing beneath the needle sharp gush of hot water, he let the force refresh him. Yet his mind refused to let him relax, and he finally turned off the tap and wrapped a towel around his waist.

He smeared the condensation from the flyblown mirror and began to shave. His short stay on Bellbird had brought back memories of his youth, and especially of his mother and grandmother. Miriam had crept into his heart despite her sharp tongue and demanding ways, and the news of her illness had come as a terrible blow. He seemed fated to lose the people he loved the best.

His hand stilled and he stared at his reflection in the mirror. Why should he care so much about a stranger? Why did Mim and her family have to complicate his life? He'd liked it fine before making his way out here. His career was progressing well, and he'd been made a partner in the law firm only last year. Now he was about to do something that could wreck everything – just for the sake of one recalcitrant old woman who probably wouldn't even thank him for it.

He shook his head as if to dismiss the dark thoughts and carried on shaving.

Miriam wouldn't be the only one he'd miss, he realised with a jolt as he strode through the door and found Fiona waiting for him. 'G'day,' he said with an over-cheerful smile as he clung to the towel around his waist and prayed it would remain in place.

'How y'goin'?' she replied as her gaze swept from his bare feet to the towel and up to his naked chest.

'Good,' he stammered as he tried to edge past her. 'Find anything yet?' Why was it that the women in this place had a habit of catching him on the hop, he thought as he juggled with wash bag, towel and discarded pyjama trousers. He might have known he'd come a cropper – why the hell hadn't he put his pyjamas back on?

Fiona blocked his way. She squinted in the early sunlight and was obviously trying not to laugh at his discomfort. 'Nothing that will help Gran's case,' she said with that throaty texture to her voice that shot bolts of electricity through him.

Jake felt foolish standing there buck-naked in the yard with only a strip of towelling between him and the loss of his dignity. 'Was there something you wanted?' he prompted. 'Only I'm in a bit of a hurry.'

She smiled up at him, her eyes bright with impish delight. 'Mim wants to see you,' she said unsteadily. 'But I suggest you put on your strides first. We aren't all impressed by the naked male form, you know.'

Jake reddened, grasped the towel and stalked back into the shack. He could hear her giggle as she walked away. 'Bloody women,' he muttered as he pulled on strides and shirt and cleaned his feet. 'How come they know just how to make a bloke feel like a complete drongo, when all a bloke's trying to do is get clean?'

It wasn't until he was dressed and booted and halfway across the yard to the homestead that he saw the humour in the situation. He smiled and rubbed his chin as he climbed the steps to the verandah. Fiona might have said she wasn't impressed, but he'd noticed the gleam in her eyes when she'd looked him over. Perhaps it wasn't all bad.

The family were in the kitchen eating breakfast. An instant silence greeted his arrival and Jake saw the looks of merriment pass between Chloe and her daughters. So Fiona had told them, he thought in despair. He heard the muffled giggles, felt the heat rise in his face and turned swiftly to help himself to a cup of tea.

Miriam broke the silence. 'Take no notice of them,' she ordered. 'It's only a bit of fun – and you should be pleased you've brightened their day.'

'Comes to something when a bloke can't take a shower in peace,' he muttered.

'Fair go, Jake,' exclaimed Fiona. 'You asked for it, going into the yard like that.'

'You can bet I won't be doing it again,' mumbled Jake as he chewed toast.

Miriam fixed him with a beady glare. 'I need to talk to you in private,' she said. 'When you've finished breakfast, come into the other room.'

An hour later Jake had packed the utility and was on his way. As he closed the final gate and climbed back into the ute, he eyed the package on the seat next to Eric. Miriam had given him an awesome responsibility. He just hoped he was worthy of her trust.

They spent the next week sifting through the endless boxes. Miriam had found letters and photographs she'd forgotten about, and had wasted time poring over them, explaining them to the family and reminiscing. She was surprised at how much of the contents in the cases and boxes were her own, and it was like unearthing a treasure trove of memories.

Here was an old photograph album with scenes from the mining camps, and faces long forgotten. There were diaries she'd written in those early days in Sydney, and the ones she'd kept here on Bellbird during the dark days of both world wars. She set them aside to read later, for her family didn't need to know the personal details of her life – the heartache and sorrow she'd experienced – for she'd found consolation in those diaries during the long, lonely nights.

Chloe dreamily unfolded the tiny baby clothes that had been stored in tissue paper in a trunk, and shed a tear as she found the girls' first shoes, their christening gown and the feather light shawl the three of them had once been wrapped in. Fiona and Louise unearthed favourite toys and books, arguing happily over who had owned what and remembering similar fights they'd had as children.

Leo sat contentedly in the middle of the chaos, a glass of brandy at his side as he sifted through old newspapers that proclaimed the death of Victoria, the abdication of Edward and the crowning of George. 'An entire century mapped out,' he rumbled as he carefully turned the pages of a wartime issue. 'You should store these properly, Mim. They could be worth something one day.'

Miriam shrugged. 'Have them if you want,' she said. 'They're of no use to me.'

'Look what I've found,' said Louise as she pulled a box from the bottom of the case. 'I wonder what's in it?'

Miriam leaned forward. She recognised that box. It had once held chocolates. 'That was mine,' she said quietly as she reached for it. 'I kept my special things in it for safe-keeping. I didn't realise I'd put it up in the attic.'

'Open it then,' said Fiona eagerly.

Miriam lifted the lid and felt a tug of sadness. The letters were still there, tied with ribbon, and yellowed by the passing years. She lifted them out and held them to her face. She could still smell the lavender she'd kept with them.

'What else is in there?' Louise came to kneel beside her.

Miriam put the precious letters in her lap. She didn't know if she had the courage to read them again, for they would only serve as a reminder of the anguish, the lost hope, the devastating finality of this circle of life they all had to join. She returned to the contents of the box, wishing it had not been found – for the memories it had evoked were suddenly more real than the present.

'Here's something you might find interesting,' she said as she gathered up the smaller package. The ribbon was faded, the thick vellum of the envelopes brittle to the touch. 'Be careful with them, they're very delicate,' she warned as Louise took them.

'Bloody hell,' breathed Fiona as the contents of the envelopes were revealed. 'These have to be worth a small fortune, Mim. Why on earth have you hidden them away all this time? Stuff like this at auction has gone for hundreds of thousands of dollars.'

Miriam retrieved them and put them with the letters. 'The ultimate price has already been paid,' she said softly. She ran her fingers gently over the brittle reminders of a time when life had seemed infinite. She'd been so young, so happy – but the shadows were already darkening the sky and all too soon her world had been plunged into night.

Edward stayed on Bellbird for almost eight weeks. Apart from a few mundane conversations and the exchange of shy glances as he and Miriam worked together, Kate and George had made sure there had been little chance for them to be alone. Now his contract was finally at an end and he would be leaving tomorrow.

Miriam waited until Kate was occupied in the kitchen and George was in his usual chair on the verandah smoking his evening pipe. She brushed her hair until the curls shone like the wing of a crow, then slipped out of her window and ran barefoot through the grass to the paddock behind the stables.

What she was doing was against all the rules, yet she had to know if Edward felt the same as she – and the only way to find out was to ask him.

Edward was sitting beneath a coolibah tree, the Stetson pushed back from his forehead as he smoked a cheroot and watched the grazing horses. He got to his feet as Miriam came round the corner of the stables. 'Evening, ma'am,' he drawled as he tipped his hat and stamped out his smoke with the heel of his boot.

Miriam hesitated. Was she about to make a complete fool of herself? Edward seemed mildly pleased to see her, but was that enough? She dug her hands in the pockets of her working trousers and decided she had nothing to lose but her

227

pride. Better to know the truth and be done with it. 'I came to say goodbye,' she said finally.

'That's mighty nice of you, little lady,' he replied. He smiled and indicated they should share the grassy patch beneath the tree. 'Set and talk awhile,' he offered. 'That's if you've a mind to?' He turned so he could look directly into her eyes.

Miriam's pulse raced and she was certain he must be able to hear the thud of her heart banging against her ribs. She ran her hands over her rough trousers, her eyes downcast. 'I reckon I would,' she managed.

He gave a soft laugh and leaned back on his elbow. His eyes were violet in the deepening shadows, the cleft in his chin emphasised by a day's growth of beard. 'I guess we didn't have much chance of talking before,' he said softly. 'And that's a shame. Don't you think?'

She saw him raise a brow. Noticed the colour of his eyes and the way his mouth moved when he talked. 'Yeah,' she murmured. She began to pluck the grass and twist it in her fingers. 'Will you be coming back?' she asked. Hope was interlaced with fear as she waited for his answer.

He remained silent, his eyes fixed upon her with a strange intensity. 'I'm a drifter, Miriam,' he said softly. 'Just a no-good old boy who happens to have a way with mustangs.' His hand covered her fingers, stilling them. 'It's better we leave it at that.'

Miriam thought her heart would break as the full meaning of his rather sweet rejection hit her. 'You know how I feel, don't you?' she asked as she blinked away the tears. 'I'm sorry to be such a fool, but I thought you felt the same.'

'I never said different,' he murmured. 'But I ain't what you might call reliable.' His face was very close to hers and she could feel the magnetism of him. 'Your mom and dad don't approve of me, and they have every right. I'm a nomad, Miriam. A man who likes nothing better than to ride free. Your folks have other plans for a lady like you.'

He cupped her chin with his fingers and drew her close

228

until they were a breath apart. Fiona noticed the tiny freckles that dusted his nose, and the way his eyes were prisms of many shades of blue. 'I don't care what they think,' she breathed. 'Or what plans they have. I want to be with you.'

He gave her a fleeting kiss and drew away. Standing, he slapped his hat against his thigh and then placed it back on his head. 'I care,' he said as he firmly looked out over the pasture. 'There ain't no profit in trying to change things, Miriam. I ain't ready to settle yet.'

Miriam softly followed the curve of her mouth with her finger. She could still feel that kiss. It was as if she'd been branded. 'So you do feel something?' she persisted.

He finally turned to look down at her as she sat there on the grass at his feet.

'Oh, yes,' he breathed.

Then he was suddenly all business and bustle. He pulled her to her feet and then turned his back. 'But we'll both get over it,' he said firmly before walking away.

Kate was on the verandah six months later, finishing the last of her letters so they would arrive before Christmas. She still wrote home frequently and kept in touch with her wide-spread family. They were all married now, but for her baby brother who'd recently taken his vows and joined the priest-hood. How sad it was that Mam and Da were no longer alive – for they would have been so proud of all of them.

The slums of Dublin were far behind each of them as they followed Kate's example and went out into the world. Now there were three sisters in America, two in Canada and a brother making a name for himself as a master carpenter in London. Another sister had married an Italian and was living in Venice, happily running a hotel and looking after her large brood of children.

She sat there, the stack of letters set to one side as she thought about the years since she'd left home, and the changes those years had wrought. From maid to partner in a business – from a single woman to a wife and mistress of

Bellbird Station, her progression through life had given her so much.

Wealth had eased things after Isaac died and left her everything, but not the loneliness, and after Henry's untimely disappearance she'd invested all her love in Miriam, his child. Then George had come into their lives and she realised she had never really loved before – not so deeply, so trustingly – and her one regret, a deep ache that refused to leave her, was that they'd had no children together.

Her gaze drifted over the paddocks, the stables and holding pens. Bellbird Station had become her sanctuary, her home, and although her life here was ordered and happy, she could still feel the pull of adventure. There were so many places she had yet to see and explore – so many journeys yet to be made – and in the past few weeks she'd come to realise that Bellbird was in danger of becoming her prison. So she'd begun to make plans, secret plans that she would reveal as soon as they were complete.

She hugged her waist and grinned. How surprised George would be when she showed him what she'd done – and how exciting to have the opportunity to shop in a city again, for she would need a whole new wardrobe, and there was nothing Kate liked more than shopping for clothes and shoes and hats. It was all very well grubbing about in working clothes every day, but now and again she longed to be feminine.

On the edge of her vision she caught a movement. It was Mim, carrying water buckets to the stables, head down, shoulders drooping.

Kate sighed. If only love at that age wasn't so painful, she thought. It had been six months of agony for the girl, surely she must soon come to realise it wouldn't have worked between them? Edward had been wise beyond his years by turning her down, and although Kate was sad for Mim, she was grateful to the young American for leaving. Next year they would hire another breaker – an older man with a wife and several children to support.

Kate left the shade of the verandah and was busy hoeing weeds in the vegetable patch with Miriam when they heard a rider approach.

Shielding her eyes from the sun Miriam watched the visitor slow his horse to a trot and then a walk. It was only as he drew out of the watery mirage that she recognised him.

'Edward,' Miriam said politely. 'We weren't expecting you.'

He climbed down from his horse and took off his hat. 'I had to come back, ma'am,' he said to Kate. Then his gaze drifted to Mim who was standing beside her. 'You see I left something very precious behind.'

Kate looked at Miriam's face and saw hope in her eyes and joy in the colour of her cheeks. She regarded Edward, ready to send him packing, but recognising the look in his eyes, remained silent. Miriam was old enough to make her own choices.

'We check the bunkhouse regularly,' said Miriam hesitantly. 'There was nothing there. Certainly nothing of value.'

'I've found it,' he said softly. 'Right here in front of me.'

Miriam looked up at him. 'Oh,' was all she could manage.

'Miriam Beecham, I have come back for you. I can't promise that life will be easy with me, but I will love and cherish you until I die.' His hair glinted fire in the sunlight as he knelt in the dirt and took her hands. 'Will you marry me, Miriam? Will you put your trust in me and make me happy again? For I'm lost without you.'

Miriam swayed on her feet, the tears rolling down her face as she placed her hand against his cheek. 'Yes, oh yes,' she breathed.

Kate moved away as the two young people embraced. They wouldn't miss her, she realised as she hurried back to the homestead. Probably had no idea of even where they were at this moment. She felt the emotion rise and brushed away the tears, for the moment had reminded her of when she'd finally accepted George's proposal.

'Edward's back,' she said breathlessly as she caught up

231

with her husband on the back verandah. 'He's proposed to Mim and they're spooning out in the vegetable garden.'

George laughed and slapped his thigh. 'Good on 'em,' he said. 'I knew that boy had brains.' He dropped the newspaper he'd been reading and stood up. 'This calls for a celebration. Break out the champagne, Kate.'

'Don't you think you're being a bit hasty?' she asked. 'Edward's a horse-breaker. Mim will either be left alone while he goes walkabout from job to job, or she'll become a gypsy and follow him. It's no kind of life for the girl – and she's too young.'

George took her hands and nuzzled her cheek. 'I'll never forget the look on your face when you first came here,' he said softly. 'I was so afraid you'd turn around and walk away.' He put a finger under her chin and made her look him in the eye. 'But you didn't. You and Mim rolled up your sleeves and made the best of things. And that's what Mim will do now.'

Kate looked away from him, the tears blinding her. 'I suppose so,' she said grudgingly. 'But I was hoping for so much more for her.'

George slipped his arm around her waist and held her close. 'You mean the Taylor boy?' His laughter rumbled in his chest. 'That was never coming to anything, my darling girl. The Taylors are set on him marrying the Pearsons' daughter. Their properties share the same boundaries and it makes good sense to form an alliance between the two families.'

Kate stepped away from his embrace. 'You men have no romance in your soul,' she muttered. 'Alliances, land, shared bloody boundaries. My girl wants to marry a Texan drifter.'

'Hush, Kate,' he whispered as he drew her back into his embrace. 'If that's what she wants, then we must give her our blessing. She's become my daughter too, you know – and I don't want to see her as unhappy as she has been these last few months.'

He took out a handkerchief and dabbed at her tears.

'Now come on, let's celebrate and plan a Christmas wedding.'

Much to Kate's disappointment, neither of the youngsters wanted a fancy wedding in the city, choosing instead to arrange for the priest to marry them on Bellbird Station. Edward's parents declined the invitation, citing difficulties in making the long journey, but made up for their absence by sending a large parcel containing two hand-crafted Mexican saddles with silver-tipped pommels that were much admired by the drovers.

The verandah was decked in flowers and ribbons, the floor swept and covered in a red carpet. A small altar had been set up on a table at one end, and an odd assortment of chairs had been placed at the other for their guests. The wedding breakfast would be taken on the grass beneath the spreading poinciana tree in home pasture, and the dancing would follow in the marquee.

Miriam stood in bridal white beside Edward as they exchanged their vows and he placed the ring on her finger. Her dress had been especially made in Sydney, along with the satin shoes and the gossamer veil. She carried a spray of roses from Kate's garden that were still spangled with dew despite the rising heat.

She looked into his eyes and repeated the vows, knowing this was the man she would grow old with. This was the man of her heart, the father of their unborn children. And she loved him so much it almost hurt.

There were a lot of guests, for a wedding was an occasion to meet old friends and make new ones – an opportunity to gossip and swap rumours and pick out partners for their offspring. The outback was a vast world within the shores of Australia, but the community was small and tightly knit.

When the champagne had been drunk and the cake cut, Edward led Miriam on to the specially laid dance floor beneath the marquee. The musicians soon had everyone on their feet and it was almost four in the morning before Kate could make her surprise announcement.

'As Mr and Mrs Strong have decided not to have a honey-moon,' she began. 'I have decided we should leave them in peace for a while and to let my own husband into a little secret.'

She turned to George who was sitting beside her trying to get his breath back from a particularly fast polka. 'We shall be leaving Bellbird for a couple of years, knowing that Mim and Edward will take good care of it in our absence.'

'Leaving?' spluttered George. 'Where are we going for two years, woman? What contorted plans have been made up in that wild Irish head of yours?'

'You'll find out soon enough, George. Now be quiet and let me finish.'

This statement was greeted with laughter and cheers and everyone had another drink. It was some time before she could bring them back to order.

'I've decided it's been long enough since I've seen my family,' she told the audience. 'We shall be leaving Sydney harbour in three weeks time and will visit Singapore, Ceylon, Aden, Port Said and Lisbon where we will disembark and join the Orient Express. After visiting the South of France and Venice, we will go to London to see my brothers. Then we will sail to Ireland for a short break before returning to London again for a very special engagement.'

She smiled down at a bemused George. 'We will then sail to America to visit not only the rest of my family, but Edward's as well.' She raised her glass. 'To the future,' she said clearly into the stunned silence. 'Or as a very good friend of mine once used to say – *l'chaim* – to life.'

Miriam and Edward joined a speechless George. 'When did you plan all this?' she asked in amazement.

'I started long before Edward came back here and proposed,' said Kate with a giggle. 'I suddenly realised I hadn't seen all the things I wanted to see, or done all the things I wanted to do.'

'But, the money . . .' George protested. 'It must be costing a fortune.'

Kate shrugged. 'Can't take it with you, George. Why not have some fun while we still can? You never know what's around the corner.'

Miriam looked at Kate and recognised the glint of secrecy in her eyes. 'What's the special engagement in London, Kate?' she said and laughed. 'Or is that private? For George's ears only?'

Kate sipped her champagne, making them wait for just long enough to bring protests. She finally put down the glass and opened the beaded evening bag that hung from her wrist. With the flourish of a magician, she drew out a letter and two ornate tickets.

'I've booked passage on a very special ship to take us to America,' she said in a breathless rush. 'It's called the *Titanic*.'

Chapter Thirteen

Miriam replaced the postcards and letters Kate and George had sent home during their epic tour back in the chocolate box and closed the lid. 'I remember how excited Edward and I were when we got them,' she said. 'Kate and George had visited so many places, had seen so much and forged such friendships during their long tour, that these mementoes can never be replaced. They come from an age that sadly, will never return.'

'But the tickets, and the headed notepaper from the *Titanic* are worth a fortune, Mim,' protested Louise. 'If you don't want to sell them, then at least make sure they're insured and put somewhere safe.'

Miriam put the box on the table beside her. 'They're probably covered on the property insurance, and as no one knows I have them – and we live out in the middle of nowhere – I'm unlikely to get burgled.' She smiled at them. 'When it's your turn to look after them, you can make your own arrangements.' She paused. 'In fact, if you're so concerned, why don't you take them back with you when you return to Brisbane? They'll soon be yours anyway.'

Louise looked stricken. 'That wasn't what I meant,' she protested.

Leo came to her assistance. 'I think we'd all feel easier if they were placed in a fireproof safe, or something similar,' he rumbled. 'A bushfire's quite likely, as you well know.'

Miriam had tired of this conversation. 'I suggest we pack this trunk again and return it to the attic. It's obviously most of my junk, and unless you wanted anything in particular, it can all stay where it is.'

A threadbare teddy was plucked out by Louise, and a couple of books retrieved by Fiona. Leo stacked the old newspapers carefully and wrapped them in brown paper, whilst Chloe regretfully folded the baby clothes again and placed them back in the trunk. Then the trunk was hauled out of the room and put in the hall until Frank could help Leo get it back up the steep ladder and into the attic.

'Right,' said Mim. 'Why don't you all clear off and do something else? I need to have a bit of a rest and we've done enough for now.'

Chloe was instantly concerned. 'Don't you feel well, Mum? I told you all this was too much.'

'Not at all,' Miriam lied. 'I'm perfectly fine. It's a beautiful day, so why don't you and Leo go for one of your walks, like you did when you were courting?' She turned to the girls. 'There's a couple of horses needing some exercise. Go on, clear off and leave me in peace. Tea will be yesterday's leftovers, so we can help ourselves when we're ready.'

She waited for them to finish their protests, but could see the idea was already appealing and they were eager to leave the house. Her daughter and granddaughters had never been the kind to sit indoors on such a day, and she was pleased with herself for having thought of a way to get rid of them.

When they had gone she took another two pills and washed them down with a slug of whisky. The combination was probably lethal, but what the hell, she thought. I'm dying anyway.

Her bedroom was glowing with the diffused light that poured through the muslin curtains. Miriam placed the chocolate box next to the Harlequin and Columbine music box on the dresser, then slumped on to the bed and with a sigh of relief collapsed into the pillows. She would read the letters tonight, when she could be sure of no interruption, but

237

for now she needed to rest. The pain was making her weary, constantly nagging and pulling at her, drawing her down.

She closed her eyes and willed the medicine to kick in. The last few days had been too much, she admitted silently. Perhaps she was tempting fate by trying to achieve everything before she went. And yet it was unfinished business and her orderly mind wouldn't allow her to leave things undone.

Miriam sighed as she thought of those letters from Kate. They had arrived long after the priest had delivered the terrible news that neither of them had survived, and it had been some time before she'd been able to pluck up the courage to read them.

Kate had sounded so happy, so excited, so in awe of the unsinkable floating palace. She'd described their stateroom and the magnificent ballroom, and was looking forward to dinner that night at the captain's table before they docked in Ireland. How tragic that it should all have come to an end in a freezing ocean. The only consolation was that they had died together, yet that knowledge hadn't assuaged the pain and the void they had left behind.

Edward had been her anchor during those dark days. He'd dealt with the banks and the solicitors and had taken on Frank as a manager to help run Bellbird. His days of nomadic horse-breaking were over.

Kate's will had been drawn up along with George's before they'd left Sydney. Had she known she would never return, Mim wondered, or was it just Kate being organised? She liked to think it was the latter, for Kate had been so joyous when she'd left Bellbird for the last time. Miriam inherited Bellbird as well as Kate's fortune, but in her sorrow she hadn't realised the significance of the old music box, or the letter she'd found in Kate's desk.

This letter was a personal message to Mim, telling her how much she loved her, and how proud she was of her. On the last page, Kate had added that she had a surprise gift for Mim's twenty-first, which would be celebrated after their

238

return. She didn't say what it was, merely hinted the music box had something to do with it.

Miriam found nothing in the music box and, assuming Kate hadn't actually done anything yet about her birthday, had tucked the letter away with the rest of Kate's belongings out of sight, but never really out of mind, in the attic. The memories were still too vivid, the pain of their departure still too raw. She had to learn to get on with her life – and she could only do that if she focused on the future and Edward.

Miriam dozed, but her thoughts refused to let her rest, and as the pain finally ebbed, she climbed off the bed and fetched her hat and boots. Lying here thinking morbid thoughts wouldn't do any good, she realised, as she picked up her rifle. She too needed to get out into the sunshine and enjoy this perfect day.

Having checked the rifle was loaded, she wondered if perhaps she could bag a roo. It had been a long time since she'd gone hunting, and it might be fun to give it one last try. Striding into the stable-yard, she almost collided with Frank as he emerged from the tack room. 'Tack up Old Blue,' she said, ignoring his horrified face. 'I'll get the buggy.'

'You'll do no such damn thing,' Frank muttered. He grabbed a passing stable-lad. 'Get the buggy out for Mrs Strong, and make sure the wheel's safe.' He turned back to Miriam. 'If it isn't, then you're not going,' he said firmly.

She looked up into his lugubrious face and tried not to smile. Dear Frank, he acted like a father, but in fact there were only a few months between them. 'I checked the other day,' she told him. 'The wheel's been fixed.'

Old Blue was a chestnut trotter who, in his time, had won many races both here and in America where harness racing was popular. Now he was just one of the many old horses Miriam didn't have the heart to sell off or put down. He shook his head and opened his mouth to display tombstone teeth in a horse laugh, as Miriam held the bridle and waited while the lad fixed the harness and buggy into place.

'Silly old bugger,' she said fondly as she fed him an apple. 'You can see the funny side of all this, even if Frank can't.'

'You're crook, Mim,' muttered Frank as he tugged the brim of his hat in frustration. 'You got no darn business in a buggy. Blue might be old, but he still gets the wind in his nose and plays up. You ain't got the strength to hold him back no more.'

Miriam ignored him, placed the rifle in the leather sheath at the side of the buggy and climbed up. It was an ancient memento from the early days, and much like the one George had used to bring them here that first time. The once shining red leather was cracked from heat and use, the wood needed a new coat of varnish and the springs creaked arthritically with rust. Miriam thought it suited her purpose well, for they were of an age, and neither of them in a fit state to go very far.

'Which way did the others go?'

Frank rammed his hands in his pockets and stared balefully at her. 'Chloe and her husband went off over that way and the girls have taken the two mares down to the billabong.'

'In that case,' she said as she slapped the reins over Blue's hindquarters. 'I'm going this way.' She left the yard and headed out into the pastures.

The swish of the grass beneath Blue's hoofs joined the rhythm of the buggy's two wheels and the soft rasp of the springs. She adjusted her hat and leaned back against the padded leather. It was indeed the most glorious day, the sun bright but not too hot, the breeze cool without being cold. The pills and whisky had done their duty and the weariness swept away – all was right with her world. She urged the old horse to greater speed, relishing the feel of the sun and wind on her face, and the scent of the crushed grass rising from beneath his feet.

Blue also seemed to be enjoying this rare escape from the paddocks, and with his ears pricked and head erect he picked up the old familiar rhythm and trotted towards the distant hills that lay in a purple haze on the horizon.

Miriam looked around her, the reins loose in her hands. The Wet had brought the greenness back, and now the trees no longer seemed to wilt, and the outback pastures were a blaze of colour from the wildflowers that had appeared. It happened every year when the Wet arrived, and she never tired of the sight of those white and yellow daisies, the pink parakeelya and delicate spider orchids. Kangaroo paw waved red and green amongst the taller grasses, and here and there she could see the tiny blue stars of the royal bluebells that clustered beneath the slender and rather elegant gum trees.

She became suddenly aware that Blue was on a mission. He'd picked up speed and was racing across open country, heedless of the bumping and jouncing of the buggy he trailed. 'Whoa,' she shouted as she pulled on the reins. 'Slow down, you mongrel before you do us both a damage.'

Blue ignored her and didn't break stride.

Miriam felt a jolt of fear as she realised they were heading straight for the creek at the end of the open country. It was narrow, but steep-sided, and because of the buggy the old horse wouldn't be able to jump it.

She gripped the reins, hauling back on them until she thought her wrists would snap. 'Stop you bloody idiot,' she yelled. 'Whoa, there. Whoa!'

The creek glittered as it meandered its serpentine way through the narrow gully. Blue faltered. Miriam pulled hard on the left rein in an attempt to turn him. Then a white cockatoo shot out of a nearby tree, shrieking its fury at being disturbed.

Blue, half-turned from the creek, took fright and bolted.

Miriam, thankful that at least they weren't headed for the creek any more, held on grimly to the reins. She was being thrown about like a pea in a bottle, and knew that neither she, nor the buggy could take much more of this. All she could do was pray that the wheel had been fixed, and that Blue would soon run out of steam.

'Bloody, bloody hell,' she breathed through clenched teeth. 'If I come out of this I promise not to lie any more.' She ignored the fact this promise had been made many times over the years – and consistently broken.

Blue finally slowed and allowed Miriam to rein him in. She clambered down from the buggy and leaned against his heaving sides to get her own breath back. 'Stupid bugger,' she said crossly. 'Nearly killed the pair of us.'

Blue shook his head and showed his teeth before blowing a raspberry in her face.

'Come on, better get home before anything else happens today,' she muttered. 'Fair shook me up, you old bastard.'

They rode sedately back to Bellbird as if their outing had been entirely unadventurous, but Mim knew that the horse, the buggy and indeed, herself, would never do this trip again. It was an end to an era – and that made her sad.

Yet she refused to be brought low by her thoughts and looked forward to a cuppa and a lie down before tea. It wasn't until she steered the buggy into home yard, she realised how long she'd been away. The yard was silent and deserted, the men and horses out for the last ride of the day. The cook was probably at his stove, but he wouldn't be much use to her, he was as thin and feeble as she was. Even the black jackaroos seemed to have disappeared, she noticed crossly as she fumbled with the buckles and finally released Blue from the traces. After giving him a cursory rub-down, she set him free in home paddock and left the buggy for the men to haul back into the big barn – she'd had quite enough for one day.

With her rifle in her hand she paused a moment to catch her breath. It had been one hell of a ride and she was still trembling from the effort it had taken to stop Blue running away with her. Frank was right, she thought grimly. I'm a stupid old woman and I should learn to take advice. If that wheel had come off it would have been curtains – then she would never see justice done.

She leaned on the top rail of the corral and admired her surroundings, relieved she was still around to do so. The homestead had been freshly painted in honour of her birthday party, the corrugated-iron roof smart in its new coat of red. Vibrant lime pepper trees drifted their fronds over the roof and the amethyst jewels of a jacaranda gave shade to the verandah. The hum of bees was a soft backdrop to the dry rasp of the crickets and the chatter of the budgies and the scent of warm grass and eucalyptus filled the air with their delicious perfume.

Mim smiled and was thankful she would never see the inside of some dreadful old folk's home. This was where she belonged. She looked around at the deserted bunkhouse and cookhouse, at the barns and stables and the machinery shop. It was so still now the men were out with the horses – a rare moment of peace in what was usually a bustling environment.

A pair of mares grazed with their foals in the paddocks beneath the spreading poinciana tree as black swans flew overhead towards the billabong. The dogs yapped in the kennels, pigs grunted in the sties behind the stables and her vegetable garden was flourishing now the new boy had taken over. She had everything here, and if she dropped dead this minute she couldn't think of a nicer place to do it.

'Bit inconvenient at the moment,' she muttered as she began to walk towards the homestead.

Miriam was about to climb the steps up to the verandah when she caught sight of an unfamiliar utility parked in amongst the stand of trees on the far edge of home yard. The utility meant visitors. Uninvited visitors. For those who came on honest business wouldn't have tried to hide their presence.

She hesitated and glanced over her shoulder. The men hadn't returned and there was no sight of her family. She would have to deal with this alone.

Miriam had never known timidity and had lived her life following gut instinct. It had never yet let her down. She pulled back the bolt and cocked her rifle.

Grasping the railings, she hauled herself slowly up the steps to the verandah. The rifle was steady in her free hand and pointed at the screen door. She waited and listened for a moment, but all she could hear was the thud of her pulse. With her feet planted sturdily on the verandah, she waited to one side of the screen. 'Come out,' she ordered. 'Show yourself, or I'll shoot.'

There was a moment of silence, swiftly followed by the rasp of scurrying boot heels inside the homestead.

Miriam licked away the sweat from her top lip, but her hands remained steady on the rifle. There were at least two of them. 'Come out of there you thieving mongrels. Let me see you.'

The screen door slammed open and hit the homestead wall. Miriam's finger twitched on the trigger. A burly figure emerged from the gloom and ran straight into her, knocking her back against the railings. The blast of the shotgun echoed around the yard as Miriam's breath was punched from her lungs and she fell to the floor.

The bullet hit an overhead branch with a sharp snap and brought down a shower of leaves and twigs. Birds rose in startled flight, and shadowed the sun.

Miriam heard the pounding footsteps as the men ran down the steps and across the yard. She was on her back, dazed, breathless and utterly incensed. Stranded like a bloody turtle, she couldn't seem to get herself upright. Then anger gave her the strength and she rolled on her side, jammed a bullet up the chamber and fired off a second shot.

The recoil punched her shoulder and she cried out in pain and frustration. The bastards were getting away and there was nothing she could do about it but reload and fire until she'd run out of bullets.

She lay there cursing and furious as dirt kicked up from beneath the utility's wheels as it shot out of the yard. The bullets zipped and zinged but the utility was soon out of range and heading for open country.

Struggling for breath and determined not to be found in such humiliating circumstances, she used the last of her strength to grasp the old wicker chair and haul herself into it. Slumped against the cushions she fought to get her breath back and her pulse on an even keel. The shock, coming so swiftly after the hectic buggy ride, had just about done her in, and she ached in places she'd forgotten she possessed.

'If I'd been younger they wouldn't have got away with it,' she gasped as she watched the diminishing cloud of dust that followed the utility's trail. 'Bastards,' she hissed as she shook her fist at them. 'That's no way to treat an old woman.'

She closed her eyes. The shock had now set in and she felt more vulnerable than she had ever done. The pain in her back was awakening, flexing its fingers, drifting into her ribs and shoulder and the bruising on her hip. The enormity of what had happened brought tears and her hands trembled as she angrily brushed them away. Tears wouldn't solve the dilemma – neither would feeling sorry for herself – but by god she was scared.

The heat diminished along with the sun as Miriam returned to the verandah after calling the police. Yet the chill of foreboding had little to do with the dying day. Nothing like this had ever happened before – but then she hadn't begun a lawsuit against Dempster before. The two had to be connected.

Jake was sitting in his office, his mind far from his work as he stared out of the window on the sixteenth floor of the high-rise overlooking the river. Brisbane sparkled in the dying sunlight and as the lights came on in the houses on the south bank his thoughts drifted to Bellbird Station. He'd felt he'd been going home as he'd arrived there, and now he'd been drawn into Mim's family circle he couldn't resist thinking about them.

He smiled as he realised he was only fooling himself. It was Fiona who haunted his dreams as well as his waking hours. He kept seeing her smile, the way her hair became a halo when she stood against the light, and the soft, sensual giggle that curled his toes and did strange things to his insides. He sighed. His work was suffering, that was for sure, but he just couldn't get her out of his head.

He swivelled his chair back to face his desk. The papers had been drafted and filed at court, the summonses sent out despite his better judgement. And because of Miriam's frailty the judge had agreed to the preliminary hearing being held in a week's time. All he could do now was wait. If the deeds didn't show up, then the case would most likely be thrown out, and he would have to face Miriam with his first failure.

Deciding to finish for the day, he began to stack the files and return the law books to their rightful place on the shelves that took up three walls of his office. His secretary had already left, and the outer office was deserted. He would go home to Eric, eat a solitary dinner for one and then go out for a beer. He wasn't in the mood for a session in the gym, and certainly in no fit state to go for his usual run along the river bank.

The telephone rang as he was about to close the door behind him. It made him hesitate as he decided whether to answer it or not. It was the end of a long day, he was tired, fed up and slightly depressed – he didn't need any more to think about. Yet the quality of the ringing tone seemed to hold an edge of urgency. It was certainly demanding, he thought as he picked up the receiver on the twentieth ring. 'Jake Connor,' he snapped.

'It's Fiona.'

He smiled and was about to ask her how she was when she carried on with breathless urgency. 'We've had a break-in. Mim got hurt and they got away.'

He gripped the receiver. 'What did they do to Mim? Is she all right?'

'She's wound up like a clock, but apart from a few bruises she's assured us she's fine. But you know Mim, so we called the doctor, and he's on his way.' She giggled. 'Mim shot at them with her old hunting rifle. Even managed to reload twice. Unfortunately she didn't hit the bastards, and the damn thing has a kick like a mule. You should see the bruise on her shoulder.'

Jake smiled. 'Annie Oakley rides again,' he murmured. The old girl had guts, that was for sure. 'Did they take anything?'

'We can't tell, and the police were absolutely no help whatsoever.' Fiona's voice was sharp with frustration and anguish. 'It's as if a tornado has ripped through the house. Everything is everywhere, and we hardly know how to start clearing up. The police don't hold out much hope of catching anyone, there's a hundred back roads and tracks out here, they could be anywhere.'

'Slow down, Fiona,' Jake said firmly. 'Had you found the deeds, or anything else to do with the case?'

'No,' she replied flatly. 'But we've only been at it a week. There are still boxes and cases and a thousand other places to look yet.' Her voice broke. 'The deeds must have been what they were looking for when Mim disturbed them.'

'I only filed the papers in court this morning,' he said to reassure her. 'It can't have been anything to do with that. No one else knew what Mim was planning.' He thought of the package Mim had entrusted him with and breathed a deep sigh of gratitude for her forward thinking. At least that was safe.

'Burglaries aren't usual all the way out here,' she retorted. 'We're miles from anywhere and no thief in his right mind would raid a place like this when the risk of getting caught is so high. On a normal day there are at least thirty people around the property, and nearly always someone in the house.'

Jake didn't like the thoughts that were whirling in his head. 'Looking at it from that point of view, it certainly

247

appears to make sense,' he admitted. 'It sounds as if the place was being watched, and they struck at the optimum moment.' He paused. 'Where was everyone when this happened, Fiona?'

'Mim wanted us out of the house,' she said with a sniff. 'I think she was tired, and wanted a bit of peace. Louise and I went for a ride and Mum and Dad were off on a long walk.' Her voice wavered. 'Mim sneaked out and went off in the buggy with Blue, and because she got back while the men were out on the evening gallop there was no one there to help her. If only I hadn't insisted upon stopping for so long at the billabong. If only Mum and Dad hadn't decided to walk so far.'

'It's pointless trying to blame yourself,' he consoled. 'You couldn't possibly have known what was going to happen.'

'I know. But that doesn't make it any easier.' She paused and Jake heard her blow her nose before she spoke again. 'I reckon you could be right,' she said finally. 'If they had been watching the place, then that was the time to break in. Not that they would have had much trouble, the place is never locked up.'

'And as far as you can tell there's been nothing stolen? No valuable jewellery, none of that priceless china or the figurines?'

'Nothing.' Fiona sighed. 'And if they did find any evidence, we'll never know because they'll destroy it.'

Jake told her about the preliminary hearing in a week's time. 'I can't think how anyone else knew what Miriam was about to do – but if they did, then this robbery, or whatever it was, has proved something,' he said finally.

'What?' Her tone was sceptical.

'It proves that someone else thinks there must be proof against the Dempsters – and they were sent specifically to find it – why else go to all that trouble and risk?'

Her voice was excited at the other end of the line. 'So we could be closer than we think to getting justice for Mim?'

She fell silent for a moment. 'That's if they didn't find any-thing.'

The pitch of her voice rose. 'You'll have to come back. We need as much help as we can get, and you're the only one who might recognise something useful.'

'I can't just drop everything,' he protested as he riffled through his diary and tried to work out which cases could be passed on to the other partners, and which appointments he could change. Luckily he wasn't due in court for a few days, so it might be possible.

'Mim's asking for you,' Fiona said firmly. 'And as she's paying you, you can put it all down to expenses. We need you here, Jake.'

He couldn't resist.

Brigid Dempster-Flytte sat on the edge of the chair, her back straight, chin imperious as she listened to Brendt's part of the telephone conversation.

'They failed.' Her tone was flat as Brendt put down the receiver.

'Yes, damn it,' muttered her son as he shoved his hands into his trouser pockets and turned away to stare out to the ocean. 'They were disturbed by Miriam, and didn't have enough time to do a proper search.'

Brigid's thin eyebrows lifted. 'I would have thought two men could have handled someone like Miriam quite easily,' she stated coldly. 'Unless she's changed, she can't weigh more than a wet Pomeranian. Why didn't they just tie her up and get on with the search?'

Brendt gave a bark of laughter, it was harsh and held little humour. 'Miriam was shooting at them,' he said. 'Caught one of them in the thigh and punctured a hole in the radiator. They were lucky to make it to the nearest town.'

Brigid didn't care about the two men. They'd been paid well and understood the risks. 'I did warn you,' she said stiffly. 'Now we've shown our hand, there's no telling which way they'll jump.' She fell silent. 'We're no closer to finding the deeds. But they may already be lodged with her solicitor,' she said after a moment of thought. 'The deeds might not even be what we're looking for. Yet she has to have some proof of ownership, otherwise, why go to court? Get Black on to it.'

Brendt turned from the window, his face grim. 'Already have,' he said as he plucked a cigar from the humidor and peeled off the wrapper. 'But there's two ways to skin a cat, and I have a contingency plan.'

His mother smiled. It was always interesting to see how her son's mind worked, and it rarely disappointed her. 'Go on,' she said softly.

Brendt lit his cigar, then drew up a chair and sat beside her. When he'd finished speaking they sat and looked at one another in silence.

'It could just work,' breathed Brigid. 'And I'd love to see that bitch's face when she discovers how it was achieved.'

He smiled for the first time that morning. 'I knew you'd appreciate my plans, Mother.' He patted her hand before he stood and left the room.

Brigid stared up at the portrait of her father. Like her mother, Teresa, she'd never feared him, for she'd understood the workings of his mind, and had been a willing accomplice in his schemes. She smiled; a tight little smile that barely touched her lips. Paddy hadn't been as clever as he'd thought. The proof should have been found and destroyed years ago – now it could bring ruination.

She bit her lip as she remembered the last time she had seen Miriam and Kate at the diggings. If only she'd managed to find the deeds when she'd searched Miriam's tent. If only there had been time to go through Kate's things properly – but the blasted woman had packed up and gone so swiftly after Henry's disappearance that she'd had little chance of more than a cursory search.

Paddy had been furious, but there was nothing either of them could do. Then, as the years passed and there was no word from Kate, no demands for Miriam's share in the

Dempster fortune, they had assumed the deeds to be lost and they held no claim. Kate and Miriam disappeared from Sydney and it was to be many years later before Brigid recognised her in a newspaper photograph following her triumph in the Melbourne Cup.

Yet something had triggered off this lawsuit – and if it wasn't the deeds, then what the hell could it be?

With a deliberate effort, Brigid slowed her thoughts and examined them one by one. The memories of those long-gone days were clear, and she knew the clues had to be there. Perhaps, if she thought about that last day on the diggings more carefully, she might realise that an action, a previously discarded incident or casual conversation might prove to be the answer.

Her smile was grim. Miriam Strong would soon discover what a powerful enemy she had made, and Brigid was determined to see her silenced for good.

Chapter Fourteen

Miriam permitted the doctor to examine her, but remained silent as he gave her a long lecture about the stupidity of tackling intruders on her own, the dangers of drinking alcohol with strong painkillers and the sheer lunacy of riding out in an ancient buggy.

She folded her arms and waited until he'd finished. She'd known him a long time, and nothing he said would come as a surprise. In fact, she thought, he just liked the sound of his own voice.

Yet, when he finally left the homestead she sank into the pillows and gave in to the weariness, the shock and the pain. She was staring mortality in the face – had been forced to realise she couldn't do the things she had once found so easy – had finally accepted that if she was to see this court case through, she would have to slow down.

'But I'll never give in,' she muttered as she reached for the box of mementoes.

The letters were yellowed with age, the ink faded to ochre, the folds so delicate they were in danger of disintegrating. She left them in the box, her fingers lightly touching them as her eyes closed and she was transported back to a time when the sun was overshadowed by the threat of war.

Things had changed on Bellbird now Miriam and Edward were in charge. There were still vast mobs of cattle grazing the pastures, still the bustle and excitement of the annual round-ups and the long droves to market – but Edward had begun a new enterprise. His knowledge and experience of breaking horses was put to good use, and now he'd turned his hand to training.

Miriam had discovered a natural aptitude for dealing with these newly broken colts, and although the majority were sold to stockmen and drovers, some were kept on Bellbird and trained as racehorses. As word of their successes grew, Miriam and Edward put a breeding programme in place, and soon Bellbird gained a reputation for strong bloodlines and promising foals.

Frank married Gladys, whom he met at the picnic races in 1912, and their first child was born in the little wooden cottage Edward had had built on the outer fringe of home yard. This cottage was enlarged as twins arrived next, and Miriam wondered when it would be her turn to have the baby she so longed for.

After two miscarriages, Chloe was born on a hot summer night in February 1914. But the shadows were already looming over their outback Eden, for there was a great deal of unrest in Europe.

Edward was sitting at the kitchen table, poring over the newspapers that had finally been delivered that morning along with the mail. Like the letters, they were weeks old, for they were delivered by horse and wagon from the nearest mail centre, which was over two hundred and fifty miles away.

'It looks as if the entire world's in trouble,' he said as he folded back the page and placed the newspaper on the battered table. 'England has an Irish rebellion on their hands as well as a miner's strike. Germany is getting edgy over a possible French-Russian alliance, because the French are financing Russia's building of railways along the German borders. The Austrians are having more trouble in Bosnia-Herzegovina and are threatening to crush any Serbian agitation within their borders.'

253

'Kate always said a short, sharp war had a way of clearing the air and relieving the tension.' Miriam was feeding Chloe by the fire. The tug of that tiny mouth on her nipple sent waves of love and tenderness through her that banished all thought of the world outside Bellbird Station. 'And it's about time the Irish got their home rule.'

'I guess so,' replied Edward sounding unconvinced.

He stared into the fire and Miriam noticed how the light reflected in his hair, and how it softened the sharper contours of his face. She experienced a sudden yearning to touch him, and reached out. 'No worries, love,' she murmured. 'Europe's a long way from Bellbird. The world can fight its wars and squabble over boundaries as much as it pleases. We're safe here.'

'Not if the British decide to put in their two cents worth,' he replied.

She looked at him, startled by his vehemence. 'But why should it concern you, Ed? You're an American. Britain has no call on you.'

He grinned and his face lost the weary lines and became a youthful twenty-six again. 'I guess you're right, honey,' he said as he took her hand and kissed it. 'But we Texas boys are as downright ornery as any okker, and if there's to be a war, I ain't gonna sit it out here. I've lived in Australia for too long not to regard it as my home, my country.'

Miriam saw the glint in his eyes and felt a chill of foreboding.

That chill deepened just after her twentieth birthday.

On 28 June 1914, the Austrian heir apparent, Franz Ferdinand was murdered in Sarajevo, and four weeks later war was declared on Serbia. Russia mobilised with the Austria-Hungarian Alliance. Germany declared war first on Russia and then on France in August. Their invasion of neutral Belgium brought a demand from Britain to withdraw, and when this was ignored, they too declared war on Germany on 4 August.

Miriam was grim-faced as they sat in the drawing room

254

and listened to the news being relayed over the two-way radio. 'You can't go,' she said firmly as he finally cut the link between the outback stations. 'Our government has already passed a law so it can buy the national wheat and wool harvests – it'll only be a matter of time before the same will apply to the beef. I'm going to need you here.'

His blue eyes were dark and thoughtful as he stared out of the window to the yard. 'I've already had an order from the army for horses,' he said. 'Seems they can't get enough.'

'Don't change the subject,' she snapped. 'Why should we fight Britain's wars? We're a new federation, only fifty-eight years from our first democratic government. Britain expects too much.'

Edward stood and leaned on the mantelpiece. His ornately tooled boot scuffed at the ashes in the hearth. 'Germany poses a threat to world peace, honey,' he said with studied care. 'Britain and Australia have joint defences here – our army and navy have been trained by the Brits – and if Britain should be defeated we'll lose the Royal Navy's protection. Australia is too isolated. She will be easy prey.'

Miriam could see the logic in his argument but refused to be convinced. 'You've got important work here,' she said stubbornly. 'We'll have to increase the herd and I can't manage on my own – not with a six-month-old baby to look after.'

Edward came to kneel at her feet. He took her hands and briefly lifted them to his lips. 'America and Australia are very similar,' he began. 'But America has had her trial by fire in the civil war and can feel the pride of belonging to a special nation. Australia is still too new, has still to find a collective pride in nationhood, has never been tested by any real trial. This war will give us the chance to not only help the "Mother Country", as you call it, but to unite us as Australians.'

She looked at him, the bleakness of his message making her shiver. 'What you really mean is, you'll get some excitement out of it. It's an adventure – a way of confirming how

255

tough and brave you are and to hell with anyone else who just might give a damn.'

Edward grinned. 'There's that to it, I guess. But, Mim, my American heritage is the same as any Australian's. The pioneering spirit is as alive here, as it is in Texas. We take our resourcefulness from the backwoodsmen, the miners and ranchers, and grapple with our objectives even against authority. Our basic creed is that a man must stand by his mate – stand up for the weak no matter what. This war will be Australia's chance to show the world what we're made of, and in the process build ourselves into a great Nation that one day will stand up and be counted.'

Miriam remembered the terrible stories her father and Kate told her about their experiences at the hand of the English. She had no loyalties but to Australia. Her tears blinded her and she tore her hands away. 'England isn't my "Mother Country",' she rasped. 'And it's not yours either.'

She stood up and folded her arms around her waist as the tears finally rolled down her face. 'Don't go, Edward,' she whispered. 'Please don't go.'

His hands were gentle as he held her arms and turned her to face him. 'Would you prefer I stay here when my buddies are fighting in Europe? Would you be able to look the other women in the eye when they accuse me of cowardice? How will you feel when they hand me a white feather and shun us both when we go into town for our supplies?'

She looked up at him, the horror dredging the colour from her face. 'They wouldn't?'

'Yes,' he replied. 'They would. There are already stories in the newspapers of men shamed in front of their wives and families by an army of women determined to see they do their bit.' He took a deep, trembling breath. 'But that's not the point,' he added sharply. 'I'm going because I want to. My sense of duty to my country will not let me stay here and do nothing.'

She was about to protest when he silenced her with a fleeting kiss.

'I won't be gone for long,' he murmured. 'The war's expected to be over by Christmas.'

He held her close, drawing her into the circle of his arms until she rested her head against his chest. She could hear the steady rhythm of his heartbeat, could smell the scent of the stables in his clothes and the soap in his freshly washed hair.

'How can you be so sure?' she asked finally.

'Our world has changed rapidly over the last decade,' he said into her hair. 'Mobilisation, weaponry, the telegraph system and railways has made war a short affair.'

She pulled back from his embrace and studied him. 'How come you know so much?' she asked in awe.

He grinned shyly. 'I majored in history at college, so it's become a habit to read the newspapers from front to back, and listen to the news whenever I can. My family have always been interested in politics, so although you can take the boy out of Texas, you can't take Texas out of the boy – not when my Mom sends me reams of cuttings from political journals.'

'And I just thought you were a horse-breaker,' she teased as the tears threatened once more.

Fiona crept into the room and looked at the frail little figure on the bed. Mim appeared to be asleep, but there was a smile on her face as if her dreams were pleasant. She was about to close the door again when Mim's voice stopped her.

'Come in, darling. I'm awake and could do with the company.'

She felt a stab of remorse, but did as she was told. 'I didn't mean to wake you,' she said as she hovered beside the bed. 'I'm sorry. You looked as if you were having a lovely dream.'

'It was, and it wasn't,' she replied. 'But it's a dream I'll always have, so it doesn't matter if it's disturbed.' Miriam patted the bed. 'Sit down. Let's talk like we did in the old days. Or are you too grown up now?'

Fiona perched on the end of the bed, careful not to crush

257

her grandmother's legs. 'Never too old to forget the little girl inside,' she said softly. 'How are you feeling, Mim? Are you very sore?'

Miriam shrugged. 'I've felt better,' she admitted sourly. 'But enough about me. Have you found the deeds yet?'

Fiona shook her head. 'We've been through five boxes and several suitcases. There's nothing remotely connected to great-grandfather except a couple of old photographs, and some letters.'

Fiona looked down at her fingers. They were laced together on her lap, the square-cut nails bare of polish. 'They weren't very nice letters,' she said finally. 'I don't know why he kept them.'

'To remind him he was better off out here,' explained Mim as she struggled to edge up the pillows and find a more comfortable spot. 'He wrote to his mother quite often. Not directly, of course, but through his sister-in-law, Emma. Miriam would reply, telling him the family news, the local gossip and the state of affairs at Beecham Hall.'

'But his father never forgave him. He found out she was writing, and put a stop to it.' Fiona had read the simple note, and it had made her so angry she'd been tempted to tear it to pieces.

' "Your father has discovered my duplicity and has threatened to divorce me. I cannot disobey him as the scandal would see me in penury. But my love will always be with you, Mother," ' recited Mim. 'Father was heartbroken. His mother had always been so strong, but she'd become too old and frail to fight any longer – and knew she couldn't carry on now there was the threat of divorce hanging over her.'

'I'd have left the mongrel years before,' muttered Fiona.

'So speaks the modern woman,' said Mim tartly. 'It was different when I was a girl – even more so for Lady Miriam. Women had no voice, no money and no position once they lost their husband. She would have had to eke out her old age as a governess, or lady's companion – in other words, she

would have been a servant. Father understood. He could forgive her.'

Fiona was thankful this was the liberated 60s and women
were free to make their own choices in life. The mistakes
would happen, as they had with Louise – but hopefully she
would grow strong and see that escape was her only choice if
she was going to have a life free from Ralph's manipulation.

'Were you never curious about your English relations?
Didn't you ever want to go over there and see them?'

Miriam eyed her with surprise. 'Why would I want to do
that?' She gave a cough of disdain. 'They didn't want anything to do with my mother, and I certainly didn't want to
have anything to do with them,' she said icily. 'Even when I
had the money and the opportunity, it never crossed my
mind to try and make contact.'

Fiona knew she was pushing her luck, but the question
had been nagging her for years. 'Surely you had the right to
inherit, though?' she asked. 'Your birth was legitimate, the
marriage between Henry and Maureen legal – and going by
those letters from Miriam Beecham-Fford, Henry's brother
never did sire any legitimate children.'

Miriam sighed and closed her eyes. 'I suppose so,' she
said wearily. 'I never really thought about it.' She opened her
eyes and regarded Fiona sternly. 'There's more to life than
money – and anything they might have left would have had
my mother's blood on it. Now, if you've quite finished, let's
talk about something else.'

Fiona blushed and looked once more at her hands.
Stubborn pride ran deep within her family, and Mim had
probably turned her back on a fortune, but Fiona could
understand why. Blood money had never appealed to her
either.

'Ralph phoned,' she said, remembering the call earlier.
'Wanted to know how the search was going and when
Louise was returning to Brisbane. I ignored the question
over the search and told him she'd be back next week, for the
court hearing.'

259

'That girl's too thin,' Mim retorted. 'Do her good to get some country air into her lungs and some decent food inside her. Won't do her any harm to get away from Ralph for a while, either. Never did trust him.' She looked at Fiona from beneath her brows. 'And what about you?' she asked. 'Any special young man waiting for you in Brisbane?'

Fiona shook her head. 'Still young, free and single,' she said brightly. 'And aiming to stay that way too. I've got a lot of things I want to do before I settle down.'

'That's a shame.' Miriam's expression was bland. 'I was rather hoping you'd taken a shine to our Mr Connor.'

Fiona got up from the bed as the blush heated her face. She turned her back on Mim and looked out of the window to the pastures. 'I hardly know the man,' she said rather more sharply than she'd intended. 'Besides, isn't there a rule against lawyers and their clients getting involved?'

'That applies to doctors and patients,' retorted Mim.

The silence lengthened and Fiona stared out of the window and tried to think of something to say. Yet her mind was filled with images of dark hair and eyes, of a naked, muscled chest and lean hips. Just the sound of his voice on the phone had done strange things to her insides.

She made a concerted effort to pull herself together and turned from the window. 'Talking of Jake, I forgot to tell you I spoke to him last night. He's coming back to help us search. Should be here tomorrow morning.'

'That's nice, dear.'

Miriam's knowing smile irritated Fiona for some reason. She walked around the bed, and keeping her back to Miriam, picked up the music box. 'I've never seen this before,' she said. 'Where did it come from?'

Miriam told her about Isaac. 'It's a lovely thing,' she said as Fiona lifted the lid. 'And probably very rare. It's unusual to have a black Harlequin.' She sighed. 'It was too much of a reminder of the old days, so I put it away. I'd almost forgotten I had it until the other day.' She looked regretfully at the scar on the base. 'Such a pity I broke it – it will never be the same.'

Fiona watched the figures dance to the music. It was a haunting, bell-like refrain she could recognise only as a waltz. 'So this is where you found the hidden clue,' she murmured. 'Must have been quite a surprise.'

'You don't catch me out that easily, my dear,' said the old lady with a knowing smile.

Fiona suddenly had a nasty thought and she closed the lid with a snap. 'Where did you hide it?' she asked. 'The clue? The intruders didn't take it, did they?'

Miriam shook her head. 'I'm not stupid enough to leave something like that lying around,' she said calmly. 'It's quite safe. Jake has it.'

Fiona put the box carefully back on top of the dresser. 'You've put a lot of trust in him,' she said. 'How can you be sure he won't let you down?'

'Because I knew his father and his grandfather,' replied Mim.

'How? I thought he was a stranger?' Fiona plumped back on the bed and tucked her feet beneath her. This was an interesting piece of news and she wanted to learn more.

'He was at first,' she admitted. 'But as we got talking and I learned a few things about him, I realised why he'd reminded me so strongly of someone else.' She gave a little laugh. 'I thought it was your grandfather at first, then realised it was *his* grandfather.'

She smiled at the memories of the handsome, dark-eyed man she'd danced with at the various gatherings before Edward came into her life. 'He and I used to drove our stock together, and met frequently at the country dances and so on. We went to each other's weddings, and then I went to his son's. I remembered Jake as a small baby lying with all the others on the homestead bed when I held a party here once. Laid out like sardines in a tin they were, and so ripper you wanted to scoop them up and cuddle them. Jake was squalling fit to bust, quite red in the face and furious he'd been left.'

261

Fiona giggled. 'I bet he doesn't need reminding of that,' she spluttered.

Miriam eyed Fiona beneath her brows. 'You were about two or three at the time, and had taken it upon yourself to look after him. You picked him up, and I just caught him before you dropped him on his head.'

Fiona pulled a face in an effort to hide her giggles. She had no recollection of the event, but it was interesting to know they'd met before – interesting to discover she was actually older by a couple of years.

Miriam collected her thoughts. 'Jake's parents were regulars at the local country dances and parties, and I remember the shock we experienced when we heard she'd died. She wasn't much past thirty when she left those three little kids motherless. None of them were past nine years old at the time.'

Fiona digested this information and felt a tug of pity for the little boy bereft of his mother at such a tender age. 'Poor Jake,' she murmured.

Miriam seemed to be tiring, for she slid back down the pillows. 'Give me my pills, dear,' she ordered. 'I think I'd like to sleep now.'

Fiona held the glass of water to her mouth as she swallowed the tablets, then plumped the pillows and tucked the sheet under her chin. 'Mim,' she said hesitantly. 'I don't want you to die. Please say this was all a terrible mistake and that you'll be with us for ages yet.'

Miriam took her hand. 'I wouldn't lie about something like that, my darling,' she said softly. 'Let's just make the most of the time we have, and not waste them with tears.'

Fiona bent to kiss the soft cheek, and Miriam gripped her arm with surprising strength. 'Follow your heart, darling,' she whispered. 'That never lies either.'

Miriam settled into the pillows. She was exhausted, but it had been good to talk to Fiona. Good to get certain things off her chest. She smiled as she remembered the girl's face when she'd talked about Jake – her instinct hadn't failed her, even if her body had. Fiona and Jake might not remember their childhood meetings, but she was certain that a spark had been lit, even then. Now, as adults, perhaps they would find it again.

The letters were still lying in the box beside her on the bed, and as sleep overcame her, she felt Edward's presence, heard his voice and knew he was still with her – waiting just out of sight until it was time to join him.

The buggy had been polished and the leather seat waxed to a shine. The horse had been groomed until his coat gleamed in the early sunlight, and she could hear the jingle of the harness, even from the bedroom.

Miriam stood in front of the pier glass and eyed her reflection. The long skirt and neat little jacket were the palest grey, a disastrous colour for the long, dusty journey ahead, but it was her best suit, and she wanted to look well for Edward. She flounced the waterfall of lace at her throat before pinning Kate's cameo brooch on the neck of her blouse, and screwing the pearl studs on to her earlobes.

Edward came to stand behind her, his arms holding her around the waist so she had to lean against him. He kissed her ear. 'You look even more beautiful than on your wedding day,' he murmured.

Miriam closed her eyes, willing herself not to cry. It was hard enough for him to go, but to see her distraught would make it worse. 'I'm going to miss you,' she replied softly. 'Promise me you'll take care and come back as soon as you can.'

He turned her within the circle of his arms and looked into her face. 'I promise to never stop loving you,' he said before he kissed the tip of her nose. 'Now, come on, or we'll never get to Baringun in time.'

Miriam picked up Chloe and they left the house. She'd noticed Edward's clever evasion, but said nothing. For how could he make such a promise when fate held the only key to their future?

The horse stamped and snorted in the chill of the early outback morning, and Frank held tightly to the throat strap to stop him running off. 'G'day,' he drawled. 'Reckon it's gunna be dry for your journey.'

Miriam grasped his hand for a moment and looked up into his long face. Frank would be leaving soon, and apart from a few older men there would only be women and children left on Bellbird until war was over. 'When are you going, Frank?'

He took off his hat and smeared his forehead with his shirtsleeve. 'Reckon I'll be leaving next week,' he drawled. 'Me and the missus is going down to Burke to visit with her family for a few days, then I'll be going up to Baringun on me own.'

Miriam climbed up into the buggy, her emotions in such turmoil she could no longer speak. She placed Chloe in the large wicker basket on the floor and watched through her tears as the two men shook hands.

'See yer, mate,' rumbled Frank.

Edward nodded, his brown hair glinting copper lights. 'You too, mate,' he replied.

Frank's wife, Gladys came out of the cottage with a baby on each hip. The eldest little girl peeked from behind her skirts. She drew a handkerchief from the waistband of her skirt and dabbed her nose, gave a swift wave and went back into the shadows of the house.

Edward climbed up beside her and took up the reins. He sat there for a long moment, looking at the house, the yards, the pastures and the stables, then without a word, he slapped the reins over the horse's rump and they were off. It would take all day to get to Baringun.

The sun was already setting when they finally drove down the dirt street to the hotel. Firebrands had been erected on either side of the street and they cast an eerie, dancing glow over the milling crowds. Cheerful bunting slapped in the wind, and the noise coming from the hotel bar could be heard at the other end of the street. Women holding placards

264

urged the men to fight for the flag – the British Union Jack – their voices raised against the demon drink and cowardice. Posters were plastered on shop fronts along the boardwalk, and every window displayed a picture of the King.

Edward steered the horse around the back of the hotel to the stables, and they climbed down. As the grooms hurried to release him from the buggy, the horse drank deeply from a bucket of water, and shook off the sweat of their long journey.

Edward patted his neck and ruffled his mane, muttering to him, saying his goodbyes. He gave the groom a bob for his troubles and told him to make sure the horse was rubbed down properly and fed only the best oats. Then he swiftly turned away, took up Chloe's basket, and with his free hand tightly grasping Miriam's, headed for the hotel.

Their love-making that night was tender and sweet and achingly precious. Miriam clung to him as he clung to her, and they garnered strength in their oneness. Whispering in the dark, kissing, familiarising themselves with each other's touch, and scent and the way their bodies melded, they loved one another until the light began to cast grey shadows in the corners of the room.

Their whispers turned to silence as they lay spent within each other's arms and watched the sun seep through the shutters. Miriam knew he was suffering as much as she – knew she would never demand he stay – knew he had to return. For a love like theirs could never be wiped out on a battlefield. It was too strong.

The sun shot beams of light through the shutters, sending dust motes drifting around them like ochre confetti. The noise from the streets down below told them it was time to leave their haven and face the awful day.

Edward reluctantly drew his arm from beneath her head and threw back the sheets. Naked, he reached down into the basket at the side of the bed and picked up Chloe. Holding her to his chest, he breathed in the warmth of her, relishing the sleepy heaviness of her head on his shoulder and the sweet clasp of her fingers around his thumb. He kissed her downy head, murmuring his love as the tears sparkled on his eyelashes.

Miriam sat up in the bed that was still warm from their lovemaking and couldn't stop the tears that were pouring down her face. She loved him so much it was a physical ache. They had never been apart since their marriage – how would she live without him for the months it might take 'for him to come home? How could she remain alone on Bellbird and not see him in every corner, every pasture and yard? The prospect was daunting and it took all her will not to cry out and beg him to change his mind.

Edward handed Chloe to her and began to pour water from the jug into the bowl. He lathered the brush and began to shave, his hand not quite as steady as usual, the tic in his cheek the only other outward sign of tension.

Miriam watched him dress as she fed the baby, her hair shielding her face, falling over her shoulder in a veil. Was the tension nervous, or excitement, she wondered. Yet she didn't ask. Edward was fighting his own mental battles – it wouldn't be fair to burden him with hers.

She had tied her hair back in a ribbon and was about to get up and dress when Edward stopped her.

'Please don't come down with me,' he urged. He sat on the bed and caressed a strand of her hair before leaving it to drift to her breast. 'I don't want to say goodbye with a hundred others watching,' he murmured. 'This is our time, our last few moments together for quite a while, and I don't want to share it with anyone else.'

Miriam put her arms around his neck as he kissed her. The longing for him rose up through her and she clung tightly to him. She wanted to carry his scent with her, the feel of his arms, and the memory of the way his hair curled just below his ears. Needed to hear the drum of his heart once more, to feel his warmth and his strength.

All too soon he'd pulled gently away from her. Now he stood before her, handsome in the uniform of the AIF. His

266

hair gleamed beneath the brown slouch hat, but his blue eyes were dark with pain, his face ashen. 'It's time,' he said softly.

Miriam clambered off the bed, naked but for the ribbon in her hair. She was drawn softly into his embrace. Kissed hard, his hands cupping her face, crushing her ever more deeply as if he needed to consume her. Then he was gone.

Miriam started as the door banged behind him. Stood there in the dust motes, isolated and bereft as she heard his boots clattering down the stairs.

She finally took a deep, trembling breath and began to dress. She fumbled with the buttons on her blouse, cursed the tangles in her hair and finally dragged on her boots and fought with the button hook. Grabbing Chloe from the bed, she opened the shuttered doors. Edward had asked her not to go down to see him off, but he'd said nothing about going out onto the verandah – and she couldn't just sit inside waiting until he'd gone – not without seeing him one more time.

From high above the main street she had a perfect view. The noise and the dust rose up to greet them as she stood by the railings with Chloe in her arms.

A brass band was playing marching tunes, horses were stamping and snorting at their tethers, and rattling trucks spewed clouds of foul-smelling fumes over the crowds. Men were shouting their farewells and women were standing in isolated misery with their children clinging to their skirts. Firecrackers startled the horses and the bunting snapped and flapped in the wind. The racecourse was bright with the coloured tents of the volunteers who were handing out wool and knitting needles so the women left behind could do their bit for the brave boys they were sending to war.

And all the while the army men were taking names, shouting orders, issuing rations and pointing to the truck that would take them away from this outback town. The tough country boys were the cream of Australian manhood. They were sunburned and strong, with skills on horseback and with a gun that would never be matched – and a sense of mateship that would never falter, even in the darkest hours.

Miriam scanned the faces, hoping for a glimpse of Edward. But from up here all she could see was an ocean of brown khaki swirling through the kaleidoscope of colourful hats, flags and banners. If Edward was still down there and had guessed she would be watching from the verandah, he gave no sign. For not one face was lifted towards her. Not one familiar, darling face sought her out for that last farewell.

The tears blinded her as she sank her chin softly on to Chloe's head and watched as the sun travelled across the sky and one by one the trucks left in a cloud of dust.

All too soon they were gone. The streets had quietened, the milling crowds intent upon returning home. 'And that's what we must do,' she whispered to Chloe. 'We must go home and make sure everything is perfect for when Daddy returns.'

Chapter Fifteen

Jake had travelled through the night. He'd hurried home, thrown a few essentials in a bag, grabbed a disgruntled Eric and set the burglar alarm. With a few stops for coffee and food, and bathroom breaks for Eric, he'd rested for a couple of hours in the car park of a roadhouse before setting out again. It was evening when he caught the first glimpse of Bellbird Station, and the dying sun cast a golden haze over the hills and valleys, making it almost surreal.

He stood for a moment by the imposing gates, drinking in the view, feeling his weariness drain away. It was a pretty place, and aptly named, he thought as he heard the single, perfect note of the bellbird and saw the horses cropping beneath the wilgas. There was a serenity here that couldn't be found in the city – a calm acceptance of life and the progression of the seasons that hadn't changed in almost two centuries of settlement. This aura of stability and serenity filled him with a sense of wellbeing and vigour. It was almost as if he was coming home.

'Don't be ridiculous,' he muttered as he closed the gates behind him and drove up the long lane. 'You've been here once – hardly a homecoming.' And yet the sense of home remained with him as he looked out at the jacaranda's purple haze, and the scarlet blossom of the poinciana trees. Their familiarity welcomed him, drew him in, like the embrace of a much-loved friend. He realised he was in danger of getting

269

over romantic, and pulled his thoughts in order as he drove into the yard and parked in front of the verandah.

Miriam was issuing orders to Frank. Bolstered by pillows in the battered cane chair, her face animated, she riffled through catalogues and files, pointing out various items of interest.

Jake couldn't hear what she was saying above Eric's demands to be let out of the ute, but took the opportunity to observe her. Her dark, greying hair was brushed away from her face in soft waves, and the purple bruising on one delicate cheekbone enhanced her frailty. Yet the spirit was obviously strong – he could see it in her eyes – and, as he climbed out of the car, she greeted him with a broad smile and a wave of her hand.

Eric jumped down to the yard and sauntered off. He was obviously on a mission, and Jake hoped he didn't plan on getting into any more fights. Should have had him neutered, he realised, but the thought of doing such a thing to a fellow male, even if he was a tomcat, made him shudder.

'That's all, Frank,' Miriam said to the man beside her. 'See what you can do and let me know.'

Jake and Frank acknowledged one another with a knowing glance, a nod of the head and a 'G'day'.

'City life too tedious for you, eh?' she teased. 'Good to see you again, Jake.'

He had the feeling he was attending a royal command and almost took her hand and kissed it, but instead, took off his hat and flopped into a chair. 'Jeez, I'm done in,' he sighed. 'That's a long trip.'

Fiona emerged from the gloom of the house, slamming back the screen door as she carried out the tray of tea things. 'G'day, glad you could make it,' she said as she put the tray on the table. 'There was a phone call for you, by the way.' She looked unusually solemn. 'Your unit's been broken in to.'

'When?' Jake sat up, alarmed.

'Sometime last night,' she replied as she poured the tea.

270

'Seems our mutual friend is determined to find something.'

'Why should they think I've got anything they might want? I'm hardly likely to leave vital evidence in an empty flat, even if I do have a security alarm.' Jake took the proffered cup and set it down on the table. 'And that's another thing,' he added. 'The alarm is state of the art – how the hell did they trip it?'

Fiona shrugged. 'Your neighbour saw lights and knew you were away, so she called the police. She didn't hear a thing before then, so I suppose your system isn't as good as you think.'

Jake knew it was, but remained silent. Only a highly skilled professional with inside knowledge could have bypassed that alarm. He thought about it for a moment as they sipped their tea, but deemed it wiser not to share his suspicion that someone had tipped them off.

'Seems our Mr Dempster is getting anxious,' he said finally. 'I'm surprised the office hasn't been turned over as well.'

The silence was profound and he saw the colour rise in Fiona's face. 'It has,' she admitted with soft regret. 'Happened about an hour after the unit break-in. The police have been informed, but your partners can't find anything missing.'

She reached across and almost touched his hand. 'Sorry, Jake. I should have told you sooner, but . . .'

'Bugger,' he swore softly. He caught Mim's eye and blushed. 'Sorry. But it's one hell of a thing to hear when you're hundreds of miles away and can do damn all about it. I'll have to ring Bill tomorrow.'

'I hope you didn't leave anything for them to find,' said Miriam.

'Give me some credit,' he snapped. 'Sorry,' he added swiftly – his second apology in less than two minutes, it was becoming a habit. 'Didn't mean to be rude.' He scrubbed his face with his hands and sighed. 'How are you doing with the search for the deeds?'

'We aren't.' Louise pushed through the door followed by her parents. 'We've searched trunks, cases, boxes and bags. There's nothing but accumulated junk and mementoes that would mean zilch to anyone but the family.'

'So, what now?' Fiona put down her cup and looked at him.

Jake was aware of five pairs of eyes turned upon him and fidgeted in the chair. He didn't really have a clue, but it looked as if he'd been chosen as leader and font of wisdom – not something he relished – and he didn't want to let them down.

'We look again until we're positive the deeds don't exist,' he said with rather more assertion than he felt. 'But Dempster's reaction makes me suspect they do – or at least *he* seems convinced they're still around.'

He drew himself up and stretched. He was dog-tired and aching for sleep. 'At least that's a positive way of looking at things. What we've got to do is out-think him – be one jump ahead. If the deeds are around, we have to find them before he does.'

He fell silent for a moment, his thoughts in a turmoil. 'I checked with the ministry of mining, in the hope that there might be a copy of the original deeds tucked away somewhere. But a lot of records went missing in the early days because of bush fires, floods and just downright carelessness. They were usually kept locally, and the powers that be didn't begin to centralise the mining permits until much later.'

'What about diaries, journals, letters? The pioneers were particularly good at keeping all three, and I'd be surprised if neither Kate, nor Henry left some sort of record of those days.' Chloe's voice drifted into the silence as the sun finally went down and night fell with its customary speed.

'Kate's diaries.' Mim's sharp interjection made them start. 'I remember now. I put them in the hatbox.'

'What hatbox?' Louise asked. 'We've been through the attic and there's nothing else up there – let alone a hatbox.'

272

'Have you tried behind the chimneystack? That was always my favourite hiding place, even as a girl. I'm sure I put it there.' Miriam struggled to get out of her chair and was firmly told to stay where she was.

Jake quickly rose and followed the two sisters into the hallway.

'You'll need this,' said Fiona as she thrust him a torch. 'Black as hell up there.'

Jake smiled at her, noted how beautiful her eyes were and swiftly looked away. She was a complication, and that was the last thing he needed if he was to keep a clear head.

The ladder had been put aside and he hauled it back to the loft opening and climbed up. Fiona was right, he realised. It was black, and almost unbearably hot beneath the low roof despite the night's approach. He could already feel the sweat trickle down his back and bead his face. It was a good thing he didn't suffer from claustrophobia.

Bent almost double, he shone the torch on to the far wall and the stone chimney stack. If there was anything behind it, he couldn't see, but as he shone the torch over the floor, he realised the journey from here to there was fraught with difficulty. The narrow wooden joists were dry with age and probably full of worm, and the lathe and plaster between them looked as delicate as bone china. One false step and he'd end up down on the floor below – probably with a broken neck, he thought dourly. And that was if he was lucky.

'Can you see anything?' shouted Fiona from below. 'What are you doing up there?'

Jake licked the sweat from his top lip as he balanced on two joists. 'Wait on, woman,' he shouted back. 'This isn't easy you know.'

'Hurry up, Jake. You've already been ages.'

He wobbled as he flashed the torch towards the loft hatch. Fiona had climbed up the ladder and was perched on the edge of the opening, legs dangling. 'I'd get this done quicker if you didn't interfere,' he said through gritted teeth.

Aware of her amused scrutiny, he took the next three steps

a little too quickly and only just made it to the floorboards that had been laid around the chimney.

'Can you see anything yet?'

Jake clamped his lips together. If she asked him that once more, he'd . . . he'd . . . The torch flickered and died just as he saw the dark shape in the corner. 'Great,' he muttered. 'Just what I flamin' need.'

'I'll get another torch,' offered Fiona with a giggle.

'Don't bother,' he grunted as he stretched out on his belly and reached for the hatbox. 'I've got it,' he said triumphantly.

'Good on ya,' she said. 'Chuck it across.'

Jake smeared sweat from his face and tugged at his sodden, filthy shirt. Like hell he would, he decided as he began to feel his way back to the hatch opening. He'd done this much, there was no way he was letting her get her sticky mitts on it.

He finally reached Fiona, the large and rather cumbersome hatbox clasped to his chest. His glare of determination silenced any comment she was about to make and she slid back down the ladder to let him through.

'Phew, am I glad to get out of there,' he breathed as he ruffled his hair to get rid of the cobwebs and dust. 'It's like a bloody oven, and those joists are being held together more by luck than anything else.'

'Don't worry about that,' said Louise impatiently. 'Let's see what's in the box.'

Jake kept the hatbox clasped in his arms as they returned to the verandah where Leo, Mim and Chloe were discussing the forthcoming horse sales in Burke. He set it down on the table in front of Mim.

There was an expectant silence as they watched her run her fingers over the aged leather. The hatbox was rounded on three sides and flat on the fourth. It was obviously meant for a lady's hat, for it was larger than one for a bowler or top hat.

Miriam's fingers traced a pattern through the dust as she familiarised herself with it. 'This was one of only two of

Kate's cases they found after the *Titanic* sank. The contents were ruined of course, but it didn't seem right to throw it out – not after knowing what had happened to it. So I used it to store Kate's journals and diaries.'

All eyes were on her as she fumbled with the locks. They were rusted and reluctant to shift until Jake eased them back with a penknife.

'Bloody hell,' breathed Fiona. 'It'll take us months to read that lot.'

They all stared down at the collection of diaries and notebooks and packets of letters. 'Better get started then,' said Miriam. 'We've only got five more days before we leave for Brisbane.'

Chloe helped her mother get ready for bed. As she turned out the light and closed the door, she felt an unbearable sadness sweep over her. Mim was such an anchor, such a driving force in her life – how on earth would she cope without her? Seventy-five was no great age. Life just wasn't fair.

'Is she asleep?' Leo's familiar voice made her turn. She nodded. 'It's been a long day,' she whispered. 'A long week, really – and it's not over yet.'

Leo put his arm around her shoulders. 'You're tired too,' he murmured. 'We all are. Even Louise has given up for the night.'

Chloe turned in her bedroom doorway and looked up at her handsome husband. They might be divorced, but she still loved him – still relied on him for so many things. 'Do you think we'll ever find the deeds?' she asked. 'Or is it just wishful thinking?'

He smiled down at her and kissed her gently on the forehead. 'Who knows? But it has brought us all together again, and that can't be bad, can it?'

She smiled back at him and shook her head. 'We've always been a united family, but this has strengthened those ties. We're talking and not fighting, Louise is eating and looking happier than she's done in an age, and Fiona's falling in love, although she doesn't realise it yet.'

He raised one snowy brow. 'So you noticed as well,' he said with a glint of humour in his eyes. 'About time she found someone. Life shouldn't be lived alone.' He paused and his gaze became intense. 'Loneliness has a way of making us selfish,' he murmured. 'It's no life for people like us.'

She pulled away from him, her hand poised to close the bedroom door. 'You've never been lonely,' she retorted. 'In fact, no one could accuse you of being solitary – not with the amount of women you've had over the years.'

He leaned on the jamb, his body blocking the closure of the door. 'I'm lonely for you,' he said. 'The other women were merely the antidote, the distraction from what really mattered. They meant very little.'

'Don't give me that,' she hissed. 'You had other women all the way through our marriage – so don't come the old soldier with me, Leo. It won't bloody wash.'

His face was a picture of rueful woe. He put his hand on his heart and shook his head. 'I am but a weak and feeble man, Chloe,' he said mournfully. 'Can I help it if women throw themselves at me and distract me from my work?'

'Good night, Leo,' she said as she firmly shut the door.

'I've changed,' he said through the door. 'I've seen the error of my ways and want you to forgive me. Take me back, Chloe, please. Life is so empty without you.'

Chloe leaned against the door and blinked away the tears. Leo was her one and only love, but he had the capacity to break her heart – not once, but over and over again. She had to protect herself from him. Had to block out her need to be in his arms, and her yearning for things to be as they once were.

'Go to your own bed, Leo,' she said through the door. 'You'll feel differently in the morning.'

His footsteps faded as he made his way out to the veran-dah and the camp bed. She had to keep telling herself that Leo would never change, that this plea for reconciliation came only partly from his affection for her, which she had never doubted, but mostly from the knowledge he was ageing, and that young girls were no longer interested in him, but for his name and his money. Perhaps Mim's illness had woken him to the fact he was mortal.

Poor Leo, she thought as she began to undress. He was going through a mid-life crisis, but she couldn't risk sacrificing her heart and her sanity for him any more. Yet, as she lay in the narrow single bed and stared up at the ceiling, she admitted it wouldn't take much for her to change her mind. She was so weak-willed when it came to Leo, so malleable and stupid – for the years apart hadn't dulled the loneliness of lying without him beside her, hadn't warmed the chill she still experienced outside the shelter of his arms. And she knew that if he asked again, she would let him back into her bed.

Fiona looked up from the diary she was reading and smiled. Jake had fallen asleep, the journal on his lap, his chin drooping to his chest. She watched him, noting how dark and thick his hair was, and how his lashes curled on to his cheek. A day's growth darkened his chin, enhancing the cleft, giving the square jaw more definition. He was beautiful, she thought with longing – but then he was probably well aware of that, she added tartly as she slapped the diary closed and made Eric leap from her lap.

'Wha . . .?' Jake opened bleary eyes and just managed to catch the journal before it spilled onto the floor.

'It's late,' she said. 'Everyone else has gone to bed and you've been snoring.'

'I don't snore,' he said defensively. 'Even my wife didn't complain about that.'

'Wife? What wife?' Fiona experienced a sensation similar to that of being dropped by parachute into the jungle – something she'd done once on her trip into Brazil and really didn't relish doing again.

He eyed her for a long moment, his sleepy lids giving him

277

a sensual, almost vulnerable appeal. 'It's late,' he said finally through a yawn. 'Come on, Eric. Time for bed.'

'What wife?' she demanded.

He turned and smiled at her over his shoulder. 'The one I married nearly ten years ago,' he replied. 'Goodnight.'

Fiona stood there and listened as the screen door whined and his boot heels rapped on the floor. She heard the murmur as he and Leo said goodnight, and then there was silence.

'Well,' she breathed. 'That's put me in my bloody place, hasn't it?' She grabbed her cardigan from the couch and snapped off the light. 'Bastard,' she hissed. 'Making eyes at me, leading me on. Who the hell does he think he is? God Almighty?'

'What the hell's the matter with you?' Louise grumbled as her sister got into bed. 'I was asleep, if you don't mind.'

'Sorry,' Fiona snapped. 'Go back to sleep.'

Louise raised herself on her elbow. 'I'm awake now. What's eating you, Fiona?'

'Men,' she said crossly. 'Bloody men.'

Louise lay back down. 'Oh,' she said softly. 'You mean Jake?' She giggled. 'What's he done now?'

'Nothing,' snapped Fiona.

'Perhaps that's the problem,' muttered Louise.

Fiona shot upright. 'No, it bloody isn't,' she stormed. 'He's married, Lou. The bastard's married.'

'Yeah, I know,' began Louise. 'But . . .'

'Then why the hell didn't you warn me?' Fiona fell back on the pillows and crossed her arms. She was fuming.

Louise looked over at her and giggled again. 'Oh, dear, you have got it bad, haven't you?' She dodged her sister's slap. 'He was married,' she said through her laughter. 'But Mim told me he's been divorced for ages. I don't know what you're getting so het up about, Fee. It isn't as if you are in love with him or anything. Is it?'

Fiona sat up and glared. 'Divorced? Then why did he let me think he was still married?'

Louise shrugged. 'Beats me.'

Fiona slumped back into the pillows. 'Bastard,' she breathed.

'Fair go, Fee. You can't have it both ways.' Her giggle was smothered by the pillow Fiona put over her face. When she'd re-surfaced, she leaned on her elbow. 'Poor bloke probably doesn't know which end is up with you,' she said as she spat out feathers. 'Perhaps he just needs a bit of time to sort things out. You can be a little . . . overpowering.'

Fiona was still awake long after Louise had fallen asleep again. If Jake Connor thought he could play games with her, then he was mistaken. But it might be interesting to see just how far he was willing to go in his deception – and perhaps teach him not to play games with her.

Miriam lay in the darkness and listened to the others as they settled for the night. She heard the deep rumble of Leo's voice outside Chloe's door, and his footsteps plodding down the hall after a short altercation. When would those two discover they couldn't live without one another, she thought sadly. It was such a waste of the chance for happiness. Such a waste of life not to be with the one you loved when all that stood between you was pride.

She propped herself up on the pillows as she heard Jake and Fiona talking. The ring of his boots on the wooden floor and the squeak of the screen door heralded his departure. Minutes later she heard the girls talking, giggling, perhaps arguing. She couldn't make out what they were saying, but Fiona certainly sounded put out about something.

She smiled. 'I bet a cent to a dollar it's got something to do with Jake,' she muttered.

Leaning back on the pillows she realised how lovely it was to have the house full again. Her family would squabble and jostle for position, but that only brought life back into the old timbers again and made the echoes disappear from the darker corners. There had been too many years of silence, of long lonely periods when she'd needed someone close to talk to. Frank was a friend, a good friend, but it wasn't the same as family, and now and again, she'd yearned to have them all close to her.

Miriam closed her eyes. This would be the last time they would be together on Bellbird. The last time she could take strength from them and capture the spirit of youth and vitality that had kept her going over these past few days. Her time was near, and if she had one regret, it was that she was leaving them behind to carry on without her. Leaving them to grow older, and hopefully wiser. Leaving them to find their own way, their own successes and failures and the different kinds of love they would surely experience.

How deeply she wished she could remain beside them and be a witness to all that. To know how they fared, and to see her great-grandchildren come into the world. 'You're getting maudlin,' she muttered as she took another pill. 'Just because you're about to kick the bucket doesn't mean they can't survive without you.'

As she waited for the pain-killers to kick in, she thought of life and death and the ability of the human psyche to cope. Time and distance were healers – and although the newly bereaved didn't want to believe it, thankfully the old adage was true. The agony eased, the tears dried, and one day you managed to get through twenty-four hours without thinking of the one you'd lost. Those few hours finally extended to days, and then weeks, months and years. You no longer looked for them in familiar places, no longer thought you heard their voice. Their memory lived on in the mind, but their features were lost, growing hazy as time passed, like old photographs left to fade in the sun.

Frank returned with Gladys and the children after their visit in Burke, and then rode alone into Balingun to join the second AIF.

The two women stood and watched the dust cloud diminish, and when it was finally gone they turned around and went into the homestead. Ashen faced and dry eyed, they sat over their cups of tea as the children played around their feet.

A friendship was forged that day. It was to sustain them until Gladys died in her sleep nearly fifty years later.

Bellbird Station sweltered in the heat of that summer of 1914 and as Christmas came and went they realised their men wouldn't be coming home yet. Through newspapers and radio reports they learned that this war was different to any other. It was being fought by armies of an unprecedented size, with terrible new weapons. Machine guns, tanks, poison gas, airplanes and submarines were the tools of slaughter, and a single battle could claim hundreds of thousands of lives on both sides.

For the first time in history, the civilian population of the protagonists were targeted. While the British blockade tried to starve the Germans and their allies into submission, German submarines were doing the same to Britain. The war effort demanded support and sacrifice from whole nations, and the women and children of the outback grew wheat as well as raising sheep and cattle for the meat markets. Wool was at a premium, the prices for a whole wool clip soaring over 50 per cent above the pre-war value.

'This war will change everything for us women,' remarked Miriam as the two friends sat on the verandah with their knitting. It was May 1915, and a pile of socks, vests, mittens and mufflers lay on the table beside her, waiting to be sent to the front.

Gladys unpicked a row of uneven stitches from her daughter's woollen tangle and gave it back to her. 'How?' she asked.

'We've learned what it's like to be independent,' she replied. She put down her knitting and stroked the swell of her pregnancy as she stared out to the paddocks. The calves were bellowing for their mothers, and the cows in the further pasture were lowing back. The bullocks looked sleek and fat as they milled around in the pens waiting for the drover to take them to market in the morning. There were fewer horses now, for like the men they'd gone to war. Yet, despite the fear that Edward may not return, she felt a deep sense of satisfaction for all they'd achieved since their men had left – and a sorrow that they couldn't be here to witness those achievements.

'Women are working in the factories, in the shops and schools and even in offices. We've learned to fend for ourselves. Learned what it's like to have wages in our pockets – our own money.'

Gladys grimaced as her three-year-old daughter decided she was bored and threw the wool off the verandah and into the dirt. 'It won't last,' she said. 'The men will come back and we'll be so glad to see them we'll forget about being independent. You'll see.'

Miriam nodded as she watched a drift of dust rise in the distance. Someone was coming. It was probably the drover they were expecting. 'Maybe,' she sighed. 'But the younger ones won't give up their freedom easily. It's different for us. As long as Edward comes home safely, it doesn't matter if I spend the rest of my life leaning over a hot range. It's exhausting enough being pregnant in this heat, without trying to do a man's job all day, and look after the children as well. Thank goodness we have the jackaroos to help us.'

Gladys gave a harsh bark of laughter. 'Fat lot of good they are. Take your eye off them for a minute and they've gone walkabout.' She too saw the dust and lifted a hand to shield her eyes. 'I hope that is the drover. Those fats were absolute buggers to catch, and I don't fancy having to let 'em loose and start all over again.'

Miriam was about to reply when she realised they had been mistaken. No drover worth his salt went anywhere without his horse, and the dust cloud was too high.

'That's a car making that dust,' she said as she watched the cloud draw nearer. 'Who on earth do we know who owns a car?'

Gladys gathered up her children. 'Mim,' she said fearfully. 'The priest drives a car. You don't think . . .?'

The two women stood and waited, their children around them and in their arms, their fear etched in their faces. Father

McFarlaine was a cold fish – a man of little humour and rare compassion. He'd never failed to let it be known he thought his widespread outback parish was merely a stepping-stone to Rome. His arrival could mean only one thing.

The car came to a grinding, dusty halt, the chrome glinting dully through the veil of dirt. The door opened and the priest climbed out.

Miriam sat down hard on the chair and gathered a protesting Chloe to her chest.

Gladys stood like a statue, her hand clamped over her mouth, her eyes wide with fear. 'Who is it?' she asked through her fingers. 'Oh, God, who is it?'

Miriam sat there and felt a cold hand clutch her heart. The world was spinning out of control, weaving in and out of darkness, making the priest swim before her. She realised she was almost smothering Chloe and set her down on the floor, then her hands flew to her swollen belly as the baby kicked inside her.

'You've got a telegram.' It was a statement, the muscles in her face so stiff, she could barely speak.

He nodded and came to stand beside Gladys, but Miriam saw that his attention was focused on her and the cold hand clutched harder.

'It's my sad duty to inform you that your husband was killed in the battle of Gallipoli,' he said stiffly. 'He showed courage beyond duty and has been awarded a commendation.'

He brushed dirt from his black soutane and stared at some point beyond Miriam's shoulder. 'The first AIF were glorious in their defeat, giving their lives with courage and fraternity. Australia has shown that she is finally a great nation. You must be very proud.'

The world tilted, went black and grey in swirls of ever-increasing speed. She was only vaguely aware of hands grasping her, of being half-carried to the day-bed in the corner of the verandah, and of a cold cloth being pressed to her head.

283

All she could hear were his words ringing in her ears. All she could see was Edward, his hair glinting fire in the sunlight as he worked the horses in the corrals. It couldn't be true. He wouldn't leave her. She would have known if he was dead. Would have somehow felt he was gone forever.

The priest's voice came to her as if from a great distance. 'I wouldn't have come if I'd known her condition,' he said. 'How soon before . . .?'

'Four weeks, maybe less after this shock,' snapped Gladys. 'You could have done this in a kinder way.' She paused and her voice trembled. 'What of Frank, Father? Is he safe?'

'No news is good news, my dear,' he said with a patronising heartiness. 'I've heard nothing.'

Miriam sank into the welcoming darkness, gathering it into her, letting it caress her and carry her into a world without pain, without thought and feeling. Her sense of time and place were lost in those dark, enfolding clouds, and it was only the urgent, demanding pain that dragged her unwillingly back to the present.

Edward's son was born on the day-bed as the dust settled behind the priest's departing car. He lived just long enough for her to kiss him and call him by name, and then Edward Henry Strong was buried in the tiny cemetery on the hill behind the house.

Miriam and Gladys stood holding hands in silence. It was early morning of the following day and the tiny white cross gleamed against the red earth and pale grass. The flowers they had placed on the little mound of earth were dewed and sparkling in the glow of sunrise, and the haunting song of the bellbird drifted over the land like a beautiful psalm.

Miriam fell to her knees, unable to bear the agony any longer. The dam was breached and the agony poured out of her in a long, agonised wail that rebounded off the hills and echoed around her, magnifying the anguish, filling Bellbird valley with her sorrow. It was to be the last time she cried.

Miriam opened her eyes and was surprised it was still dark. The reality of those memories was still with her and she thought she could feel the warmth of the sun, and feel the nomadic breeze that had seemed to caress her that awful day.

She realised she'd been fooled, and brushed her eyes with her fingers and sat up. It was cold and dark, the quietest time of the night. Never one for religion, she struggled to remember the piece from the Bible that she'd been made to learn at that awful dame school.

'A time to live, and a time to die. A time to speak and a time to stay silent,' she whispered into the night.

This was her time to remember, to garner all the sorrows and joys of her life and examine them. She'd had no one to bury, but her son – no tangible evidence of their existence but for her memories. Father had disappeared. Kate and George were immersed in the ocean, and Edward had never come home.

A calm acceptance drifted over her. Soon, she thought, I will see them again.

Chapter Sixteen

Jake had slept well and had even managed to get through most of another of Kate's diaries as the sun came up. The writing had been difficult to decipher, and a lot of it was faded, but the diaries were a wonderful source of history and he'd come to admire the tough little Irish woman who'd achieved so much.

Showered and dressed, Jake strode across the yard. He was looking forward to breakfast. Perhaps Fiona would be there, he thought hopefully. I was a bit crook teasing her like that last night.

'I want a word with you.' Miriam appeared from out of the drooping fronds of the pepper tree. 'Quick, in here, and keep quiet.'

Jake grinned. There was nothing like a bit of cloak-and-dagger first thing in the morning to sharpen the appetite. Mim was obviously recovering from her shock and looked on sparkling form.

'Come on, hurry up. I haven't got all morning,' she hissed.

Jake pushed aside the weeping fronds and stepped into the cool shadows. He would play along with her if it made her happy. 'What on earth is it?' he whispered. 'Have you found something?'

'Yes and no,' she replied with enigmatic sharpness. 'Read that and tell me what you think.'

Jake took the notebook and scanned the page. It wasn't a

diary, he realised, but a record of Kate's purchases and sales during her travels around the diggings. The writing was meticulous as were the details. 'I don't see what this has to do with anything,' he said, his puzzlement clear in his eyes.

'Turn the page,' ordered Miriam.

He did as he was told and then realised why she'd become so excited. 'I see what you mean,' he said thoughtfully. He looked into her face and saw hope and excitement there and had no wish to disappoint her – but how to tell her it wasn't enough?

'It's not what you expected, is it?' she asked, crestfallen. 'I can tell by your face.' She shook her head, the disappointment clear in her eyes. 'You don't have to mollycoddle me, Jake. I'm old enough to take it on the chin.'

'This is excellent background information and, coupled with one or two entries in the diary I'm reading, I will probably use it in court. The defence will no doubt see it as inadmissible and ask for it to be thrown out, but we'll see.' He closed the book. 'I'm sorry I can't promise anything more.'

She took a step toward him, her voice low. 'You're a good man, Jake. I'm glad I've got you on my side.' She patted his arm and pushed her way through the fronds.

Jake stood there for a moment and listened to the hum of the bees that swarmed within the pepper tree, too busy to take any notice of his intrusion. His thoughts were spinning. Perhaps the records could be used, he decided. It was risky, but without the deeds he had little choice but to try. In conjunction with the only other piece of evidence, this record book could make quite a significant statement.

Fiona watched her sister demolish a plate of scrambled egg and crispy bacon and wash it down with a mug of sweetened tea. Louise had already lost the pinched look of someone half-starving themselves, and the outback air and sunshine had brought a glow to her cheeks. Her temperament had changed too, and Fiona was glad she had the old Louise back again after so long.

She finished her toast and pushed the plate aside, her appetite gone. She would have to tell Mim she was leaving, and although she knew her timing was lousy, she couldn't afford to miss the interview back in Brisbane. With so much happening over the past week, she'd forgotten it entirely, and had only been reminded this morning when she checked her own diary. She eyed her grandmother, hoping she'd understand her reasons for leaving, but dreaded having to tell her.

She was momentarily rescued by Jake's appearance. 'What's that?' she asked as she watched him lock the book in his briefcase.

'Just something Mim thought I might find interesting,' he said in a non-committal tone.

Fiona took a deep breath. She was getting sick and tired of being kept in the dark. She was about to speak when the telephone rang and made them all jump. 'Bellbird,' she snapped.

'It's Rafe. Put Louise on.'

'She's busy,' Fiona said sharply.

'Who is it?' Louise asked.

Fiona told her and reluctantly handed over the receiver. Louise took the telephone into the hall and closed the door.

Chloe and Fiona exchanged looks across the table. 'I hope he's not planning on coming back,' whispered Chloe. 'Louise looks so well. It's obvious he's not good for her.'

Miriam nibbled toast and sipped from her mug of tea as she turned the pages of Kate's diary. 'Time is wasting,' she grumbled. 'Get on with your reading.'

Fiona was halfway through Henry's diary of the voyage from England. It was fascinating reading and although she knew she would have to leave soon, she was eager to learn what life had been like back in the days of steam and sail.

She turned the page. It was blank – and so were all the others.

'Anyone got Henry's diaries? He seems to have given up on this one.'

'He didn't keep one after Maureen died,' said Miriam through her toast. 'Lost heart, I suspect.'

She eyed Fiona over her spectacles. 'I don't know why you're wasting time going that far back. We need to concentrate on 1906 and perhaps a few years later.' Reaching out, she selected a thick diary with a heavy clasp. The leather was tooled with gold, and the date on the cover was 1906. 'Try that,' she ordered.

Silence fell as they became absorbed, and all that could be heard in the kitchen was the ticking of the clock and the rustle as pages were turned.

Louise came in and put the telephone back on the shelf. She edged around the table and sat down.

Fiona looked up when she heard her sniff. 'What's happened?' she demanded.

Louise blew her nose. Her eyes were puffed from crying and her skin was blotchy. 'Nothing,' she said defensively.

'Bullshit,' declared Fiona in her usual bald manner. 'What has he said to you, Louise? Has he been bullying you again?'

'Fiona,' warned Mim in an absent-minded tone. 'Mind your language.'

Louise picked up the diary she'd been reading and scraped back her chair. 'It's none of your damn business,' she snapped. 'I'm going out on to the verandah where I can get a bit of peace.' She slammed the chair back into place. 'And don't even think about following me, because I refuse to discuss it with you.'

The telephone rang again as she was passing and she snatched it up, her face alight with hope. 'Rafe?' She listened, obviously aware of everyone watching, and her expression turned dour. 'It's for you,' she said holding out the receiver to Jake. 'Someone called Bill.'

Fiona watched Jake listen to the man at the other end of the line. It was obviously important as well as long-winded. She tried to gauge what was being said by his replies, but Jake was playing it close to his chest as usual, and giving nothing away. When he finally replaced the receiver and turned to face them, she knew it was bad news.

'I'm sorry, Mim. That was my partner. Dempster has lodged a counter-suit for libel. His lawyers are demanding two million dollars compensation plus costs.'

Miriam felt her heart thud painfully in her chest. Two million dollars was an impossible sum to find even if she tried selling Bellbird. And she would never do that. Could never give up her beloved home to pay off a snake like Dempster.

'Oh, god,' she moaned. 'What have I done?'

'It's not too late, Mim,' said Jake as he sat beside her and took her hand. 'If you withdraw the suit, and write a formal letter of apology, the Dempsters will withdraw their claim.'

'Never,' she gasped. 'I'll never apologise to any of them.'

'Mum.' Chloe's voice was uncharacteristically sharp. 'You can't go on like this. It's become an obsession. Give the man what he wants and forget all about this silly court case. You're in no fit state to be taking him to court anyway, and to risk all that money is just plain stupid.'

Miriam looked across at her daughter, stunned by her vehemence. 'I can't,' she said. 'It might seem like an obsession to you, but it's all I have left to fight for the justice my father never had.'

'Chloe's right,' rumbled Leo. 'Things have gone too far. It's time to pull back and retain some dignity. You're not well enough to deal with all this, and two million dollars isn't exactly a drop in the ocean.'

Miriam turned to Fiona. 'What do you think?' She was almost afraid of the reply, but she had to know.

Fiona sat in silence for a long moment, her eyes clouded in thought. 'I reckon Dempster's trying it on,' she said eventually. 'The very last thing he needs is for this to go to court. Mud sticks, regardless of who wins.'

Miriam felt a surge of hope. How clever her granddaughter was – how analytical. She watched as Fiona leaned back in her chair, arms folded, brow furrowed in thought. At her age, she realised, she'd have been motivated by gut instinct – but Fiona's way was better. She thought things out, didn't open her mouth until she was certain that what came out of it was sensible.

'It's as if he knows we don't have anything to fight the case with,' said Fiona into the silence. 'This counter-suit and demand for two million is designed to frighten you off. The demand for an apology is merely his spiteful way of shaming you.'

Miriam nodded, deep in thought. 'It looks that way, certainly. But he's taking a risk. How can he know for certain we don't have proof against him?'

'Men like Dempster thrive on risk,' retorted Fiona. 'It's the only way they can amass such fortunes. Little people like us can be scared off quite easily when they start throwing their money about.' She paused. 'But I'm surprised he's shown his hand.'

Jake cleared his throat and all eyes turned to him. 'Have you considered the possibility that Dempster did indeed find what he was looking for? Even he isn't arrogant enough to risk court action unless he had some certainty of winning the case.'

'Jake's right,' breathed Chloe, her eyes wide with horror. 'Do as he says, Mum. Give it up before we lose everything.'

Miriam sat there for a long moment and eyed her family. Her thoughts were clear, her mind set. 'No,' she said firmly. 'I prefer to believe Fiona's opinion is right. Dempster's running scared. This counter-suit is to stop me going any further. He's trying to frighten me.'

'I'm sorry,' came the sob from the doorway. 'It's all my fault. I've let you down.'

'Louise?' Chloe pushed away from the table and went to her daughter. Putting her arm around the trembling shoulders, she tried to make sense of what the girl was saying. 'Hush,' she said firmly. 'Calm down and tell me how you could have possibly let us down.'

Louise smeared away the tears and blew her nose on the

proffered tissue. 'I never thought things would go so far,' she sobbed. 'I didn't mean to say anything, but it just slipped out.'

Miriam felt her spirits tumble. 'You've been talking to Ralph.' It was a statement, not a question, and she knew what the reply would be.

Louise nodded. 'We were talking and I told him about the search for the deeds.' She blew her nose again. 'He knew what we were doing of course, he was here when we decided to look for them. But I didn't think it mattered if I told him we'd found nothing.'

Leo came to embrace her alongside Chloe as Louise sniffed and wiped her eyes.

'Fiona was furious about Mim giving Jake something to take back to Brisbane. She was eaten up with curiosity as to what it was, knowing only it had something to do with the case.' Louise looked across at Jake. 'I'm sorry, but how was I to know an amusing anecdote could cause so much trouble?'

'So, Ralph's been using you to get information so he could curry favour with Dempster.' Fiona's face was grim. 'No wonder we've all been burgled and frightened half to bloody death. What a bastard.'

'Language, Fiona,' muttered Miriam automatically.

'I'm so sorry,' wept Louise. 'But Rafe has a way of making me say things I don't want to say, of telling him things I know should be kept secret. I didn't for one minute think he'd go to Dempster with anything – until this morning, that is.'

'Why, what happened this morning?' Miriam was glad she was sitting down. There were only so many shocks she could take in one day.

'He let slip he knew about Jake's break-in,' she sobbed. 'Then tried to cover it up by accusing me of having an affair with him.' She blushed hotly as she shot a glance at Jake before turning to her father. 'He accused me of such terrible things, Dad. He said I was deliberately hiding things from

292

him. Working against him so he couldn't get the contract with Shamrock Holdings, and going behind his back by plotting with my family against him. He's always known that none of you like him, and before I knew it I'd told him everything.'

Miriam's love went out to her and she grasped her hand in an effort to convey the emotion. 'There wasn't really very much to tell him, darling, and I suspect Dempster's none the wiser. Dry your tears and sit down. We have a lot to discuss.'

Louise sat in dumb misery as they all began to speak at once. She felt like an outsider, a traitor. She'd hurt the people she loved the most, and could never forgive herself – or Ralph. Why had she been so malleable, so blind to the man he really was? Fiona had tried to warn her, but she'd refused to listen. How stupid was that?

She pulled a cigarette from Fiona's pack on the table and lit up. It would be a first for years, and in a way, a sort of defiance against Rafe.

The talk was lively, going around the table as ideas and suggestions were mulled over, put aside or dismissed. Yet she was only partly aware of the conversation, for her mind was fully occupied with thoughts of her marriage and the man she'd suddenly discovered was a stranger.

She had just begun to emerge from a disastrous relationship with a fellow actor when she'd met Ralph at a cocktail party fundraiser for the little theatre she'd been involved with for three years. Her acting career was beginning to take off, and she'd had dreams of one day playing in the National Theatre on the south bank.

Ralph had flattered her, courted her with lavish treats and gifts, and swept her off her feet. She'd been only too happy to receive the attention and advice from one so urbane and obviously destined for great things – and had mistaken that fleeting need for a boost to her ego as love. She could see it all now, so clearly, why the hell hadn't she been more aware at the time?

When he'd casually suggested that acting and banking didn't really go with each other, she'd given up the stage and the friends that went with it to marry him. Looking back, she could see how manipulative he was, and how easily he'd turned her into a shadow of her true self. Ralph had taken her over. Had chosen her clothes, her hairstyles, even her make-up. He'd bought their house with no reference to her needs, had decided they couldn't have children in case they interfered with their lifestyle. He'd refused to let her go out to work, and handled all the bills as well as the money, hired and fired the staff and expected her to be grateful.

And she had been – until these past few days. Now, in the chill of acceptance, and the clear-eyed view of her marriage, she knew Ralph had never loved her. That their marriage was a sham. He'd used her because she was weak, and he'd enjoyed controlling her. The weaker she became, the more he took over, until she'd simply faded into the background.

Life here on Bellbird had opened her eyes to what real love meant, and to how much she'd missed out on that family unity by marrying Ralph. Fiona had been right, she admitted silently. He'd driven away her friends, her acting ambitions, even her family – isolating her completely so that she had no one else to turn to but him. She'd become his toy, his puppet. Pull a string and see Louise dance.

Fresh tears threatened and she wiped them away. It was too late to feel sorry for herself. She had to find a way out of his shadow – find a way to make amends to this family she adored. And eventually find the real Louise.

'If you're determined to go on with this madness, then I'll have to go back and see what I can do,' said Leo. 'Two million is a lot to find, but I've favours due, and it's time I called them in.'

'I'll go with him,' said Chloe. 'You don't mind, do you, Mum? Only I've got a bit stashed away and it'll take some time to free it up.'

'I'm not expecting to have to pay this blood money,'

retorted Miriam. 'And I certainly don't want you bankrupting yourselves because of this. It's a personal fight between me and Brendt, and if push comes to shove, I can always sell Bellbird.'

'Over my dead body,' snapped Fiona. 'Bellbird is ours. I couldn't bear to think of Dempster taking it over.'

'I think we're all getting a bit carried away,' said Jake calmly. 'Dempster has to prove you've libelled him. The case will probably be heard by a jury and they will have to have a majority decision. If there's the slightest doubt he has cheated your family, then he'll lose, or worse – he could find his compensation cut to a dollar which will show the court's contempt and cast doubt on his reliability.'

Miriam nodded. 'It will mean washing his dirty laundry in public,' she said flatly. 'And he won't want to do that. As one of you said, mud sticks.'

'Better to be safe than sorry,' rumbled Leo. 'Chloe and I will go back and sort out the finances just in case.' He turned to Louise. 'What are you going to do, darling?'

Louise dragged herself from her misery. 'I'm staying here,' she said firmly. 'The last place I want to be is Brisbane.'

'I have to go back unfortunately,' said Fiona. 'I've got an important interview the day after tomorrow that I've completely forgotten about until now. I can't miss it – it could be an offer of a really good job.' She reached across the table and took Mim's hand. 'I'm sorry, Mim,' she said. 'I feel mean about leaving you, but it is important.'

Miriam patted her hand. 'Of course I don't mind, darling. Life goes on and if it's that important, of course you must go. As long as you don't forget to come and support me in court on Monday,' she added.

'Well at least Louise will be here,' said Jake as he picked up the briefcase. 'I don't want Mim left alone.'

'Where are you going?' asked Fiona. 'Back to the wife?' She bit her lip. That was a bitchy thing to say, and she was immediately ashamed.

295

He eyed her sharply, his brow raised in query. 'I'm needed at the office,' he said. 'Now Dempster's posted a counter-claim, there's a lot of paperwork to go through.' He reached out and took up three of the ledgers. 'They might shed light on a couple of things, so I'll read them when I have a spare minute.'

He turned to Miriam. 'I'm sorry to run out on you, Mim. But if we're to be prepared I can't stay any longer. Poor old Bill's been left to carry the can long enough.'

Miriam stood on the verandah an hour later and watched her family leave. Leo drove sedately out of the yard as Chloe dabbed away her tears and waved mournfully out of the window. Fiona kick-started her noisy motorbike, and after blowing Miriam a kiss, roared off in the same direction. They had all taken a diary or a journal and would ring the minute they found anything.

'I seem to have lost Eric,' said Jake as he came back from the barn. 'Damn cat. Never around when you want him.' He looked at his watch, then ran his fingers through his tousled hair. 'I have to leave,' he muttered crossly. 'Where the hell's he got to?'

Miriam sat down in her customary chair and smiled. 'Leave him here,' she offered. 'He obviously feels at home.'

'But he's my cat,' he muttered. 'Not fair to burden you.'

Miriam smiled up at Louise and they shared a knowing look. 'He'll come back to the homestead when he's good and ready,' said Miriam. 'I'll bring him to Brisbane for you.'

Jake took one last look over home yard and the surrounding paddocks. 'I suppose so,' he said quietly. Then he grinned and rubbed his chin. 'Thanks, Mim. Sorry to dump him on you like this, but it's important I get back to the office and prepare for Monday.'

Louise came to sit beside her as they watched Jake collect his things and climb into the utility. 'He's certainly good looking,' murmured Louise as they waved goodbye and watched the dust cloud rise and ebb behind the ute. 'And nice with it, too. Makes you wonder what's wrong with him – it's unusual for a man to be that perfect.'

Miriam eyed her eldest granddaughter and tried not to laugh. Jake certainly had a gift for stirring up the women in her family. 'He has his problems, just like anyone else. I think he's terribly insecure when it comes to anything outside his career. Had an awful childhood, you know. Father hit the bottle after his mother died, and the kids were spread hell west and crooked for a while until their grandmother took over.' She smiled. 'Reckon he had his share of grief even before his divorce,' she said. 'But there's a stillness about him I like, a certain steadfastness that I find comforting.'

'It's rather touching he's so fond of that damn cat,' said Louise. 'Pity he doesn't feel the same about Fiona.' She giggled. 'She's obviously besotted.'

Miriam kept her thoughts to herself. If Jake and Fiona hadn't made the first move by the end of the trial, then she would have to do something. Just as she would have to make sure her daughter and Leo were re-united. They were far too old to be behaving like a couple of spoilt children. 'Come on, let's get reading. I don't expect we'll find anything, but there's nowhere else to look, so we might as well plough on.'

'You made a mistake,' said Brigid as she took the glass of wine from her son. 'Never show your hand before the endgame. I thought you knew better.'

'If nothing else it might frighten the old bitch off,' he muttered, as he turned away and looked out of the window. The sun was glinting on the water and sailboards were racing through the choppy waves. The view usually brought him pleasure, but today he almost didn't notice it.

'Nothing frightens Miriam,' said his mother dryly. 'She's tough, and when her back's up against the wall she doesn't give in – she comes out fighting.'

'Perhaps I should have made the compensation charge

even higher,' he snapped. 'We can't let her go through with this case. It will ruin us.'

Brigid put her glass of wine on the small table at her elbow. 'Our reputation will be damaged, certainly. That's why it was so important to keep a low profile until we knew for certain she wouldn't actually have enough to take us to court.' She gave a deep sigh and fingered the row of exquisite matching pearls at her throat. 'Without any evidence the case will be thrown out – will never be heard, and we have enough contacts in the press to stifle any scurrilous reports.'

'And if there is something?' His usually florid face was ashen, his eyes dark embers glowing with malice – and, she suspected, fear.

'I think it's highly unlikely,' she said with a firmness that belied the squirm of doubt. 'Ralph would have told us, and our searches would have revealed something.'

'But he said the lawyer brought something back to Brisbane,' Brendt persisted. 'I'm damned if I know what it is, or where it is. The office has been bugged, and the clerk paid a fortune to pass on anything of interest, but no one's saying anything. It's so damn frustrating.'

'Calm down, Brendt.' Brigid's tone was icy.

'I wish grandfather had pushed her down the same mineshaft as her father,' he muttered. 'Would have saved us all a lot of trouble.'

Brigid picked up her glass and sipped the wine. She said nothing, but her thoughts were legion.

Chapter Seventeen

It was one of those perfect mornings, and the Brisbane River glinted a million sunlit stars as it swept beneath Victoria Bridge. The new buildings on the south bank gleamed in the morning sun and even the heavy traffic pouring into the city along the North Quay couldn't detract from the beauty of the warbling magpies as they perched in the blossom trees of the small patch of green that looked over the river.

Fiona was the first to arrive on that Monday morning, and as she stood on the greensward and watched the traffic stream over the bridge, she wondered how the day would end. Her latest telephone chat with Mim had revealed only that Mim had decided to leave Bellbird earlier than planned and was staying with Chloe. Louise had confided that she suspected their grandmother was at last beginning to wonder if she was doing the right thing and had decamped back to Ralph. The silly bitch was going to give her marriage one last go.

Fiona fluffed out her hair – a nervous gesture that had nothing to do with vanity – and tugged at her jacket. The suit was already making her hot, but it was the only respectable item of clothing she possessed, for she spent most of her life in jeans and T-shirts. Lighting a cigarette, she tried to avoid the bird droppings and perched on the corner of a bench to wait. There was still almost an hour to go before she would have to leave the sunshine for the cool, austere surroundings of the Supreme Court.

'You're early,' said Jake as he came to sit beside her.

Startled, she turned to look at him. 'Strewth,' she breathed. 'You scrub up well.'

Jake tweaked his suit collar and fidgeted with his tie. 'Wait until you see the gown and wig,' he retorted with wry humour. 'I'm positively dashing when I'm dressed for the part.'

She giggled, then noticed the tic at the edge of his jaw and realised he was as nervous as she. 'I wish we weren't doing this,' she said as she saw the press begin to gather around the court-house.

'So do I,' he replied. 'But Mim does have a case, albeit a shaky one, and we mustn't let our own doubts beat us.' He looked across at her and smiled. 'Just remember we're doing this for Mim,' he said softly. 'She's not scared of losing – just determined to have her day in court. We're here to offer support in the best way we can.'

Fiona noticed how the sun highlighted the gold flecks in his brown eyes, and enhanced the blue-black of his hair. She cleared her throat and looked away. He was too near, his scrutiny too intense – her reaction to him far more powerful than she'd realised. 'You'd better explain what's happening,' she said gruffly. 'I've no idea what goes on in a Supreme Court.'

Jake put his briefcase on the ground and leaned back against the bench. 'A civil case is one in which a person is in dispute with another person or party, and seeks compensation. To start a civil action, we have lodged a writ in the Supreme Court. Mim is called "the plaintiff". Patrick Dempster's heirs are the defendants – the ones alleged to have perpetrated the infringement of Mim's rights to her inheritance.'

'I'm with you so far. Doesn't sound too complicated.'

Jake smiled. 'It isn't, but the legal jargon is apt to confuse the layman.' He ran his fingers through his hair, making it stand on end. 'As Mim's lawyer, I have served Dempster with a writ. He must acknowledge receipt of that writ within a certain time, by lodging a form generally referred to as "an appearance". If he doesn't do this, or raise any other objections, Mim would automatically win the case.'

'But Dempster did lodge an appearance – that's why we're here.' Fiona stared out at the river and watched the ferry cast off and chug its way up river. The tourists were standing on deck taking their photographs. She'd have given anything to be with them instead of waiting here in front of the court-house. 'So, what happens next?' she asked, bringing her attention back to the man beside her.

'I exchanged various documents, called pleadings, with Dempster's legal advisers. These included a statement of claim, which details the case and indicates the remedy being sought. Dempster may then supply a defence, which admits or denies each claim – and is then permitted to make a counter-claim.'

'Which he did,' said Fiona bitterly. She squinted into the sun. 'Will Mim get the chance to have her say? Is there enough evidence without the deeds to make a proper case?'

'She's the plaintiff, and her case is always stated first. Dempster will have his turn when she's finished, and will respond to any issues Mim raised. Mim must produce enough evidence to establish that her case outweighs Dempster's arguments. This standard of proof is known as the balance of probabilities.'

He took a deep breath. 'We can also use witness testimony or sworn affidavits. When each party has finished its submission, the judge will give his decision, either immediately, or reserve it until a later date.' Jake smoothed his hair and fidgeted with his tie. 'Of course any witnesses are long dead by now. Mim is going to have a tough time, going it alone.'

'There is one witness,' said Fiona as she caught sight of movement on the far side of the green.

Jake followed the direction of her gaze. 'I thought of that,' he murmured. 'But she's a hostile witness, and has already been summoned for the defence.'

'She'll lie through her back teeth,' hissed Fiona.

'Then it's my job to get to the truth.' He smiled and rested his hand lightly on her arm. 'I know it's a cliché, but trust me, Fiona,' he murmured.

Fiona looked deeply into his eyes and knew – that despite all the warnings to the contrary – she would.

Brigid took a deep breath as she stepped from the limousine and faced the press. They swarmed around her, yelling questions, their flashes going off as they busily clicked their cameras. She struck her most imperious pose, tucked her hand in the crook of Brendt's arm and strode through the mêlée across the courtyard. She had no comment to make. Brendt had slipped up – again – the press were supposed to be occupied elsewhere this particular morning.

As they passed the Themis Statue, she gave a wry thought that the Greek goddess of justice would not be amused by today's events. Yet the three stone pillars featuring the Queensland coat of arms and a series of plaques that traced the creation and history of the Queensland Supreme Court were enough to sober her thoughts. For the might of the law hung over them like the sword of Damocles, and although her contingency plans were in place, she didn't relish carrying them out.

Once they had gained the hushed foyer of the Supreme Court and had walked through the security arch, she withdrew her hand from his arm and adjusted the neat little hat and veil. 'I thought you'd created a diversion?' she hissed.

'A merchant banker caught with his trousers down obviously isn't enough to put them off,' he said grimly as he straightened his tie. Then he grinned for the first time in days. 'Black certainly earned his wages there.'

Brigid's smile was frosty as she fingered the pearls at her neck. The photographs were certainly lurid and the man's dignity forever lost – a fitting punishment for such a pompous ass. 'You should have gone for the paedophile lawyer – a much stronger target for the press.'

'I still need him,' said Brendt as he looked around at the gathering. 'The banker was expendable, we can use the lawyer another time.' He ran his hand over his silk tie. 'I see our family is giving us full support as usual,' he said with sourness.

'You can't make an omelette without breaking eggs,' snapped Brigid. 'What did you expect, Brendt? You've alienated the rest of the family over the years, they aren't going to break the habits of a lifetime and come to your support now.'

'I'm fighting for the corporation's very existence, here,' he hissed. 'You'd think that at least some of them would be interested.'

Brigid shrugged. Like the rest of the family she had a vast trust fund. The outcome wouldn't harm any of them except Brendt who'd been too vain to take advice and had put everything into Shamrock Holdings. 'Arabella obviously has another engagement,' she said softly. 'I'm disappointed in her.'

'My wife will be here,' he muttered crossly. 'At least she knows where her loyalties lie.'

Brigid remained silent. Arabella was a woman after her own heart, a woman who had salted away a fortune during her marriage and invested wisely. Brendt would be shocked if he realised just how independently wealthy his wife was. As for loyalties – she was loyal only to herself and her children. Brigid understood her better than she probably understood herself, and if the outcome of the case damaged Shamrock Holdings and brought them down, Arabella would be the first rat to leave the sinking ship.

Realising she was thinking in clichés, Brigid brought her thoughts to order and mentally prepared for the day. She stiffened as a swirl of activity turned heads. The opposition had arrived.

Miriam stepped through the security arch and saw her immediately. With a glare of hauteur, she returned Brigid's scrutiny and felt a small twist of satisfaction when the other woman was the first to break eye contact.

'How are you feeling, Mim?'

She looked up at Jake and smiled in delight at how handsome he was in his wig and flowing gown. 'I've had my pills and a stiff whisky. Never felt better,' she retorted. Strangely enough, she realised, her statement was true. For, despite her weakened state, she was eager to have her day in court. Eager, and full of zest for what was to come.

'Where are Leo and your daughter?' he asked searching through the crowd. 'I thought that as you were staying with them, they'd drive you here.'

'I stayed in a hotel last night. I expect Chloe's forgotten the time,' she replied airily. 'Never one to clock watch, my daughter.' She patted his arm. 'No worries, Jake,' she soothed. 'They'll be here.'

'What have you done with Eric?' he asked as he fidgeted with his wig.

Miriam had hoped he wouldn't ask. 'Couldn't find him,' she said. 'But he'll be right. No worries.'

Jake had no chance to reply as the clerk to the court called for attention. 'All those concerned with the matter of Strong versus Dempster, please take your place in Court.'

'We're on,' muttered Jake as he took her arm. 'Are you sure you want to do this?'

Miriam smoothed her hand over her freshly washed hair. 'Too right. I haven't come all this way for nothing. Lead on, Jake. Let's do battle.'

Miriam's pulse was racing as she took her seat next to Jake. She watched as the courtroom filled, and noted with pleasure the number of reporters crammed into the press box. She felt a warm pleasure as Louise followed Fiona and they filed into the rows of seats behind the lawyers' tables. Her granddaughter had obviously come without her husband. Was that a good sign? She hoped so. She smiled serenely, and tried to appear relaxed at the obvious absence of Chloe and Leo.

She turned her glare on Brendt and his mother who were in a huddle with their lawyer. Her nerves were shot, the adrenaline coursing through her at such a rate she felt light-headed. And yet this was what she'd been waiting for almost all her life – she was determined to see it through.

'The judge is Justice Fradd-Gilbert,' Jake murmured. 'She's as straight as an arrow and considered fair. Dempster's brief wanted the case heard in camera, but she refused on the grounds it was in the public's right to know when a vast corporation was suspected of fraud.' He grasped the lapel of his black gown. 'We could have asked for a jury as well, but I think we're better off with just a judge – less chance of corruption.'

As if on cue, the judge made an appearance through a side door and all rose until she had taken her seat. A tall, thin woman of indeterminate age, she regarded the assembly over the rim of her half-moon spectacles. 'If you would proceed, Mr Connor. I understand your client is unwell, so I have made provision for her.'

Jake thanked her, and guided Miriam to the witness box and settled her in the chair.

Miriam looked up at him and winked. It had been Jake's idea to play upon her frailty, and she'd refused at first until she'd seen the wisdom of his ploy – now she was grateful she wouldn't have to stand while she gave her statement. She took the oath and settled back, hands clasped lightly on her knees.

Jake's clear, deep voice rang through the silent courtroom. 'Mrs Strong, will you please begin by telling the court why you are here.'

Miriam looked across the courtroom to Brigid and her son. They sat stony-faced side by side surrounded by their legal counsel. 'I'm here to prove my entitlement to half of the Dempster family fortune,' she said firmly.

Jake waited for the rustle and buzz to die down. 'Perhaps you would clarify your claim by telling us the history behind this entitlement?'

305

Miriam took a sip of water and replaced the glass beside the small pitcher on the shelf next to her. She began to speak, the past coming back with all the clarity of something that might have happened only hours before. She told them everything that had happened during those childhood years, the privations, the sharing of finds and food and shelter. The relationships forged with Patrick and his family, and of course with Kate.

'My father and Patrick Dempster were partners,' she said finally. 'Patrick had the knowledge of mining from his time in the pits in Wales, and my father had the money to back the project – or at least for a while. The money soon ran out, but my father earned enough from his paintings to keep us all going until the next find.'

She smiled, feeling sad. 'The search for gold and gems had become a fever by then,' she told them. 'There was always another diggings, another mine, another chance to make their fortune. Australia was in the grip of a rush for wealth – a wealth hidden beneath the earth and there for the taking if only a man was persistent enough.'

'So, the partnership between Patrick and your father was well known amongst the diggers?'

Miriam nodded, knowing what was to come. 'Neither of them made it a secret.'

Jake entered Kate's diary as exhibit one, and explained Kate's relationship with Henry and Miriam. 'Will you please read out the entry for July 1894?'

Miriam felt Kate's presence as she held the much-thumbed diary and turned it towards a sharper source of light. It was as if she was standing beside her, reading the words she had written so long ago – a lone witness to the events that were to cause such heartbreak.

I have learned this day that my darling Henry has gone into partnership with Paddy Dempster. He's even shown me the legal documents relating to this partnership, and the deeds to their claim, convinced they will protect him should anything happen. I despair, but what can I do? He has found hope again after so much darkness – and only wants to make a life for himself and little Miriam. I pray Patrick is honest in this partnership, but knowing what I do, I fear the worst.

'Why should Kate have feared the worst?' asked Jake.

'Kate was in Dublin a year before she sailed to Australia. So was Patrick. She witnessed Patrick commit murder,' said Miriam.

The court was in uproar. The defence lawyers were on their feet shouting their objections, Brendt was yelling and waving his arms about and the press were scribbling notes as if their lives depended upon it. Brigid sat ramrod straight on the hard wooden bench, her very stillness isolating her from the surrounding chaos as the judge banged on the gavel.

'Do you have any proof of this accusation?' Justice Fradd-Gilbert peered over her spectacles at Miriam.

'None,' admitted Miriam. 'Only what Kate told me, and she wasn't a liar.'

'Inadmissible,' declared the judge. She glared at Jake. 'Please see your client keeps only to the evidence necessary to prove her case, Mr Connor. You're experienced enough to know hearsay cannot be admitted.'

Jake acknowledged this and shuffled papers as the noise died down and an expectant hush filled the room. 'Mrs Strong, will you tell the court what happened shortly after your twelfth birthday?'

Miriam closed her eyes and composed herself. She took a deep breath and stared out into the well of the courtroom as she retold the events of that awful day.

'My father's body has never been found,' she said finally. 'Kate packed up her belongings and we left early the next morning. I didn't understand her haste then, but I do now.'

'And why is that?' prompted Jake.

Miriam thought carefully of how she would phrase her reply. The judge had already refused to listen to hearsay, but

307

it was important she relate the truth. 'Because of her suspicions, and the previous violence Paddy had shown towards her,' she began. 'Kate was afraid for my safety.'

Defence counsel was on his feet objecting.

The judge dismissed him. 'Let this go on until I deem it inadmissible,' she said.

Miriam told the court of Patrick's rape attempt and Jake entered Kate's diary in which she'd recorded that awful night on board the *Swallow*. 'Patrick was obsessed with her, but must have realised she and my father were falling in love. He didn't help in the search for my father, neither did he show any emotion regarding his disappearance. But I was there when he threatened Kate over the deeds for the mine. You see he was claiming they belonged solely to him, and suspected Henry had given them to Kate for safe-keeping.'

She fell silent, the tears blinding her as she looked down at her hands. 'He ranted and raved and frightened us both, but Kate had no knowledge of the deeds. My father's tent had been ransacked, but obviously the deeds hadn't been found there either. We had no proof against Dempster's claim that the mine was his, and if Kate's suspicions over my father's disappearance were right, I too was in danger. That's why we left.'

Jake coaxed her through a potted history of her life following the loss of her father, and finally arrived at the day she'd asked his advice. 'Why did you contact me, Mrs Strong? What, after all the intervening years suddenly made you certain you could prove your right to inherit part of Dempster's fortune?'

'I found something that could only have come from that last digging. Something that would have given Dempster yet another motive for murder.'

All eyes were on Jake as he lifted the music box from the case beneath the table and held it aloft. 'Is this what you found?'

Miriam saw Brendt visibly relax and tried not to smile. 'Yes,' she said. 'But it was what was inside the secret compartment that made me call on you.'

'Perhaps you should explain,' said Jake, casting a swift glance over the defence who were now tensed to object.

'Before I do,' said Miriam, determined to relish every minute of this hearing, 'I should read something from Kate's later diary, written in 1911, just before she set out on her last ill-fated journey.' She opened the diary, her voice clear and steady in the silence as she read the familiar copperplate script from the yellowed pages.

I have discovered the true worth of Henry's legacy, and after much heart-searching, will do no more than give it to Miriam for her twenty-first birthday. Old enmities are better left in the past, and I want my darling girl to savour the future. Her father entrusted me with his secret, and until now, like so many others, I have believed such things to be worth no more than pennies. Perhaps she will not thank me for keeping his legacy secret for so long, but I hope the music of the Harlequin dancers will bring peace and understanding to her troubled soul, and that in time she will learn to forgive me.

Jake placed the Harlequin music box on the broad shelf of the witness stand. 'Well done,' he murmured. 'I put it back where it was originally, and you'll see the box has been repaired.' He turned and addressed the court. 'Will you please show the court what you found in this music box, Mrs Strong?'

Miriam's hands trembled as she clicked the tiny catch in the foot of the box and watched the drawer slide open. She reached for what lay on the red velvet and held it up.

A gasp went through the room like a sigh of wind through a field of corn.

Miriam looked across at the Dempsters. They knew what it was, and what it represented – she could see it in the ashen hue of their faces, and the shock in their eyes.

She swung the gem from the delicate gold chain once

309

more, before she captured it between her thumb and finger. It was at least five inches long and three or four inches wide, and cut and polished to perfection.

'This is a black opal found only in a place that I knew as Wallangulla. You will know it as Lightning Ridge,' she explained. 'But it is no ordinary black opal, as I'm sure you've realised.'

She smiled, aware she had everyone's attention. Moving the opal in the light, she let the colours play across it. 'You can see all the colours of the spectrum against the black. There are even splashes of pink – the rarest colour of them all – but that isn't the only reason this particular opal is so very valuable.'

She held it out, admiring the way it gleamed and the colours shifted in the light. 'This is what legends are made of,' she said quietly into the hush. 'For this is so rare that only a very few fortunate people have ever seen one. So rare, that some even believe such a gem does not exist except in the imagination of the old diggers.'

She looked over at her granddaughters and saw their astonishment. Noted her daughter's arrival, and after a fleeting exchange of eye contact, turned back to find Brigid's naked hatred fixed upon her. Miriam's gaze was steady on the other woman's face as she began to speak again. 'You will not be able to see from over there, but the colours are in a pattern. The same pattern as on the clothes of one of these little dancing figures.'

She opened the box and the dancers began to twirl to the haunting music. Like an actress, she made her audience wait – timing was all, and she wanted to get this moment right. As the music died and the last echo of its refrain faded into silence she once again faced the crowded courtroom.

'This, ladies and gentlemen is a Black Harlequin.'

'That proves nothing,' shouted Brendt as he shook off his lawyer's warning hand and shot out of his seat. 'Your father probably stole it from the mine.'

'Order,' demanded the judge as she banged on the gavel.

The courtroom was in uproar, people yelling, the press scrambling and fighting their way through the doors to get to a telephone.

Brendt would not be silenced. 'That Harlequin could have come from Kate's dealings with any of the other miners at Lightning Ridge – where's your proof it came from my diggings? Go on!' he yelled. 'Prove it, you old bitch.'

'I will have order in court,' shouted the judge over the babble of noise. She banged the gavel repeatedly until a restless hush fell once more. Folding her hands on the desk in front of her she glared out over the courtroom. 'I will not have these interruptions,' she said sternly to the defence counsel. 'Please remind your client that I will not support such outrageous language in my court. He will have the opportunity to have his say later. If I have any more outbursts he will be in contempt and ejected.'

Fiona was on the edge of her seat, her hands gripped on the polished wood. Mim looked tired, but euphoric, and not at all phased by Brendt's outburst. It was as if she expected it – and had an answer to his accusations. And yet how could she? Surely Kate's diaries wouldn't be enough proof? She looked across at Jake who appeared calm and in control. They exchanged a glance and she attempted to relax.

The judge settled back in her seat. 'Mr Connor, you may proceed.'

'Thank you ma'am,' he said with a stiff little bow. Turning back to Mim, he asked her to explain why she was so certain the Black Harlequin had come from her father's mine.

'I have Kate's record books here,' she said. She selected one and held it aloft. 'Kate was meticulous in keeping records of the gems she bought. She kept a record book for each mining field she visited. She listed the name of the miner, the number of stones, their quality and the price she paid. She added the details of costs regarding cutting and polishing and, in some rare cases, of setting them in silver or gold.' Mim licked her lips before taking another sip of water.

'Kate then recorded the sale of these gems and the name of the buyer.'

'And do you have a record there of the Black Harlequin?'

'Not in so many words,' she admitted. 'But I do have a record of my father giving her a parcel of opal on the night before he disappeared.'

She opened the book with LIGHTNING RIDGE tooled on the cover, and pointed to an entry halfway down the page. ' "Parcel of twelve opal nobbies. Henry Beecham, 12 May 1906. Quality unknown but thought worthless." '

Fiona saw Brendt move restlessly on the hard bench, watched him whisper fervently in his lawyer's ear and saw his negative response, the calming hand on his arm. She smiled, glad to see him squirm.

'Why would a woman of Kate's experience think this priceless gem was worthless?' said Jake. 'When on today's market it would sell for hundreds of thousands of dollars per carat?'

'You have to remember that this all took place at the beginning of this century. The miners had discovered the more common opal, what we call the fire and flash opals, at White Cliffs and Coober Pedy. The black opal was unknown until the miners found the nobbies at Lightning Ridge. Because they were unusual and there was no market for them, the buyers were taking a risk. That risk paid off in the end of course, but at the time no one knew what to do with them.'

'Which would explain why she kept them for so long,' prompted Jake.

Miriam nodded. 'Having read her diaries, I think Kate decided to keep them for me. It was the only legacy my father could leave. It wasn't until much later that she realised the worth of those stones – and decided to cut and polish them for me as a twenty-first birthday gift.'

'Do you have the other opals, Mrs Strong?'

Miriam reached once more into the music box and held them out. 'Kate made them into a pair of exquisite earrings,

312

a bracelet and a ring. These pieces alone have just been valued at two million dollars.'

Fiona slumped back on the bench. The shock took her breath away. 'Bloody hell,' she gasped. She caught Louise's eye and they stared at one another in disbelief.

Her gasp of surprise and awe was echoed all around her as people took stock of what Miriam had told them.

Jake waited once again for them to settle down. 'These gems represent a fortune already, Mrs Strong. Why are you pursuing the Dempsters for a share in their wealth?'

Miriam placed the jewellery carefully on the shelf before her, letting it wink and smoulder in the shaft of sunlight streaming from one of the high windows. 'These opals were found at Shamrock Flats, the claim my father and Patrick Dempster took up in 1904. My father disappeared before that claim proved to be one of the richest in Lightning Ridge. By 1914, the black opals of Lightning Ridge were to become famous. They would be deemed almost priceless because of their rarity. Shamrock Flats was still being mined by Patrick Dempster, and his present fortune is based upon what he found there.'

She gently touched each exquisite piece of jewellery, the tears sparkling on her eyelashes. 'These represent only a tiny part of the wealth Patrick Dempster and his family stole from me, and I'm here today to claim my rightful inheritance.' She blinked and looked up. 'My father never had the chance to defend his rights to that claim, but I still have a voice, and I demand justice.'

Fiona watched intently as Miriam wiped her eyes and blew her nose. There was something about her grandmother's demeanour that didn't look right, but she couldn't figure out what it was. Yet she had the distinct impression Mim was faking – that she was plotting something.

Jake seemed to notice it too, for he walked to the witness box and had a quiet word before turning back to the packed courtroom. 'Mrs Strong,' he began. 'You have told this court you believe your father and Patrick Dempster were in a partnership and that this was backed up by the ownership of the deeds to Shamrock Flats.'

He surveyed the courtroom. The silence was profound.

'Do you have those deeds, Mrs Strong?'

Miriam's face was ashen. She swayed as she tried to stand, then crumpled to the floor.

'Court adjourned,' snapped the judge as Jake rushed to Miriam's side. 'Inform me when Mrs Strong is well enough to proceed,' she added before sweeping out of the room.

Fiona and the others scrabbled to join Jake as he lifted Miriam in his arms and carried her through a side door. They hurried behind him as he crossed a narrow hallway and entered a room marked Juror's Lounge.

Miriam was deposited on a couch, a pillow beneath her head. Fiona and the others crowded around her, shocked at her appearance and afraid the case had finally proved too much for this stalwart matriarch.

Miriam opened her eyes and gratefully sipped from the glass Chloe held to her lips. 'Give me one of my pills,' she ordered. 'And do stop fussing. I only fainted.'

'You certainly pick your moments,' muttered Jake with a fondness that surprised none of them. 'Should be on the stage with that sense of timing.'

Miriam raised an eyebrow and glared at him. 'I don't faint to order,' she snapped. She waved her hand imperiously. 'Leave me,' she ordered. 'I need to rest and you're crowding me.'

'Mum,' protested Chloe. 'You scared us half to death. We can't just leave you on your own. What if it happens again?'

Miriam looked disgruntled as they hovered around her. 'All right,' she said grudgingly. 'You stay, Chloe. The rest of you clear off and leave me in peace.'

Fiona had the feeling something was askew here. Something intangible in the air that she couldn't capture.

She lingered a while longer, but was soon gently but firmly steered out of the room by her father. 'She'll be right,' Leo said. 'Come on girls, I'll treat you to lunch, though god knows what ghastly offerings they have in a court canteen.'

'No need,' said Jake as he led the way to a private room further down the corridor. 'I've arranged to have lunch brought in.'

The room was filled with sunshine that glinted on the silverware and crystal. Jake opened a bottle of Chardonnay as they helped themselves to the delicious seafood buffet and took their places at the table.

'Thanks for rescuing Mim out there,' said Fiona as she sat down beside him. 'And for this,' she added, indicating the sumptuous lunch. 'You seem to think of everything.' She glanced at him through her lashes. 'Is there anything you can't do?'

He smiled. 'Plenty of things,' he replied softly. 'Perhaps we could discuss them one day?'

Fiona fluffed out her hair. 'I'm leaving soon,' she said. 'Better make it quick.'

'Leaving?' His hand stilled as he was reaching for his fork. 'Where are you going?'

Fiona concentrated on her food. It was probably delicious, but it tasted of nothing. 'I got the new contract with National Geographic,' she said finally. 'They want me to do a series of articles on the disappearing coral reefs. I leave for my diving course soon, then I have to learn how to use an underwater camera.' She turned back to face him, her bright smile plastered on her face to mask the turmoil of her emotions. 'It's a terrific job. I can't wait to get started.'

His expression was enigmatic, but his eyes revealed his disappointment. 'Where is this diving course?'

'North of Cairns,' she replied. 'I'll be covering the Great Barrier Reef in the first article.' She decided she couldn't keep up the pretence any longer. Unplanned and unwelcome, she'd realised she fancied the socks off this man and could deny her feelings no longer. What was so great about being single anyway? Why not give it a go and see how they get along? 'It's not so far away. Why don't you come up and visit?'

He tilted his head, the laughter returning to his eyes and tugging at the corners of his expressive mouth. 'I might just do that,' he murmured.

Brendt was pacing the floor in his lawyer's office. 'She hasn't got the deeds,' he snapped. 'Never had the damn things in the first place. She's playing for time.'

Arabella, who'd arrived in court only minutes before Miriam fainted, crossed her slender legs and lit a cigarette. 'Calm down, darling,' she drawled, her English vowels so different to those around her. 'You'll give yourself a heart attack.'

'And where the hell were you this morning?' he snarled as he whipped round to face her. 'I'd have thought your loyalty to me and the company was more important than anything else.'

'I had things to do,' she replied in her stately manner. 'I'm here now. So stop fretting.'

Brendt turned to Brigid. 'Miriam's bluffing, isn't she?' he demanded, needing to be reassured.

Brigid shrugged. 'That was a pretty convincing collapse,' she said thoughtfully. 'She's basically an honest woman.' Her admittance was sour. 'Considering her ill-health, I think she's found this case all too much for her and was incapable of going on with her lies.'

Brigid stared back into the past, remembering the days when they'd both been young women at that awful Academy. Miriam had shown spirit and tenacity then, as she had done today – strange she had faltered so easily when her case had seemed so strong.

Gathering her thoughts, she lifted her chin. 'I suspect that when we go back into court it will all be over in seconds. The judge will find in our favour and that will be an end to it.'

'No it won't,' stormed Brendt. 'I'll sue the bitch for every last penny for what she's done today. She'll be lucky to walk out of here with the clothes on her scrawny back.'

Brigid eyed her son with distaste. Brendt had always been a bad loser – it was one of the traits he'd inherited from his grandfather Patrick – and she had no wish to see their name dragged further through the mire. 'If you decide to pursue the claim for libel, then you're on your own,' she said icily. 'I've already handed in my resignation to the board. I am now retired, as of this morning.'

He looked at her, his mouth agape, his eyes wide as the colour suffused his face. 'Why?' he rasped.

'If you need an answer, Brendt, then you have learned nothing of what I've taught you over these long years.' She picked up her handbag and left the room.

Chloe and Miriam emerged from the Juror's Lounge at the same time as Brigid closed the door further up the hall. 'Let's go the other way,' Chloe murmured, her hand on Miriam's arm.

Miriam shook it off. 'I will not walk away from her as if I have something to hide,' she said firmly. She tilted up her chin, her back straight, shoulders square as the other woman slowly approached.

Chloe eyed the grey-haired, elegant woman as she came to a standstill in front of them. Her clothes were expensive, the pearls at her neck and in her ears perfectly matched and obviously valuable. Diamonds flashed on her fingers as the manicured and painted nails tapped a tattoo on the leather handbag.

'It's been a long time, Bridie,' said Miriam. 'Still taking care of yourself, I see.'

'Some of us take a pride in our appearance,' retorted Brigid, her cold gaze sweeping over Miriam's plain cotton dress and faded cardigan. 'But then, I suppose living out in the middle of nowhere makes one careless.'

'You always were a stuck up bitch,' Miriam said with controlled heat. 'Even when your arse was hanging out of your pants and you had no shoes, you thought you were better than everyone else.'

Brigid smirked. 'I was,' she drawled. 'I knew even then that if you wanted something you had to get it for yourself before anyone else grabbed it. You and your mealy-mouthed father didn't have the guts to do anything for yourselves – you left everything to my father.'

Miriam took a deep breath and Chloe could almost feel the electricity bouncing from her as she fought to remain calm. 'How can you sleep at night knowing you and your precious family are guilty of murder and fraud?'

'Easily,' Brigid replied. 'I have nothing to feel guilty about.' She tucked the handbag under her arm. 'People disappeared in the diggings. It was a common event with so many holes in the ground, so many tunnels being dug. Your father was just unfortunate to be one of them.'

'Liar,' breathed Miriam. 'You knew what had happened – thick as thieves you and Paddy. I wouldn't be surprised if you didn't help him.'

Chloe thought she saw a flash of something in Brigid's eyes, but it was gone before she could analyse it. 'I think you've both said enough,' she said gently, trying to steer her mother away. 'It must be time to be getting back into the courtroom.'

Brigid's hand shot out and grabbed Miriam's sleeve. 'You'll take that accusation back, you whey-faced bitch,' she spat.

Miriam slapped the heavily made-up face, the ring of flesh on flesh echoing down the long, deserted corridor. 'Never,' she hissed. She took a step forward until she was almost nose to nose with her old enemy. 'If you call me a bitch again, I'll punch your bloody lights out,' she said through clenched teeth. 'I might be old, and shabbily dressed and living out in the sticks, but my right hook can still fell a biting horse in seconds.'

Brigid stepped back, her hand covering the finger-marks left on her ashen face by Miriam's slap. 'I'll have you up for assault,' she gasped.

'Ha!' retorted Miriam. 'I'd like to see you try.' She turned

318

her back and marched down the corridor towards the door to the courtroom.

Louise had left the house very early. Rafe was in a strange mood this morning and she'd needed to escape. Her attempts at patching up her marriage had started out well, but now they were back in the old routine and nothing had changed. To take her mind off her marital problems, she picked up a copy of the *Australian* that was on a side table and smoothed it out. What she saw was so unbelievable she had to look again. 'Oh, my god,' she breathed. 'Look at this.'

Startled, the others gathered around her.

Louise turned the paper around so they could all see the photographs of Ralph with his mistress. They were graphic, despite the discreet blacking out of certain areas. 'Bastard,' she moaned as she read the covering story. 'It says here he's been with this tart for several months, and there's pictures of other women as well that he's supposed to have been involved with.'

She crushed the newspaper, the tears blinding her with a rage she could barely control. 'And all these years he's been accusing me of being unfaithful. All these years he's threatened to kill me if he found me with anyone else.' She looked at Fiona and dashed the tears from her face. 'If I ever see him again it will be too soon. What a bloody fool I've been, Fee. What a stupid, ignorant idiot to believe a word he said.'

Fiona put her arms around her. 'Keep the newspaper, Louise,' she murmured. 'And every time you look at those pictures you'll see what a prat he is. I mean,' she said through the giggles. 'What man is worth crying over if he has to keep his shoes and socks on when he has sex? And as for those suspenders holding up his socks . . .' The laughter burst from her and she tried to smother it with her hand.

Louise sniffed back the tears and smoothed out the pages. She felt the renewing zest of laughter bubble through her. 'You're right,' she giggled. 'He looks ridiculous – and look at his fat bottom!'

319

She rested her head against Fiona's. The tears poured down her cheeks, but they were tears of release, of laughter and the start of a new day for Louise. For she would never look back, never regret leaving Ralph – and never again be anyone but her true self.

The courtroom filled quickly and as the judge entered and took her place, there was a rustle of eagerness amongst those assembled.

Miriam noticed Brigid's absence immediately, and felt a pang of something approaching disappointment. But she realised her old adversary was doing what she always did – protecting herself.

'Are you feeling well enough to continue, Mrs Strong?' asked the judge from her lofty seat.

'I am,' she replied. 'Thank you.'

The judge indicated that Jake started the proceedings again, and Miriam sat calmly in the witness box, waiting for the dreaded moment to arrive.

'Mrs Strong,' said Jake. 'Will you please tell the court if you have the deeds to Shamrock Flats in your possession?'

'I do,' she replied.

A shocked gasp ran around the room and Miriam couldn't help but smile when she saw Jake's startled reaction to her statement. She looked over to the crowded benches and saw her family, wide-eyed and flushed with euphoria and disbelief.

Fiona stood and punched the air. 'Way to go, Mim,' she yelled.

'Silence in court,' said the judge, banging her gavel.

Miriam almost giggled. 'Do you want to see them?' she asked with all the innocence of a new-born colt.

Jake grinned. 'If you would be so kind,' he said.

Miriam reached into her capacious handbag and pulled out three sheets of yellowing paper. Riffling through them, she chose one and held it out to Jake. 'This is the partnership deed drawn up by a solicitor in Port Philip and signed by both Patrick Dempster and my father. It is dated 3 July 1894.'

She watched as Jake took the piece of paper and studied it. Smiled as his gaze lifted finally and she saw the disbelief and awe in his eyes. Brendt Dempster, she noticed was pale, his eyes burning dark coals, fixed on the papers as if he wanted to consume them.

Miriam took out the second slip of paper. 'This is the claim the two men made at White Cliffs for a mine they called "Dove Field".' The final piece of paper was flourished. 'And this,' she said with a triumphant ring to her voice. 'This is the claim for Shamrock Flats at Lightning Ridge. It is signed by both Patrick Dempster and his partner, Henry Beecham.'

'That's not possible,' shouted Brendt above the uproar this statement caused. He lunged for Jake, his face puce as he clawed for the documents. 'My father said he'd destroyed them years ago.'

The silence was immediate. Brendt stood in the courtroom ashen faced, all rage quelled by the awful realisation of what he'd said.

'Sit down, Mr Dempster,' said the judge into the silence. 'You are in contempt, and will be charged.' She gathered up her notes, the precious slips of paper and her spectacles. 'Court is adjourned until tomorrow morning.'

Miriam made them wait until she'd had a large whisky and was settled comfortably in the hotel suite. She looked at their faces as they sat around her, and felt the warm glow of love for each of them. Her family were more precious to her than any Black Harlequin, she realised.

'Come on Mim,' groaned Fiona. 'Spill the beans. Where did you find the deeds?'

Trust her to be first, Mim thought with fondness. Fiona never could bear to be in the dark where secrets were concerned. 'It wasn't really me,' she admitted finally. 'It was your mother.'

'Mum?' Fiona and Louise turned as one to look at Chloe. 'But how? You went back to Byron Bay.'

Chloe nodded. 'I did, but of course my mind was still on the deeds. I knew they had to be somewhere, and as I sat in my studio I realised there was one place none of us had thought of.'

Miriam broke in, she couldn't bear to keep silent any longer. 'Chloe phoned me and I checked. And there they were.'

'Where?' It was an exasperated chorus from the others.

'Staring us in the face all the time,' she said, delighted to be holding court again. Loving the attention, her moment of triumph. 'The clue was obvious once I'd thought about it, and when I looked closer, I realised my father had left his own signpost as to where he'd hidden them.'

'Mum,' said Chloe softly. 'Don't you think you're over-egging the pudding, just a little?' Her green eyes were alight with laughter, her cloud of red hair a halo in the stream of light pouring through the window. Mim thought she had never looked lovelier – or happier, now she and Leo had finally called a truce and become lovers again.

'Maybe,' she murmured. She reached for Chloe's exhibition folder – a simple folder made from two squares of thick card tied together with scarlet ribbons. Drawing back the tissue paper she carefully lifted out her father's last painting.

A gasp went around the room. 'Of course,' whispered Fiona.

'We should have known,' muttered Louise.

'Well, I'll be . . .' said Jake as he shook his head.

Miriam studied the painting, holding it to the light so the delicate brush strokes could be minutely examined. Bereft of its frame, it looked quite small and almost insignificant, but of course, she thought, one should never go on appearances alone – they could sometimes turn out to be most deceptive.

'He painted this scene of Lightning Ridge during the stillness of early morning and the hush of evening. He was tired and filthy, his poor hands ruined by the digging, but he had

322

this burning need to paint. An almost feverish yearning to capture the extraordinary light of our New World. This was the last of a series he painted of the diggings both in Lightning Ridge and at White Cliffs. There were others of course, but there's no trace of them any more.'

She took a deep breath, the trauma of the day and the triumph of what she'd achieved almost overwhelming her. 'He gave this to Kate on the morning of the day he vanished. It was his last gift, and his most precious. He knew it would never be sold or given away – never be discarded. And that was why he left the clue to the deeds on the back – in case something happened to him.'

'What was the clue?' Fiona was perched eagerly on the arm of Mim's chair.

Miriam turned the painting over. The ink had faded to ochre, but it was still legible. She handed it over to Jake. 'You'd better read it, my Latin's non-existent.'

He stood with his back to the light so he could read Henry's last words.

Mens lenis perfacta lenia cognita est
Homo enim nulla re tanto proditur

'Well, I'll be darned,' he said. 'It's a quotation from Spenser.' He looked up, saw the blank faces and smiled. 'Your father was indeed a very clever man, Mim – and obviously not without humour.'

He looked around the room and must have realised he was making little sense, for he again bent his head to the writing on the back of the canvas. 'This quotation is so subtle, that unless you were looking for it, you would never have guessed what it really meant.'

'But what *does* it mean?' groaned Fiona as she squirmed on the arm of the chair. 'Bloody hell, isn't anyone around here capable of talking in anything but riddles?'

'Language, dear,' reproached Miriam with practiced tolerance.

323

Jake grinned and handed Fiona the delicate canvas. He rested his hand lightly on her shoulder as they looked into one another's eyes.

The gentle mind by gentle deeds is known
For man by nothing is so well betrayed

Epilogue

Three months had passed since the trial. The judge had ruled in her favour, and her family would never want for anything again. Not that the money mattered a bit – it was the principle of the thing, for money couldn't buy happiness, couldn't give you the love and solidity of one's family.

Miriam sat in the car and thought of her family as Frank drove north. Fiona was in northern Queensland, no doubt with Jake, as the two had been inseparable since the court case, and she suspected there would soon be a wedding.

Louise was attending counselling and had enrolled in an acting course down in Sydney. She was seeing someone – a nice bloke called Ed who was something in the theatre – but it was too early to hope it might prove important. She needed a bit of fun before she settled down again.

Jake's cat, Eric, was still residing at Bellbird and had sired at least two litters. She smiled as she remembered the day he'd so proudly marched into her kitchen. It had been a couple of weeks after the trial, and there he was, with his harem and a half dozen kittens trailing behind him. Poor Jake, she thought. He'd lost Eric, but he's got Fiona to make up for it.

As for Chloe. Her daughter had been unusually focused when she'd needed her. Miriam hugged the delight as she thought of Chloe and her husband happily squabbling over which house they would share. She sighed. It was so lovely that everything had turned out all right in the end.

Miriam was on her second wind, but realised it wouldn't last for much longer. She'd somehow found the energy to make this long, dusty journey back to Lightning Ridge, and knew it would be her last. Yet it was important she came, for there was something she had to do before her life could finally come full circle.

Lightning Ridge hadn't changed very much since the beginning of the century, she realised as Frank drove her down the main street. There were shops now, of course, and a few motels and hotels, even an estate of new houses on the very edge of town. But the heat was still unbearable, and the miners looked as if they'd stepped from old sepia photographs as they lounged in the shade. Down at heel and dressed in a collection of rags, their beards straggled almost to their chests as their curious eyes followed the car down the road. It was as if she'd been transported back into the past.

She leaned back in the passenger seat, almost overcome with nostalgia for those long lost days. And it was as they headed out of town and drove along the narrow, winding road through the scrub and the dusty trees, she felt it most keenly. For this part of the Ridge hadn't changed at all.

The mounds of mullock heaps still littered the bush, where the blood red earth poked through the salt bush, box, fake sandalwood, wilga and orange trees. Swathes of wild yellow turnip drifted and swayed, seeded by the wind, brought to life by the recent rain. Clusters of scarlet berries clung to creepers as they entwined themselves around the grey trunks of drooping gum trees, the light sifting through the leaves in a golden glow that made the place almost magical. Grey wallabies and kangaroos watched from the shelter of the bush, their ears twisting like radar beacons as they poised for flight.

Rusted corrugated-iron shelters leaned precariously on boulders beside decrepit machinery and pit wheels that screeched as they turned and hauled up the buckets of nobbies. Life was the same here as it had always been. Lightning

Ridge was unique, in that no large corporation was allowed to take it over – each claim had to be privately owned – and was guarded fiercely with intense suspicion of their neighbour.

Miriam gazed out of the window at the broken-down caravans, the stone huts and ragged tents and dilapidated wooden shelters. Utility trucks had taken the place of the mules and horses, but the spirit of the place hadn't changed, she realised as she watched a group of small children scrabbling through a nearby mullock heap. It was almost as if she was watching herself and Brigid, and it made her shiver.

'Let's go back through town,' she said as she pulled the window shut and turned up the air conditioning. 'You know where I need to go.'

'This'll bust the axle,' he warned in his usual dour tone as he steered around the cracks and humps in the dirt road and narrowly missed an enormous pothole. He changed down a gear and they crept forward.

Miriam ignored him and waited. Her journey was almost at an end, a few minutes more wouldn't matter.

The cemetery sprawled behind rusted white railings on a plateau overlooking the town. There were few trees, and the heat bounced off the hardened earth, glinting on one or two shards of broken glass or abandoned crystal stones. There was no church, no formal lines of marble headstones, merely a few wooden crosses marking mounds of red earth.

Miriam slipped the chain through the gate and pushed it open. There was a sense of desolation and lost dreams in this silent, abandoned patch, and Miriam felt its full force as she walked between those pathetic little mounds.

Here and there was an epitaph still legible, a token left by his mates to see him into the next world. A man's name, perhaps only his nickname, etched into the bleached wood – a bunch of plastic flowers faded by the sun, lying forgotten and abandoned like the men beneath this rich, red soil.

Miriam's smile was sad as she noted the beer bottles left as a reminder of the deceased's favourite drink – an inglorious end to a life that must have once been so filled with hope. She stood for a moment at the far end of the cemetery, listening to the birds chatter in the trees, watching the galahs as they flew in a pink and grey cloud towards their evening's roost. Then she turned and headed further back to the single mound of earth that was almost hidden amongst the weeds.

Frank took off his hat and scratched his head as he read the epitaph.

Miriam smiled and looked down at the pale marble head-stone that glimmered beneath its veil of wild flowers and ivy. She spent a few moments tugging at the ivy and when she'd done, she placed her posy of flowers against the exposed marble and stood there for a long moment deep in communion with the man lying beneath the salmon-coloured earth. The bones had been found several years ago and she liked to think it was him.

'You would have been proud of Chloe,' she whispered. 'The deeds were almost dust. But the other papers were in a good enough state for her to make an excellent forgery.'

The pain was returning. It was time to go home for the last of her Bellbird summers. She kissed her fingers and rested them lightly on the headstone. 'See you soon, Dad.'